TIME FLYZ

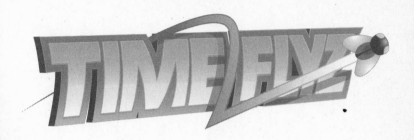

BERLIN BREAKOUT

ZONDERVAN®

Berlin Breakout
Copyright © 2008 by Ben Avery
Illustrations copyright © 2008 by Adi Darda Gaudiamo

Requests for information should be addressed to:

Zondervan, Grand Rapids, Michigan 49530

Library of Congress Cataloging-in-Publication Data

Avery, Ben, 1974-
  Berlin breakout / story by Ben Avery; art by Adi Darda.
        p. cm. -- (TimeFlyz; v. 3)
    ISBN-13: 978-0-310-71363-0 (softcover)
    ISBN-10: 0-310-71363-3 (softcover)
    1. Graphic novels. I. Adi Darda, 1972- II. Title.
    PN6727.A945B47 2008
    741.5'973--dc22

                                                                2007031011

Series Editor: Bud Rogers
Managing Editor: Bruce Nuffer
Managing Art Director: Merit Alderink

Printed in the United States of America

---

08 09 10 11 12 13 • 10 9 8 7 6 5 4 3 2 1

BERLIN
BREAKOUT

SERIES EDITOR:
BUD ROGERS

STORY BY BEN AVERY
ART BY ADI DARDA GAUDIAMO

Z ZONDERVAN®

ZONDERVAN.com/
AUTHORTRACKER
follow your favorite authors

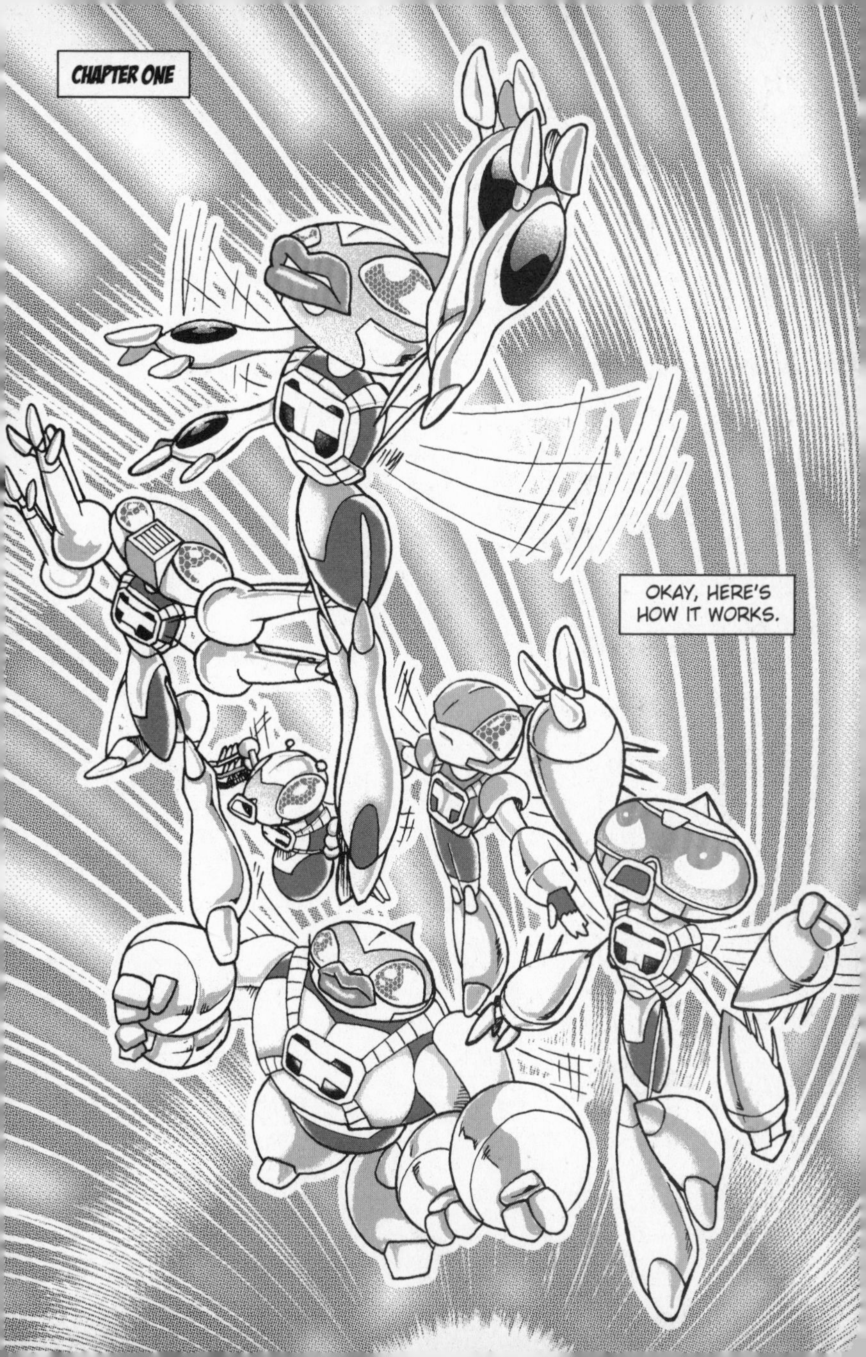
CHAPTER ONE
OKAY, HERE'S HOW IT WORKS.

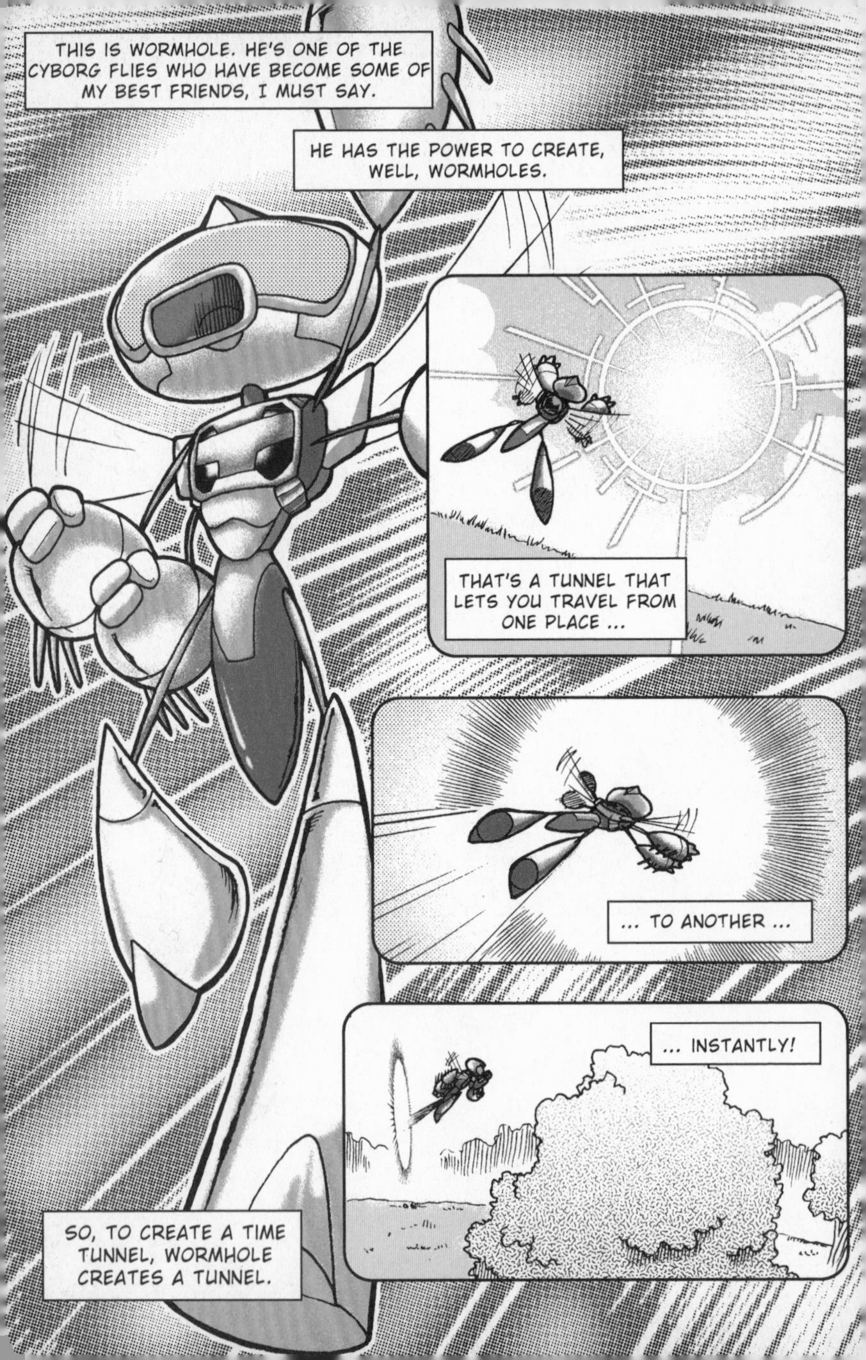
THIS IS WORMHOLE. HE'S ONE OF THE CYBORG FLIES WHO HAVE BECOME SOME OF MY BEST FRIENDS, I MUST SAY.
HE HAS THE POWER TO CREATE, WELL, WORMHOLES.
THAT'S A TUNNEL THAT LETS YOU TRAVEL FROM ONE PLACE ...
... TO ANOTHER ...
... INSTANTLY!
SO, TO CREATE A TIME TUNNEL, WORMHOLE CREATES A TUNNEL.

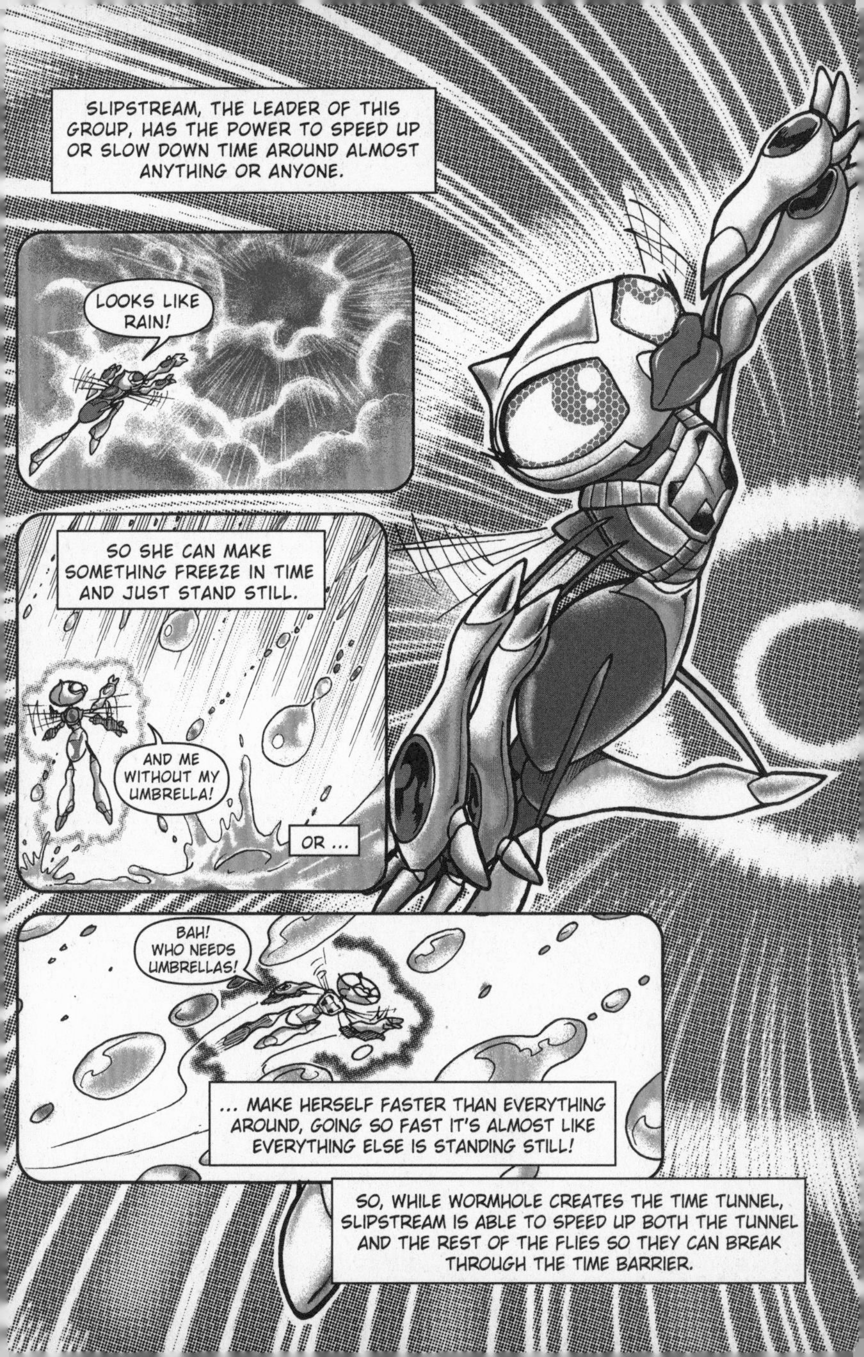
SLIPSTREAM, THE LEADER OF THIS GROUP, HAS THE POWER TO SPEED UP OR SLOW DOWN TIME AROUND ALMOST ANYTHING OR ANYONE.
LOOKS LIKE RAIN!
SO SHE CAN MAKE SOMETHING FREEZE IN TIME AND JUST STAND STILL.
AND ME WITHOUT MY UMBRELLA!
OR ...
BAH! WHO NEEDS UMBRELLAS!
... MAKE HERSELF FASTER THAN EVERYTHING AROUND, GOING SO FAST IT'S ALMOST LIKE EVERYTHING ELSE IS STANDING STILL!
SO, WHILE WORMHOLE CREATES THE TIME TUNNEL, SLIPSTREAM IS ABLE TO SPEED UP BOTH THE TUNNEL AND THE REST OF THE FLIES SO THEY CAN BREAK THROUGH THE TIME BARRIER.

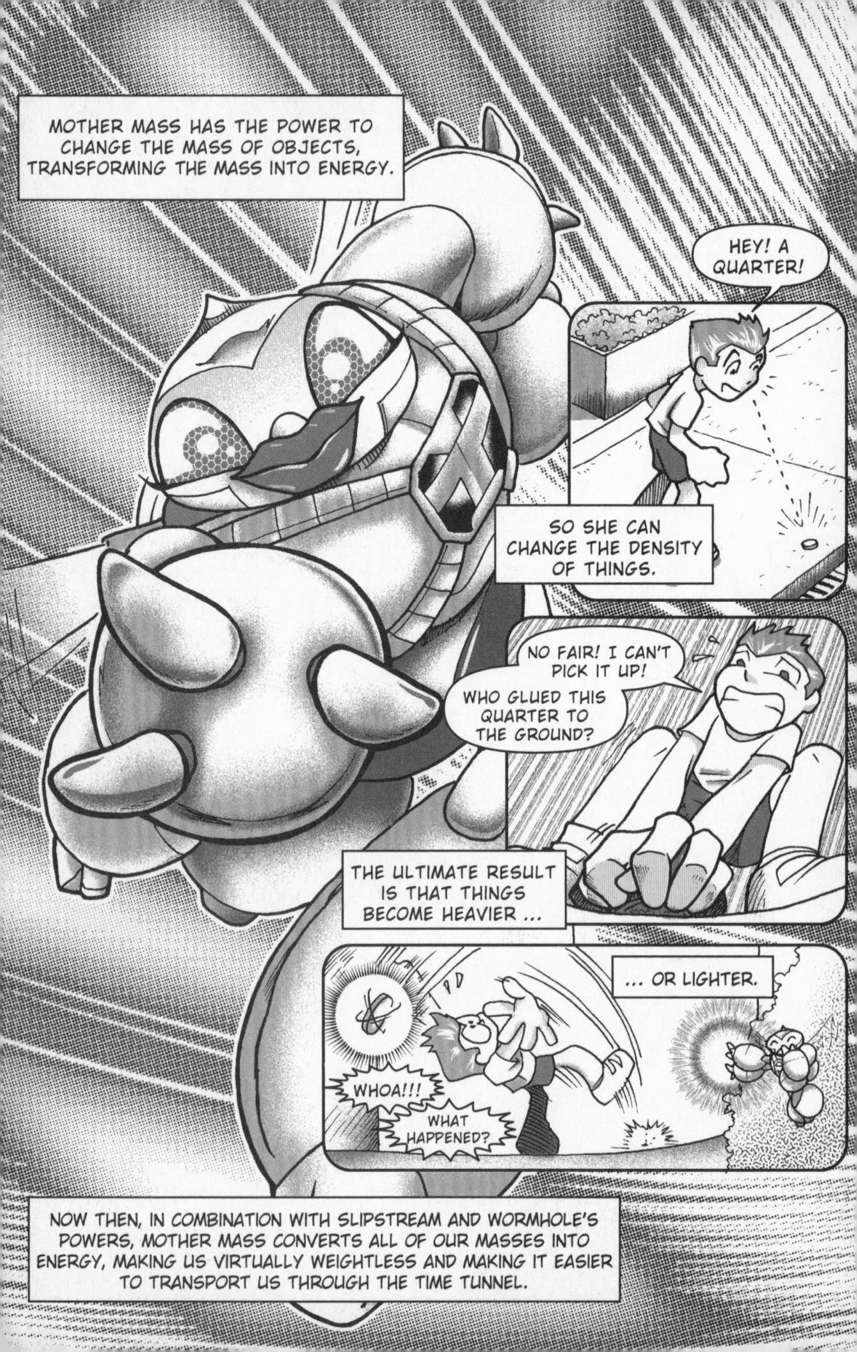
MOTHER MASS HAS THE POWER TO CHANGE THE MASS OF OBJECTS, TRANSFORMING THE MASS INTO ENERGY.
HEY! A QUARTER!
SO SHE CAN CHANGE THE DENSITY OF THINGS.
NO FAIR! I CAN'T PICK IT UP!
WHO GLUED THIS QUARTER TO THE GROUND?
THE ULTIMATE RESULT IS THAT THINGS BECOME HEAVIER ...
... OR LIGHTER.
WHOA!!!
WHAT HAPPENED?
NOW THEN, IN COMBINATION WITH SLIPSTREAM AND WORMHOLE'S POWERS, MOTHER MASS CONVERTS ALL OF OUR MASSES INTO ENERGY, MAKING US VIRTUALLY WEIGHTLESS AND MAKING IT EASIER TO TRANSPORT US THROUGH THE TIME TUNNEL.

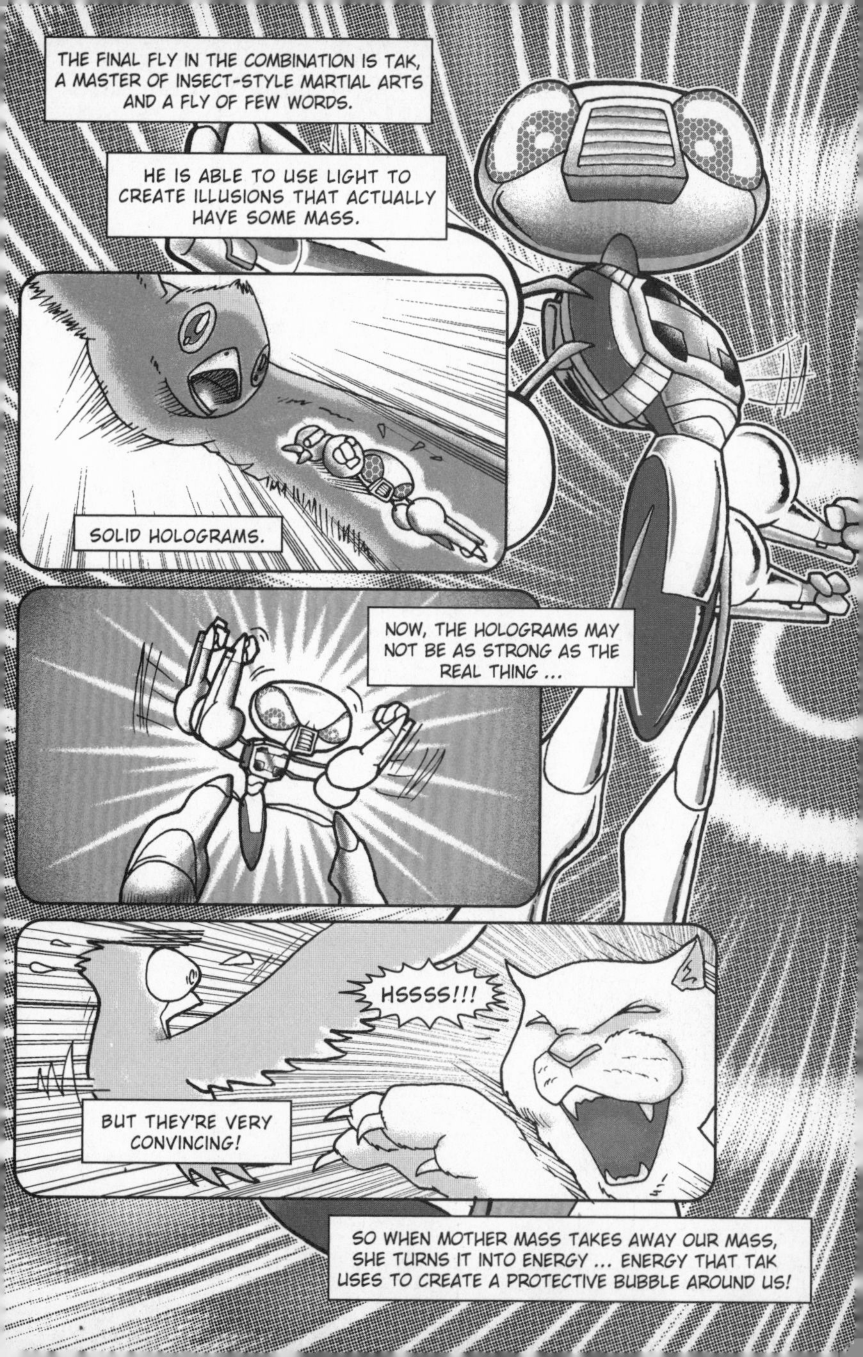
THE FINAL FLY IN THE COMBINATION IS TAK, A MASTER OF INSECT-STYLE MARTIAL ARTS AND A FLY OF FEW WORDS.
HE IS ABLE TO USE LIGHT TO CREATE ILLUSIONS THAT ACTUALLY HAVE SOME MASS.
SOLID HOLOGRAMS.
NOW, THE HOLOGRAMS MAY NOT BE AS STRONG AS THE REAL THING ...
HSSSS!!!
BUT THEY'RE VERY CONVINCING!
SO WHEN MOTHER MASS TAKES AWAY OUR MASS, SHE TURNS IT INTO ENERGY ... ENERGY THAT TAK USES TO CREATE A PROTECTIVE BUBBLE AROUND US!

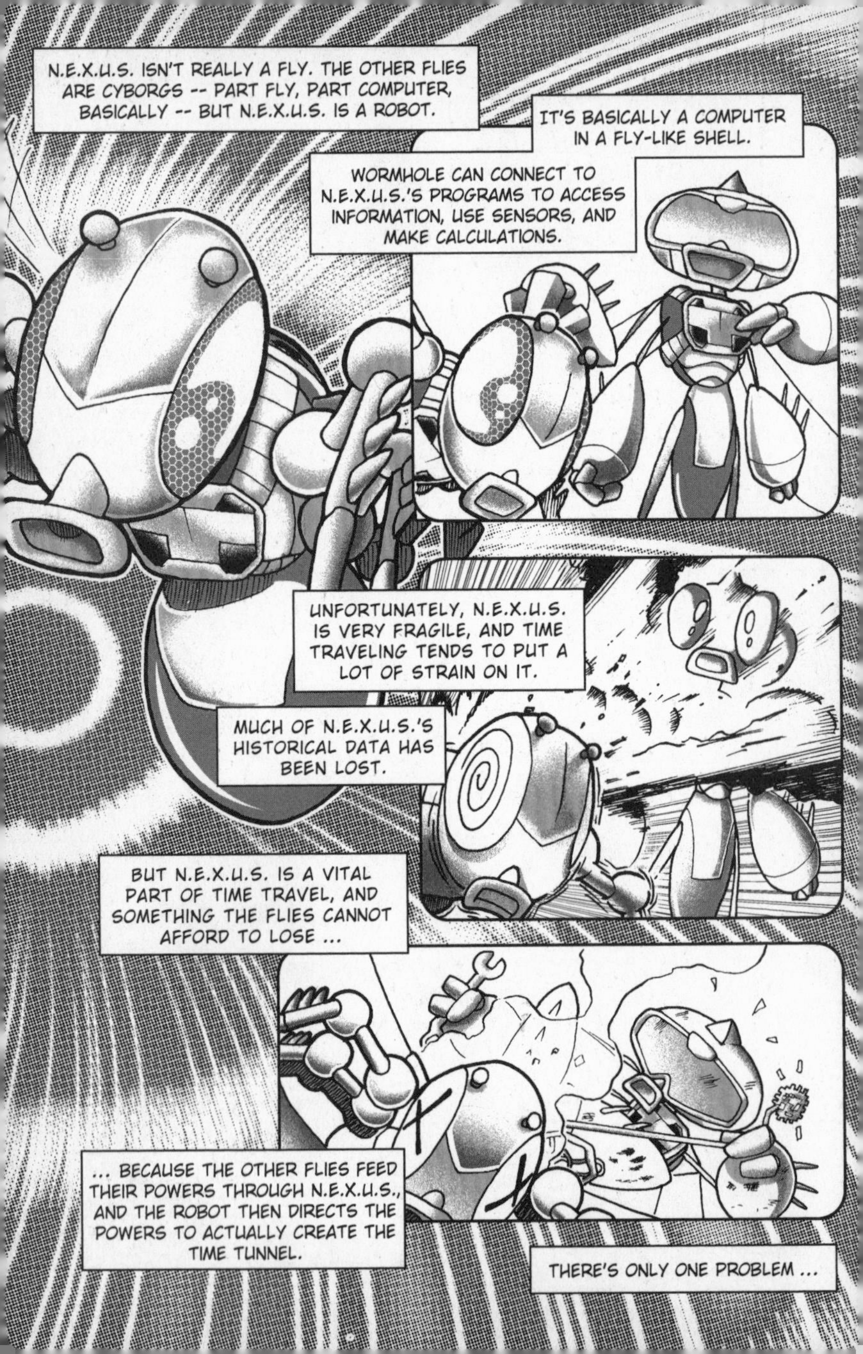
N.E.X.U.S. ISN'T REALLY A FLY. THE OTHER FLIES ARE CYBORGS -- PART FLY, PART COMPUTER, BASICALLY -- BUT N.E.X.U.S. IS A ROBOT.
IT'S BASICALLY A COMPUTER IN A FLY-LIKE SHELL.
WORMHOLE CAN CONNECT TO N.E.X.U.S.'S PROGRAMS TO ACCESS INFORMATION, USE SENSORS, AND MAKE CALCULATIONS.
UNFORTUNATELY, N.E.X.U.S. IS VERY FRAGILE, AND TIME TRAVELING TENDS TO PUT A LOT OF STRAIN ON IT.
MUCH OF N.E.X.U.S.'S HISTORICAL DATA HAS BEEN LOST.
BUT N.E.X.U.S. IS A VITAL PART OF TIME TRAVEL, AND SOMETHING THE FLIES CANNOT AFFORD TO LOSE ...
... BECAUSE THE OTHER FLIES FEED THEIR POWERS THROUGH N.E.X.U.S., AND THE ROBOT THEN DIRECTS THE POWERS TO ACTUALLY CREATE THE TIME TUNNEL.
THERE'S ONLY ONE PROBLEM ...

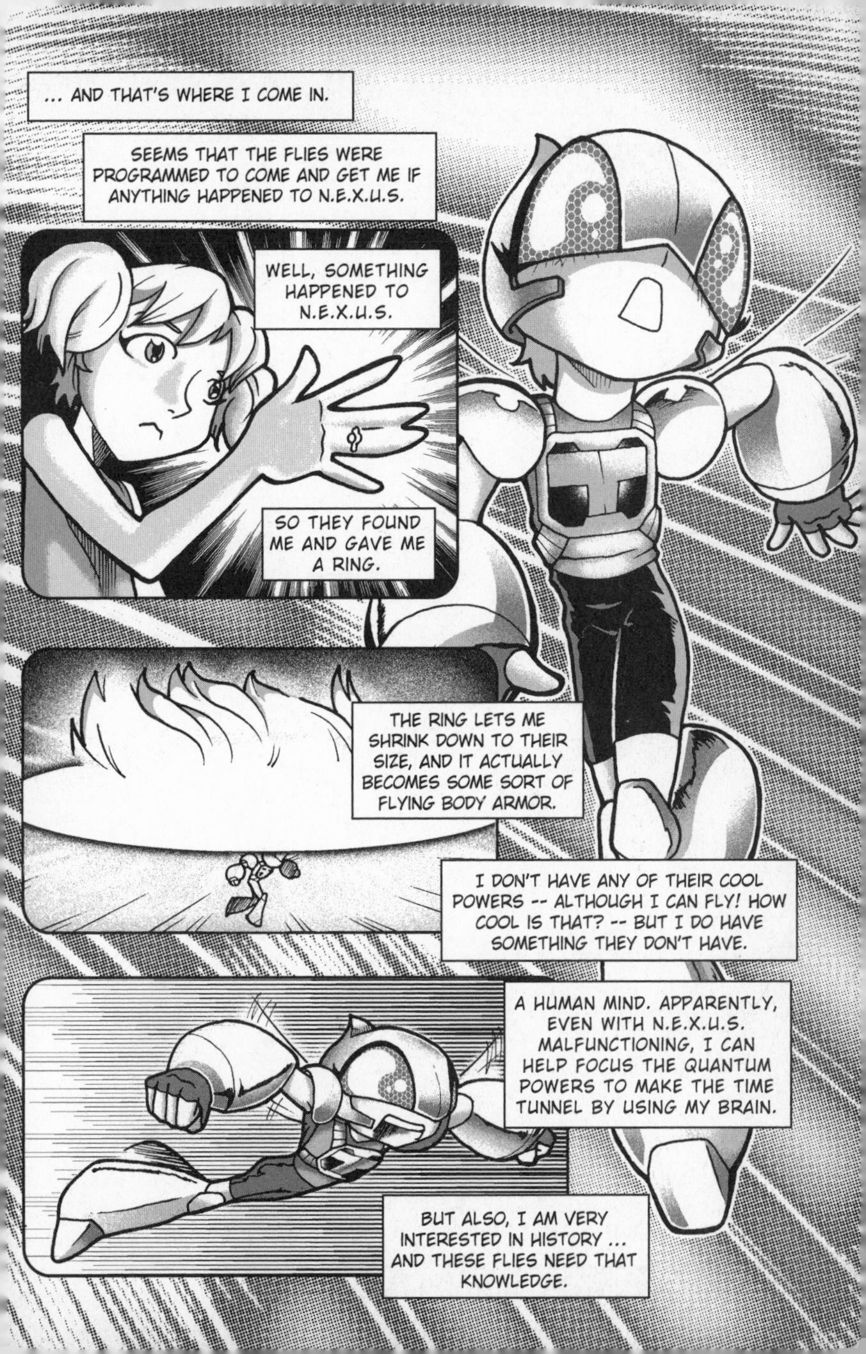
... AND THAT'S WHERE I COME IN.
SEEMS THAT THE FLIES WERE PROGRAMMED TO COME AND GET ME IF ANYTHING HAPPENED TO N.E.X.U.S.
WELL, SOMETHING HAPPENED TO N.E.X.U.S.
SO THEY FOUND ME AND GAVE ME A RING.
THE RING LETS ME SHRINK DOWN TO THEIR SIZE, AND IT ACTUALLY BECOMES SOME SORT OF FLYING BODY ARMOR.
I DON'T HAVE ANY OF THEIR COOL POWERS -- ALTHOUGH I CAN FLY! HOW COOL IS THAT? -- BUT I DO HAVE SOMETHING THEY DON'T HAVE.
A HUMAN MIND. APPARENTLY, EVEN WITH N.E.X.U.S. MALFUNCTIONING, I CAN HELP FOCUS THE QUANTUM POWERS TO MAKE THE TIME TUNNEL BY USING MY BRAIN.
BUT ALSO, I AM VERY INTERESTED IN HISTORY ... AND THESE FLIES NEED THAT KNOWLEDGE.

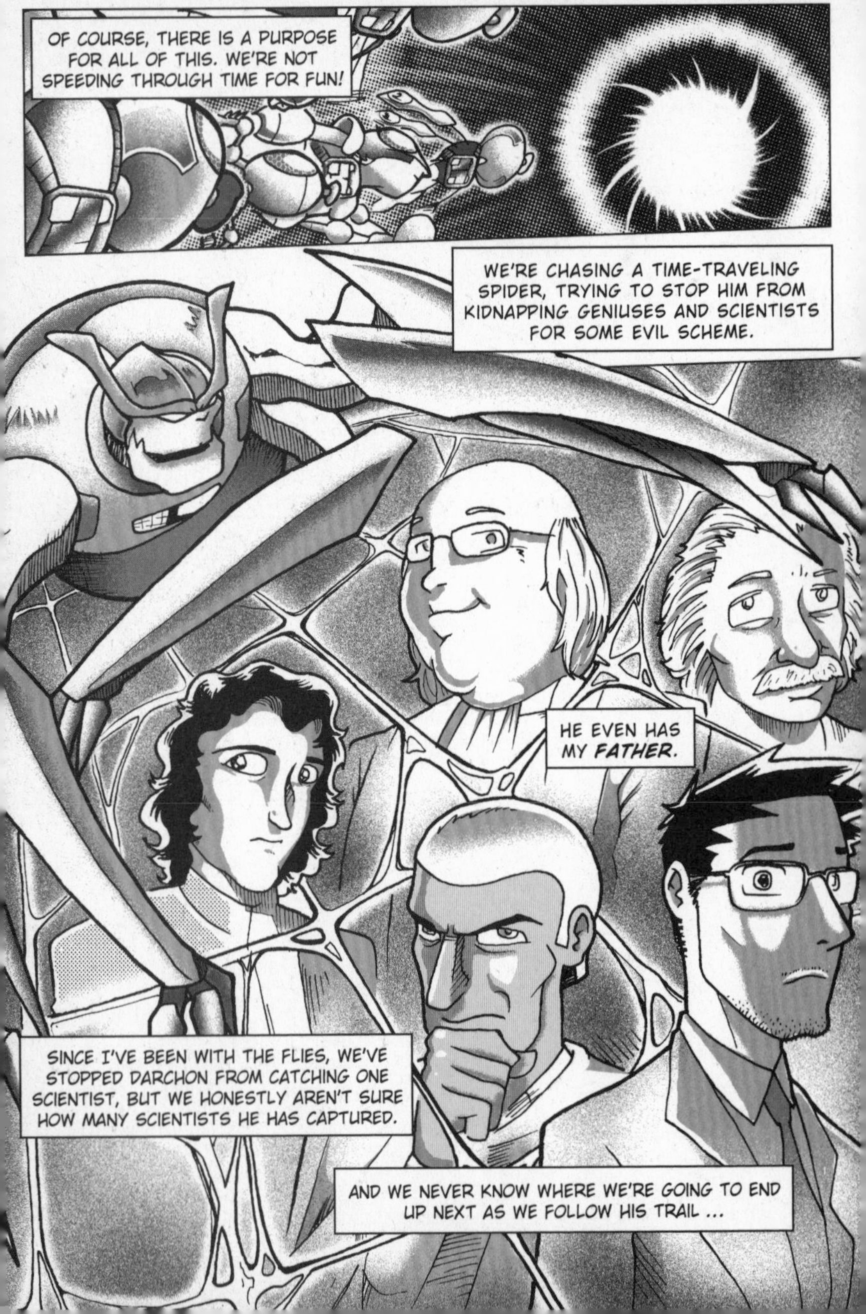
OF COURSE, THERE IS A PURPOSE FOR ALL OF THIS. WE'RE NOT SPEEDING THROUGH TIME FOR FUN!
WE'RE CHASING A TIME-TRAVELING SPIDER, TRYING TO STOP HIM FROM KIDNAPPING GENIUSES AND SCIENTISTS FOR SOME EVIL SCHEME.
HE EVEN HAS MY ***FATHER***.
SINCE I'VE BEEN WITH THE FLIES, WE'VE STOPPED DARCHON FROM CATCHING ONE SCIENTIST, BUT WE HONESTLY AREN'T SURE HOW MANY SCIENTISTS HE HAS CAPTURED.
AND WE NEVER KNOW WHERE WE'RE GOING TO END UP NEXT AS WE FOLLOW HIS TRAIL ...

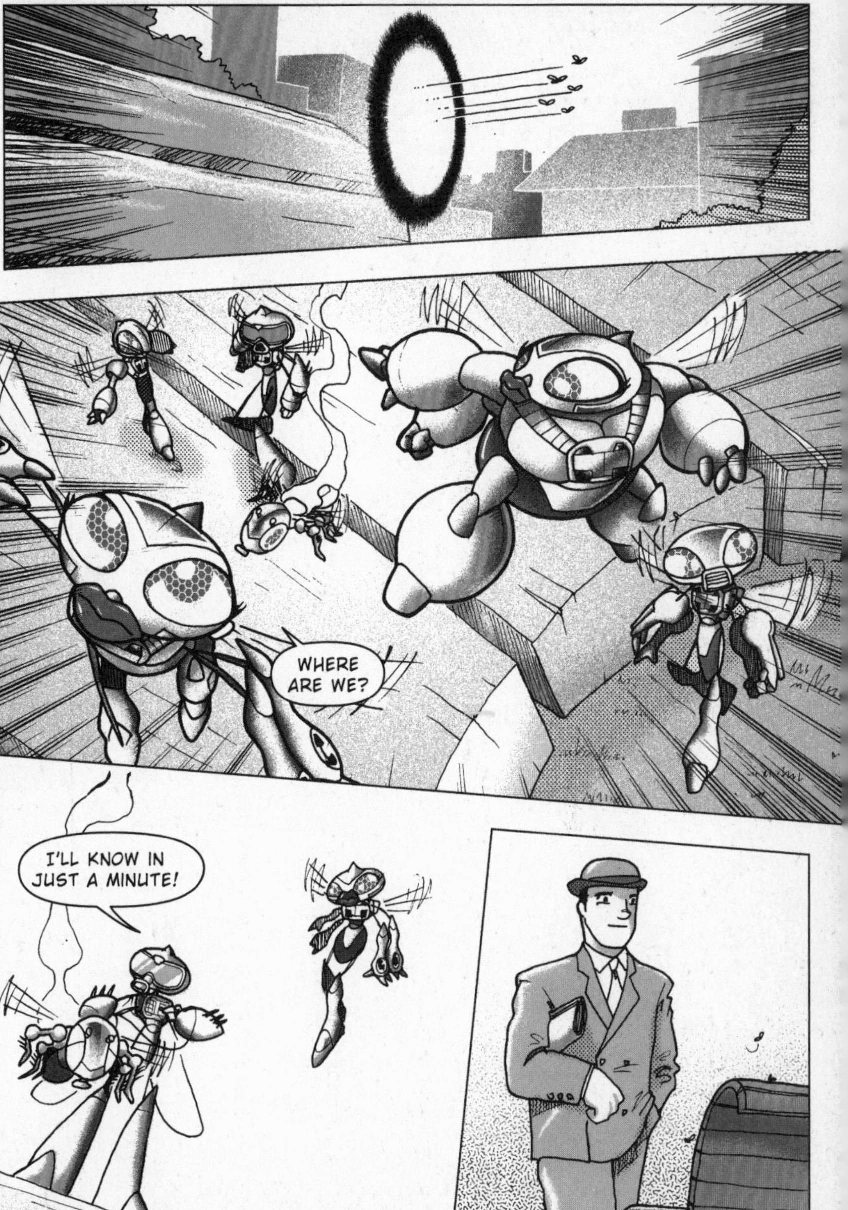
WHERE ARE WE?
I'LL KNOW IN JUST A MINUTE!

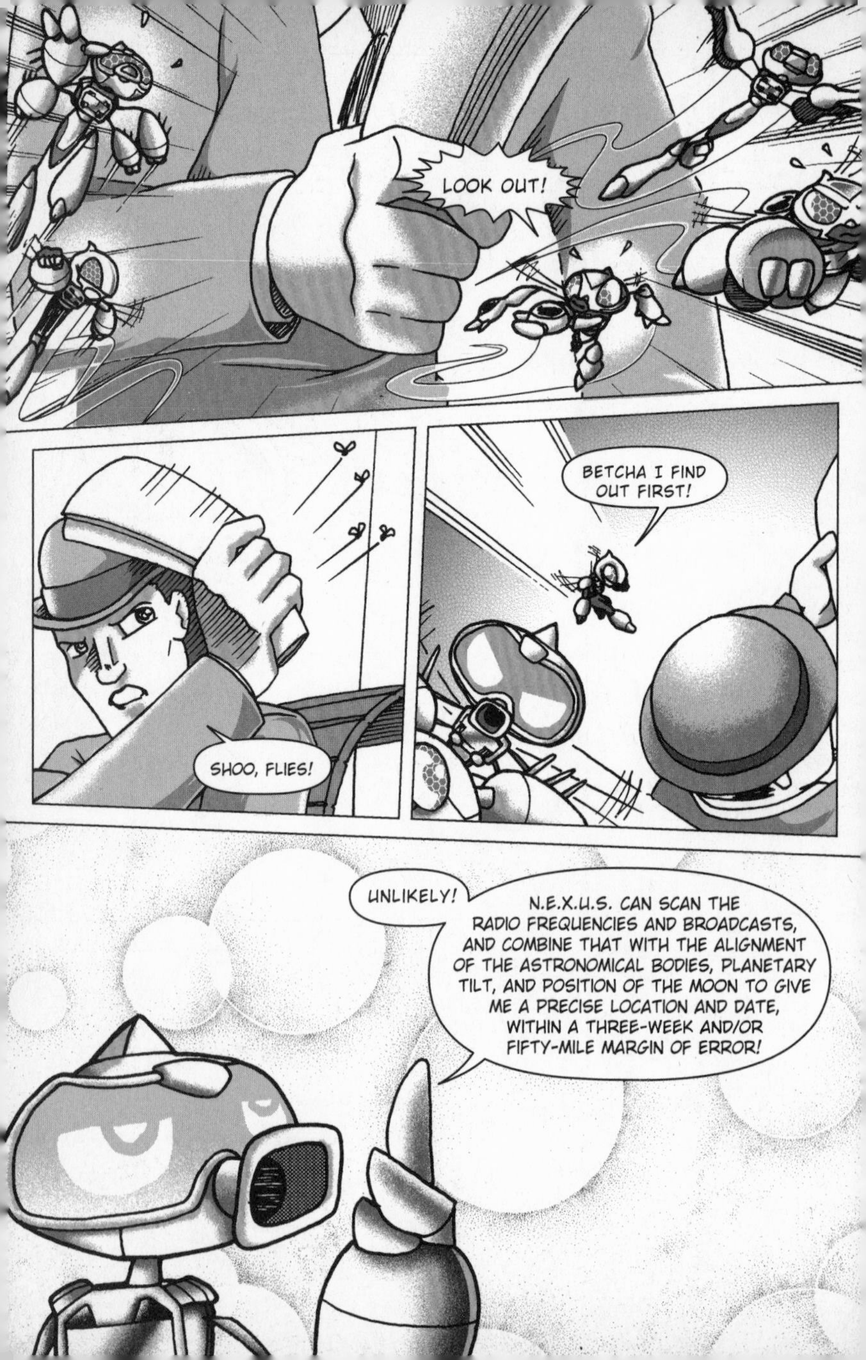
LOOK OUT!
SHOO, FLIES!
BETCHA I FIND OUT FIRST!
UNLIKELY!
N.E.X.U.S. CAN SCAN THE RADIO FREQUENCIES AND BROADCASTS, AND COMBINE THAT WITH THE ALIGNMENT OF THE ASTRONOMICAL BODIES, PLANETARY TILT, AND POSITION OF THE MOON TO GIVE ME A PRECISE LOCATION AND DATE, WITHIN A THREE-WEEK AND/OR FIFTY-MILE MARGIN OF ERROR!

ANY SIGN OF DARCHON?

~~~~~~ ~~~~~~~~~~~~~ ~~~~~~~~~~!

MORE LIKE A NEEDLE IN A *FIELD* OF HAYSTACKS, TAK!

BERLIN. JULY, 1938.

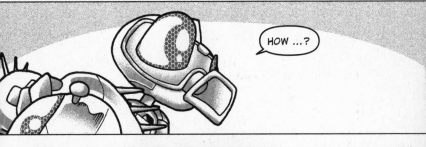

HOW ...?

I READ THE FRONT OF THAT MAN'S NEWSPAPER!

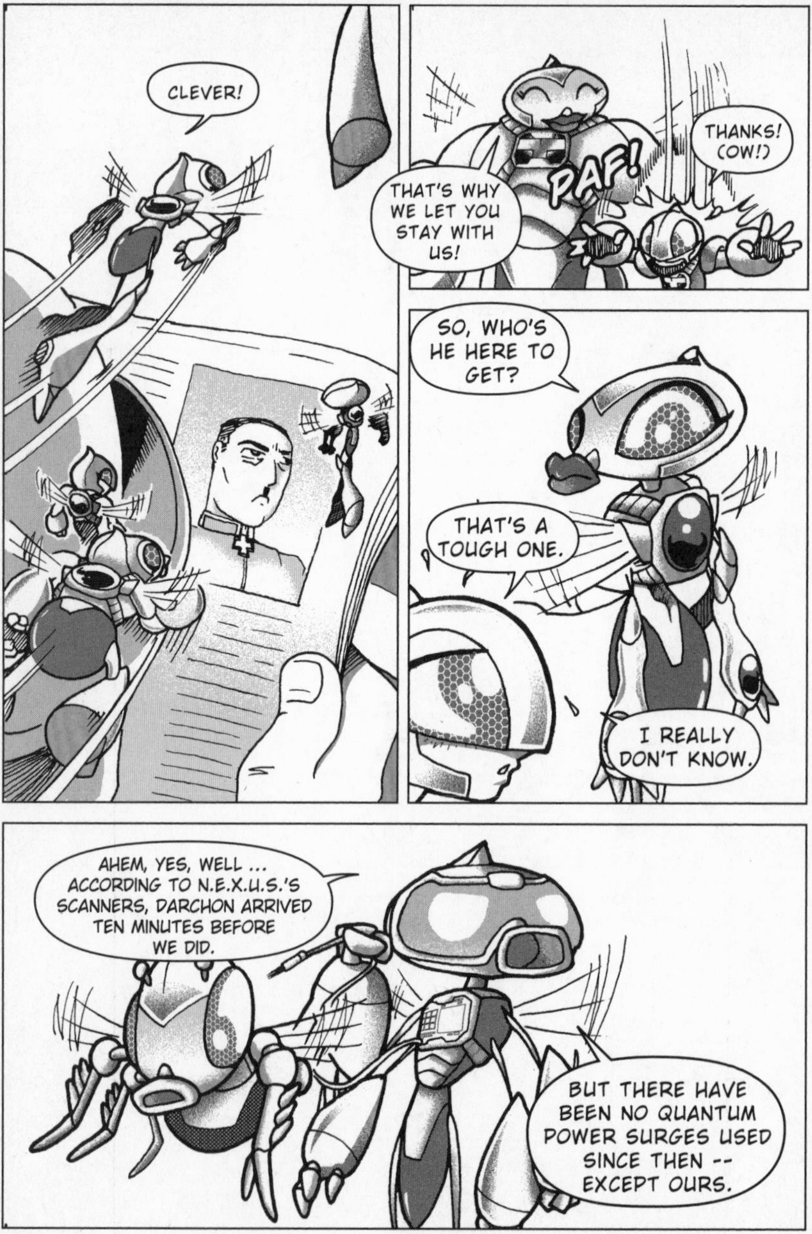

CLEVER!
THAT'S WHY WE LET YOU STAY WITH US!
PAF!
THANKS! (OW!)
SO, WHO'S HE HERE TO GET?
THAT'S A TOUGH ONE.
I REALLY DON'T KNOW.
AHEM, YES, WELL ... ACCORDING TO N.E.X.U.S.'S SCANNERS, DARCHON ARRIVED TEN MINUTES BEFORE WE DID.
BUT THERE HAVE BEEN NO QUANTUM POWER SURGES USED SINCE THEN -- EXCEPT OURS.

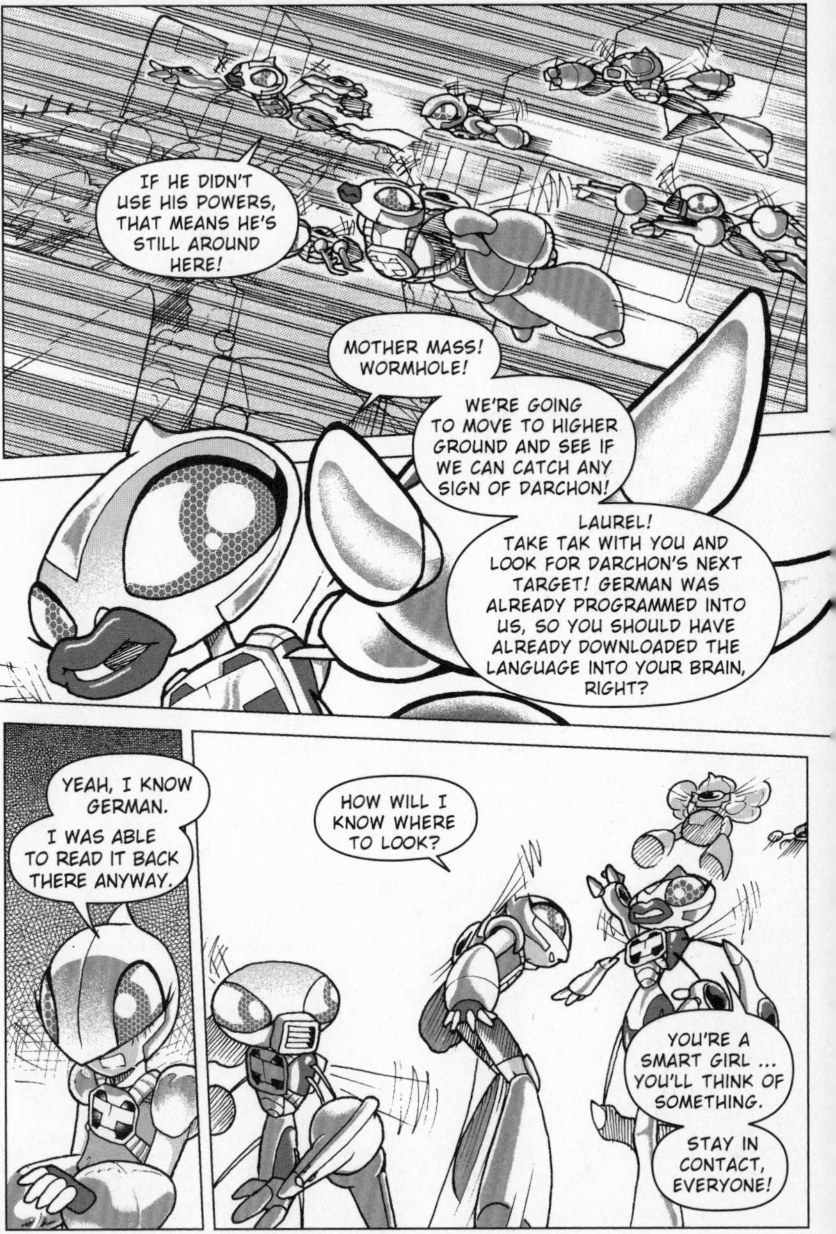
IF HE DIDN'T USE HIS POWERS, THAT MEANS HE'S STILL AROUND HERE!
MOTHER MASS! WORMHOLE!
WE'RE GOING TO MOVE TO HIGHER GROUND AND SEE IF WE CAN CATCH ANY SIGN OF DARCHON!
LAUREL! TAKE TAK WITH YOU AND LOOK FOR DARCHON'S NEXT TARGET! GERMAN WAS ALREADY PROGRAMMED INTO US, SO YOU SHOULD HAVE ALREADY DOWNLOADED THE LANGUAGE INTO YOUR BRAIN, RIGHT?
YEAH, I KNOW GERMAN.
I WAS ABLE TO READ IT BACK THERE ANYWAY.
HOW WILL I KNOW WHERE TO LOOK?
YOU'RE A SMART GIRL ... YOU'LL THINK OF SOMETHING.
STAY IN CONTACT, EVERYONE!

NOW, HOW I AM EVEN SUPPOSED TO KNOW WHERE TO START?

YOU KNOW, THERE'S A JOKE MY DAD USED TO TELL WHEN I LOST SOMETHING.

"IT'S ALWAYS IN THE LAST PLACE YOU LOOK."

~~~~ ~~~~~ ~~~~~.

I KNOW IT'S NOT FUNNY; YOU JUST HAVE TO KNOW MY DAD.

LET'S SEE ...

THIS IS 1938. JUST BEFORE WORLD WAR TWO GETS GOING ...

WASN'T EINSTEIN IN BERLIN FOR A WHILE?

~~~~ ~~~~~ ~~~~~~?

OH, BUT THEY KICKED HIM OUT A LONG TIME BEFORE THE WAR.

~~ ~~~.

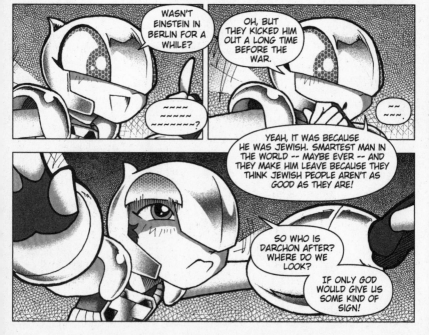

YEAH, IT WAS BECAUSE HE WAS JEWISH. SMARTEST MAN IN THE WORLD -- MAYBE EVER -- AND THEY MAKE HIM LEAVE BECAUSE THEY THINK JEWISH PEOPLE AREN'T AS GOOD AS THEY ARE!

SO WHO IS DARCHON AFTER? WHERE DO WE LOOK?

IF ONLY GOD WOULD GIVE US SOME KIND OF SIGN!

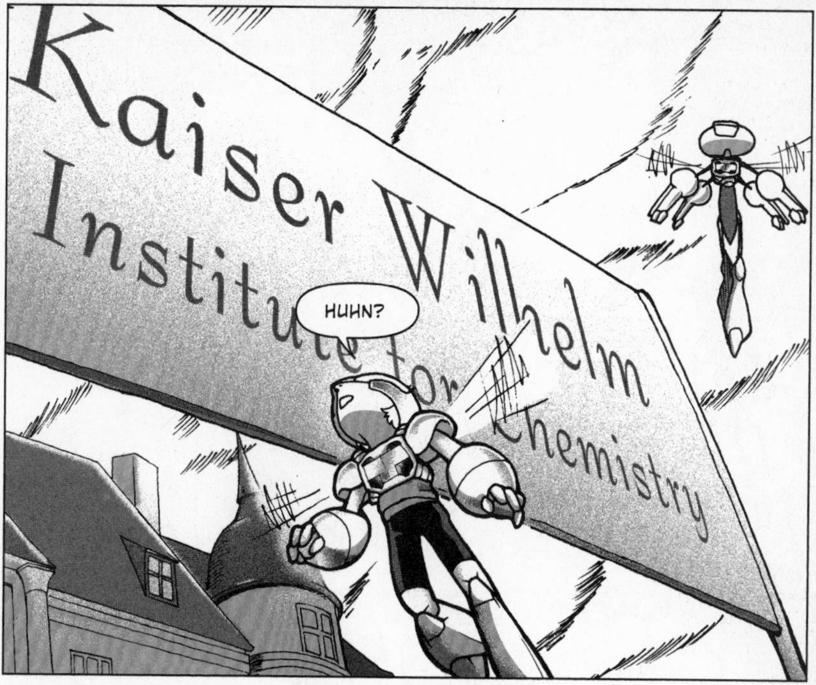
Kaiser Wilhelm
Institute for Chemistry
HUHN?

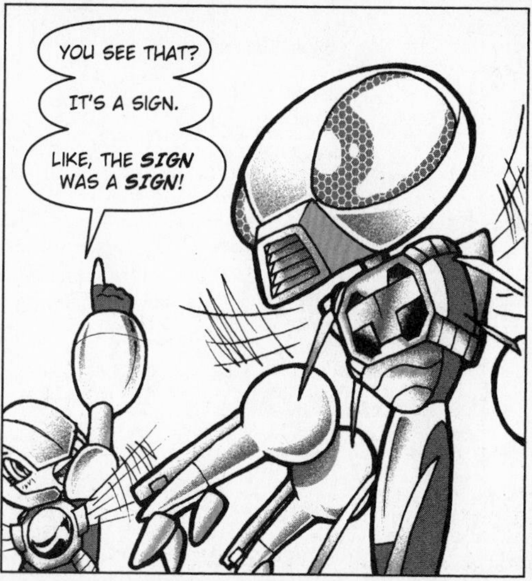
YOU SEE THAT?
IT'S A SIGN.
LIKE, THE **SIGN** WAS A **SIGN**!

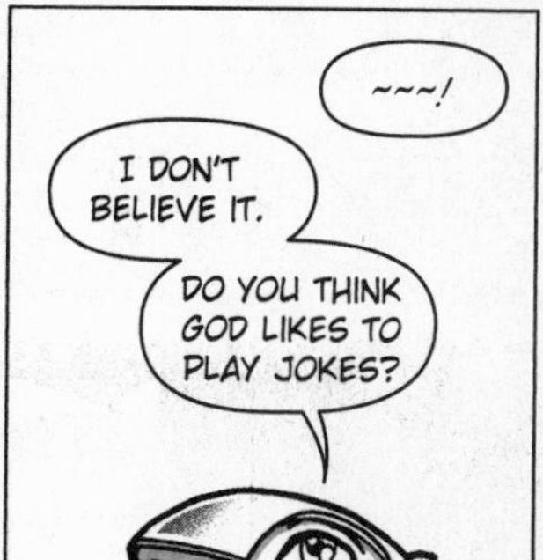

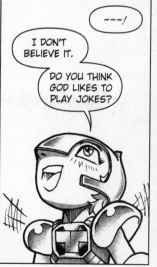

I DON'T BELIEVE IT.
DO YOU THINK GOD LIKES TO PLAY JOKES?

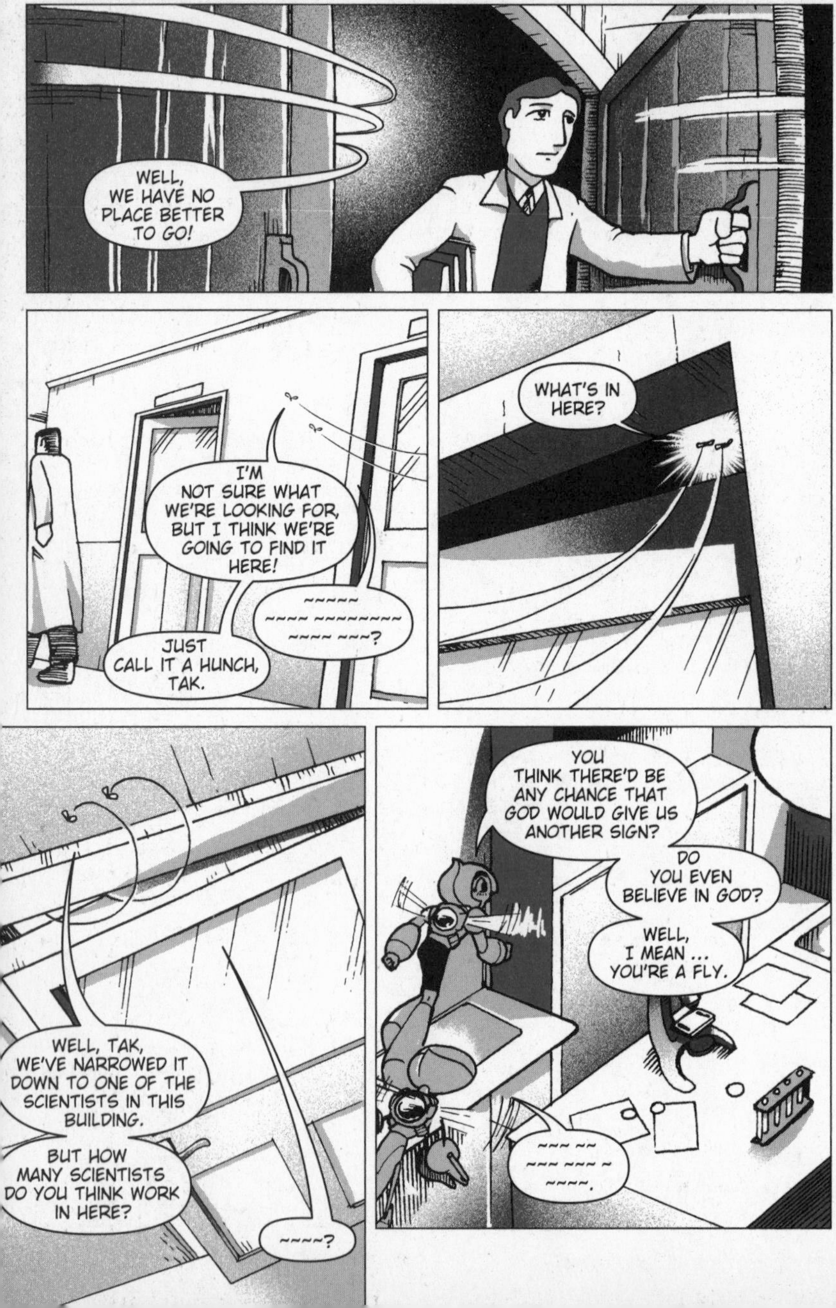
WELL, WE HAVE NO PLACE BETTER TO GO!
I'M NOT SURE WHAT WE'RE LOOKING FOR, BUT I THINK WE'RE GOING TO FIND IT HERE!
~~~~~ ~~~~ ~~~~~~~~ ~~~~ ~~~?
JUST CALL IT A HUNCH, TAK.
WHAT'S IN HERE?
WELL, TAK, WE'VE NARROWED IT DOWN TO ONE OF THE SCIENTISTS IN THIS BUILDING.
BUT HOW MANY SCIENTISTS DO YOU THINK WORK IN HERE?
~~~~?
YOU THINK THERE'D BE ANY CHANCE THAT GOD WOULD GIVE US ANOTHER SIGN?
DO YOU EVEN BELIEVE IN GOD?
WELL, I MEAN ... YOU'RE A FLY.
~~~ ~~ ~~~ ~~~ ~ ~~~~.
~~~

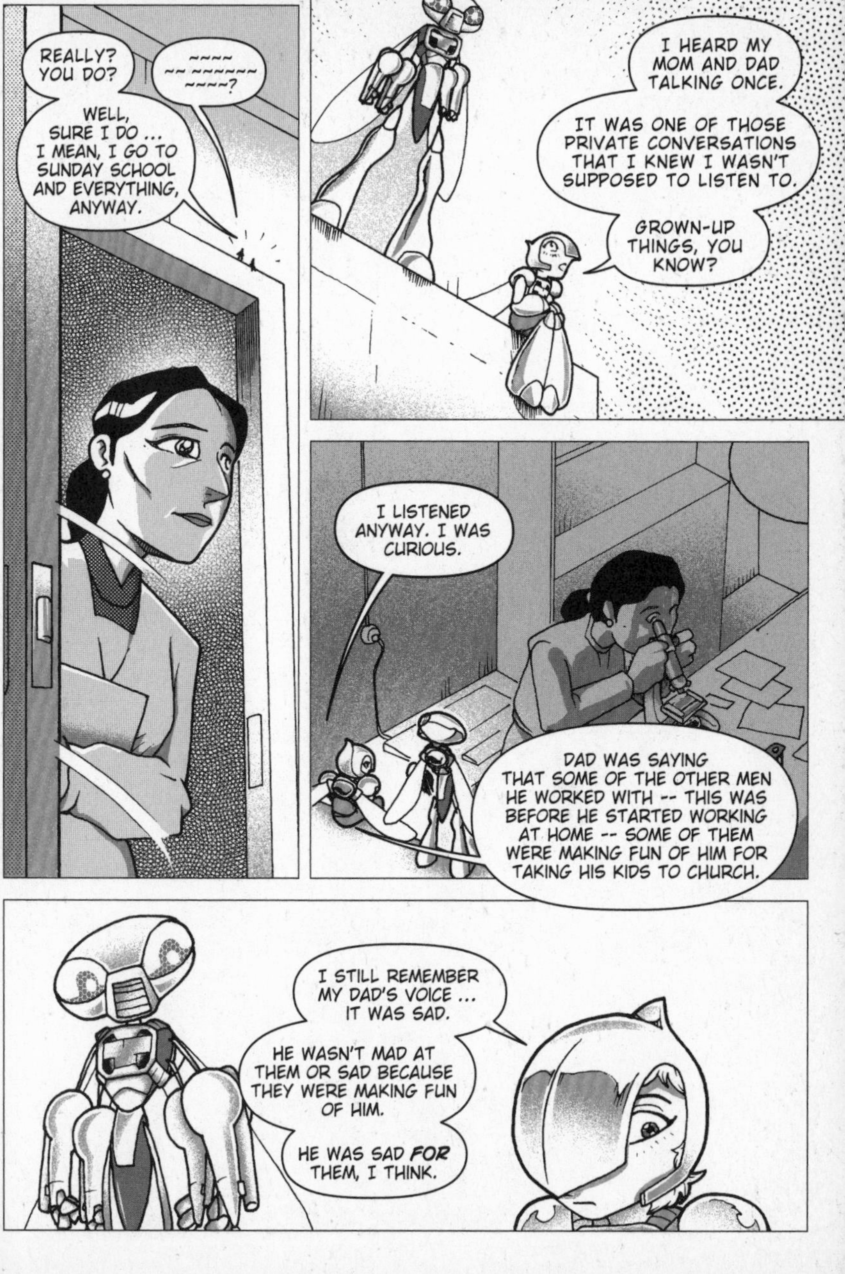
REALLY? YOU DO?
~~~~ ~~ ~~~~~~ ~~~~?
WELL, SURE I DO ... I MEAN, I GO TO SUNDAY SCHOOL AND EVERYTHING, ANYWAY.
I HEARD MY MOM AND DAD TALKING ONCE.
IT WAS ONE OF THOSE PRIVATE CONVERSATIONS THAT I KNEW I WASN'T SUPPOSED TO LISTEN TO.
GROWN-UP THINGS, YOU KNOW?
I LISTENED ANYWAY. I WAS CURIOUS.
DAD WAS SAYING THAT SOME OF THE OTHER MEN HE WORKED WITH -- THIS WAS BEFORE HE STARTED WORKING AT HOME -- SOME OF THEM WERE MAKING FUN OF HIM FOR TAKING HIS KIDS TO CHURCH.
I STILL REMEMBER MY DAD'S VOICE ... IT WAS SAD.
HE WASN'T MAD AT THEM OR SAD BECAUSE THEY WERE MAKING FUN OF HIM.
HE WAS SAD FOR THEM, I THINK.
~~~~

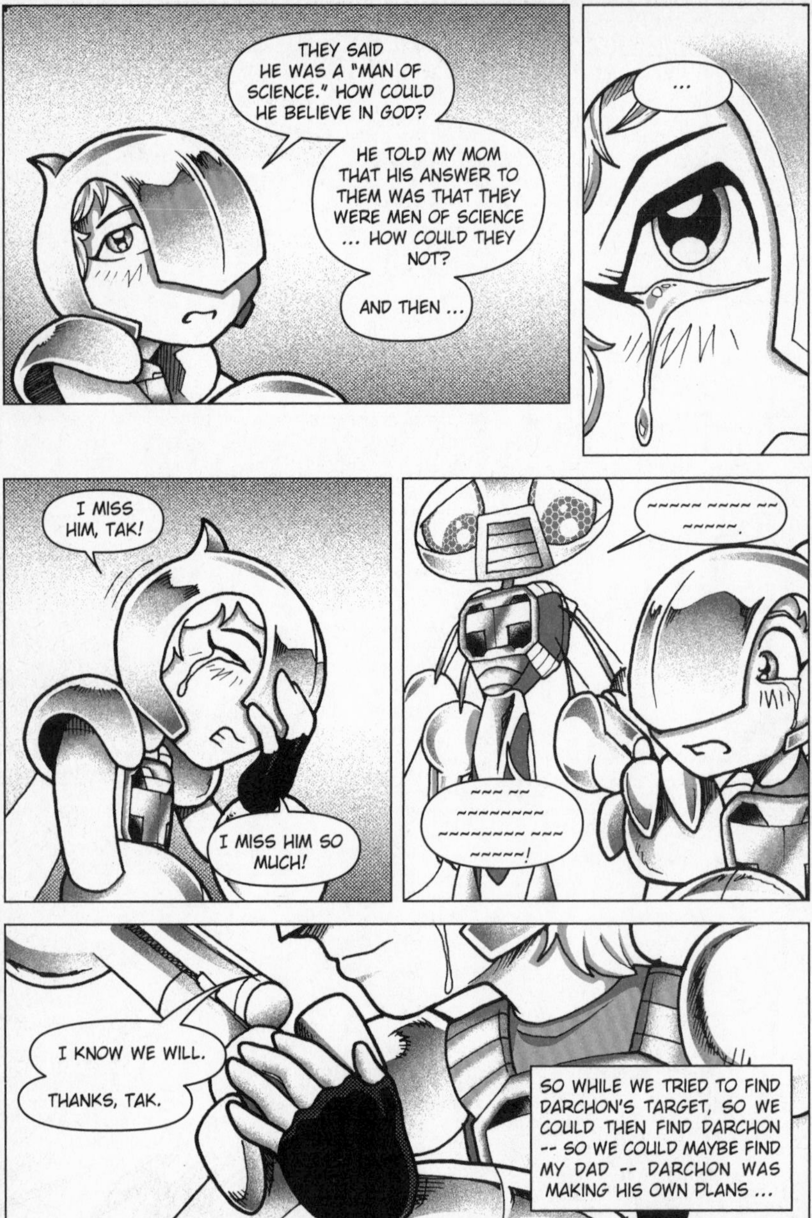
THEY SAID HE WAS A "MAN OF SCIENCE." HOW COULD HE BELIEVE IN GOD?
HE TOLD MY MOM THAT HIS ANSWER TO THEM WAS THAT THEY WERE MEN OF SCIENCE ... HOW COULD THEY NOT?
AND THEN ...
...
I MISS HIM, TAK!
I MISS HIM SO MUCH!
~~~~~ ~~~~ ~~ ~~~~~.
~~~ ~~ ~~~~~~~~ ~~~~~~~~ ~~~ ~~~~~!
I KNOW WE WILL.
THANKS, TAK.
SO WHILE WE TRIED TO FIND DARCHON'S TARGET, SO WE COULD THEN FIND DARCHON -- SO WE COULD MAYBE FIND MY DAD -- DARCHON WAS MAKING HIS OWN PLANS ...

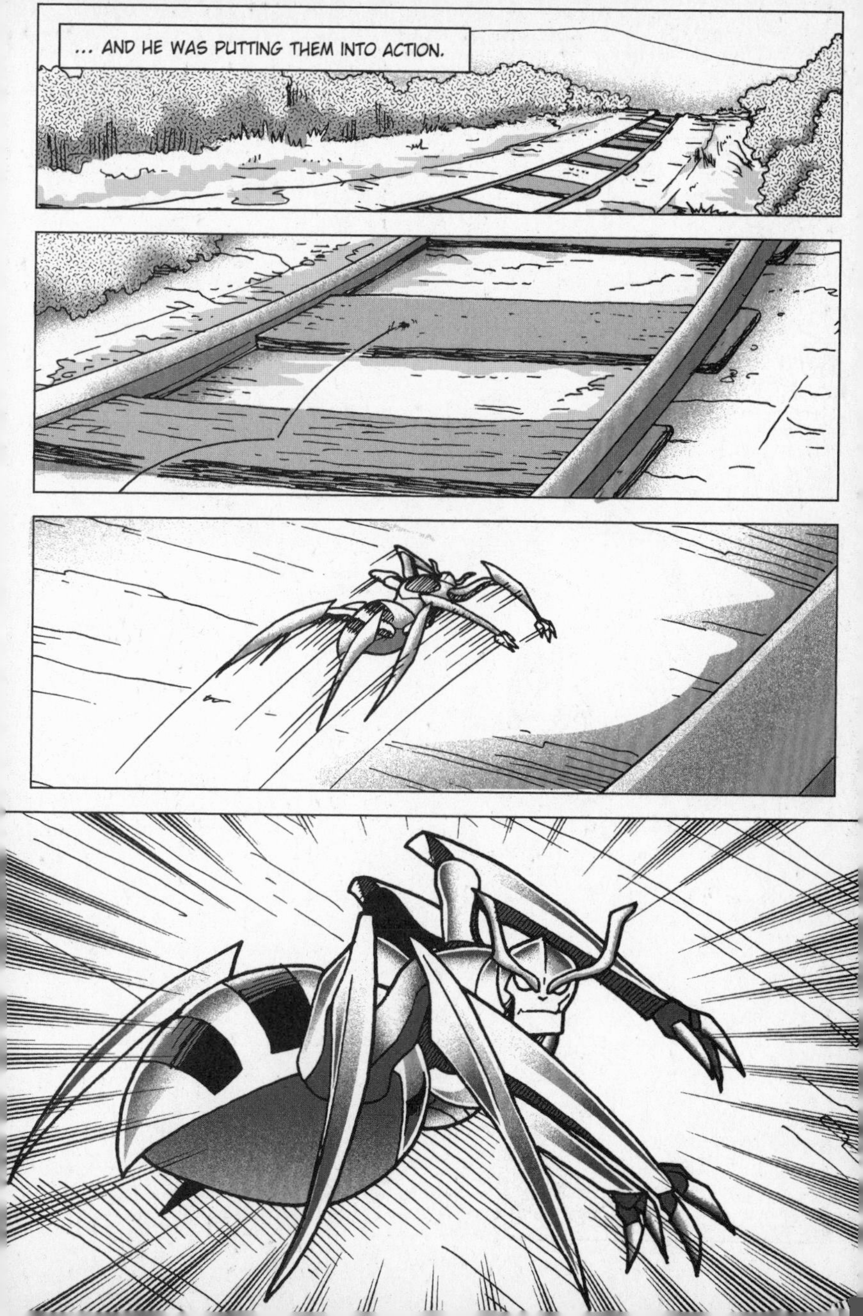
... AND HE WAS PUTTING THEM INTO ACTION.

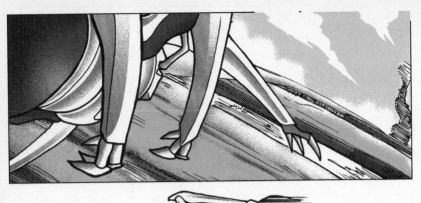

ERMMM ...

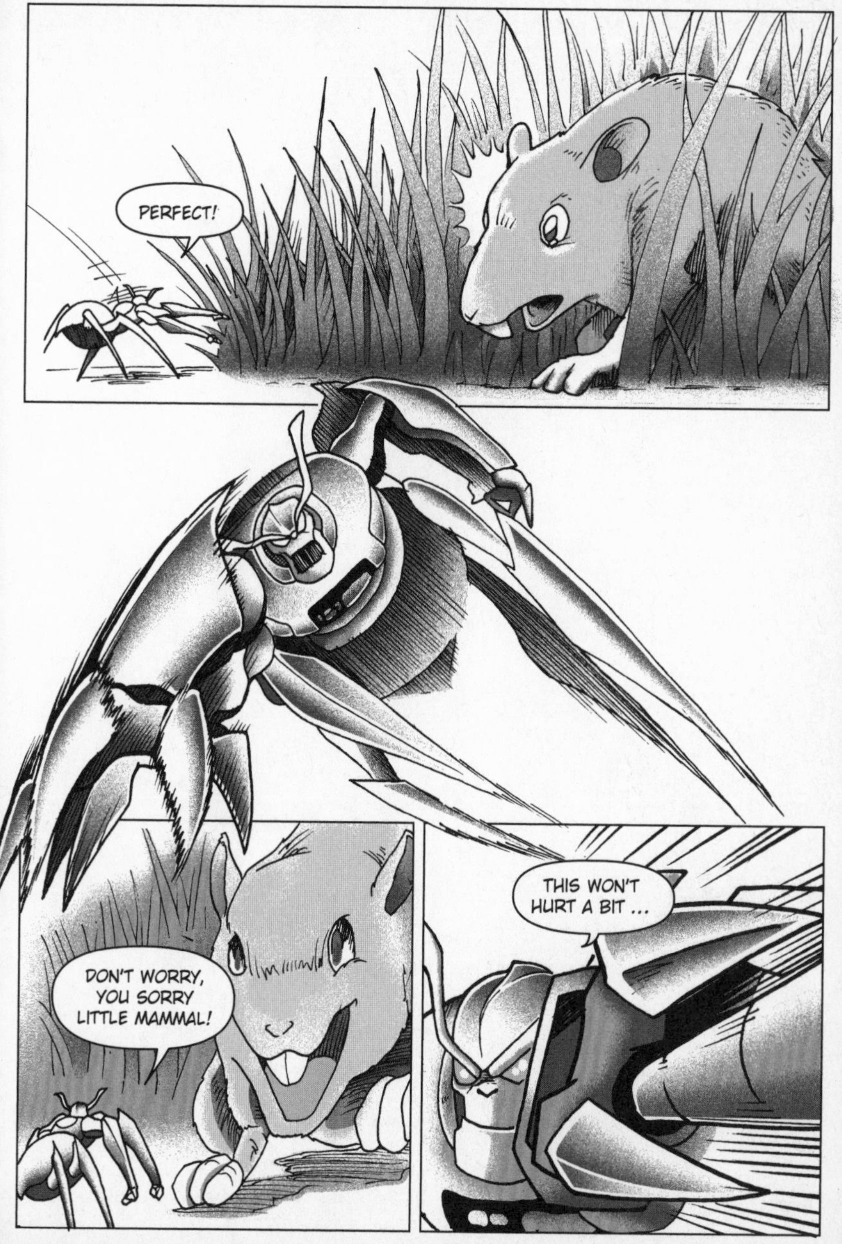
PERFECT!
DON'T WORRY, YOU SORRY LITTLE MAMMAL!
THIS WON'T HURT A BIT ...

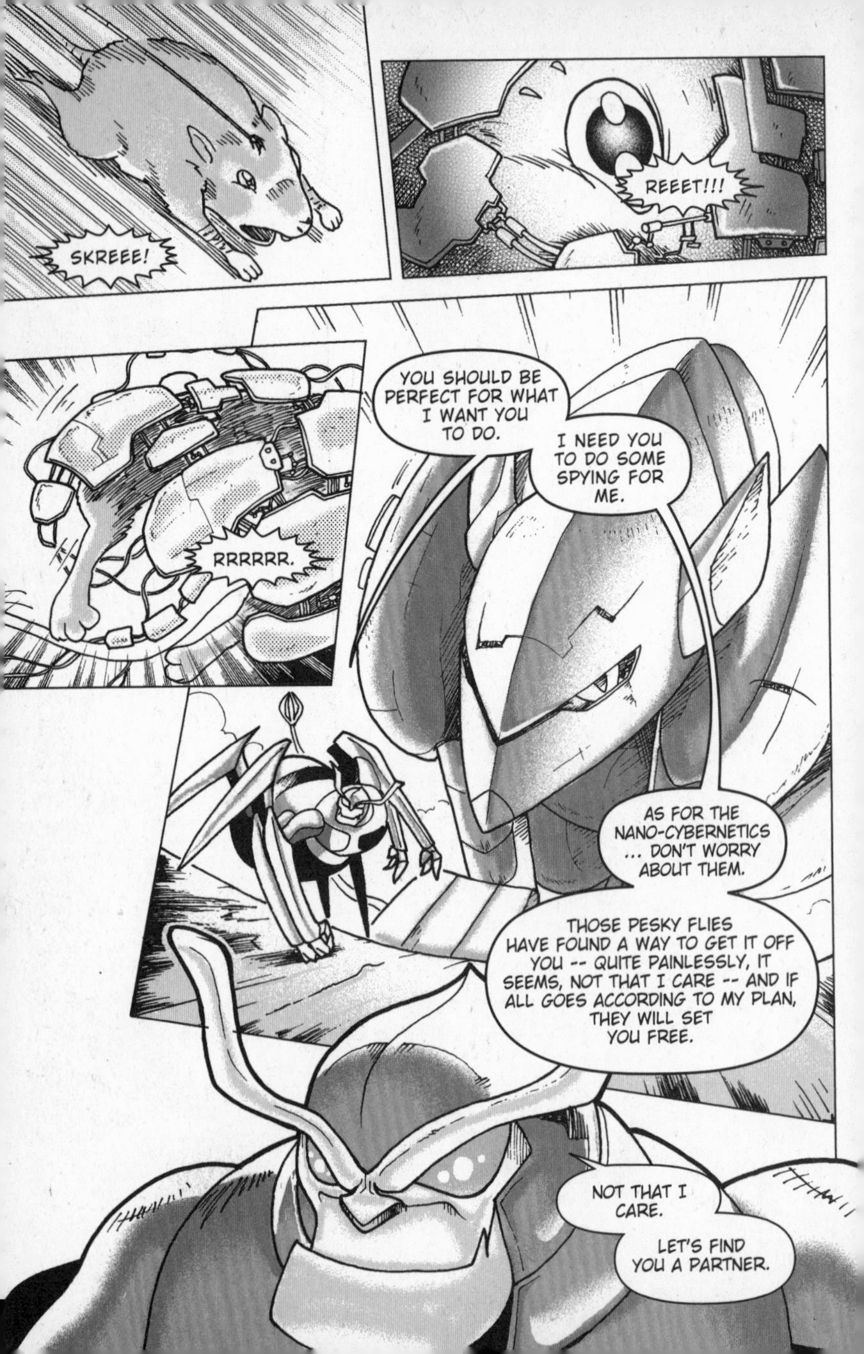
SKREEE!
REEET!!!
RRRRRR.
YOU SHOULD BE PERFECT FOR WHAT I WANT YOU TO DO.
I NEED YOU TO DO SOME SPYING FOR ME.
AS FOR THE NANO-CYBERNETICS ... DON'T WORRY ABOUT THEM.
THOSE PESKY FLIES HAVE FOUND A WAY TO GET IT OFF YOU -- QUITE PAINLESSLY, IT SEEMS, NOT THAT I CARE -- AND IF ALL GOES ACCORDING TO MY PLAN, THEY WILL SET YOU FREE.
NOT THAT I CARE.
LET'S FIND YOU A PARTNER.

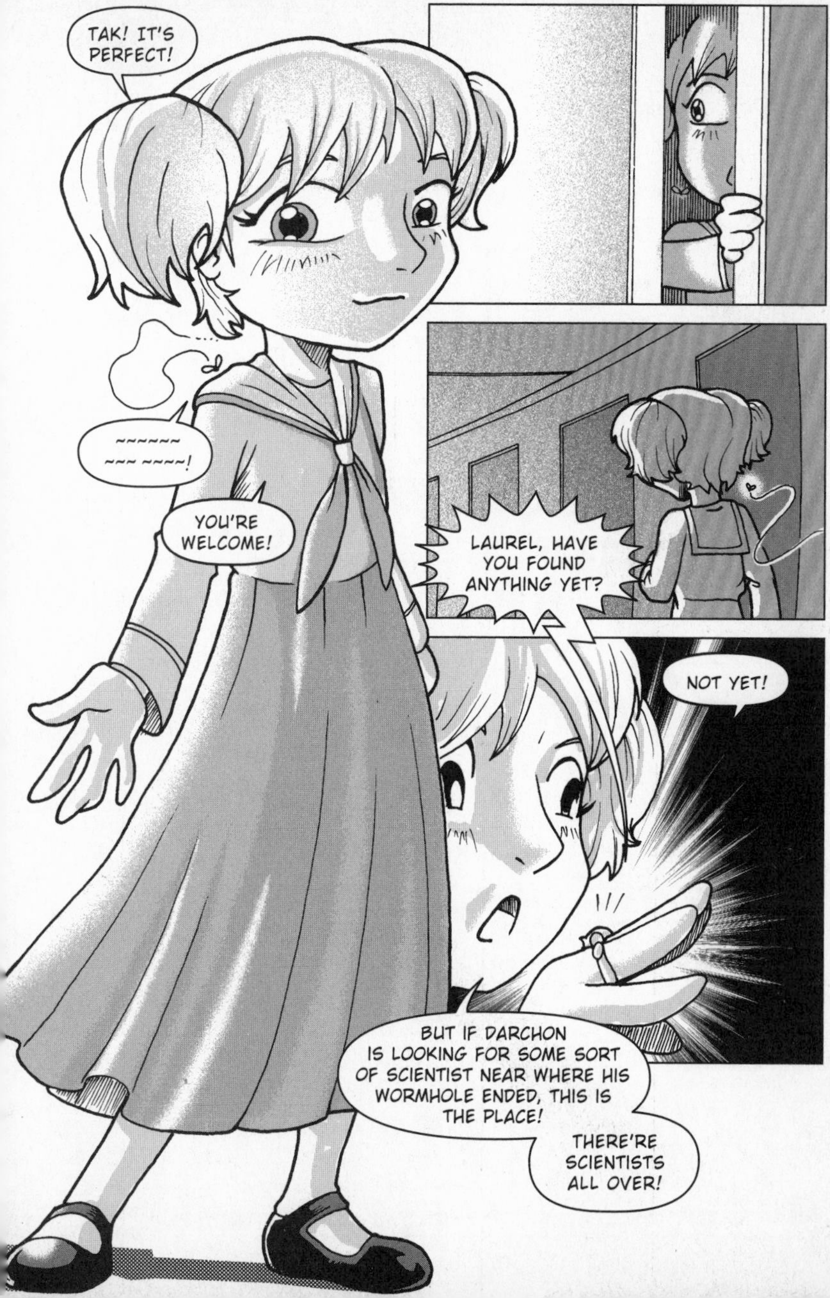
TAK! IT'S PERFECT!
~~~~~~ ~~~ ~~~~~!
YOU'RE WELCOME!
LAUREL, HAVE YOU FOUND ANYTHING YET?
NOT YET!
BUT IF DARCHON IS LOOKING FOR SOME SORT OF SCIENTIST NEAR WHERE HIS WORMHOLE ENDED, THIS IS THE PLACE!
THERE'RE SCIENTISTS ALL OVER!
~~~~~~

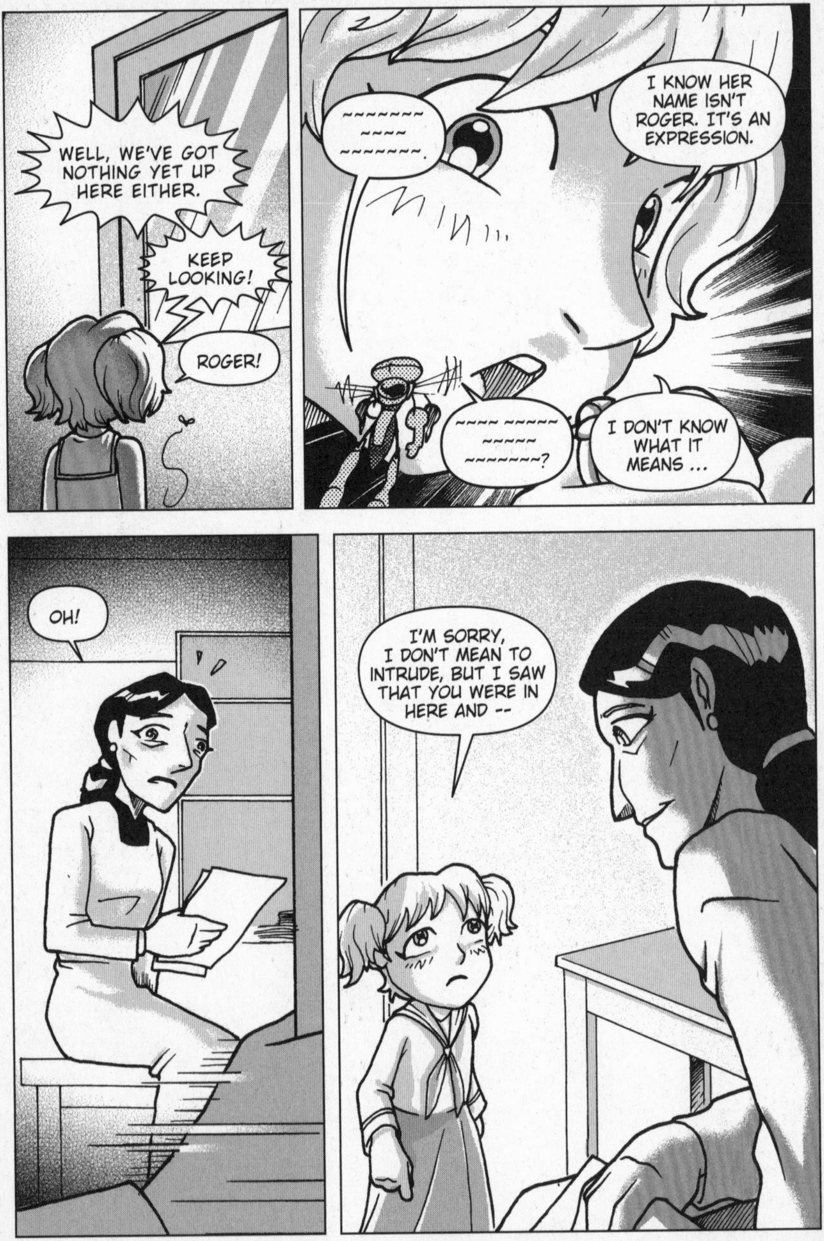
WELL, WE'VE GOT NOTHING YET UP HERE EITHER.
KEEP LOOKING!
ROGER!
~~~~~~~ ~~~~ ~~~~~~~.
I KNOW HER NAME ISN'T ROGER. IT'S AN EXPRESSION.
~~~~ ~~~~~ ~~~~~ ~~~~~~~?
I DON'T KNOW WHAT IT MEANS ...
OH!
I'M SORRY, I DON'T MEAN TO INTRUDE, BUT I SAW THAT YOU WERE IN HERE AND --

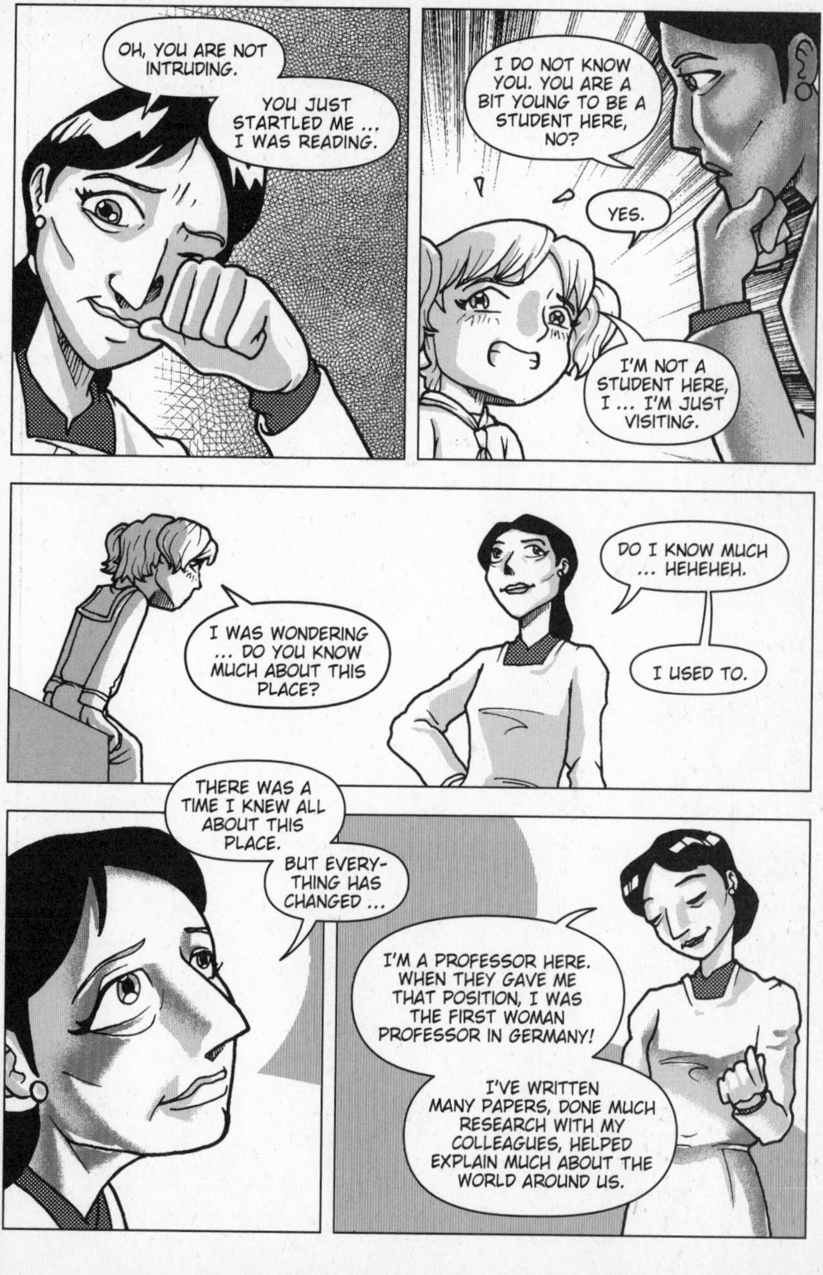
OH, YOU ARE NOT INTRUDING.
YOU JUST STARTLED ME ... I WAS READING.
I DO NOT KNOW YOU. YOU ARE A BIT YOUNG TO BE A STUDENT HERE, NO?
YES.
I'M NOT A STUDENT HERE, I ... I'M JUST VISITING.
I WAS WONDERING ... DO YOU KNOW MUCH ABOUT THIS PLACE?
DO I KNOW MUCH ... HEHEHEH.
I USED TO.
THERE WAS A TIME I KNEW ALL ABOUT THIS PLACE.
BUT EVERY-THING HAS CHANGED ...
I'M A PROFESSOR HERE. WHEN THEY GAVE ME THAT POSITION, I WAS THE FIRST WOMAN PROFESSOR IN GERMANY!
I'VE WRITTEN MANY PAPERS, DONE MUCH RESEARCH WITH MY COLLEAGUES, HELPED EXPLAIN MUCH ABOUT THE WORLD AROUND US.

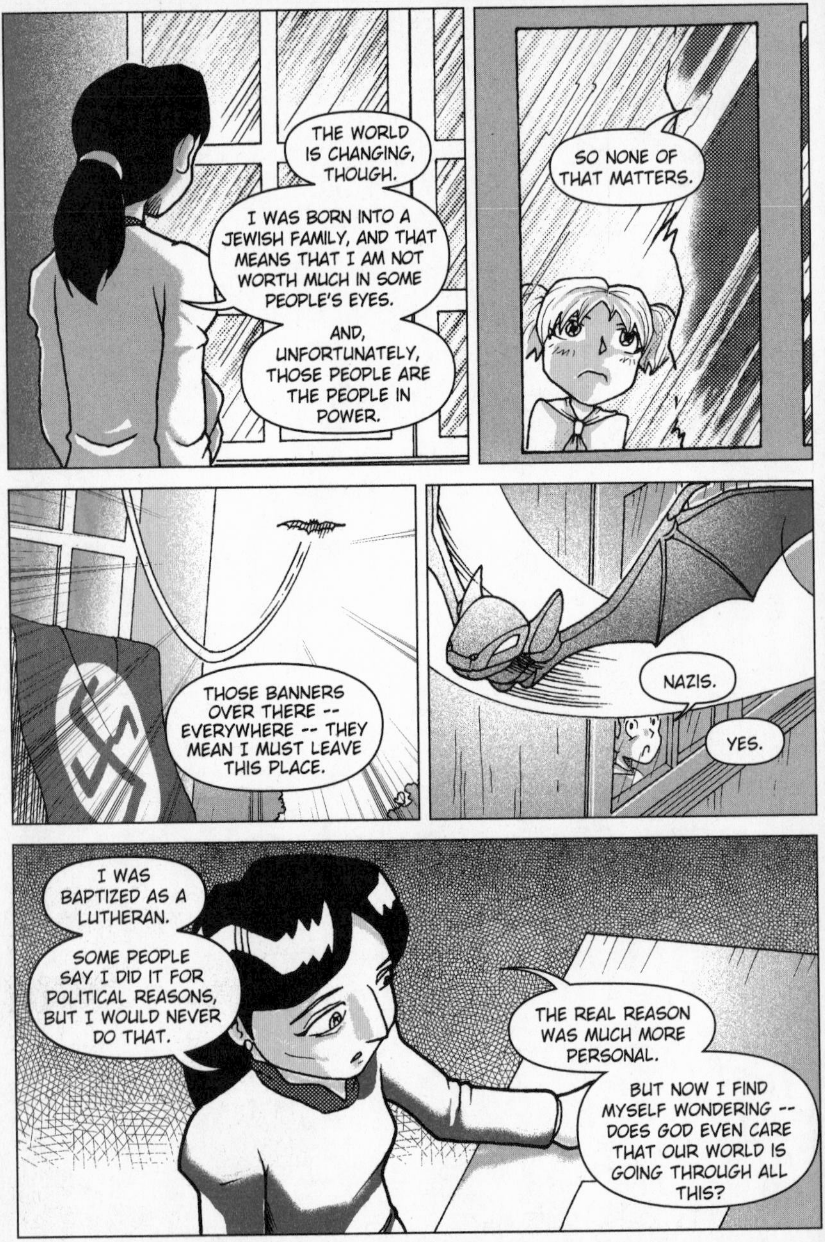
THE WORLD IS CHANGING, THOUGH.
I WAS BORN INTO A JEWISH FAMILY, AND THAT MEANS THAT I AM NOT WORTH MUCH IN SOME PEOPLE'S EYES.
AND, UNFORTUNATELY, THOSE PEOPLE ARE THE PEOPLE IN POWER.
SO NONE OF THAT MATTERS.
THOSE BANNERS OVER THERE -- EVERYWHERE -- THEY MEAN I MUST LEAVE THIS PLACE.
NAZIS.
YES.
I WAS BAPTIZED AS A LUTHERAN.
SOME PEOPLE SAY I DID IT FOR POLITICAL REASONS, BUT I WOULD NEVER DO THAT.
THE REAL REASON WAS MUCH MORE PERSONAL.
BUT NOW I FIND MYSELF WONDERING -- DOES GOD EVEN CARE THAT OUR WORLD IS GOING THROUGH ALL THIS?

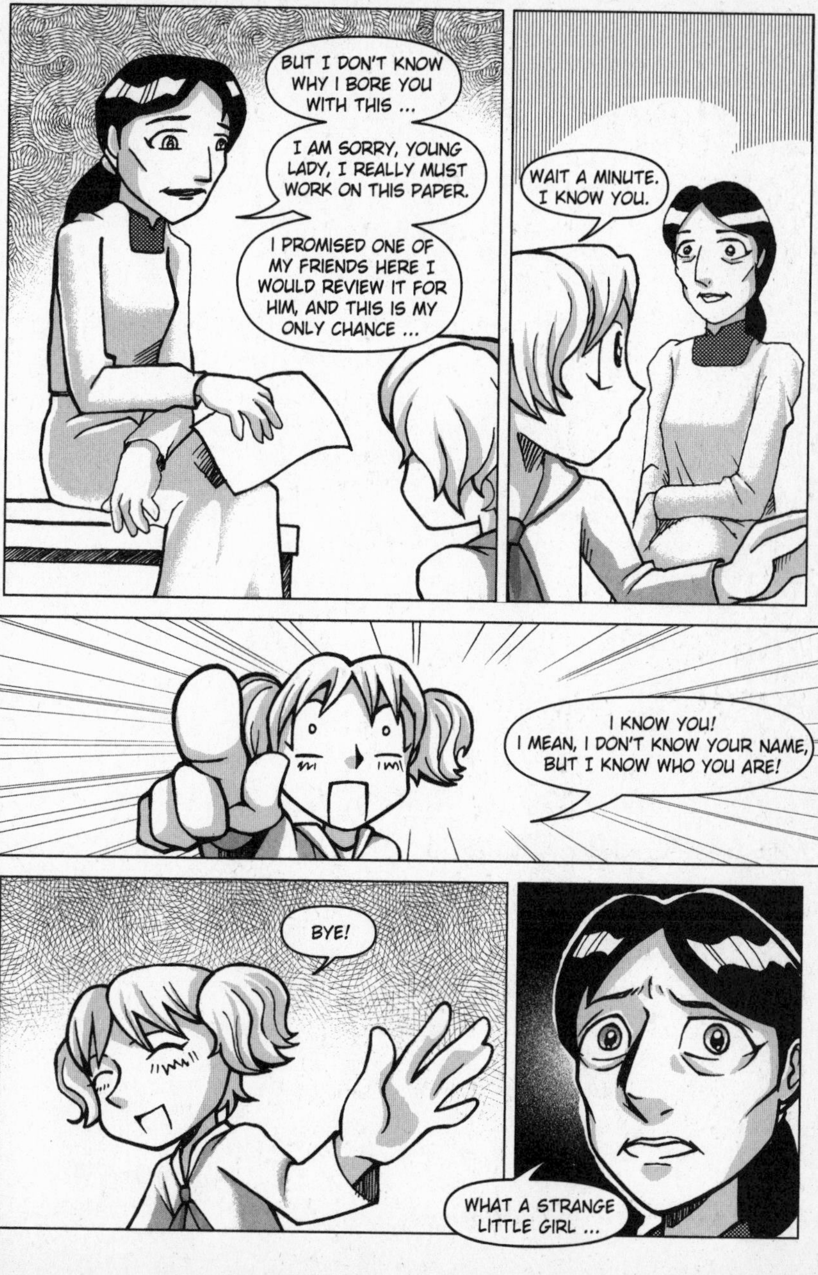
BUT I DON'T KNOW WHY I BORE YOU WITH THIS ...
I AM SORRY, YOUNG LADY, I REALLY MUST WORK ON THIS PAPER.
I PROMISED ONE OF MY FRIENDS HERE I WOULD REVIEW IT FOR HIM, AND THIS IS MY ONLY CHANCE ...
WAIT A MINUTE. I KNOW YOU.
I KNOW YOU! I MEAN, I DON'T KNOW YOUR NAME, BUT I KNOW WHO YOU ARE!
BYE!
WHAT A STRANGE LITTLE GIRL ...

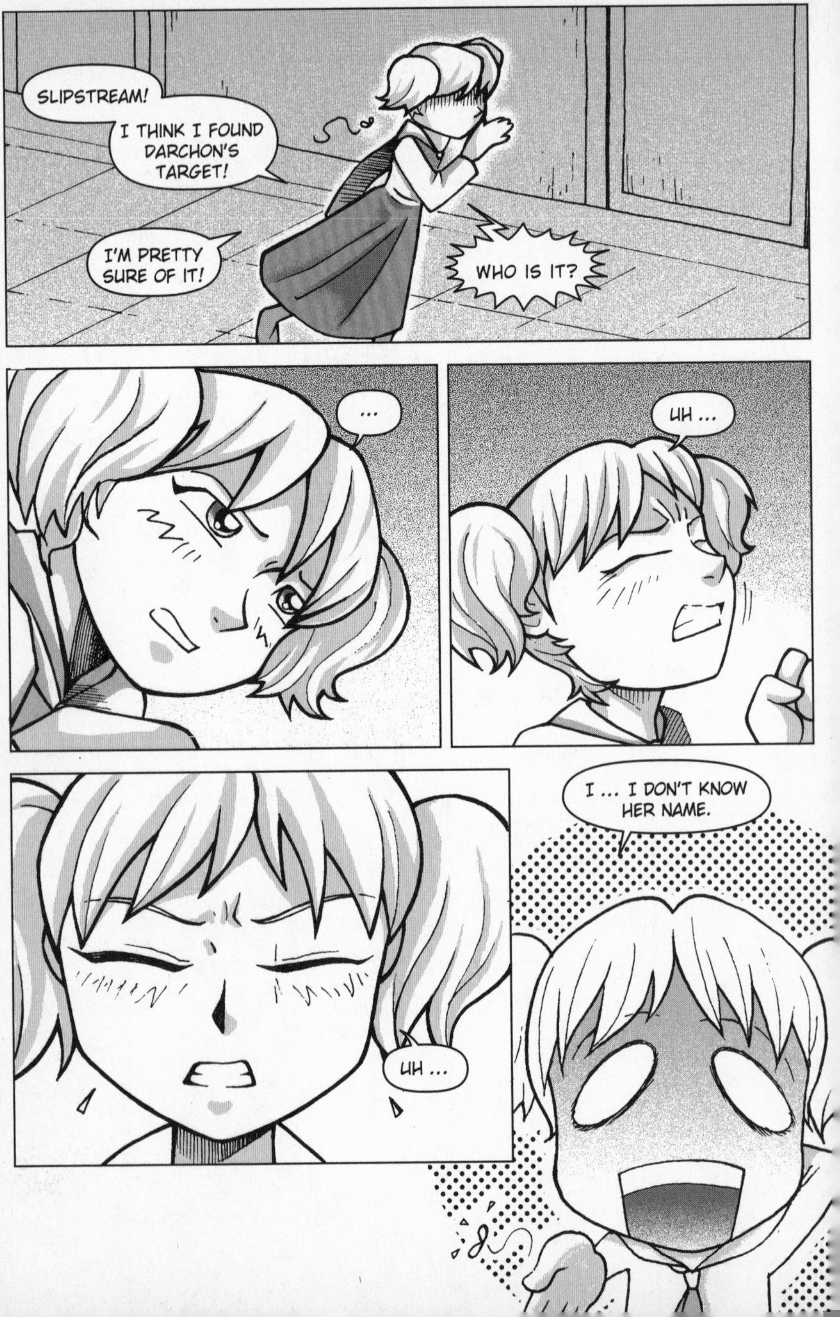
SLIPSTREAM!
I THINK I FOUND DARCHON'S TARGET!
I'M PRETTY SURE OF IT!
WHO IS IT?
...
UH ...
UH ...
I ... I DON'T KNOW HER NAME.

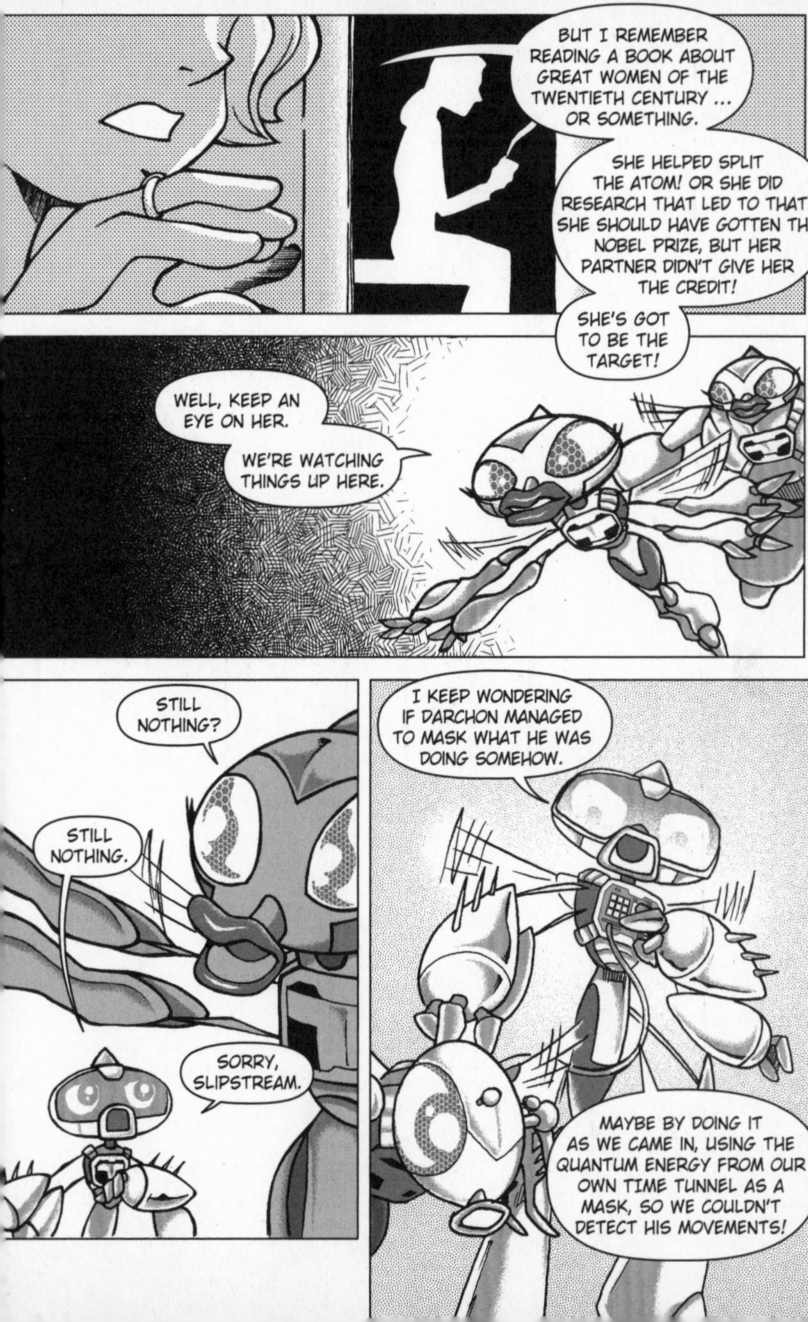
BUT I REMEMBER READING A BOOK ABOUT GREAT WOMEN OF THE TWENTIETH CENTURY ... OR SOMETHING.
SHE HELPED SPLIT THE ATOM! OR SHE DID RESEARCH THAT LED TO THAT! SHE SHOULD HAVE GOTTEN THE NOBEL PRIZE, BUT HER PARTNER DIDN'T GIVE HER THE CREDIT!
SHE'S GOT TO BE THE TARGET!
WELL, KEEP AN EYE ON HER.
WE'RE WATCHING THINGS UP HERE.
STILL NOTHING?
STILL NOTHING.
SORRY, SLIPSTREAM.
I KEEP WONDERING IF DARCHON MANAGED TO MASK WHAT HE WAS DOING SOMEHOW.
MAYBE BY DOING IT AS WE CAME IN, USING THE QUANTUM ENERGY FROM OUR OWN TIME TUNNEL AS A MASK, SO WE COULDN'T DETECT HIS MOVEMENTS!

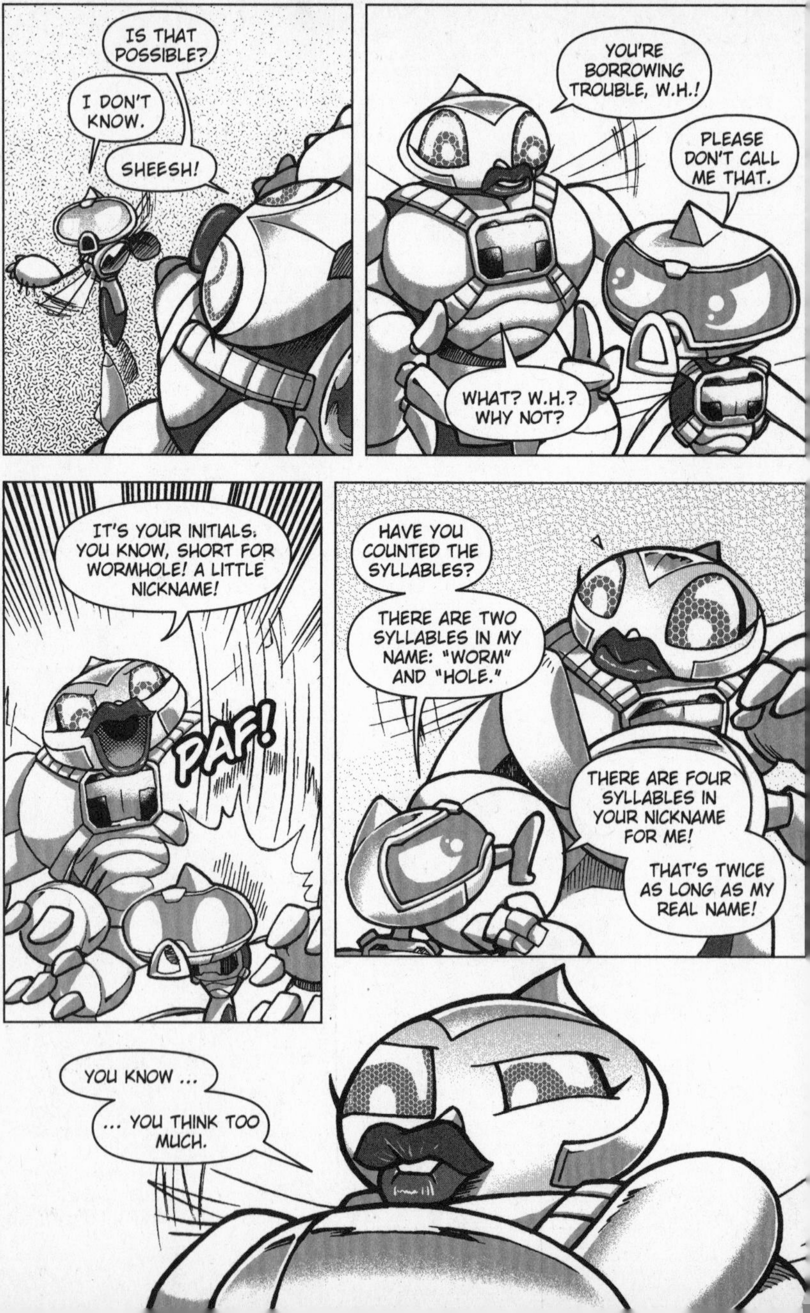
IS THAT POSSIBLE?
I DON'T KNOW.
SHEESH!
YOU'RE BORROWING TROUBLE, W.H.!
PLEASE DON'T CALL ME THAT.
WHAT? W.H.? WHY NOT?
IT'S YOUR INITIALS: YOU KNOW, SHORT FOR WORMHOLE! A LITTLE NICKNAME!
PAF!
HAVE YOU COUNTED THE SYLLABLES?
THERE ARE TWO SYLLABLES IN MY NAME: "WORM" AND "HOLE."
THERE ARE FOUR SYLLABLES IN YOUR NICKNAME FOR ME!
THAT'S TWICE AS LONG AS MY REAL NAME!
YOU KNOW ...
... YOU THINK TOO MUCH.

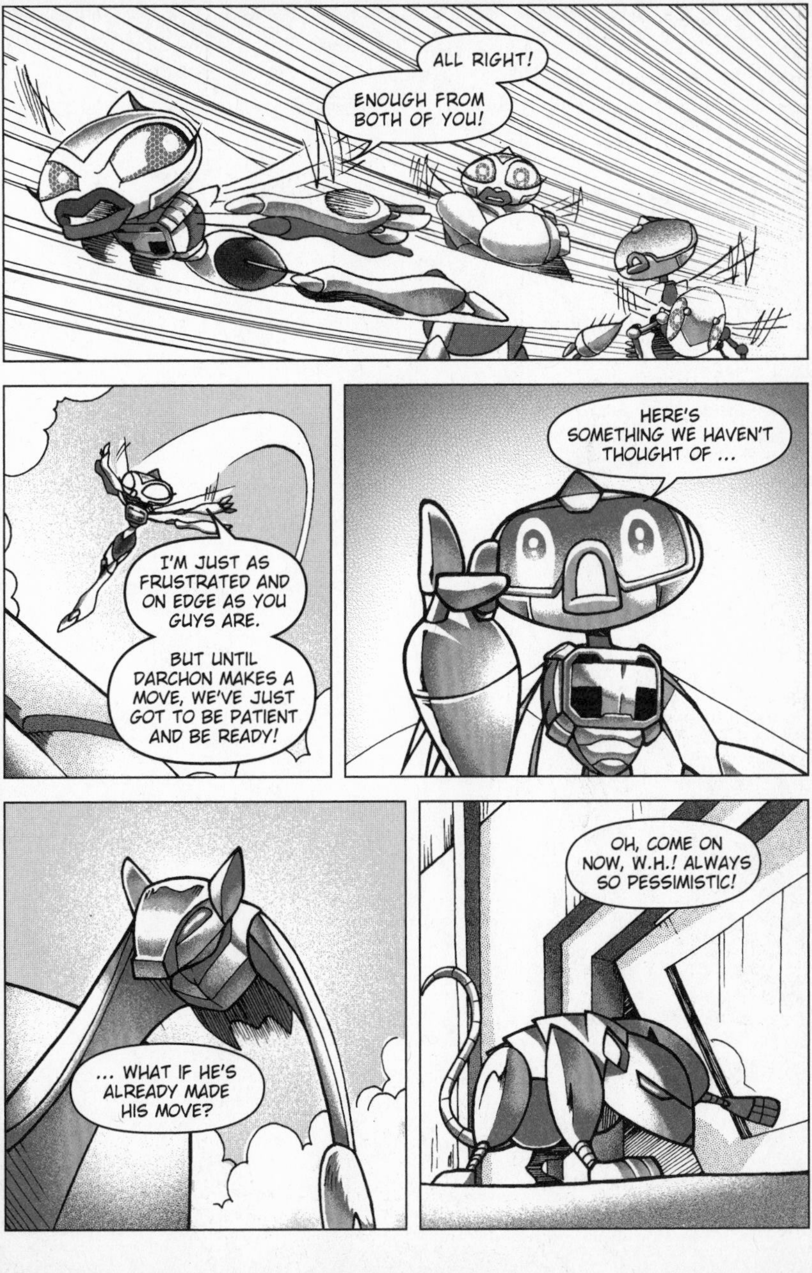
ALL RIGHT!
ENOUGH FROM BOTH OF YOU!
I'M JUST AS FRUSTRATED AND ON EDGE AS YOU GUYS ARE.
BUT UNTIL DARCHON MAKES A MOVE, WE'VE JUST GOT TO BE PATIENT AND BE READY!
HERE'S SOMETHING WE HAVEN'T THOUGHT OF ...
... WHAT IF HE'S ALREADY MADE HIS MOVE?
OH, COME ON NOW, W.H.! ALWAYS SO PESSIMISTIC!

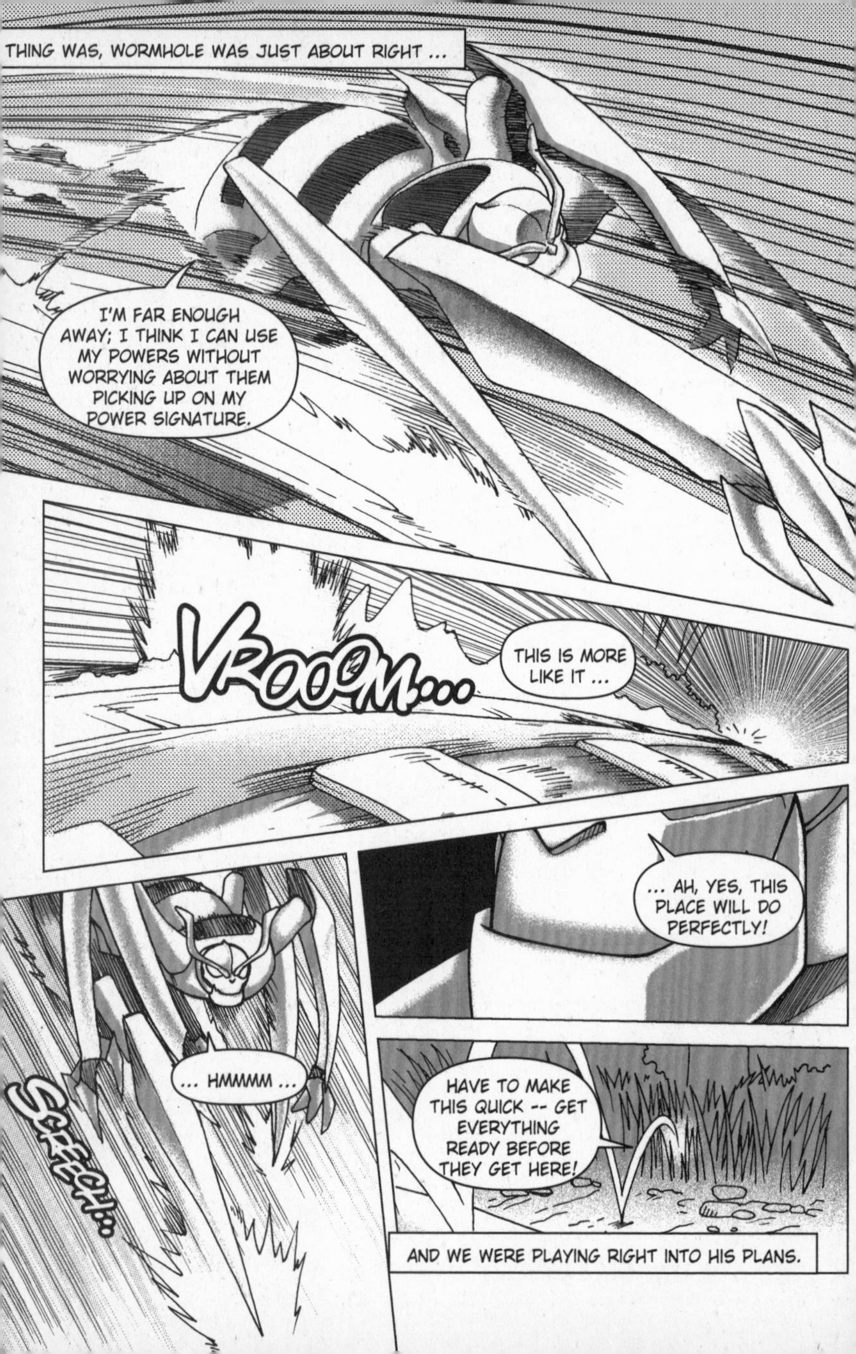
THING WAS, WORMHOLE WAS JUST ABOUT RIGHT ...
I'M FAR ENOUGH AWAY; I THINK I CAN USE MY POWERS WITHOUT WORRYING ABOUT THEM PICKING UP ON MY POWER SIGNATURE.
VROOOM...
THIS IS MORE LIKE IT ...
... HMMMM ...
SCREECH...
... AH, YES, THIS PLACE WILL DO PERFECTLY!
HAVE TO MAKE THIS QUICK -- GET EVERYTHING READY BEFORE THEY GET HERE!
AND WE WERE PLAYING RIGHT INTO HIS PLANS.

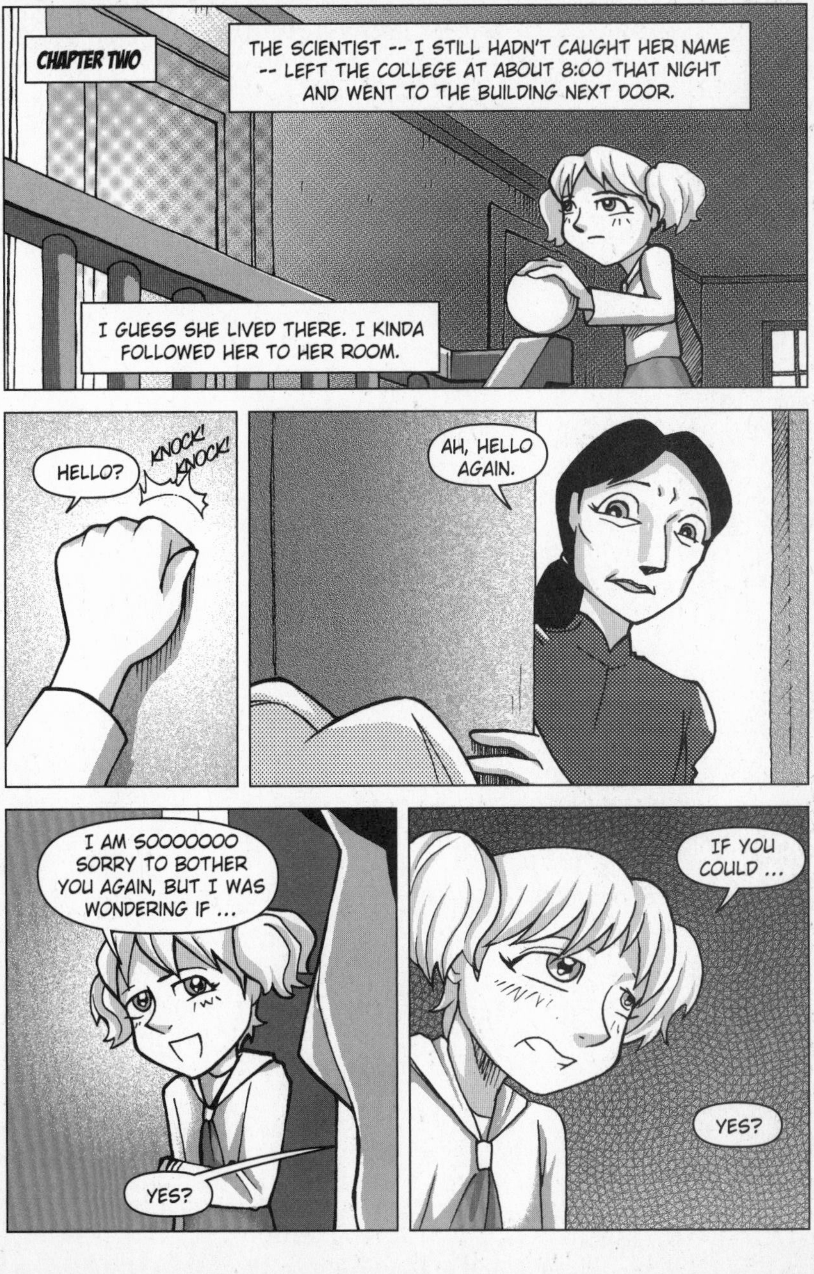
CHAPTER TWO
THE SCIENTIST -- I STILL HADN'T CAUGHT HER NAME -- LEFT THE COLLEGE AT ABOUT 8:00 THAT NIGHT AND WENT TO THE BUILDING NEXT DOOR.
I GUESS SHE LIVED THERE. I KINDA FOLLOWED HER TO HER ROOM.
HELLO?
KNOCK! KNOCK!
AH, HELLO AGAIN.
I AM SOOOOOOO SORRY TO BOTHER YOU AGAIN, BUT I WAS WONDERING IF ...
YES?
IF YOU COULD ...
YES?

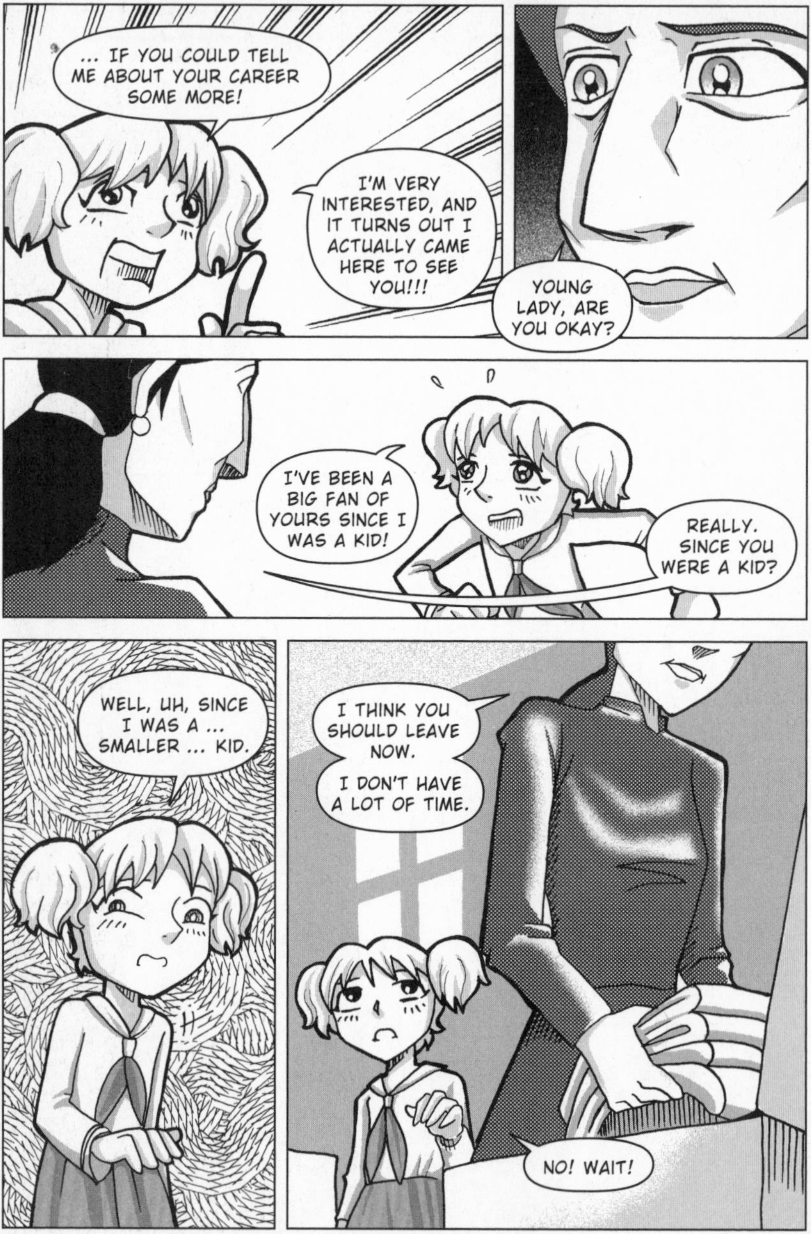

... IF YOU COULD TELL ME ABOUT YOUR CAREER SOME MORE!
I'M VERY INTERESTED, AND IT TURNS OUT I ACTUALLY CAME HERE TO SEE YOU!!!
YOUNG LADY, ARE YOU OKAY?
I'VE BEEN A BIG FAN OF YOURS SINCE I WAS A KID!
REALLY. SINCE YOU WERE A KID?
WELL, UH, SINCE I WAS A ... SMALLER ... KID.
I THINK YOU SHOULD LEAVE NOW.
I DON'T HAVE A LOT OF TIME.
NO! WAIT!

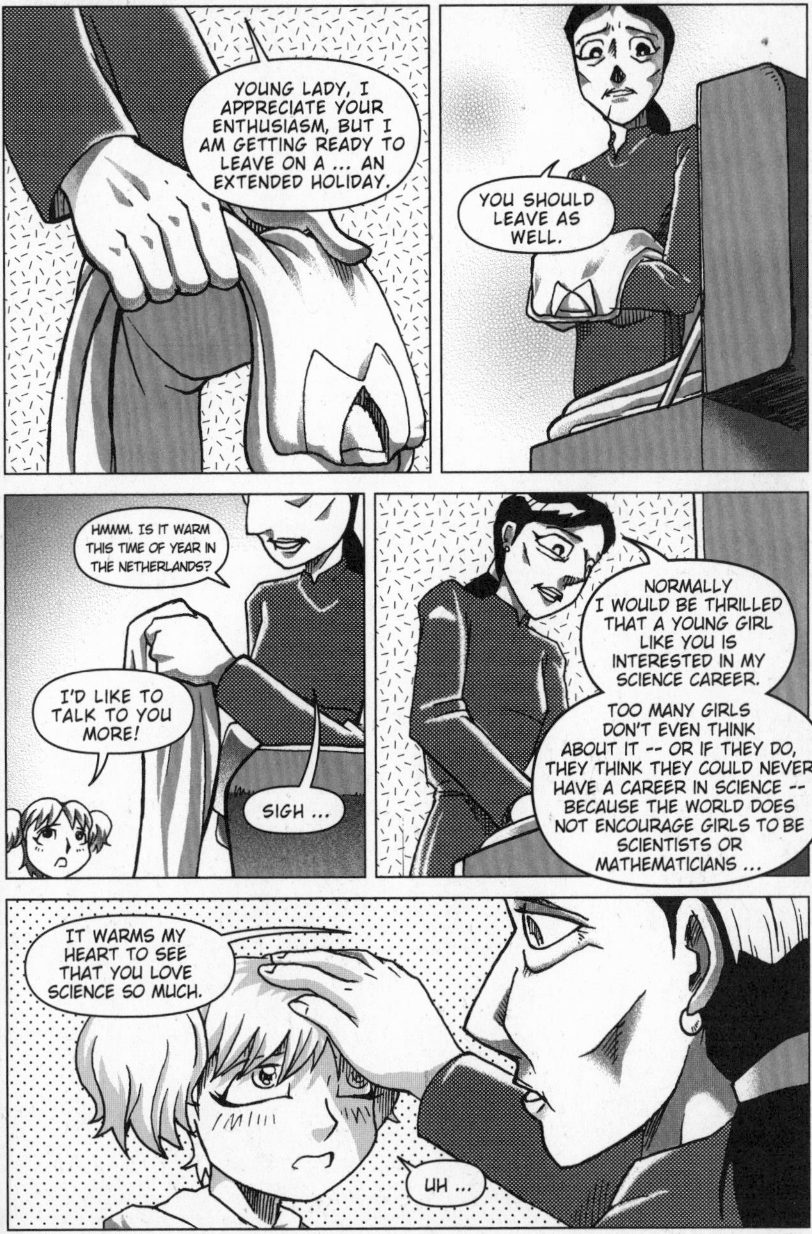
YOUNG LADY, I APPRECIATE YOUR ENTHUSIASM, BUT I AM GETTING READY TO LEAVE ON A ... AN EXTENDED HOLIDAY.
YOU SHOULD LEAVE AS WELL.
HMMM. IS IT WARM THIS TIME OF YEAR IN THE NETHERLANDS?
I'D LIKE TO TALK TO YOU MORE!
SIGH ...
NORMALLY I WOULD BE THRILLED THAT A YOUNG GIRL LIKE YOU IS INTERESTED IN MY SCIENCE CAREER.
TOO MANY GIRLS DON'T EVEN THINK ABOUT IT -- OR IF THEY DO, THEY THINK THEY COULD NEVER HAVE A CAREER IN SCIENCE -- BECAUSE THE WORLD DOES NOT ENCOURAGE GIRLS TO BE SCIENTISTS OR MATHEMATICIANS ...
IT WARMS MY HEART TO SEE THAT YOU LOVE SCIENCE SO MUCH.
UH ...

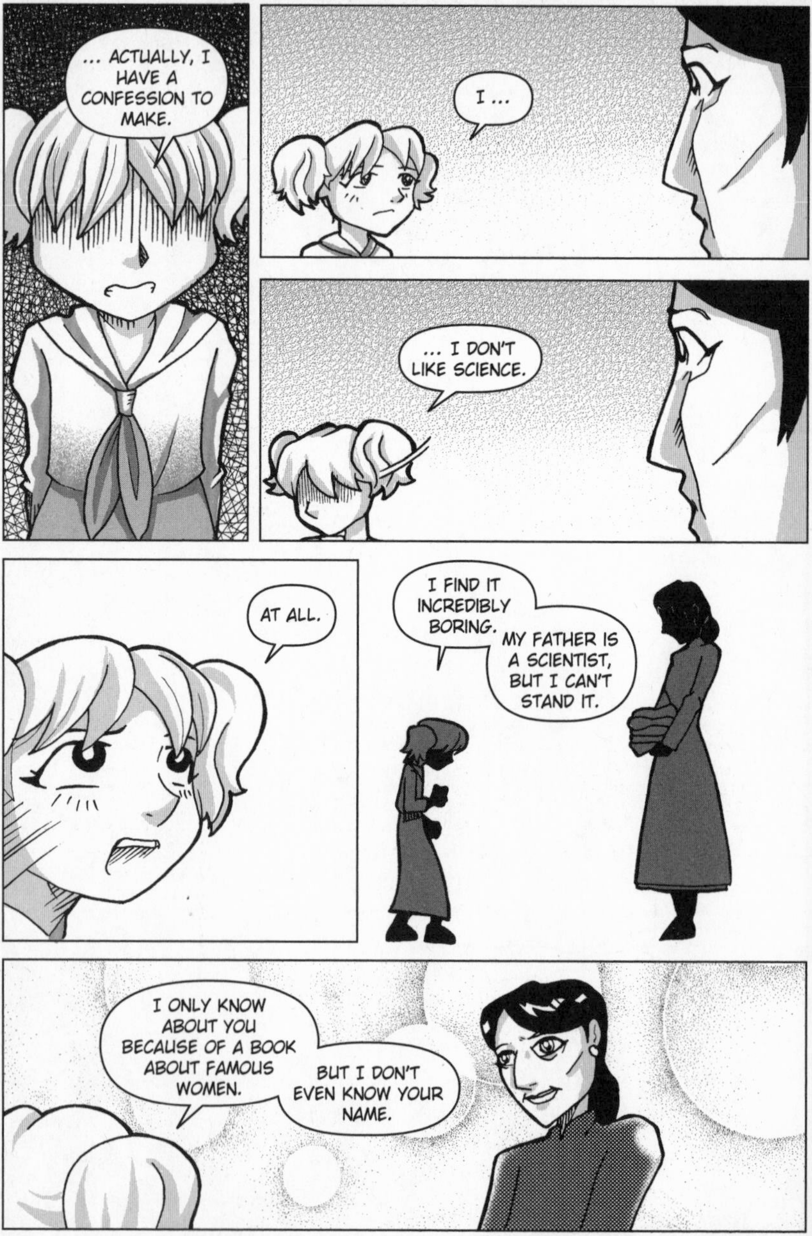
... ACTUALLY, I HAVE A CONFESSION TO MAKE.
I ...
... I DON'T LIKE SCIENCE.
AT ALL.
I FIND IT INCREDIBLY BORING.
MY FATHER IS A SCIENTIST, BUT I CAN'T STAND IT.
I ONLY KNOW ABOUT YOU BECAUSE OF A BOOK ABOUT FAMOUS WOMEN.
BUT I DON'T EVEN KNOW YOUR NAME.

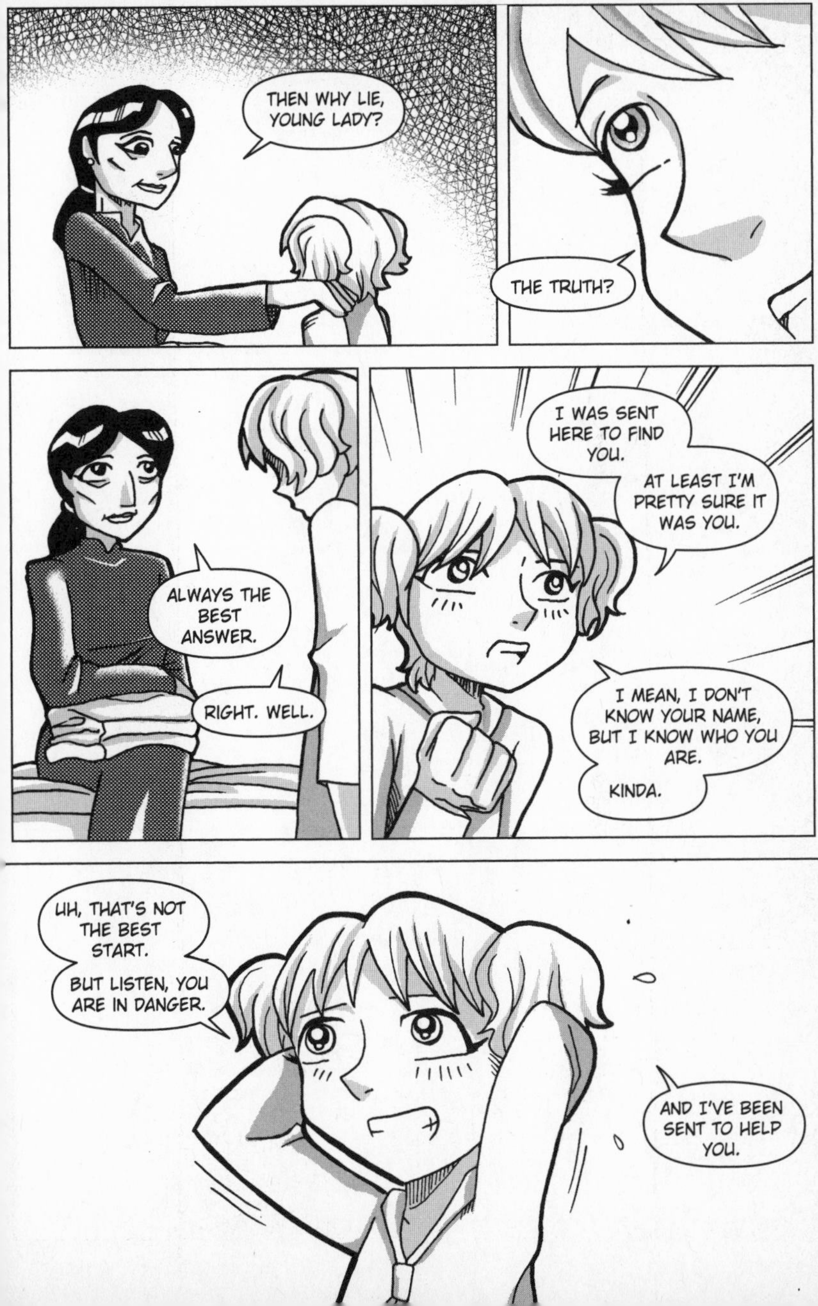
THEN WHY LIE, YOUNG LADY?
THE TRUTH?
ALWAYS THE BEST ANSWER.
RIGHT. WELL.
I WAS SENT HERE TO FIND YOU.
AT LEAST I'M PRETTY SURE IT WAS YOU.
I MEAN, I DON'T KNOW YOUR NAME, BUT I KNOW WHO YOU ARE.
KINDA.
UH, THAT'S NOT THE BEST START.
BUT LISTEN, YOU ARE IN DANGER.
AND I'VE BEEN SENT TO HELP YOU.

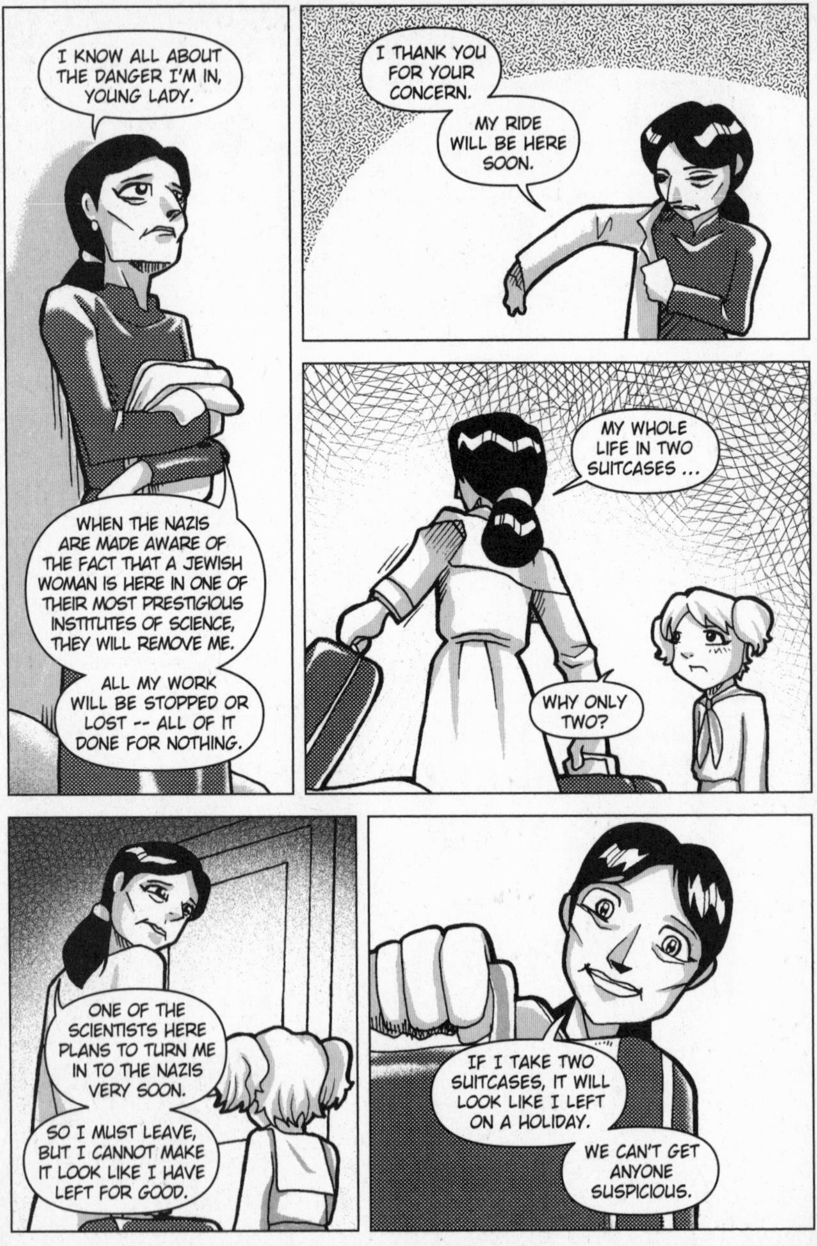
I KNOW ALL ABOUT THE DANGER I'M IN, YOUNG LADY.
WHEN THE NAZIS ARE MADE AWARE OF THE FACT THAT A JEWISH WOMAN IS HERE IN ONE OF THEIR MOST PRESTIGIOUS INSTITUTES OF SCIENCE, THEY WILL REMOVE ME.
ALL MY WORK WILL BE STOPPED OR LOST -- ALL OF IT DONE FOR NOTHING.
I THANK YOU FOR YOUR CONCERN.
MY RIDE WILL BE HERE SOON.
MY WHOLE LIFE IN TWO SUITCASES ...
WHY ONLY TWO?
ONE OF THE SCIENTISTS HERE PLANS TO TURN ME IN TO THE NAZIS VERY SOON.
SO I MUST LEAVE, BUT I CANNOT MAKE IT LOOK LIKE I HAVE LEFT FOR GOOD.
IF I TAKE TWO SUITCASES, IT WILL LOOK LIKE I LEFT ON A HOLIDAY.
WE CAN'T GET ANYONE SUSPICIOUS.

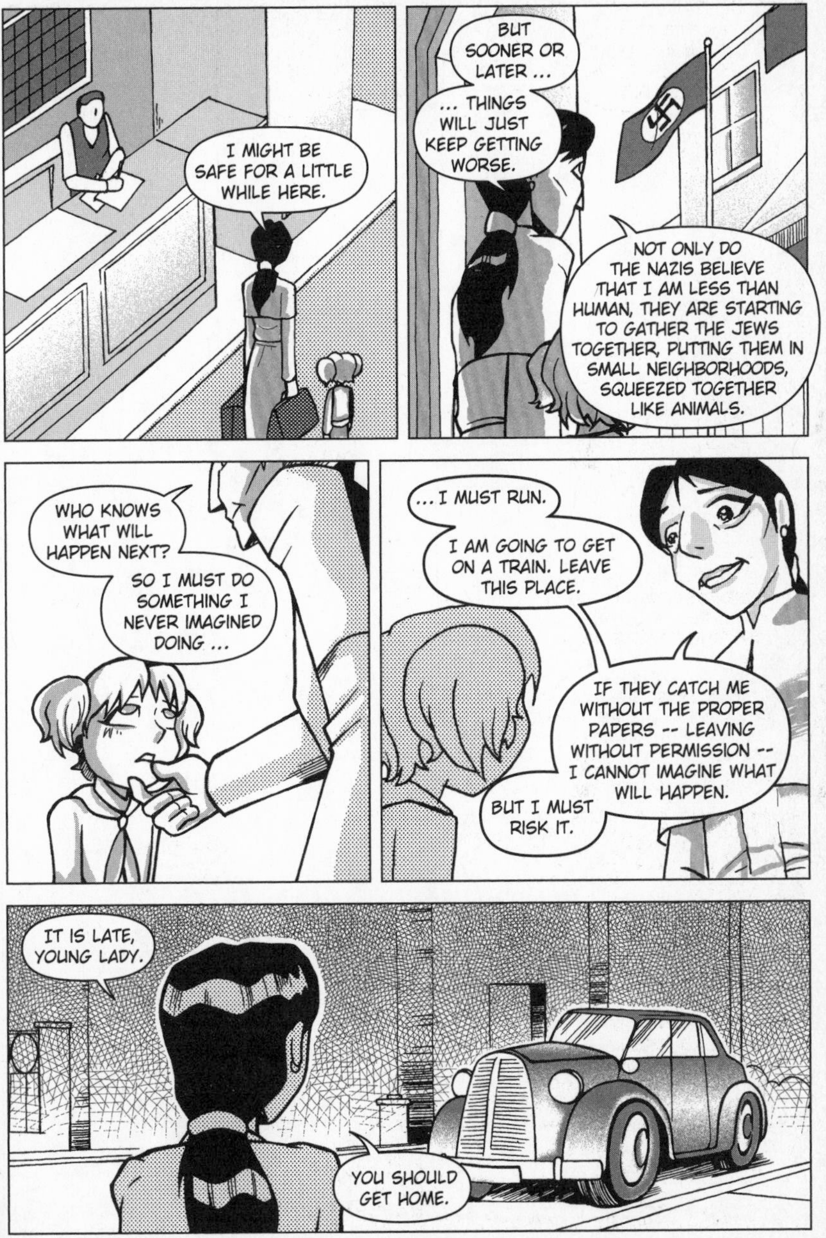
I MIGHT BE SAFE FOR A LITTLE WHILE HERE.
BUT SOONER OR LATER ...
... THINGS WILL JUST KEEP GETTING WORSE.
NOT ONLY DO THE NAZIS BELIEVE THAT I AM LESS THAN HUMAN, THEY ARE STARTING TO GATHER THE JEWS TOGETHER, PUTTING THEM IN SMALL NEIGHBORHOODS, SQUEEZED TOGETHER LIKE ANIMALS.
WHO KNOWS WHAT WILL HAPPEN NEXT?
SO I MUST DO SOMETHING I NEVER IMAGINED DOING ...
... I MUST RUN.
I AM GOING TO GET ON A TRAIN. LEAVE THIS PLACE.
IF THEY CATCH ME WITHOUT THE PROPER PAPERS -- LEAVING WITHOUT PERMISSION -- I CANNOT IMAGINE WHAT WILL HAPPEN.
BUT I MUST RISK IT.
IT IS LATE, YOUNG LADY.
YOU SHOULD GET HOME.

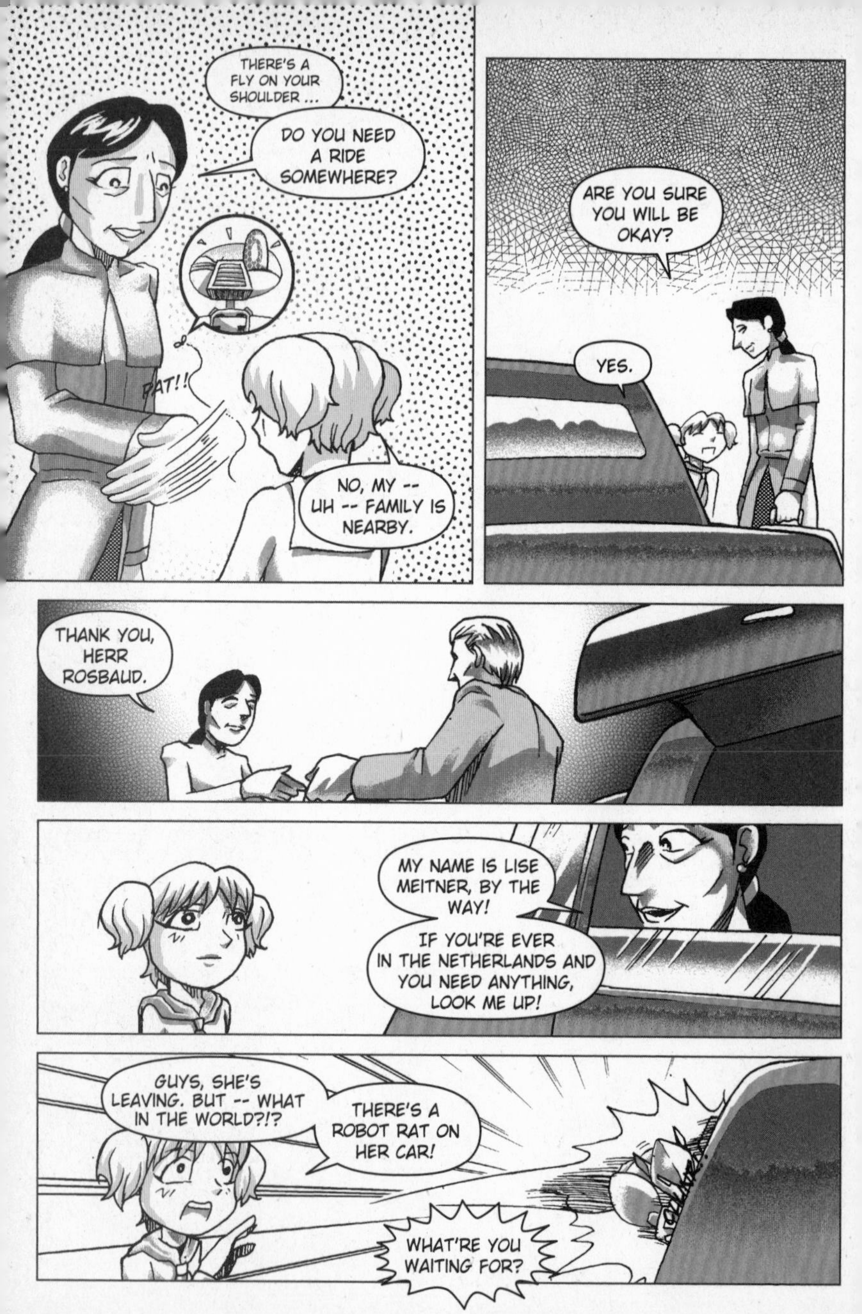
THERE'S A FLY ON YOUR SHOULDER ...
DO YOU NEED A RIDE SOMEWHERE?
PAT!!
NO, MY -- UH -- FAMILY IS NEARBY.
ARE YOU SURE YOU WILL BE OKAY?
YES.
THANK YOU, HERR ROSBAUD.
MY NAME IS LISE MEITNER, BY THE WAY!
IF YOU'RE EVER IN THE NETHERLANDS AND YOU NEED ANYTHING, LOOK ME UP!
GUYS, SHE'S LEAVING. BUT -- WHAT IN THE WORLD?!?
THERE'S A ROBOT RAT ON HER CAR!
WHAT'RE YOU WAITING FOR?

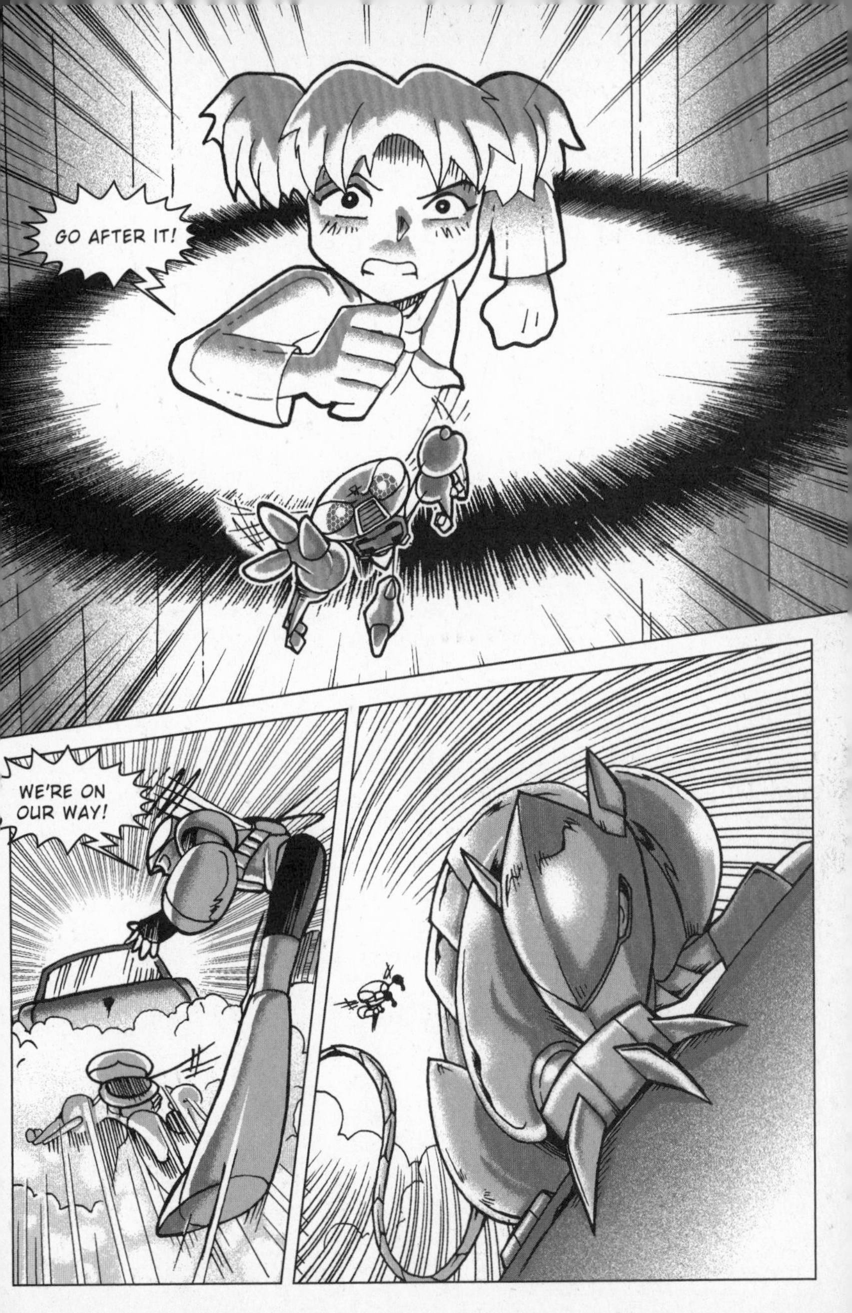
GO AFTER IT!
WE'RE ON OUR WAY!

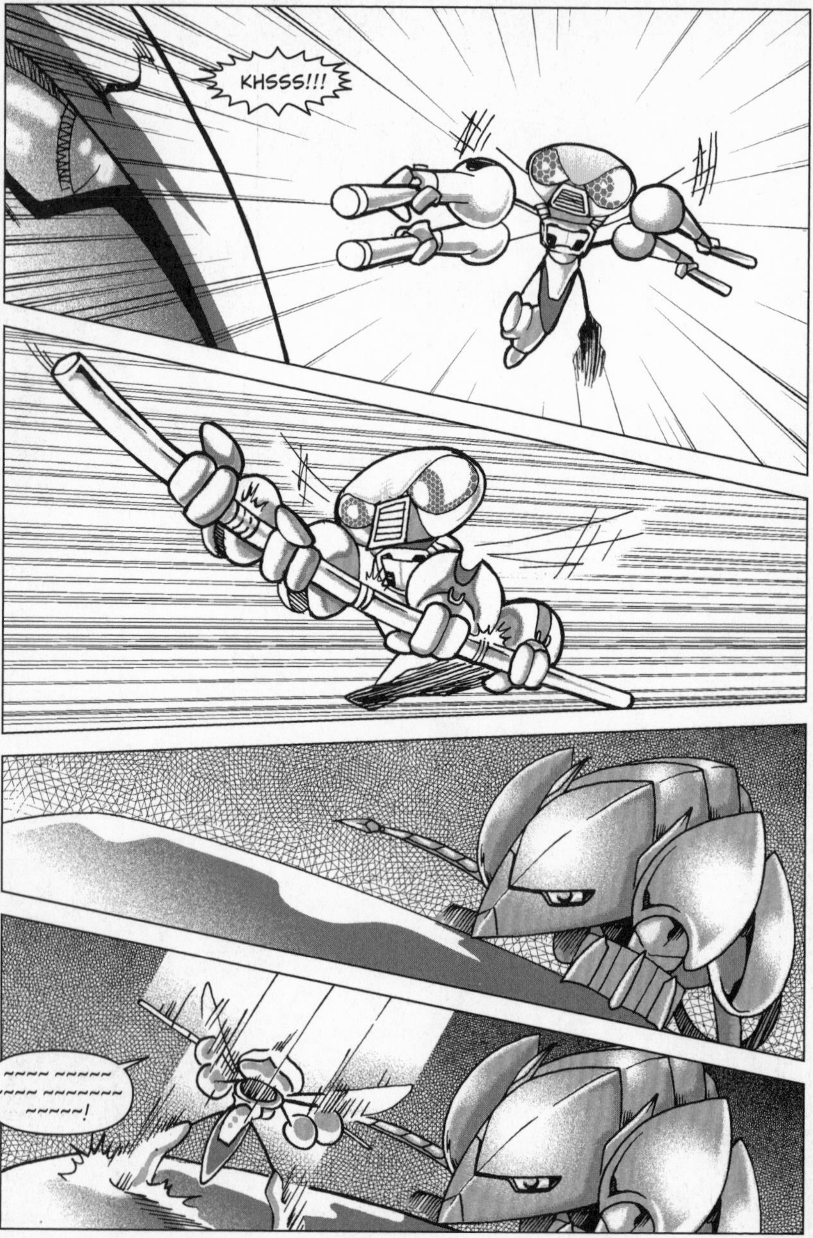
KHSSS!!!
~~~~ ~~~~~
~~~~ ~~~~~~~
~~~~~!
~~~~~

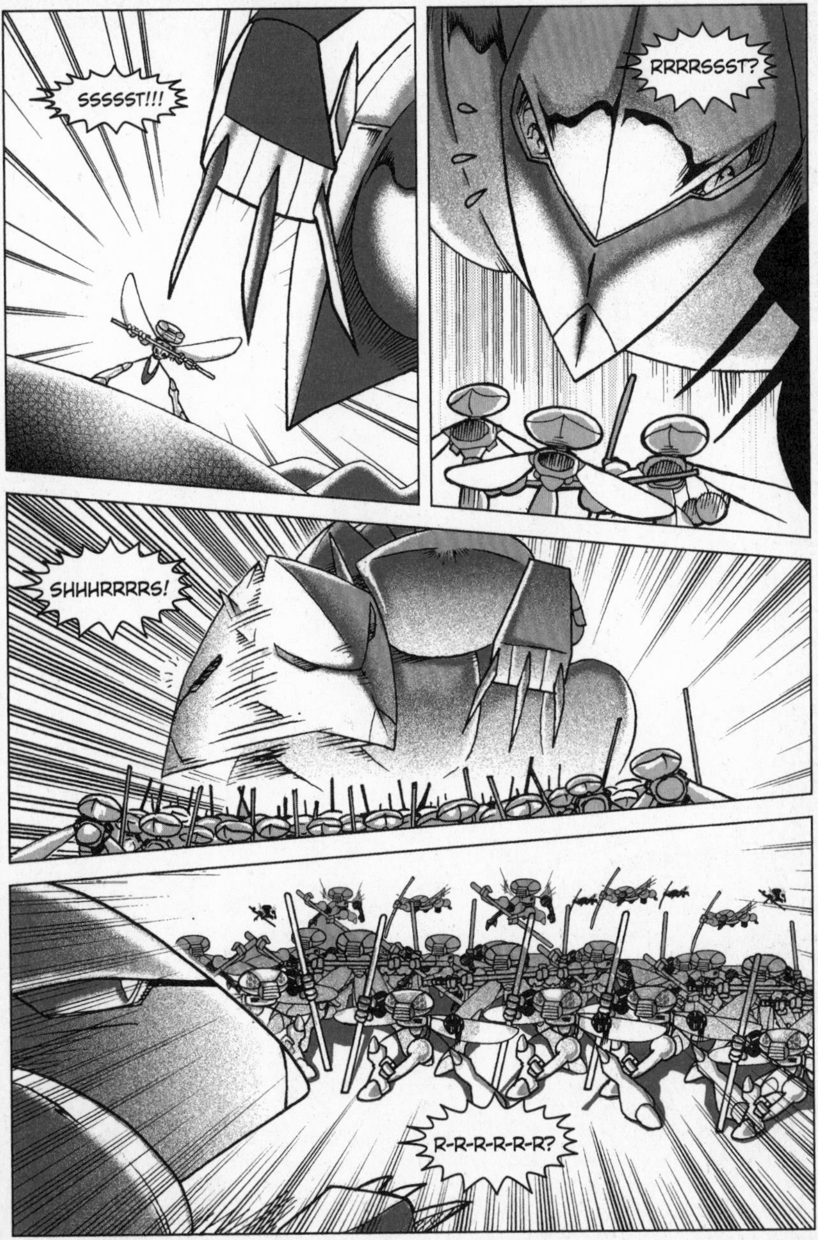
SSSSST!!!
RRRRSSST?
SHHHRRRRS!
R-R-R-R-R-R?

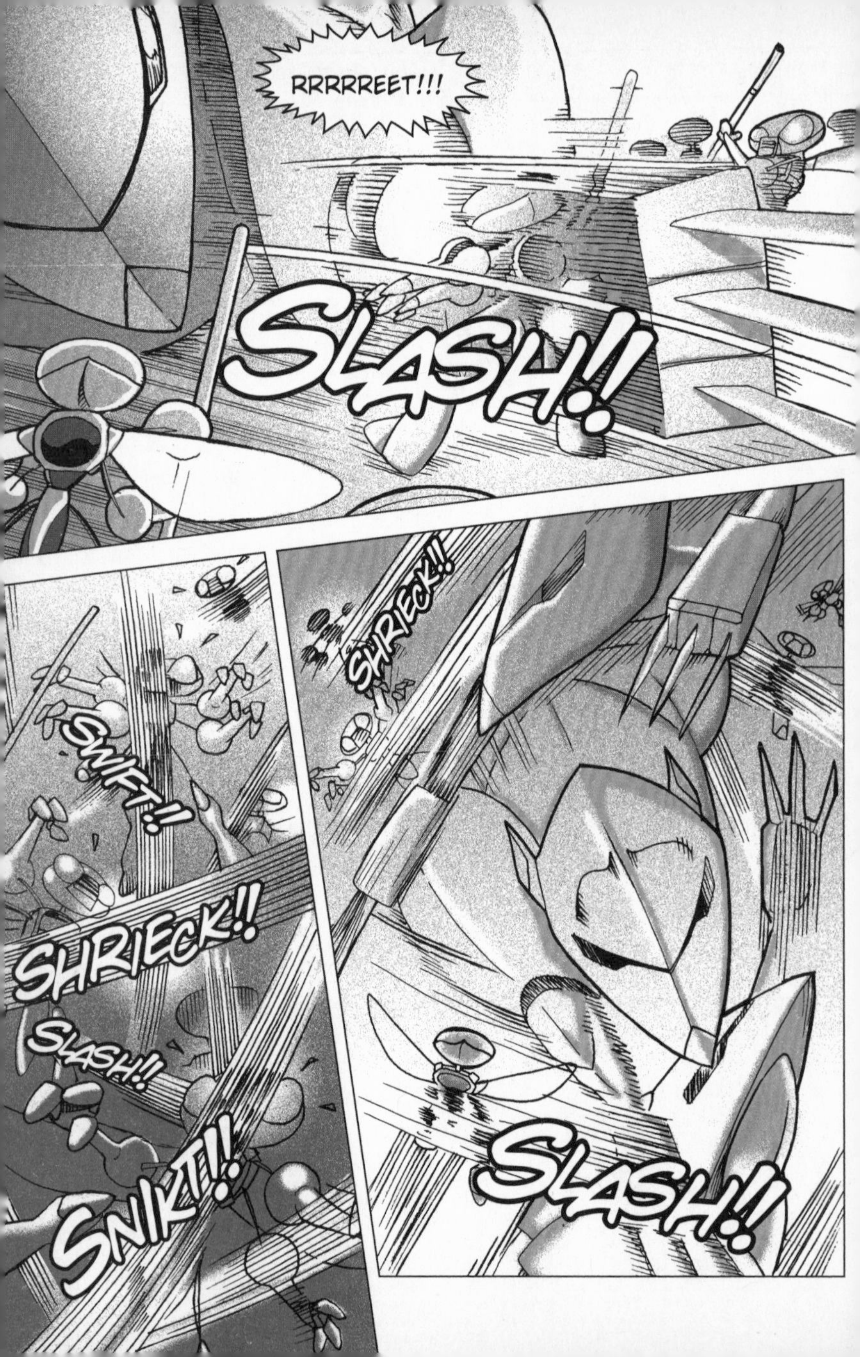
RRRRREET!!!
SLASH!!
SWIFT!!
SHRIECK!!
SLASH!!
SNIKT!!
SHRIECK!!
SLASH!!

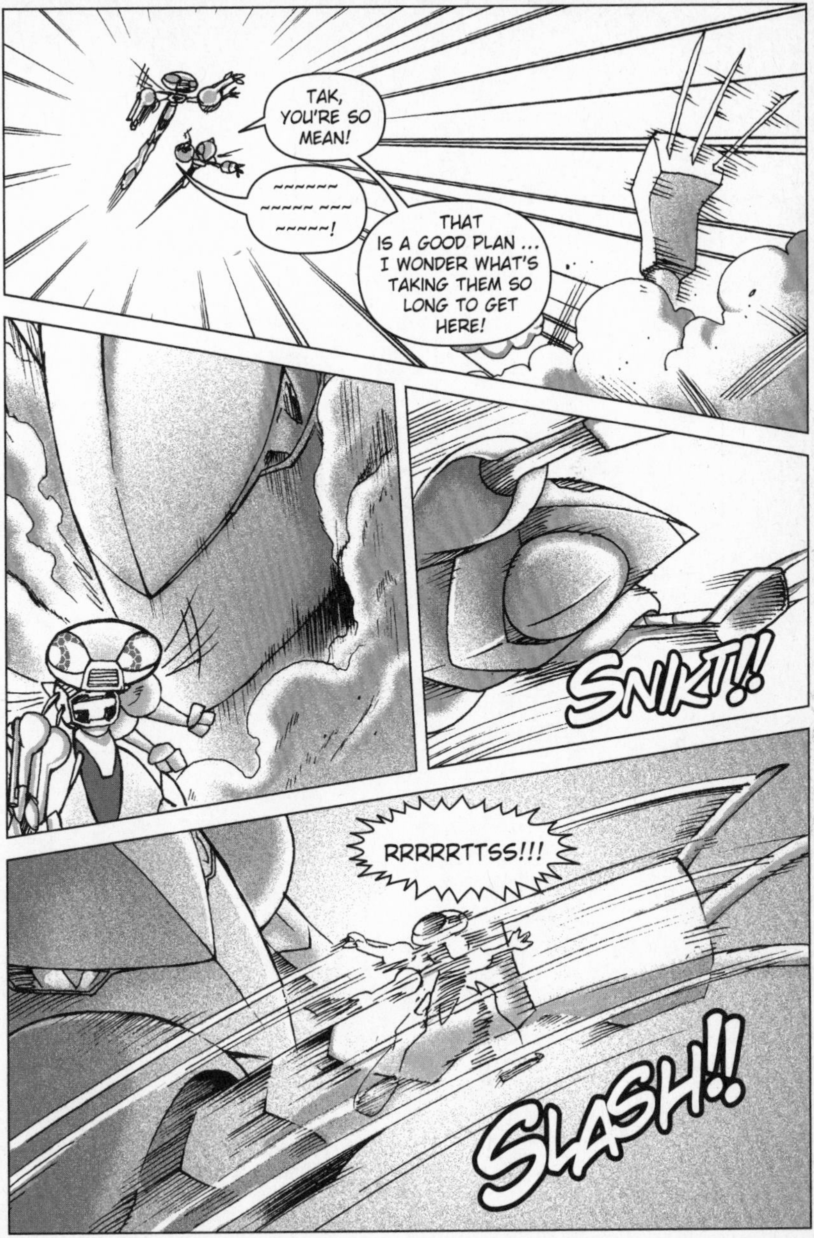
TAK, YOU'RE SO MEAN!
~~~~~~ ~~~~~ ~~~ ~~~~~!
THAT IS A GOOD PLAN ... I WONDER WHAT'S TAKING THEM SO LONG TO GET HERE!
SNIKT!!
RRRRRTTSS!!!
SLASH!!
~~~~~~

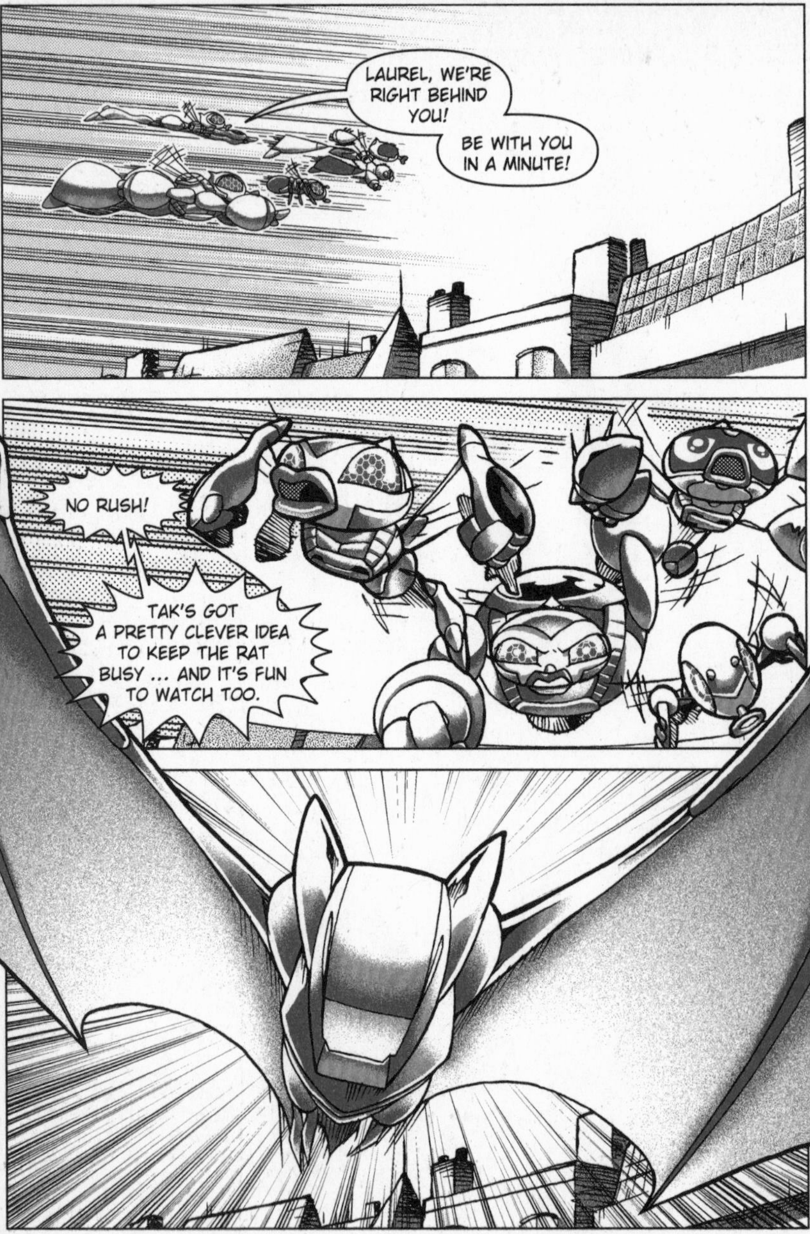
LAUREL, WE'RE RIGHT BEHIND YOU!
BE WITH YOU IN A MINUTE!
NO RUSH!
TAK'S GOT A PRETTY CLEVER IDEA TO KEEP THE RAT BUSY ... AND IT'S FUN TO WATCH TOO.

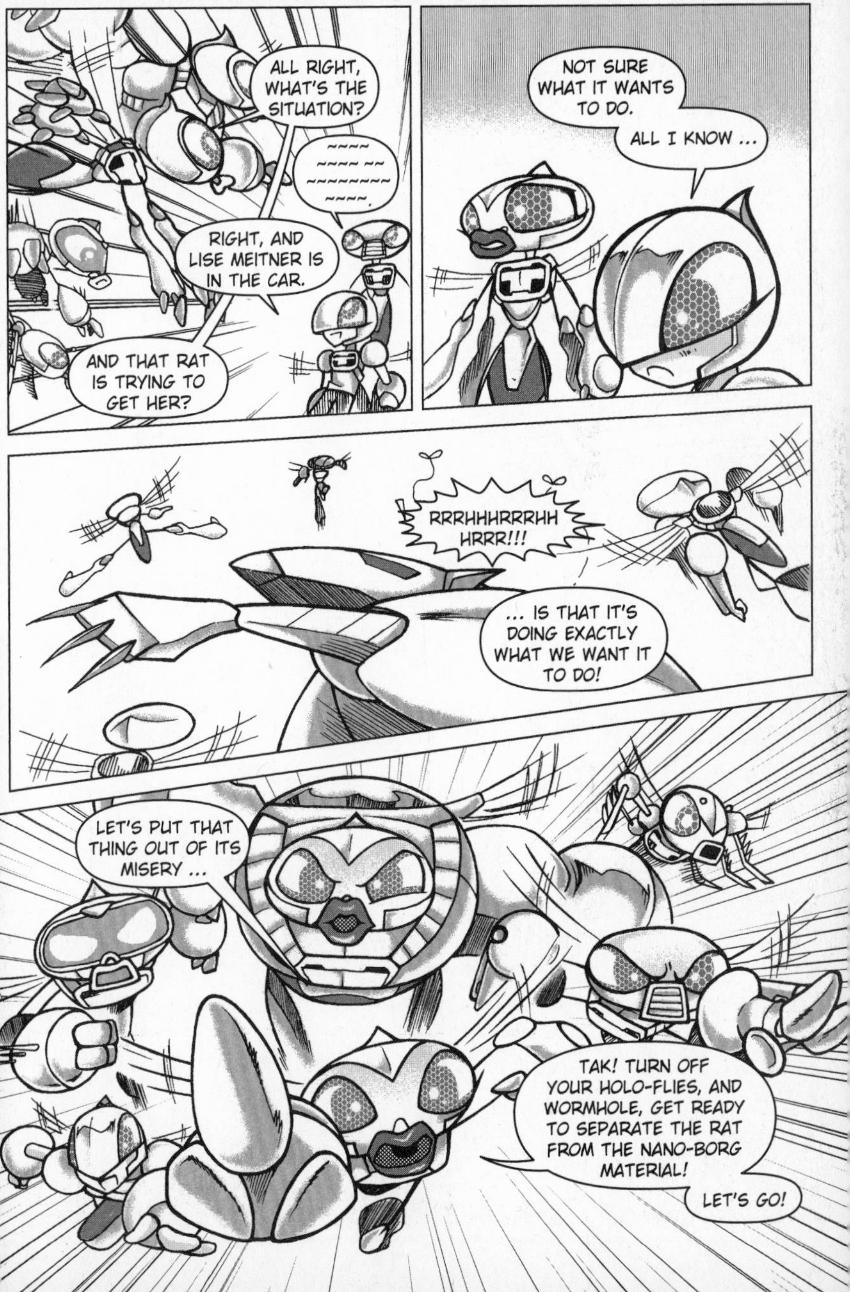
ALL RIGHT, WHAT'S THE SITUATION?
~~~~ ~~~~ ~~ ~~~~~~~~~ ~~~~.
RIGHT, AND LISE MEITNER IS IN THE CAR.
AND THAT RAT IS TRYING TO GET HER?
NOT SURE WHAT IT WANTS TO DO.
ALL I KNOW ...
RRRHHHRRRHH HRRR!!!
... IS THAT IT'S DOING EXACTLY WHAT WE WANT IT TO DO!
LET'S PUT THAT THING OUT OF ITS MISERY ...
TAK! TURN OFF YOUR HOLO-FLIES, AND WORMHOLE, GET READY TO SEPARATE THE RAT FROM THE NANO-BORG MATERIAL!
LET'S GO!
~~~~

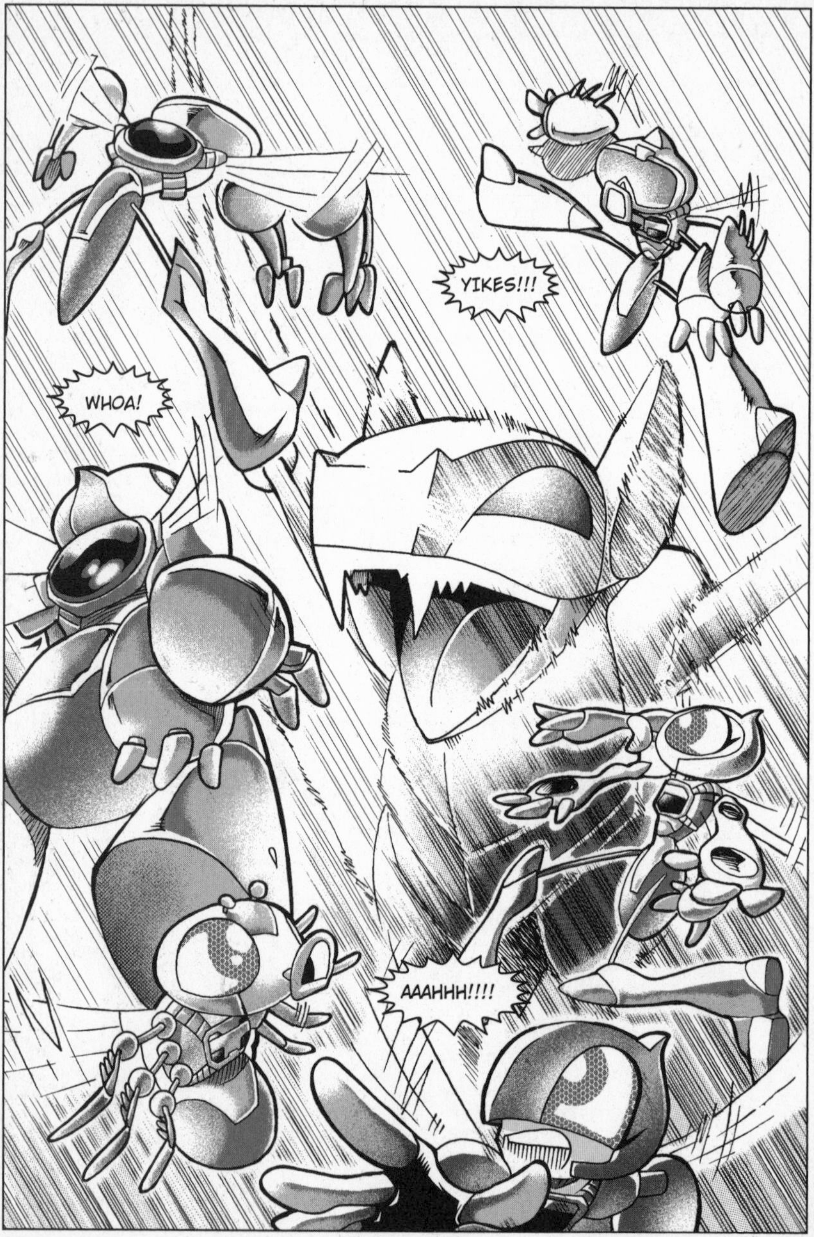
YIKES!!!
WHOA!
AAAHHH!!!!

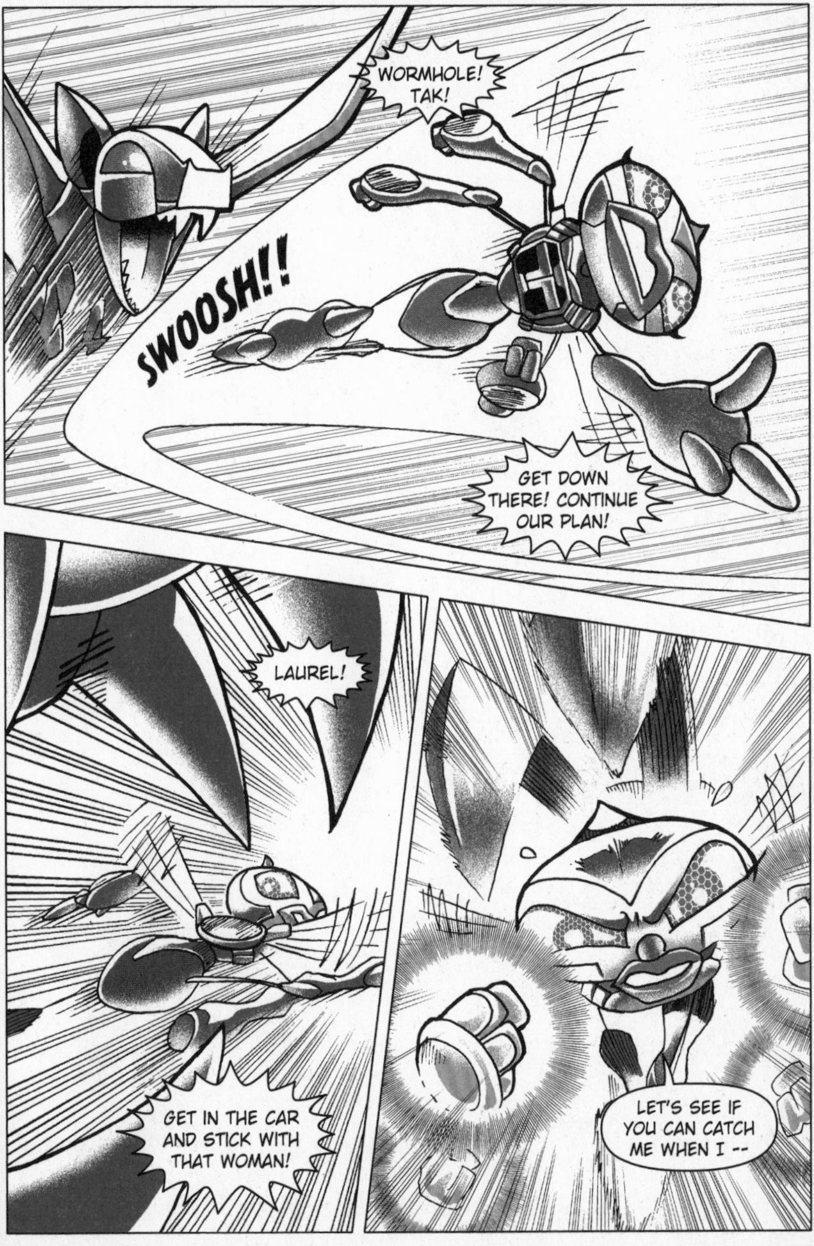
WORMHOLE! TAK!
SWOOSH!!
GET DOWN THERE! CONTINUE OUR PLAN!
LAUREL!
GET IN THE CAR AND STICK WITH THAT WOMAN!
LET'S SEE IF YOU CAN CATCH ME WHEN I --

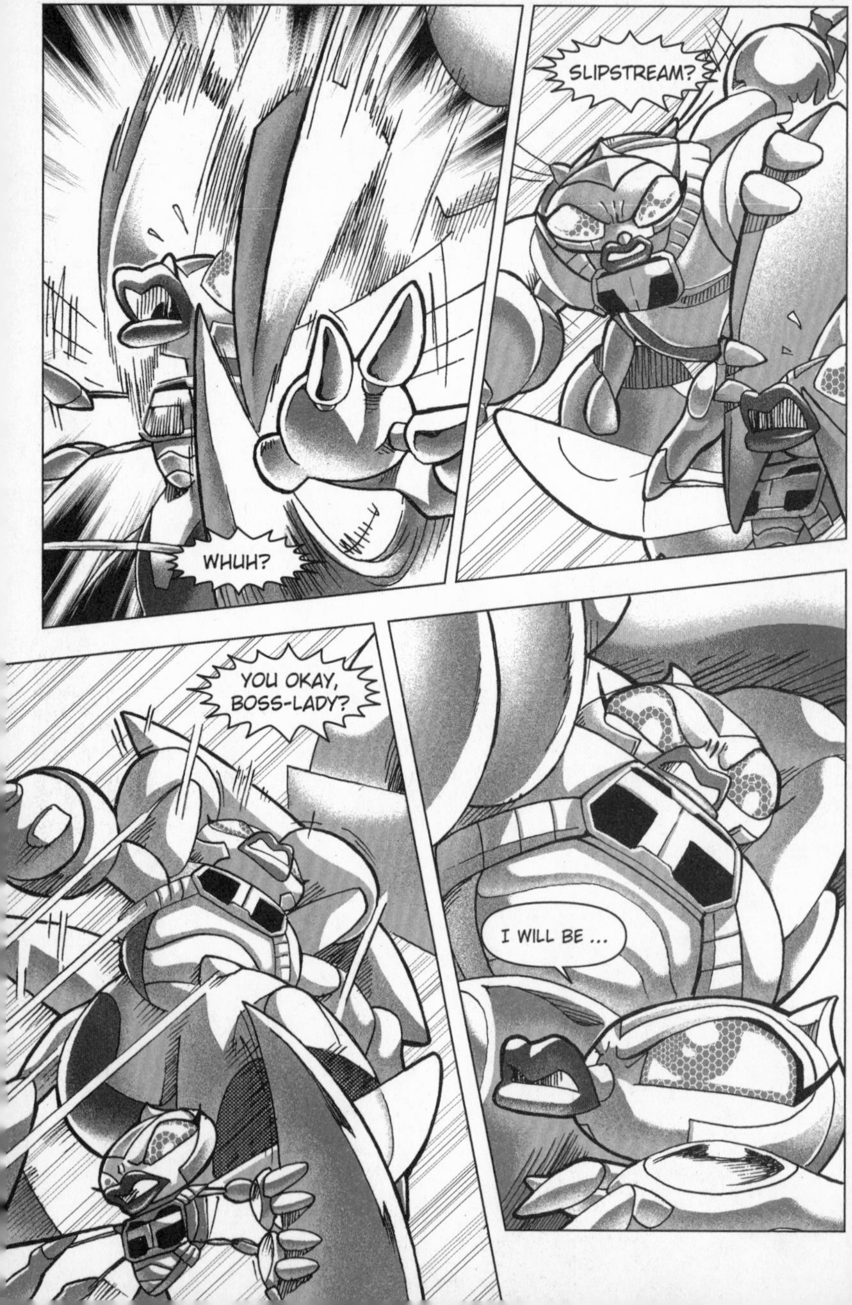
WHUH?
SLIPSTREAM?
YOU OKAY, BOSS-LADY?
I WILL BE ...

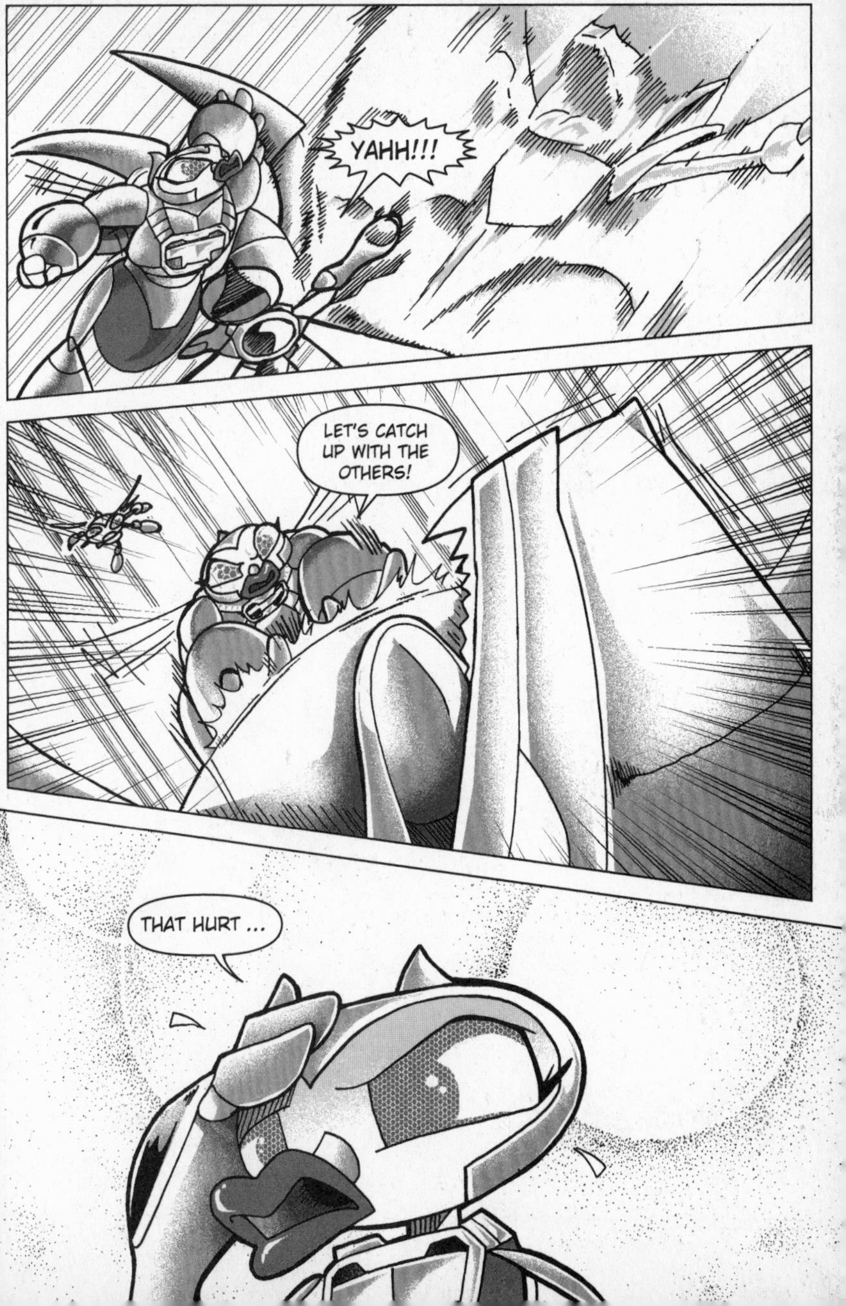
YAHH!!!
LET'S CATCH UP WITH THE OTHERS!
THAT HURT ...

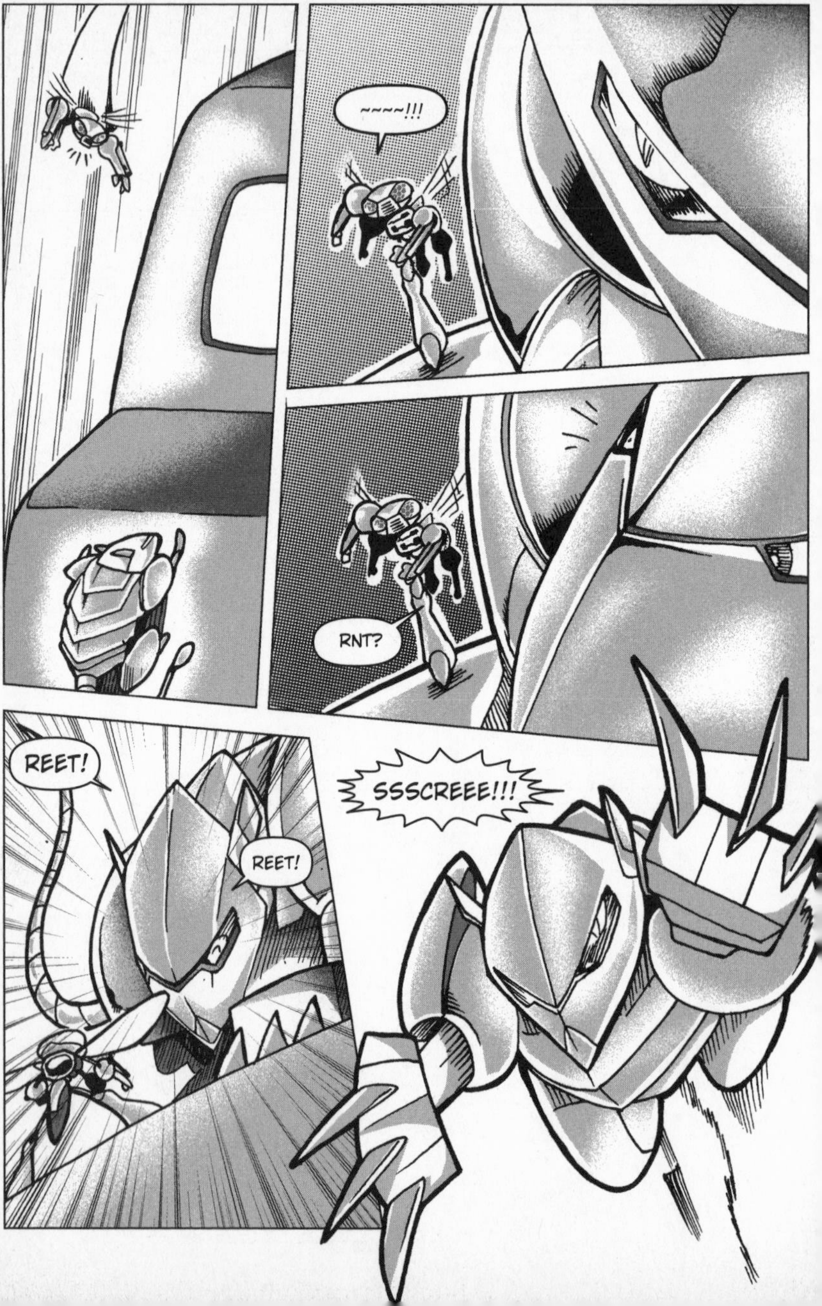

RNT?
REET!
REET!
SSSCREEE!!!

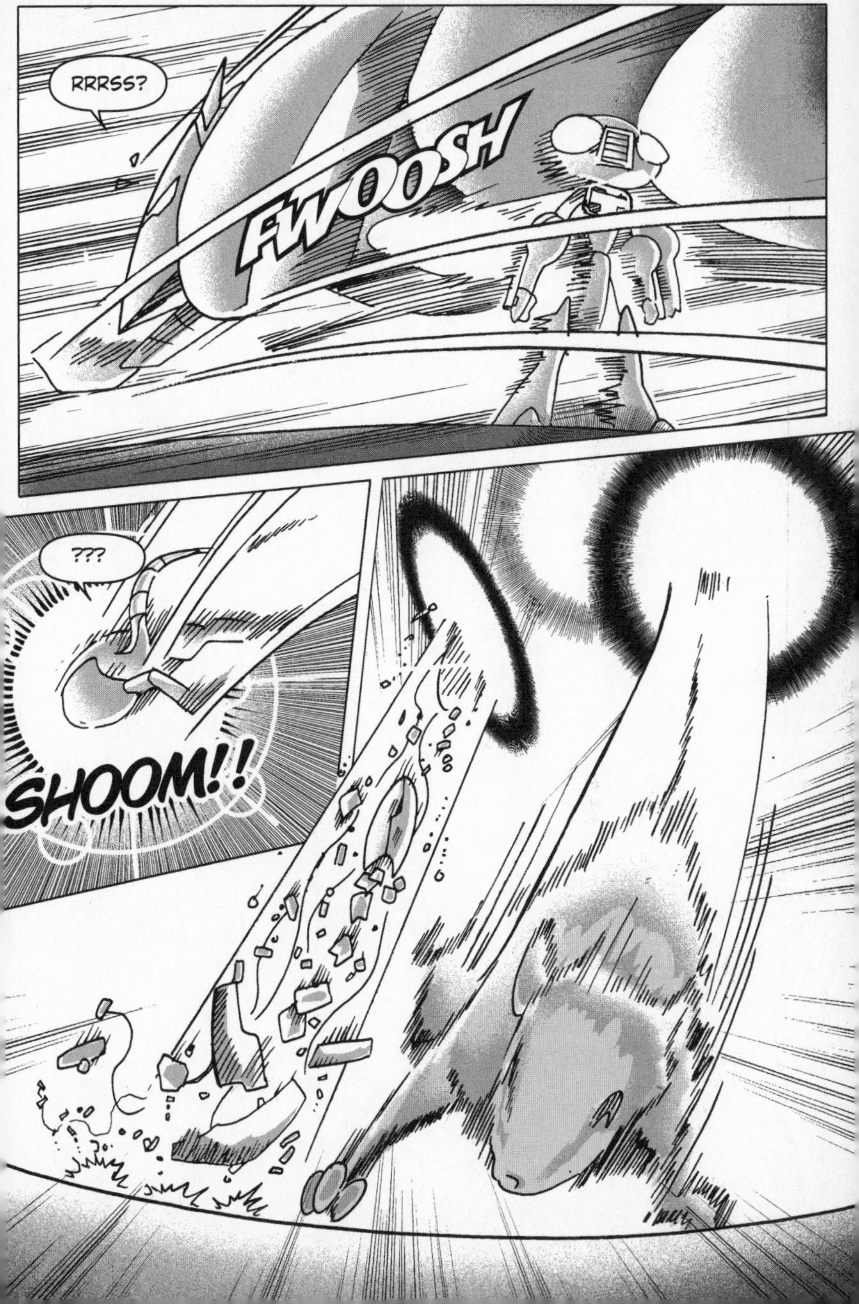
RRRSS?
FWOOSH
???
SHOOM!!

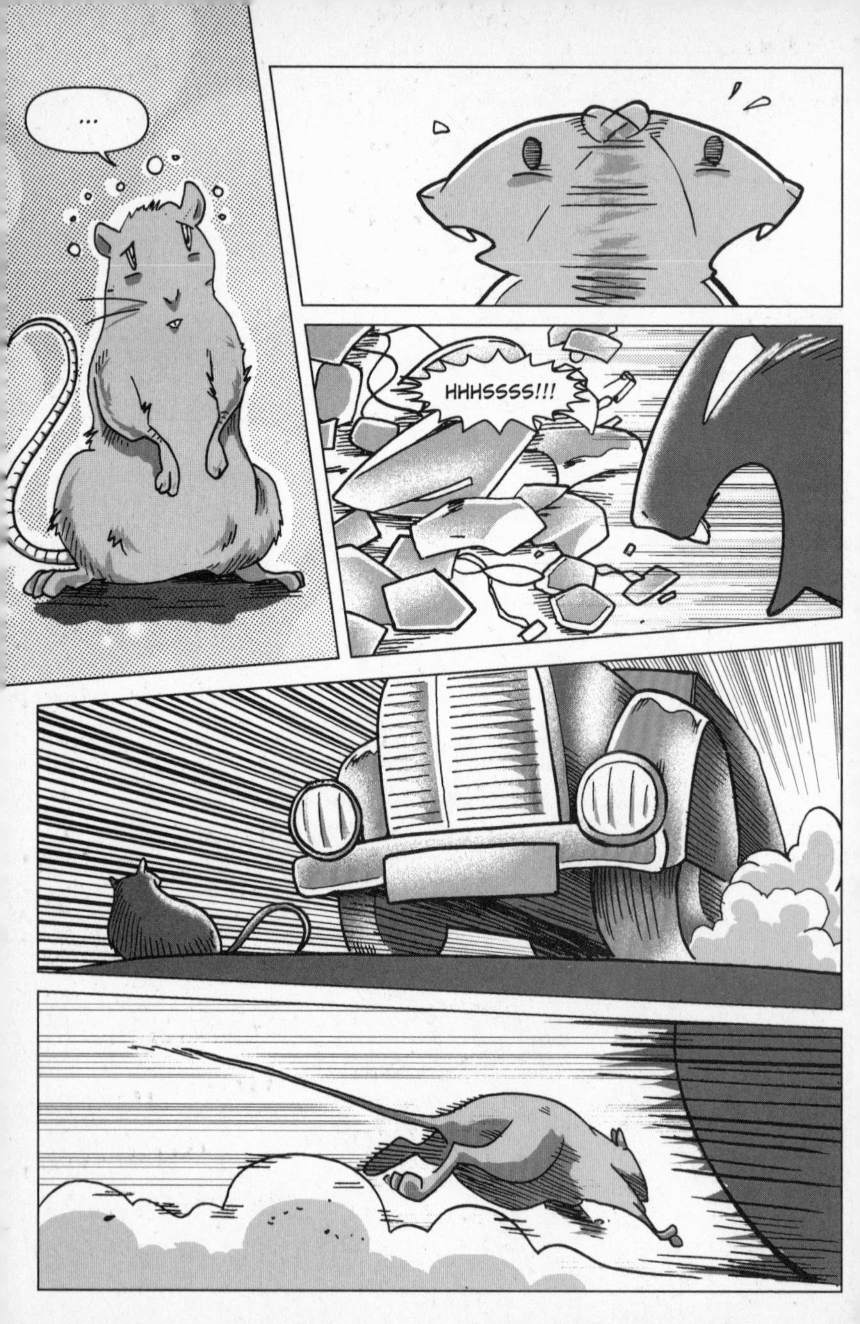
...
HHHSSSS!!!

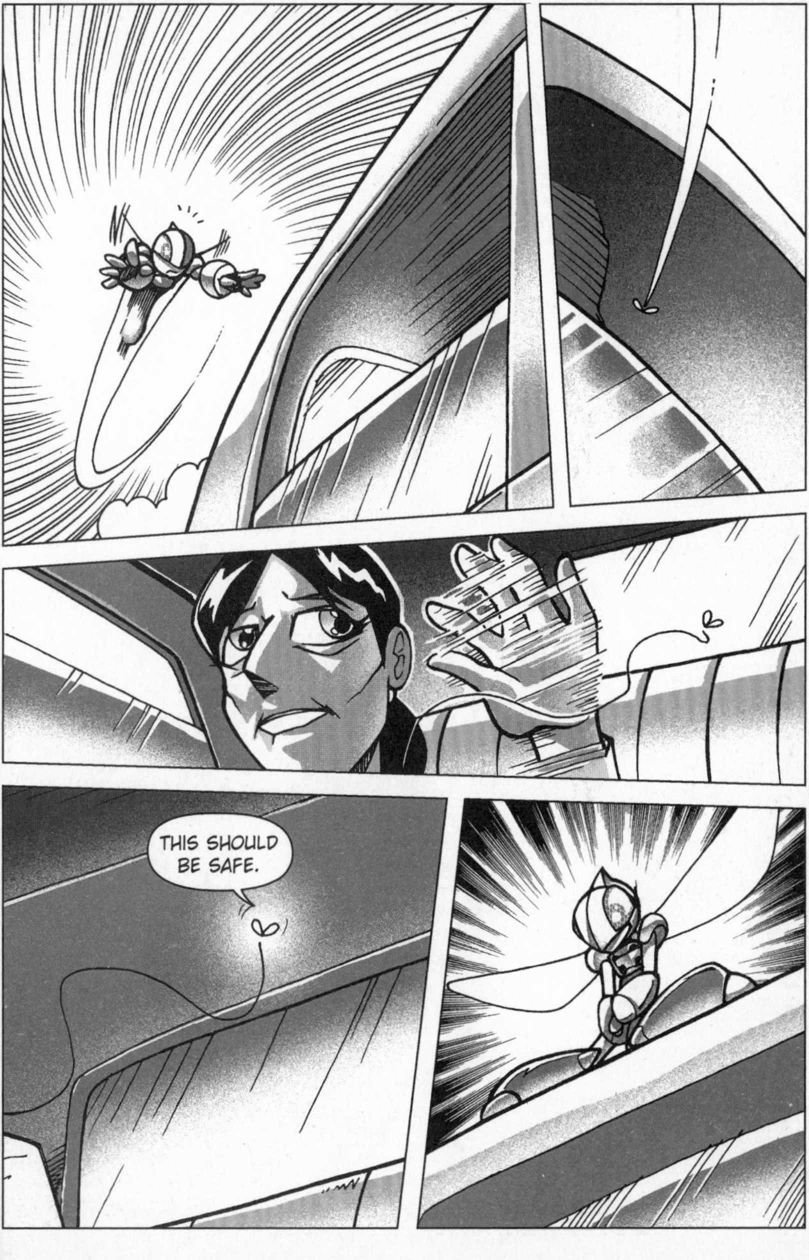
THIS SHOULD BE SAFE.

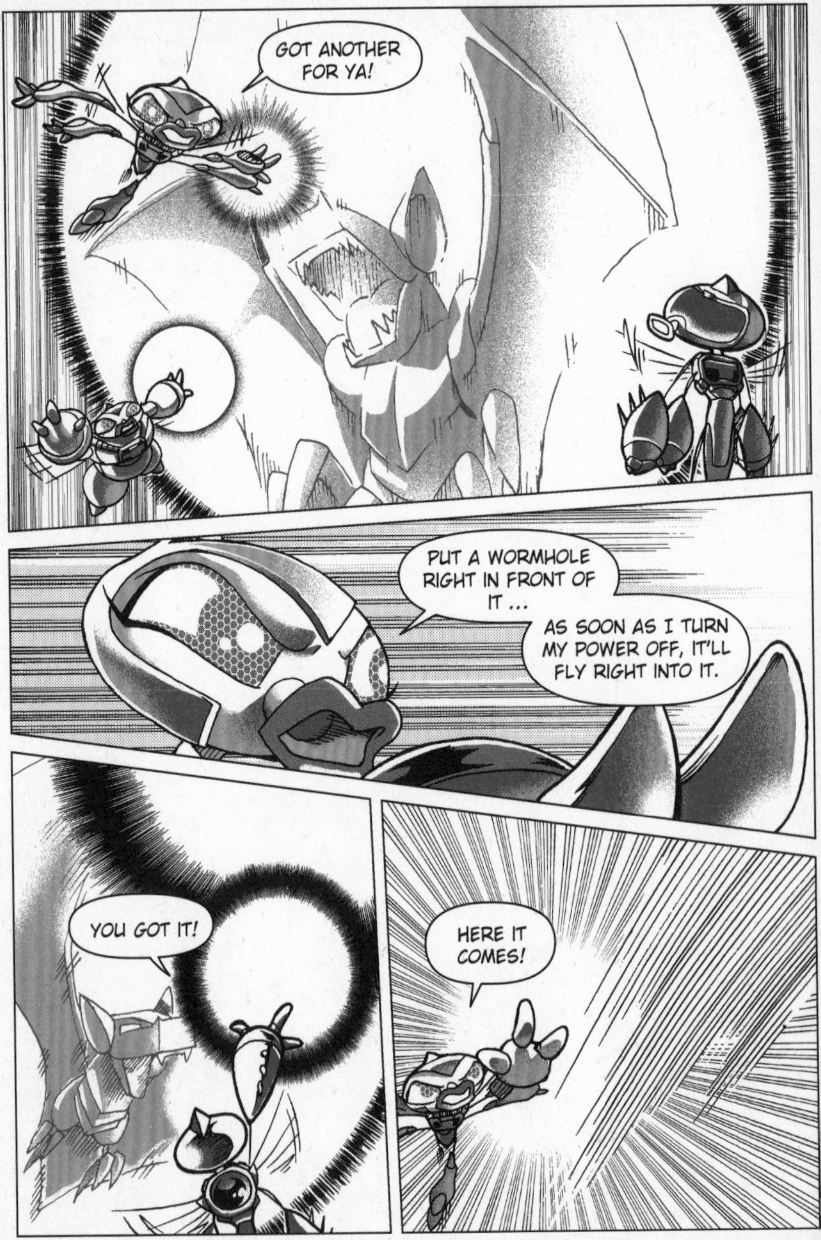
GOT ANOTHER FOR YA!
PUT A WORMHOLE RIGHT IN FRONT OF IT ...
AS SOON AS I TURN MY POWER OFF, IT'LL FLY RIGHT INTO IT.
YOU GOT IT!
HERE IT COMES!

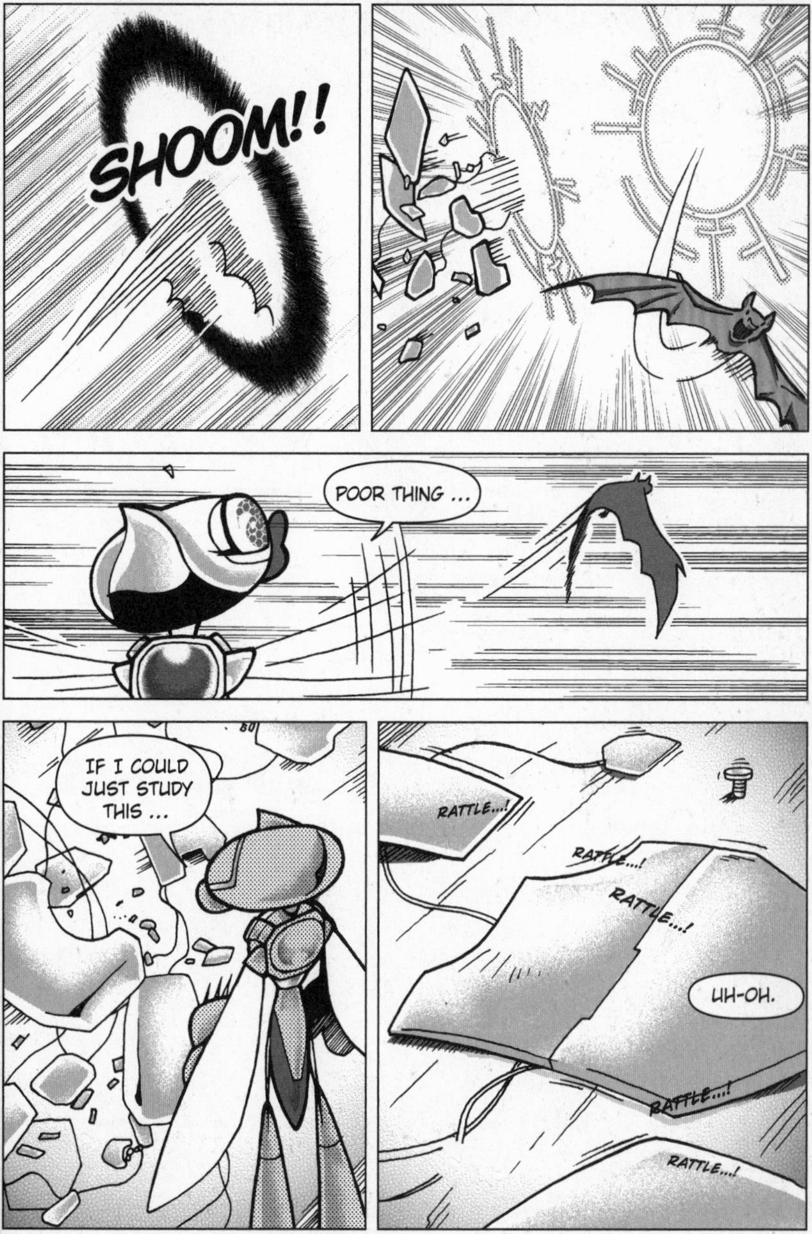
SHOOM!!
POOR THING ...
IF I COULD JUST STUDY THIS ...
RATTLE...!
RATTLE...!
RATTLE...!
UH-OH.
RATTLE...!
RATTLE...!

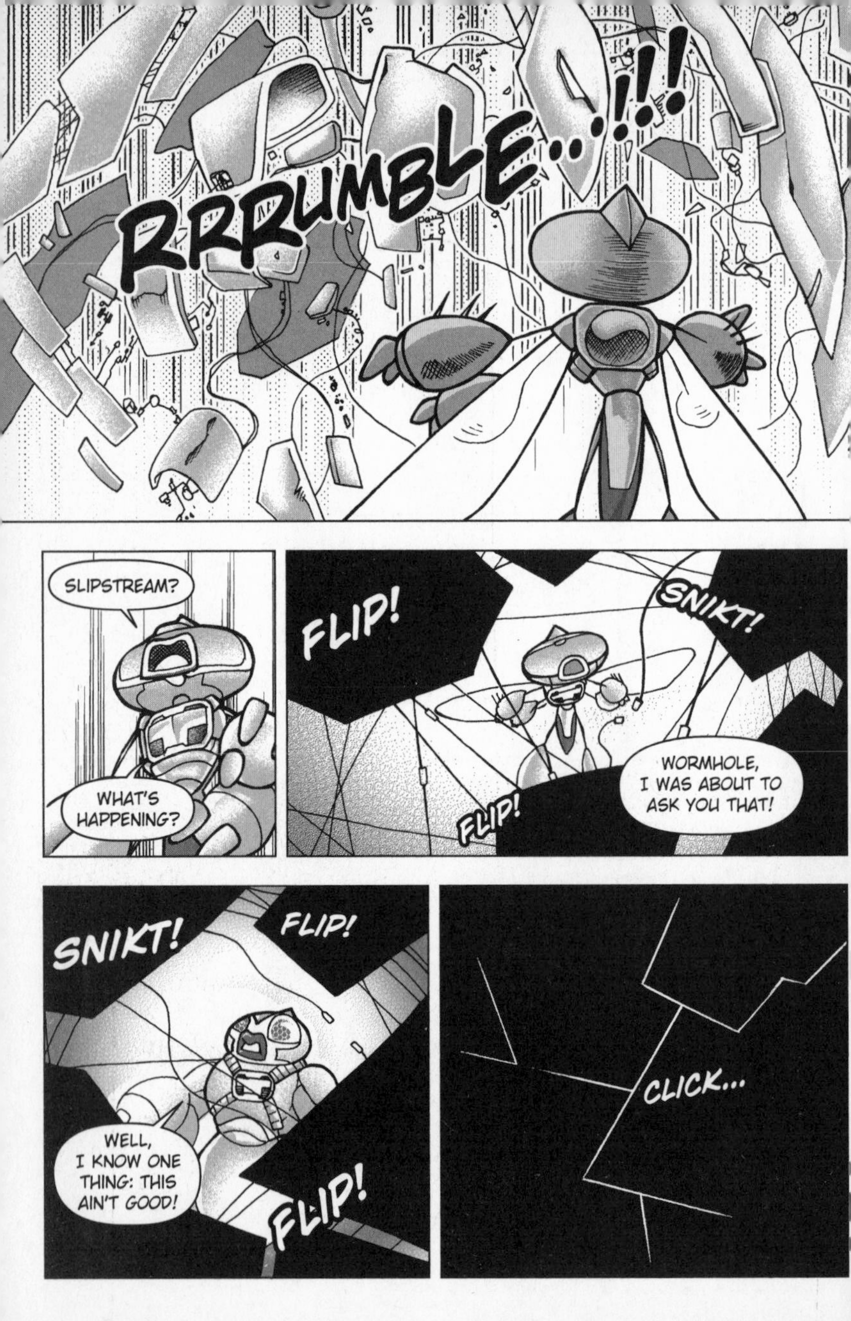
RRRUMBLE...!!!
SLIPSTREAM?
WHAT'S HAPPENING?
FLIP!
SNIKT!
WORMHOLE, I WAS ABOUT TO ASK YOU THAT!
FLIP!
SNIKT!
FLIP!
WELL, I KNOW ONE THING: THIS AIN'T GOOD!
FLIP!
CLICK...

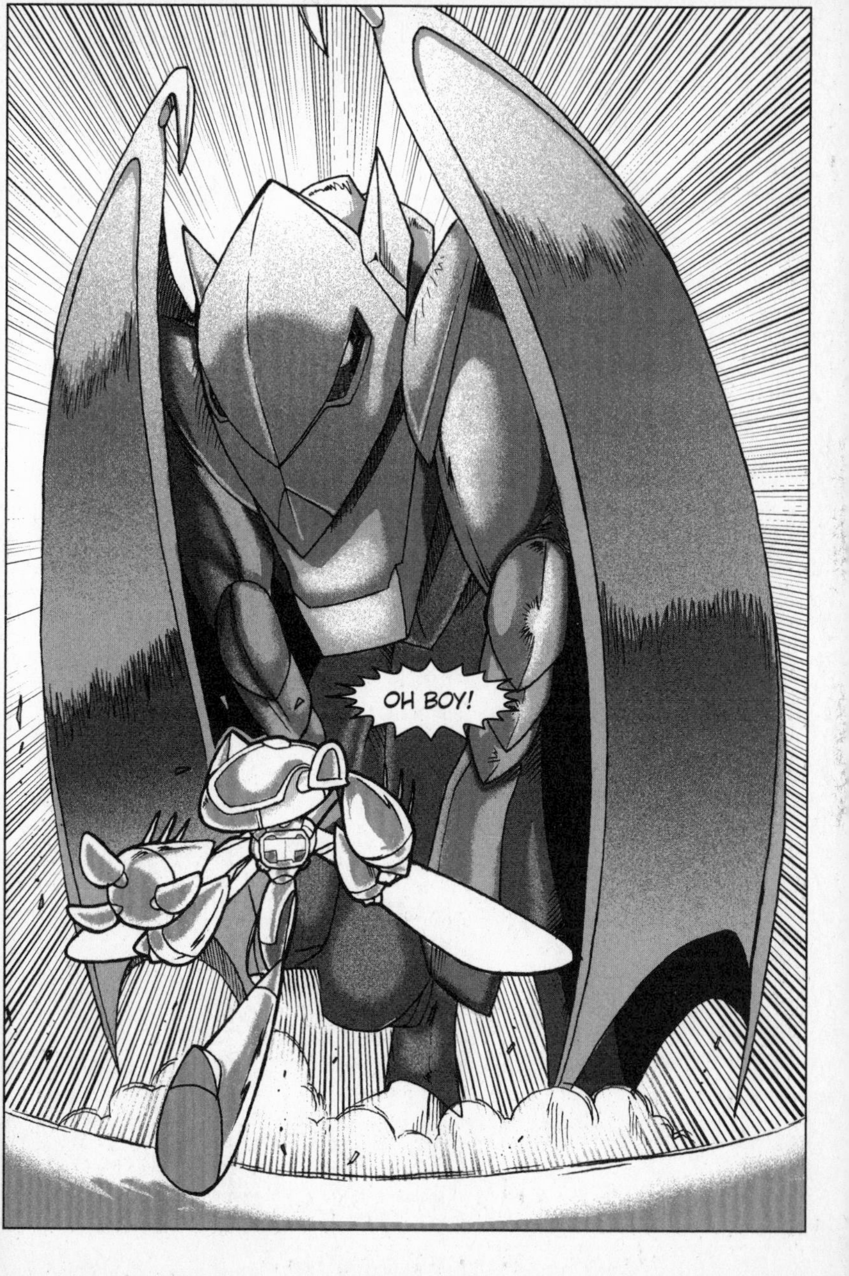
OH BOY!

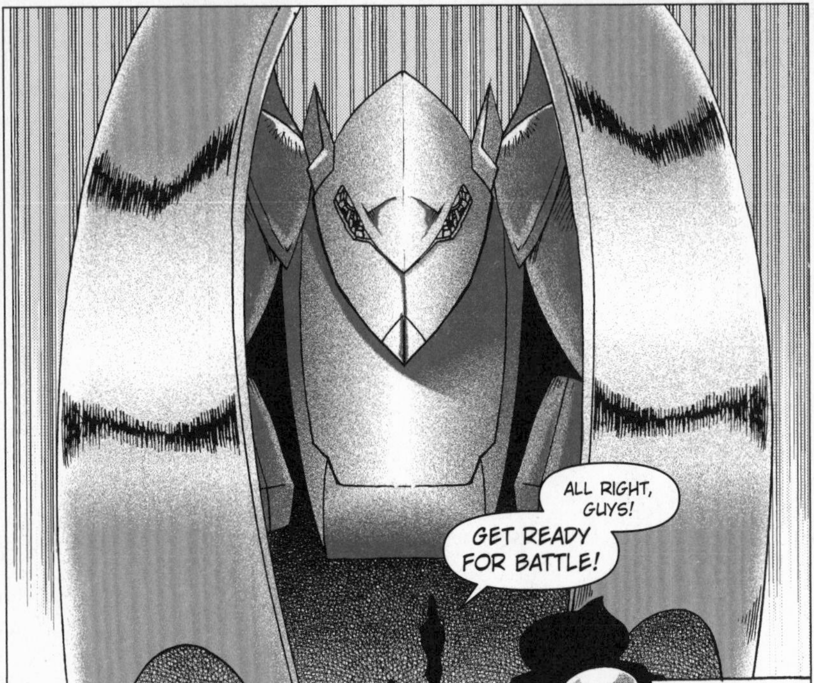
ALL RIGHT, GUYS!
GET READY FOR BATTLE!
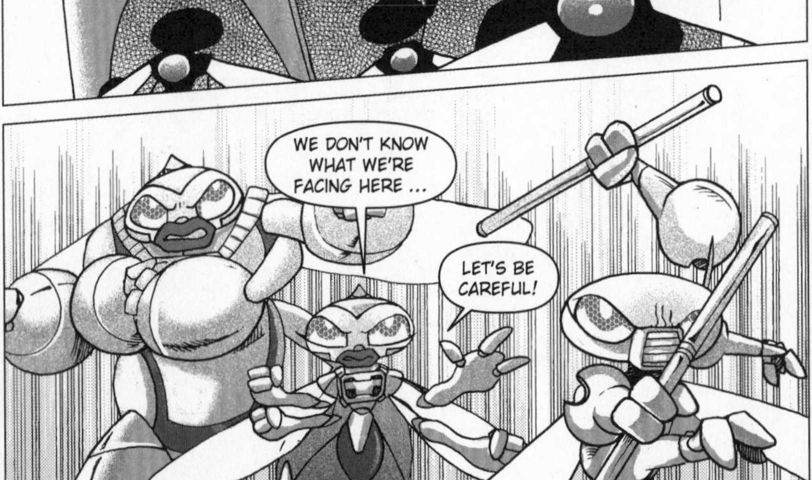
WE DON'T KNOW WHAT WE'RE FACING HERE ...
LET'S BE CAREFUL!

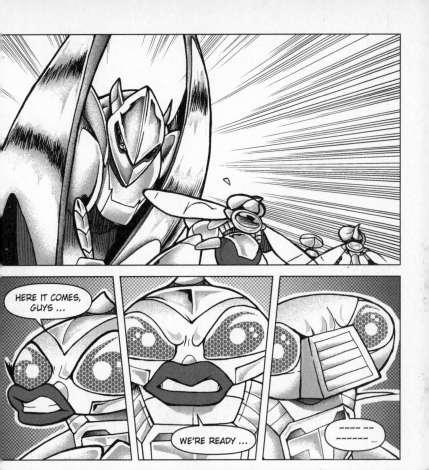

HERE IT COMES, GUYS ...

WE'RE READY ...

~~~~ ~~ ~~~~~~ ...

SWIIIP

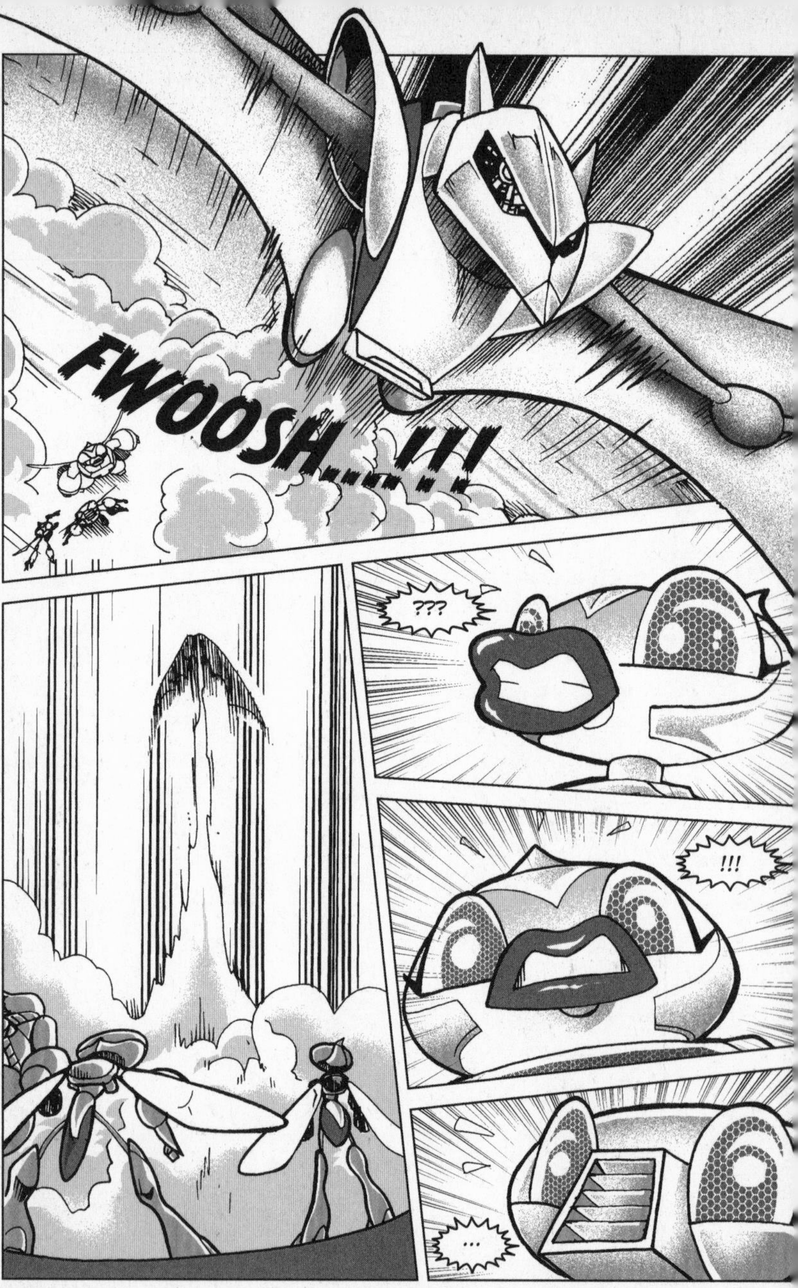
FWOOSH...!!!
???
!!!
...

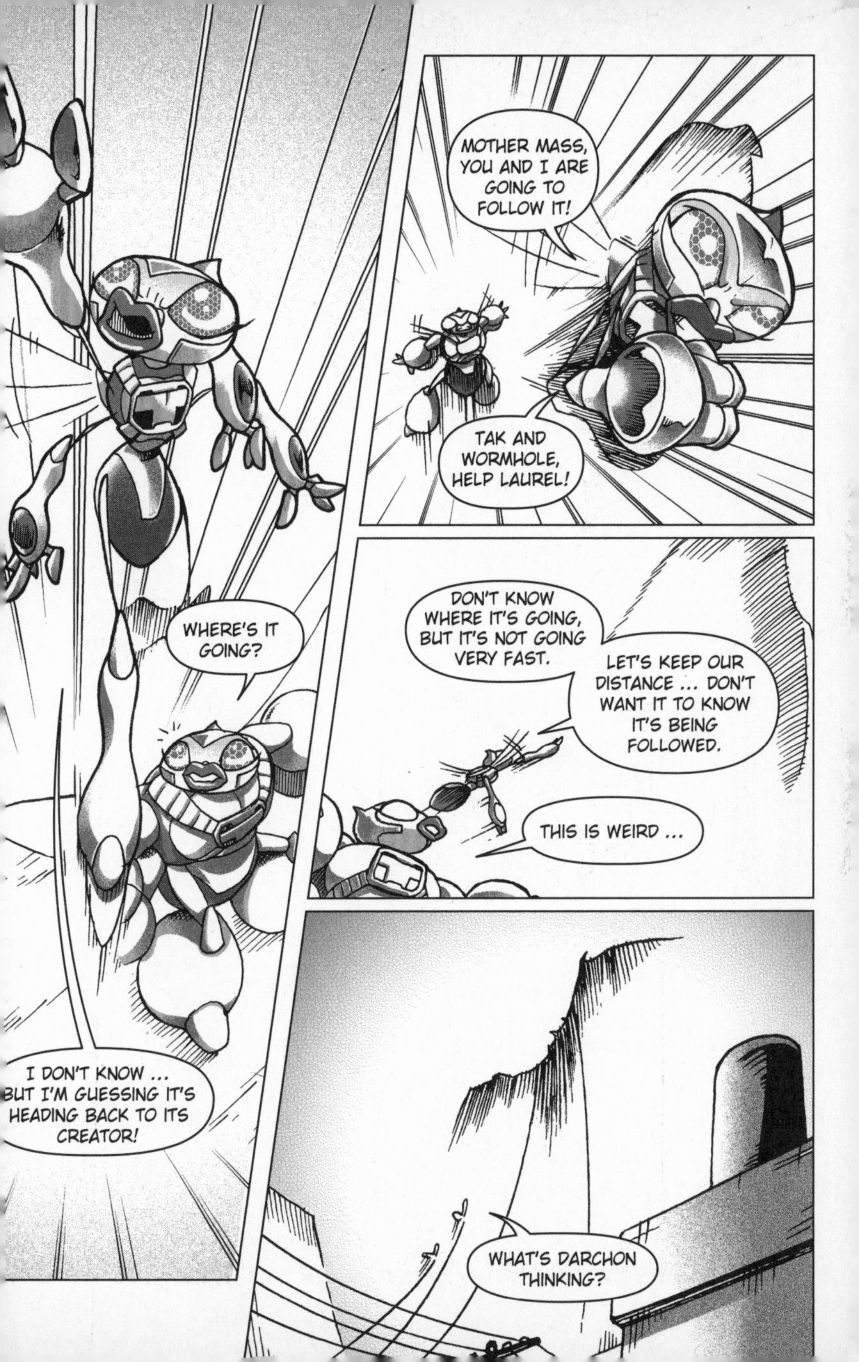
WHERE'S IT GOING?
I DON'T KNOW ... BUT I'M GUESSING IT'S HEADING BACK TO ITS CREATOR!
MOTHER MASS, YOU AND I ARE GOING TO FOLLOW IT!
TAK AND WORMHOLE, HELP LAUREL!
DON'T KNOW WHERE IT'S GOING, BUT IT'S NOT GOING VERY FAST.
LET'S KEEP OUR DISTANCE ... DON'T WANT IT TO KNOW IT'S BEING FOLLOWED.
THIS IS WEIRD ...
WHAT'S DARCHON THINKING?

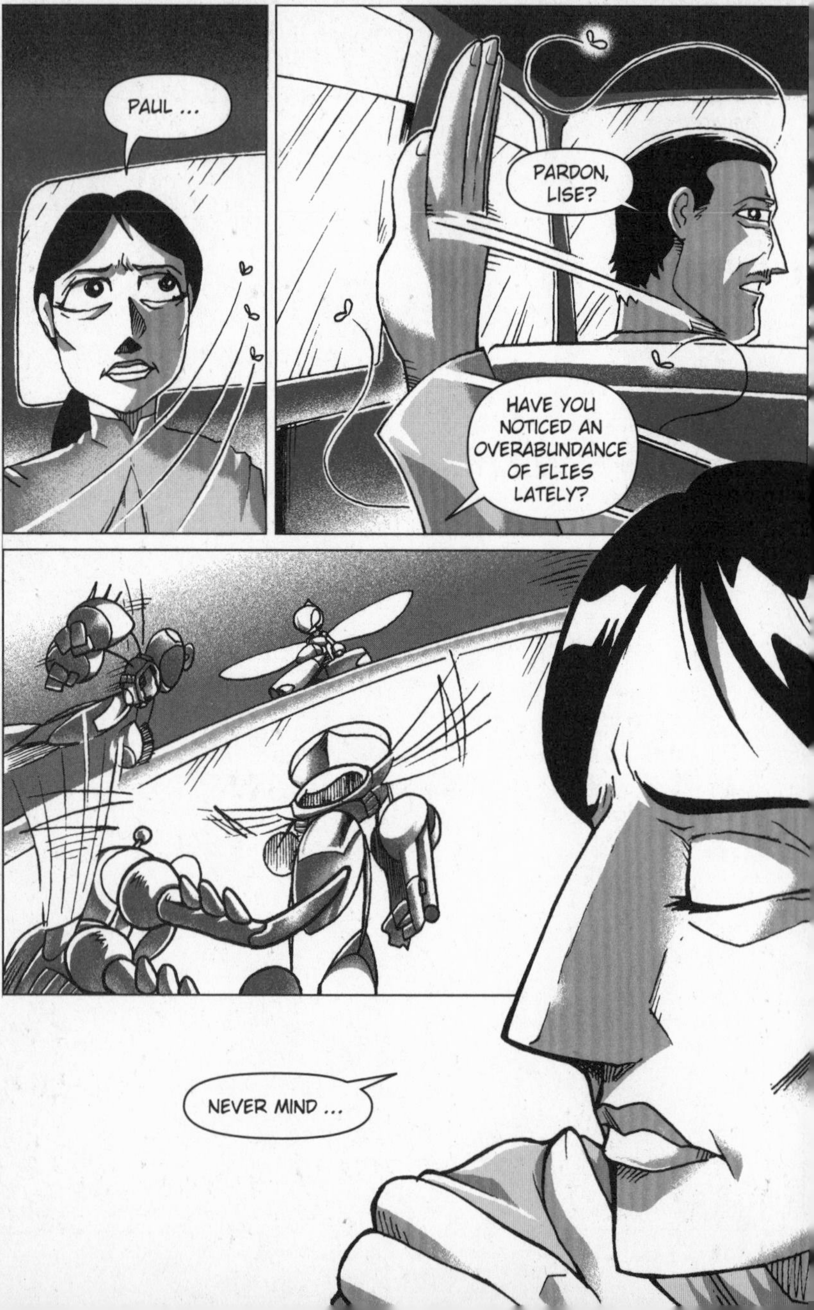
PAUL ...
PARDON, LISE?
HAVE YOU NOTICED AN OVERABUNDANCE OF FLIES LATELY?
NEVER MIND ...

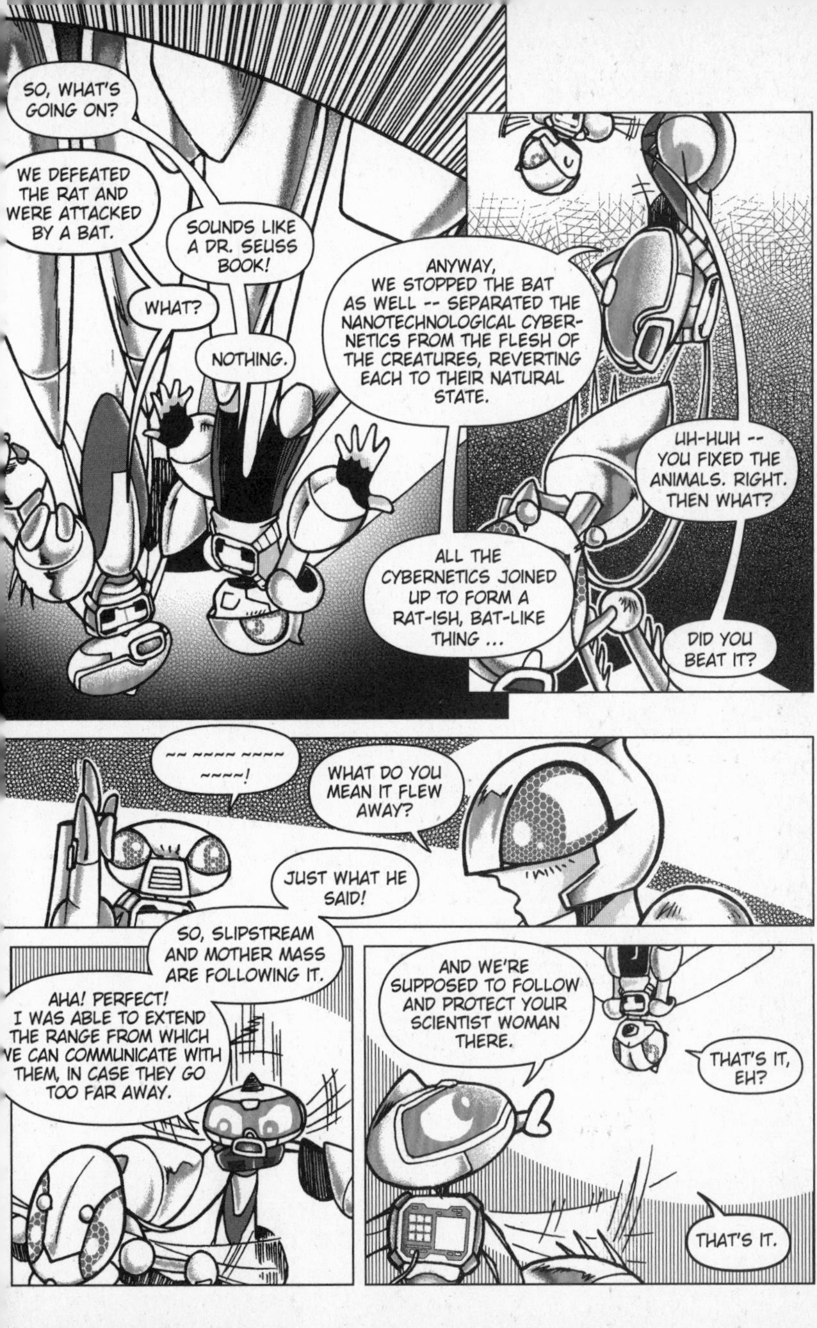
SO, WHAT'S GOING ON?
WE DEFEATED THE RAT AND WERE ATTACKED BY A BAT.
SOUNDS LIKE A DR. SEUSS BOOK!
WHAT?
NOTHING.
ANYWAY, WE STOPPED THE BAT AS WELL -- SEPARATED THE NANOTECHNOLOGICAL CYBER-NETICS FROM THE FLESH OF THE CREATURES, REVERTING EACH TO THEIR NATURAL STATE.
UH-HUH -- YOU FIXED THE ANIMALS. RIGHT. THEN WHAT?
ALL THE CYBERNETICS JOINED UP TO FORM A RAT-ISH, BAT-LIKE THING ...
DID YOU BEAT IT?
~~ ~~~~ ~~~~ ~~~~!
WHAT DO YOU MEAN IT FLEW AWAY?
JUST WHAT HE SAID!
SO, SLIPSTREAM AND MOTHER MASS ARE FOLLOWING IT.
AHA! PERFECT! I WAS ABLE TO EXTEND THE RANGE FROM WHICH WE CAN COMMUNICATE WITH THEM, IN CASE THEY GO TOO FAR AWAY.
AND WE'RE SUPPOSED TO FOLLOW AND PROTECT YOUR SCIENTIST WOMAN THERE.
THAT'S IT, EH?
THAT'S IT.

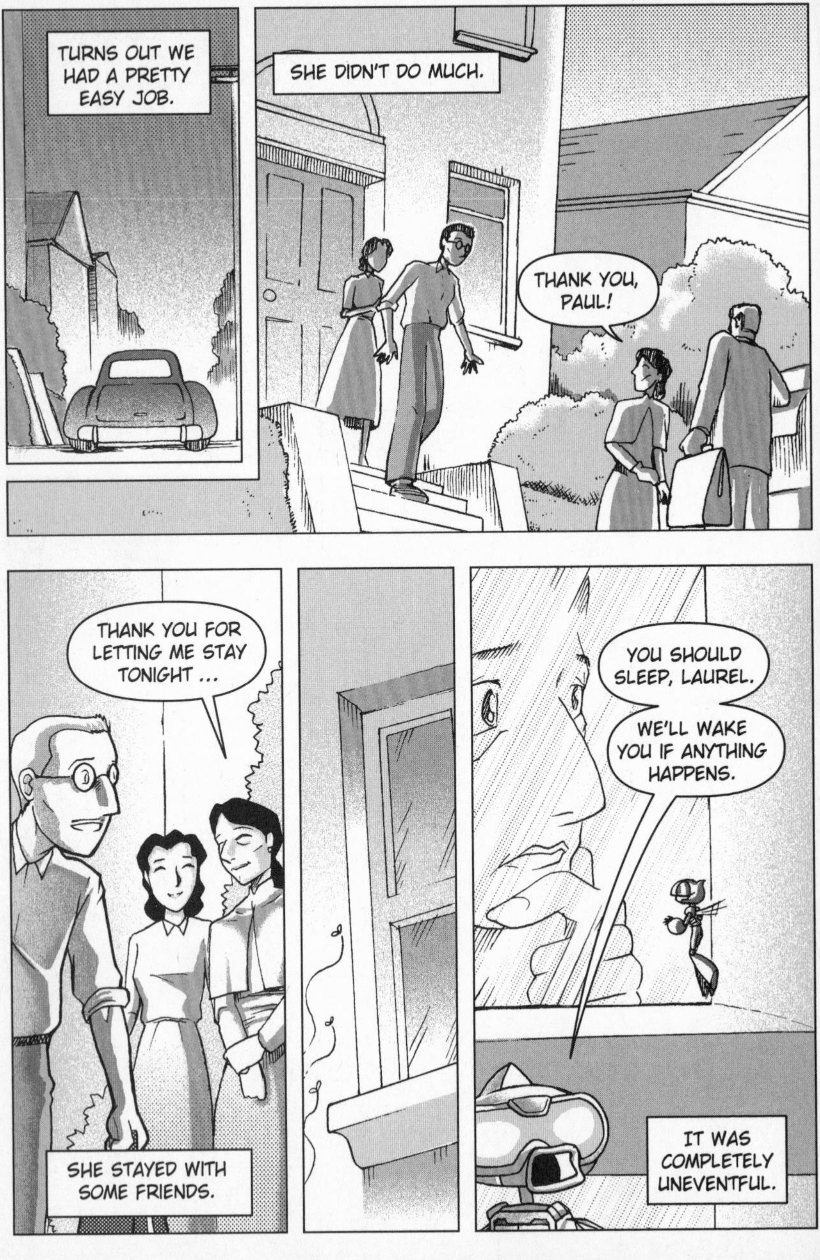
TURNS OUT WE HAD A PRETTY EASY JOB.
SHE DIDN'T DO MUCH.
THANK YOU, PAUL!
THANK YOU FOR LETTING ME STAY TONIGHT ...
SHE STAYED WITH SOME FRIENDS.
YOU SHOULD SLEEP, LAUREL.
WE'LL WAKE YOU IF ANYTHING HAPPENS.
IT WAS COMPLETELY UNEVENTFUL.

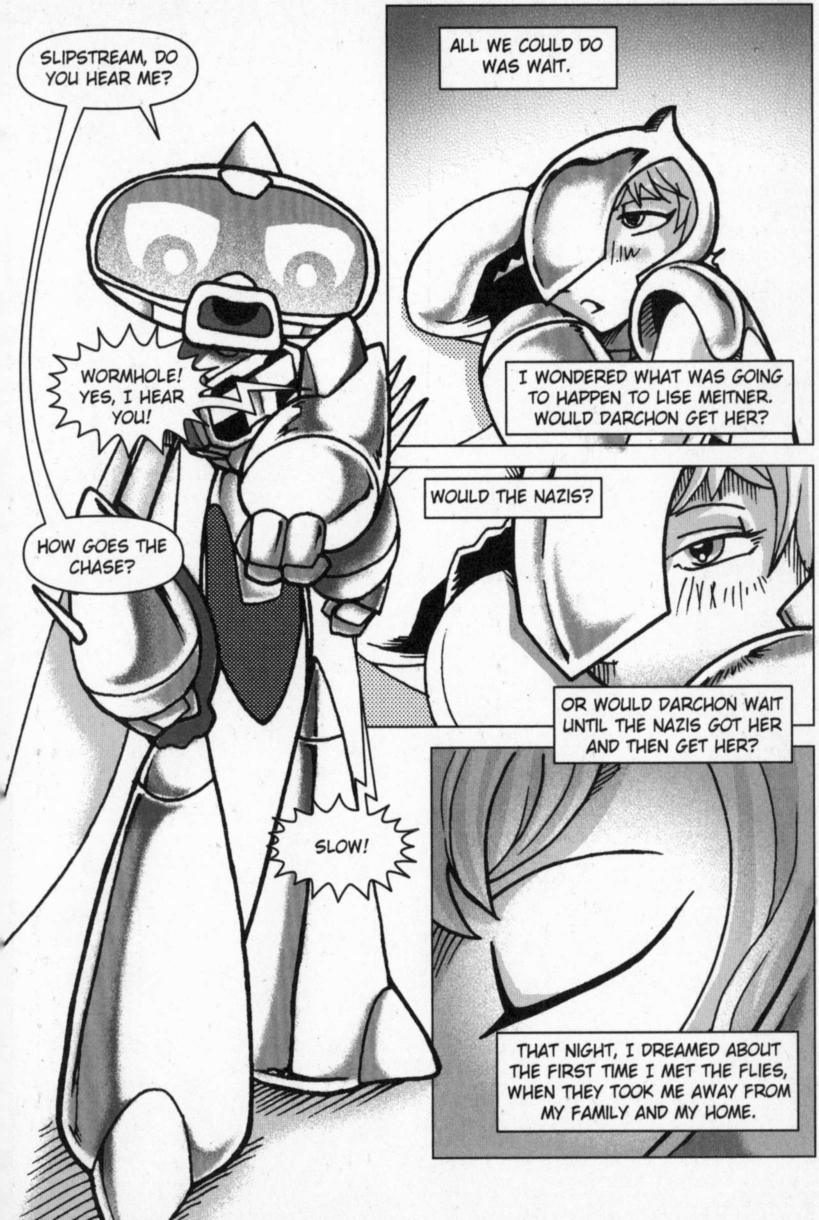
SLIPSTREAM, DO YOU HEAR ME?
WORMHOLE! YES, I HEAR YOU!
HOW GOES THE CHASE?
SLOW!
ALL WE COULD DO WAS WAIT.
I WONDERED WHAT WAS GOING TO HAPPEN TO LISE MEITNER. WOULD DARCHON GET HER?
WOULD THE NAZIS?
OR WOULD DARCHON WAIT UNTIL THE NAZIS GOT HER AND THEN GET HER?
THAT NIGHT, I DREAMED ABOUT THE FIRST TIME I MET THE FLIES, WHEN THEY TOOK ME AWAY FROM MY FAMILY AND MY HOME.

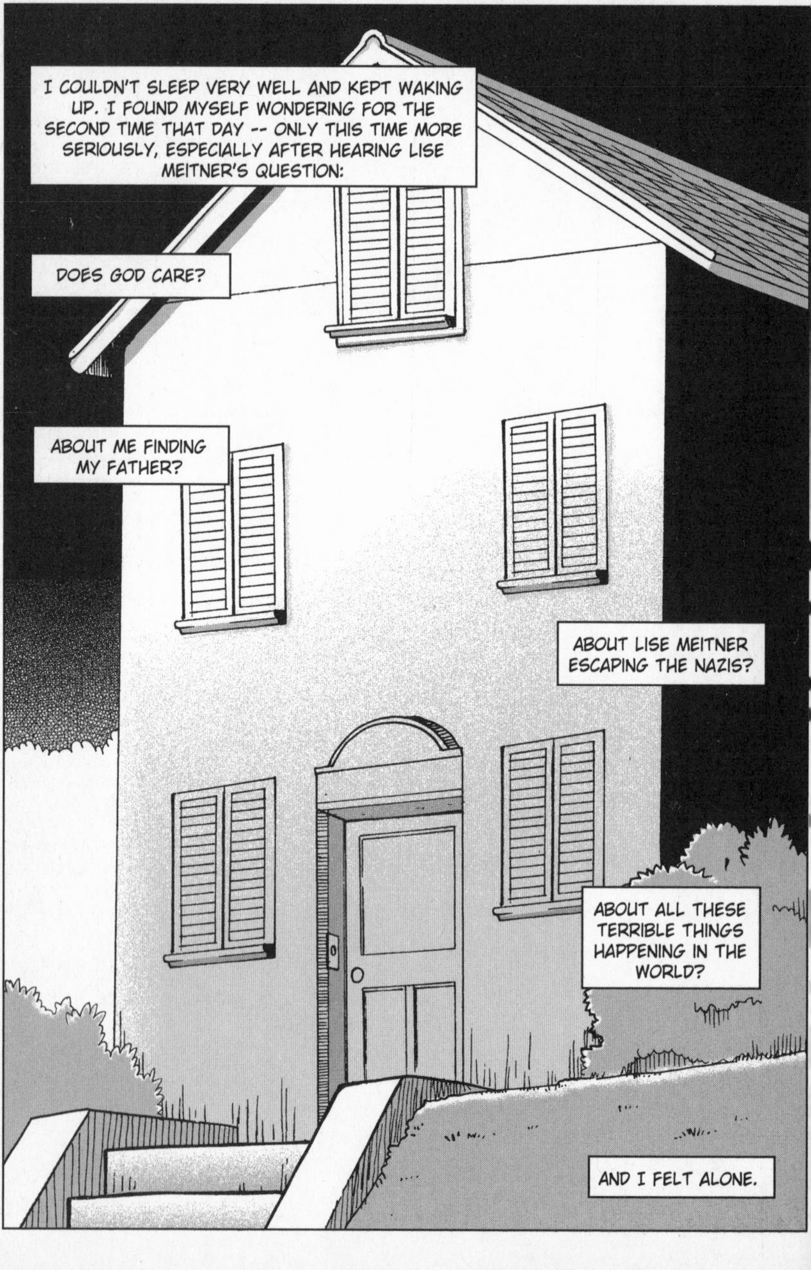
I COULDN'T SLEEP VERY WELL AND KEPT WAKING UP. I FOUND MYSELF WONDERING FOR THE SECOND TIME THAT DAY -- ONLY THIS TIME MORE SERIOUSLY, ESPECIALLY AFTER HEARING LISE MEITNER'S QUESTION:
DOES GOD CARE?
ABOUT ME FINDING MY FATHER?
ABOUT LISE MEITNER ESCAPING THE NAZIS?
ABOUT ALL THESE TERRIBLE THINGS HAPPENING IN THE WORLD?
AND I FELT ALONE.

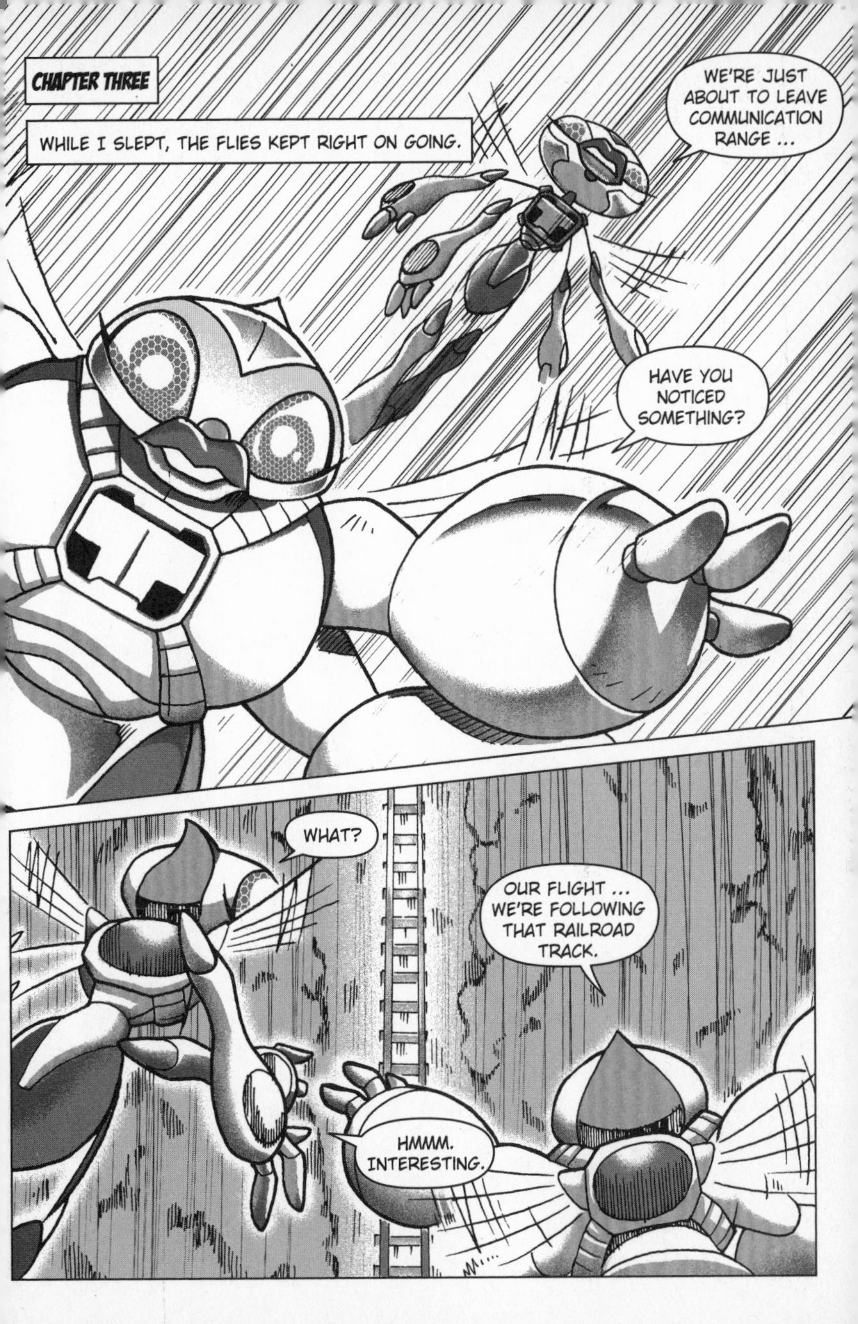
CHAPTER THREE
WHILE I SLEPT, THE FLIES KEPT RIGHT ON GOING.
WE'RE JUST ABOUT TO LEAVE COMMUNICATION RANGE ...
HAVE YOU NOTICED SOMETHING?
WHAT?
OUR FLIGHT ... WE'RE FOLLOWING THAT RAILROAD TRACK.
HMMM. INTERESTING.

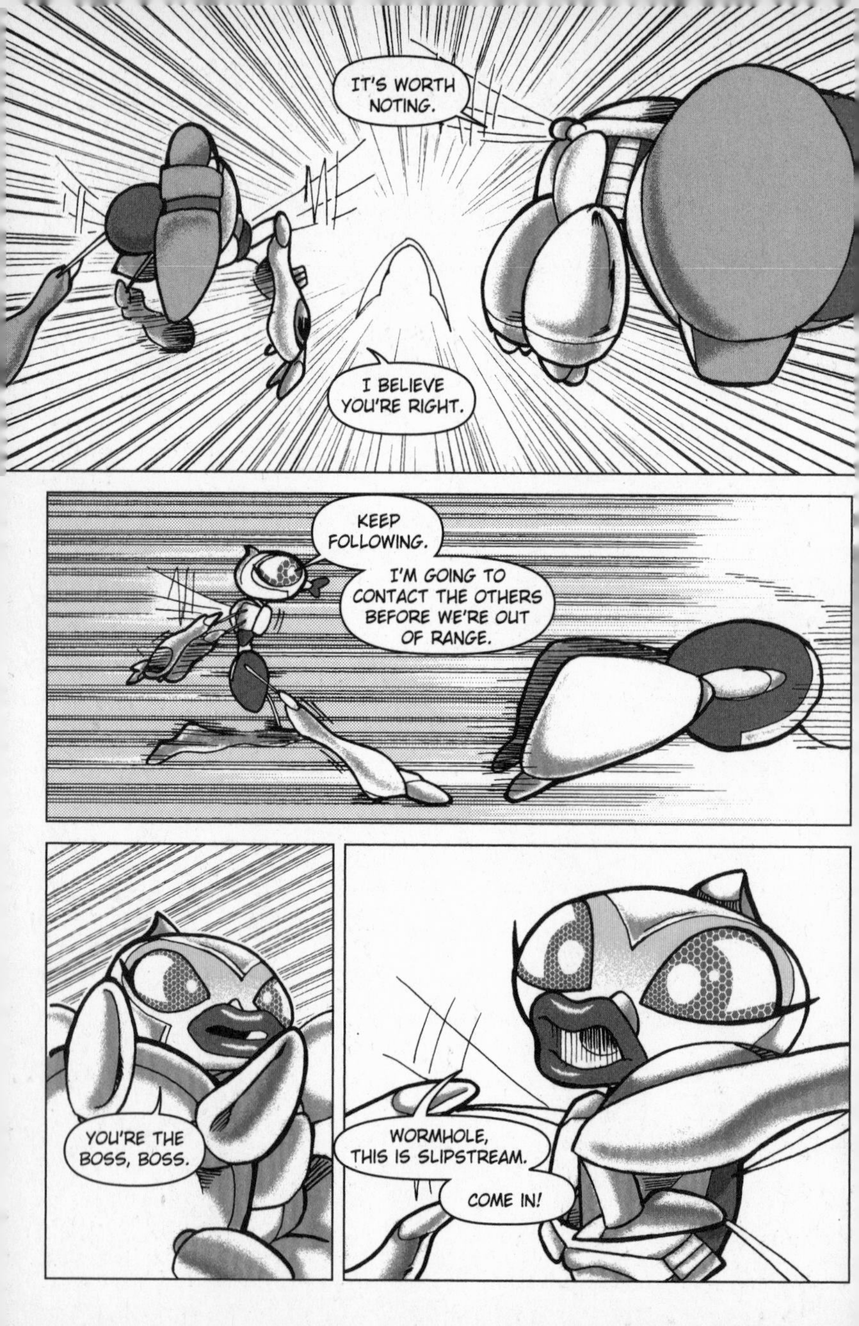
IT'S WORTH NOTING.
I BELIEVE YOU'RE RIGHT.
KEEP FOLLOWING.
I'M GOING TO CONTACT THE OTHERS BEFORE WE'RE OUT OF RANGE.
YOU'RE THE BOSS, BOSS.
WORMHOLE, THIS IS SLIPSTREAM.
COME IN!

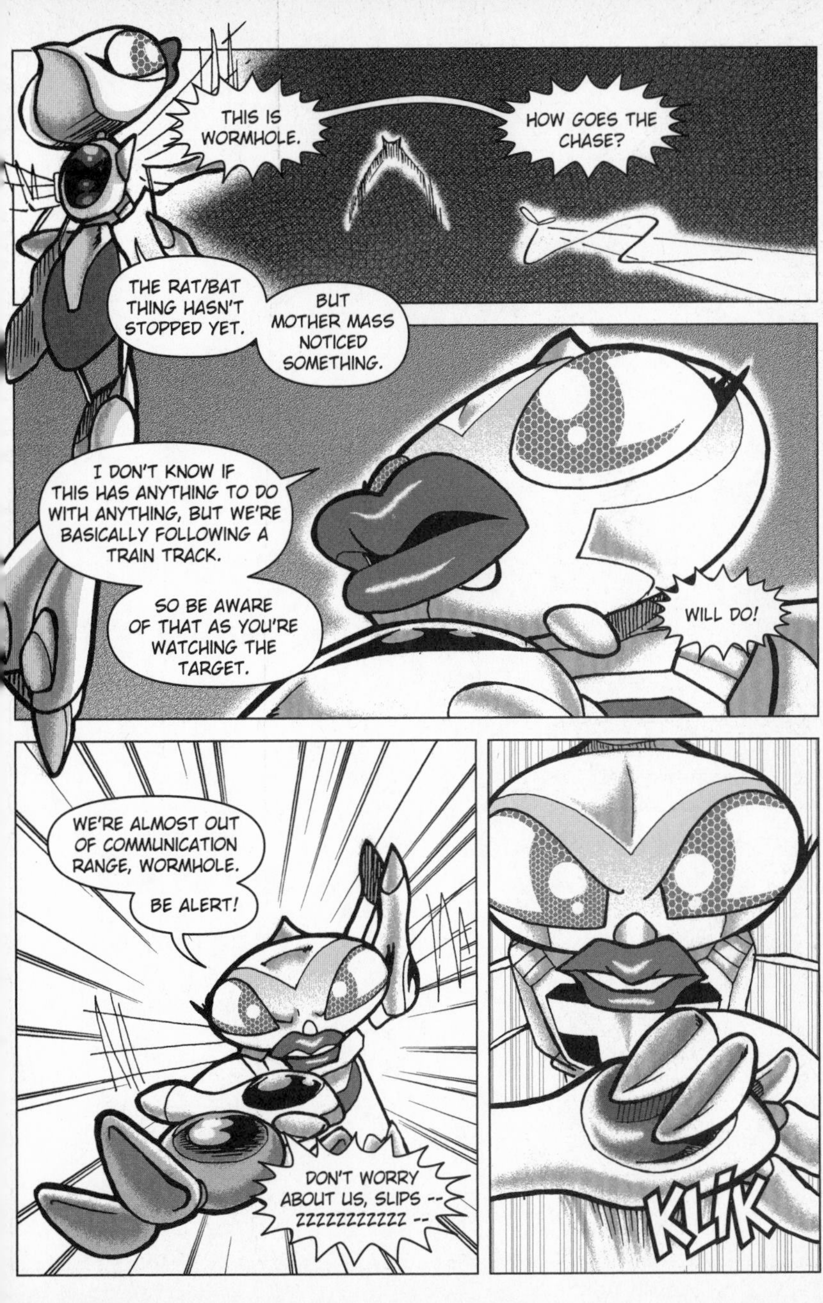
THIS IS WORMHOLE.
HOW GOES THE CHASE?
THE RAT/BAT THING HASN'T STOPPED YET.
BUT MOTHER MASS NOTICED SOMETHING.
I DON'T KNOW IF THIS HAS ANYTHING TO DO WITH ANYTHING, BUT WE'RE BASICALLY FOLLOWING A TRAIN TRACK.
SO BE AWARE OF THAT AS YOU'RE WATCHING THE TARGET.
WILL DO!
WE'RE ALMOST OUT OF COMMUNICATION RANGE, WORMHOLE.
BE ALERT!
DON'T WORRY ABOUT US, SLIPS -- ZZZZZZZZZZZ --
KLIK

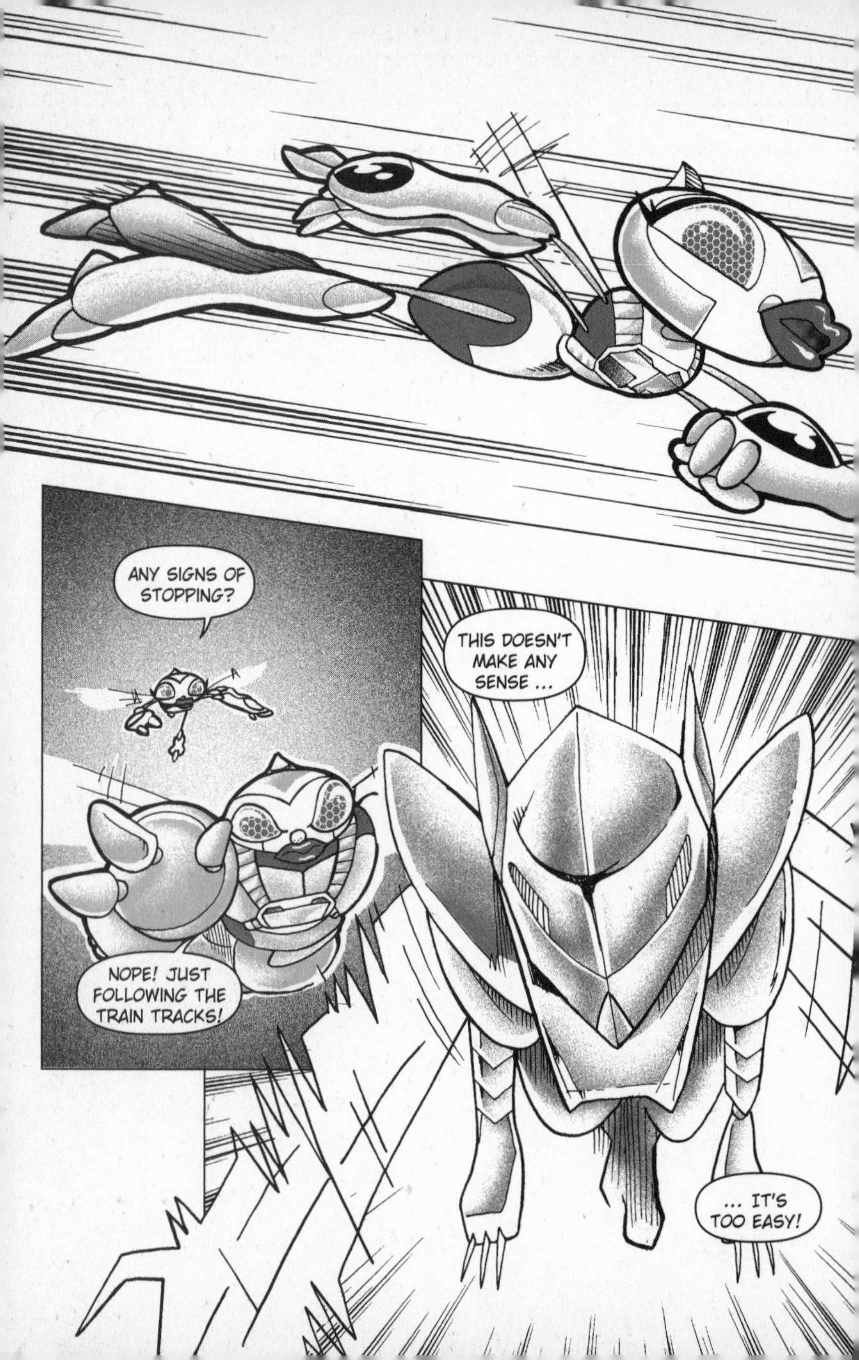
ANY SIGNS OF STOPPING?
NOPE! JUST FOLLOWING THE TRAIN TRACKS!
THIS DOESN'T MAKE ANY SENSE ...
... IT'S TOO EASY!

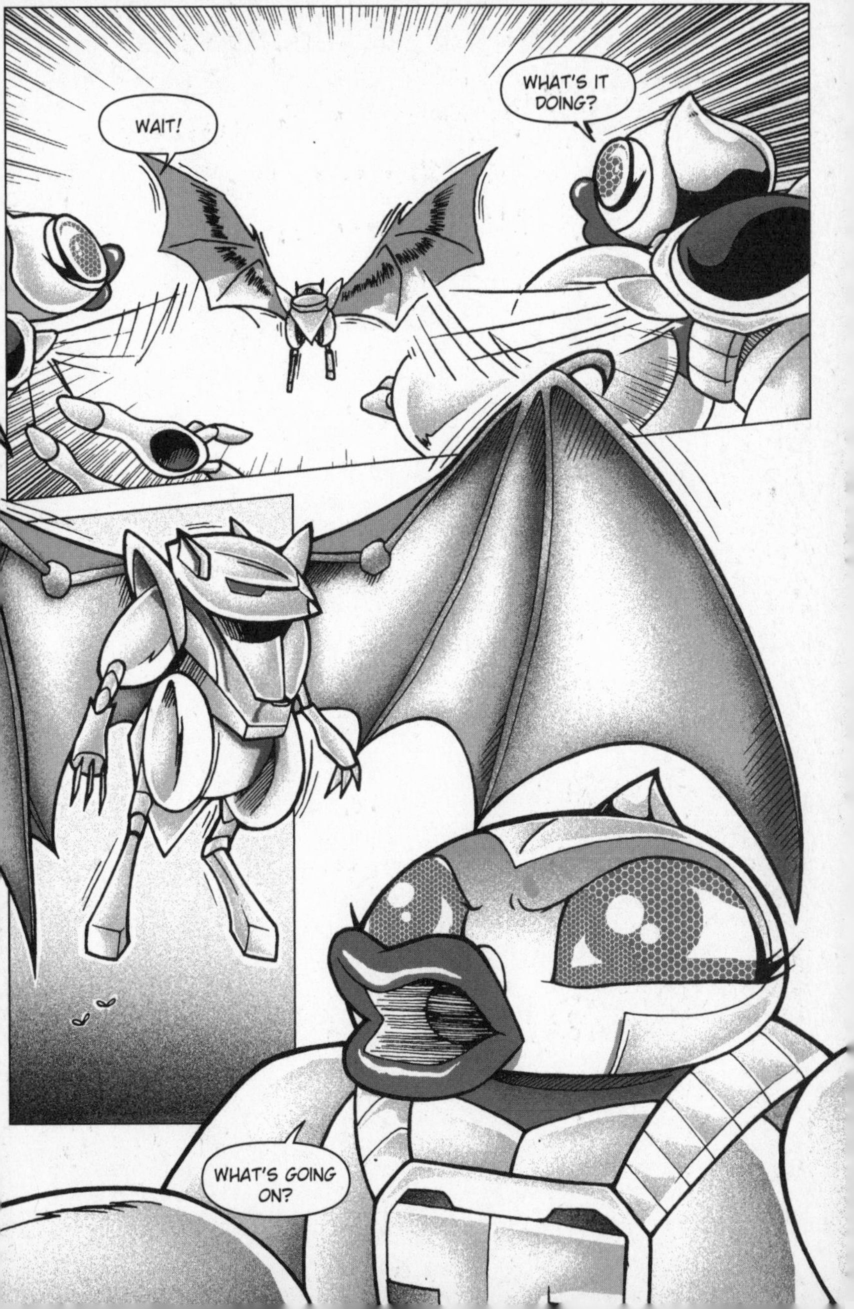
WAIT!
WHAT'S IT DOING?
WHAT'S GOING ON?

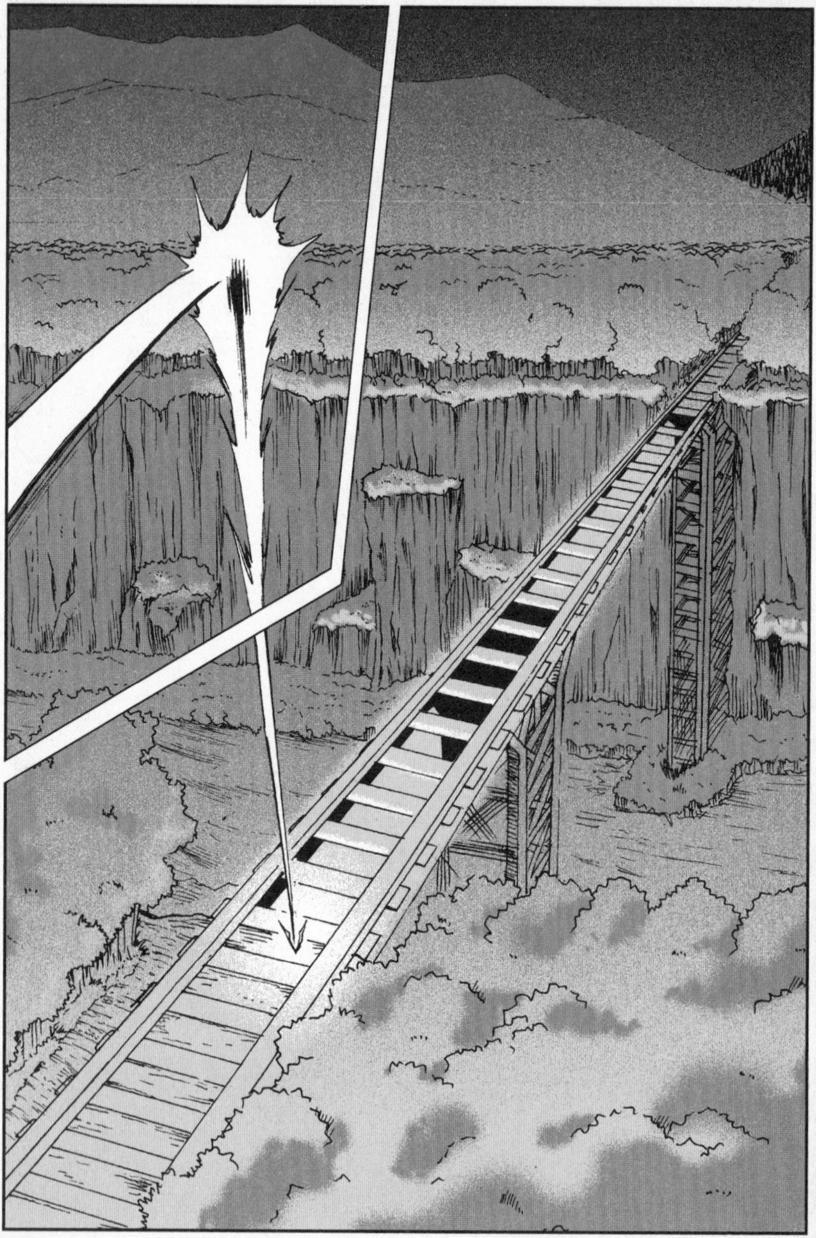

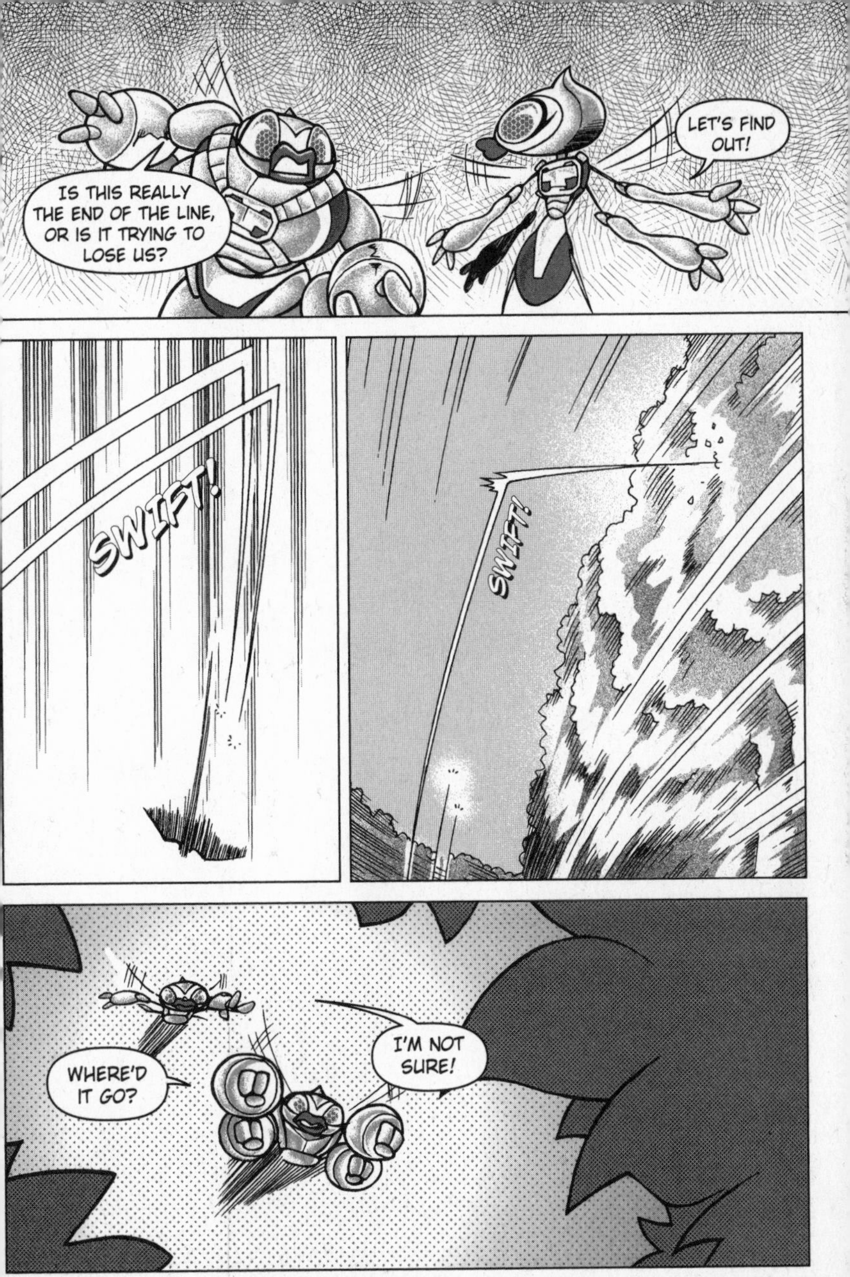
IS THIS REALLY THE END OF THE LINE, OR IS IT TRYING TO LOSE US?
LET'S FIND OUT!
SWIFT!
SWIFT!
WHERE'D IT GO?
I'M NOT SURE!

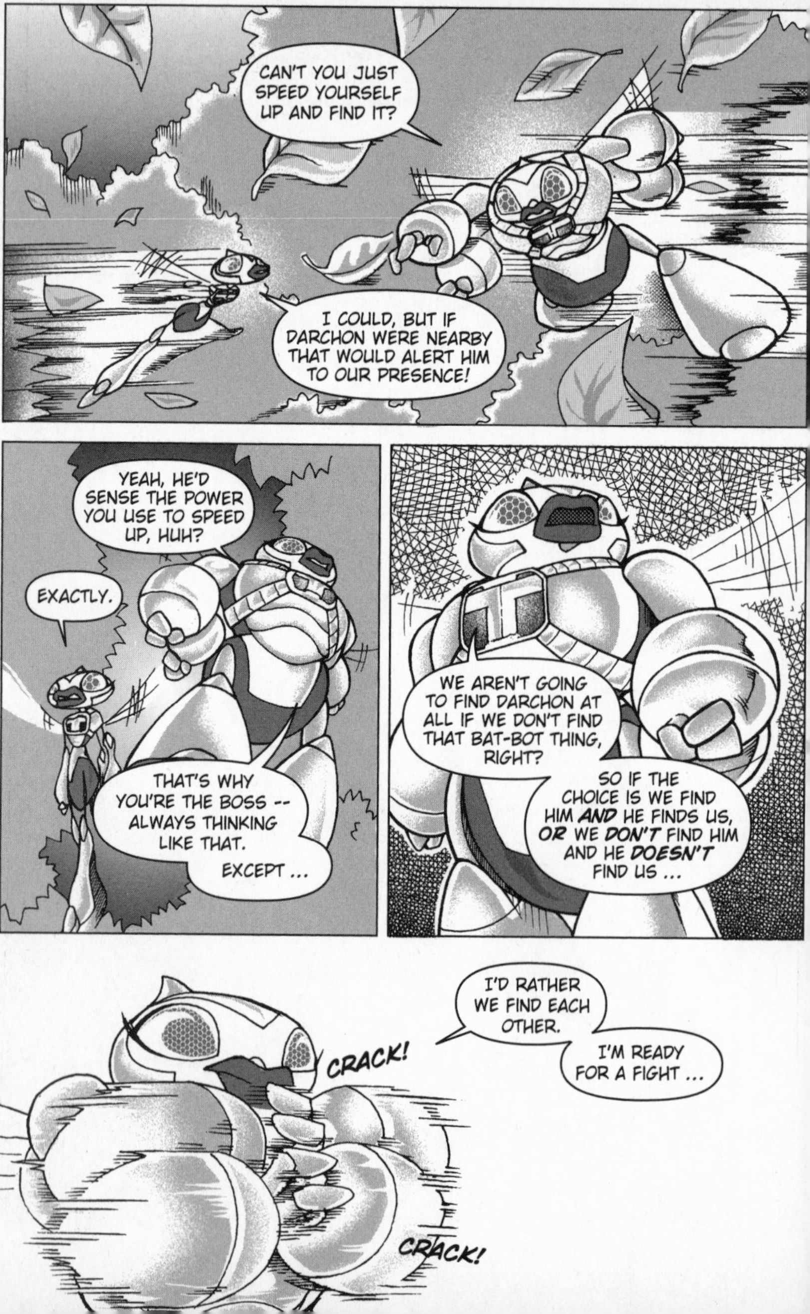
CAN'T YOU JUST SPEED YOURSELF UP AND FIND IT?
I COULD, BUT IF DARCHON WERE NEARBY THAT WOULD ALERT HIM TO OUR PRESENCE!
YEAH, HE'D SENSE THE POWER YOU USE TO SPEED UP, HUH?
EXACTLY.
THAT'S WHY YOU'RE THE BOSS -- ALWAYS THINKING LIKE THAT.
EXCEPT ...
WE AREN'T GOING TO FIND DARCHON AT ALL IF WE DON'T FIND THAT BAT-BOT THING, RIGHT?
SO IF THE CHOICE IS WE FIND HIM ***AND*** HE FINDS US, ***OR*** WE ***DON'T*** FIND HIM AND HE ***DOESN'T*** FIND US ...
I'D RATHER WE FIND EACH OTHER.
I'M READY FOR A FIGHT ...
CRACK!
CRACK!

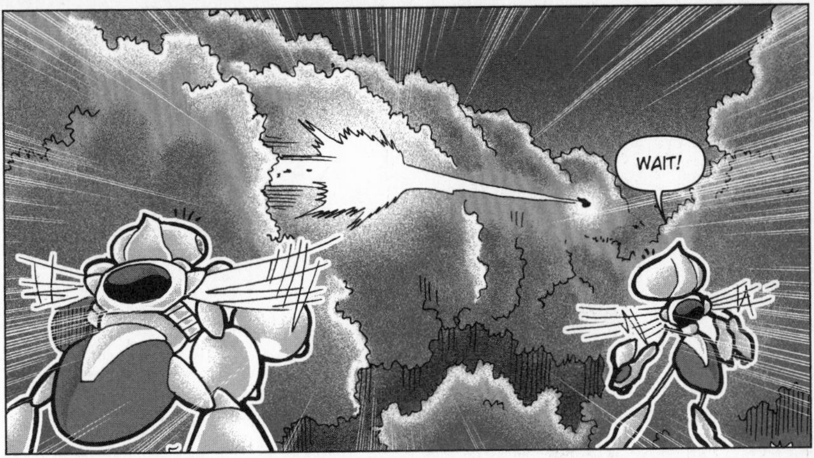
WAIT!
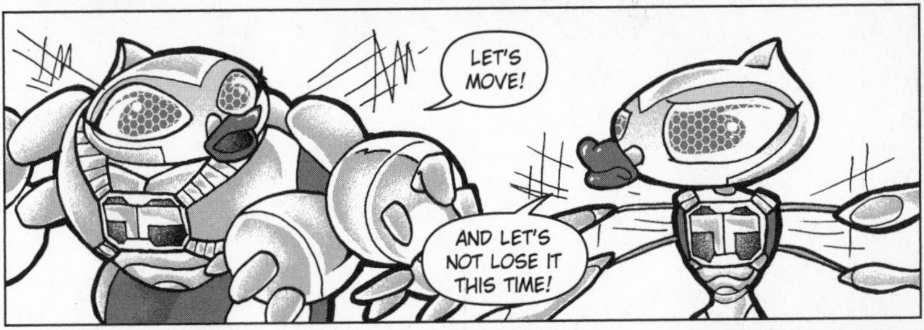
LET'S MOVE!
AND LET'S NOT LOSE IT THIS TIME!
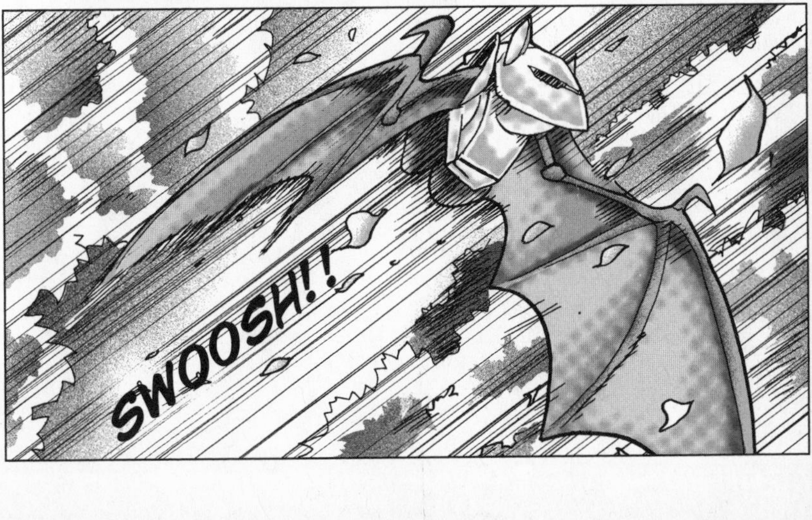
SWOOSH!!

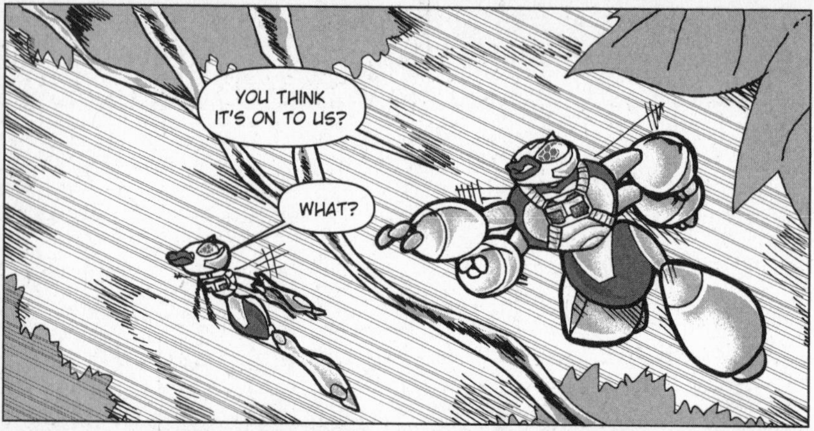
YOU THINK IT'S ON TO US?
WHAT?

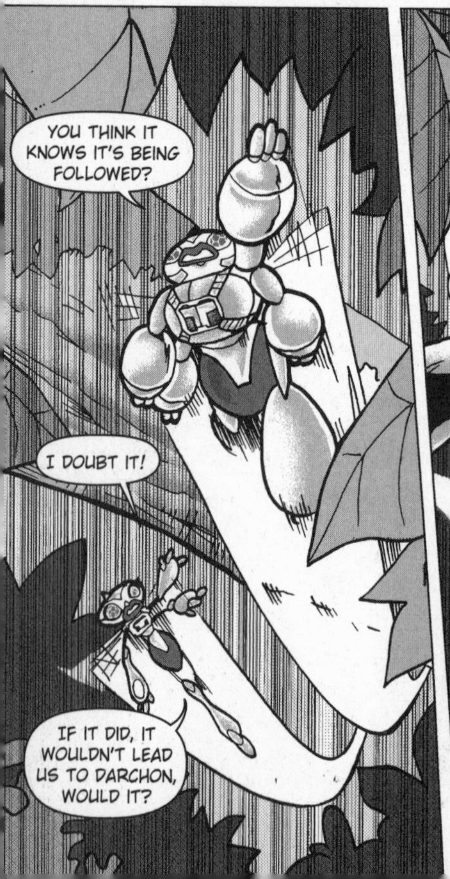
YOU THINK IT KNOWS IT'S BEING FOLLOWED?
I DOUBT IT!
IF IT DID, IT WOULDN'T LEAD US TO DARCHON, WOULD IT?

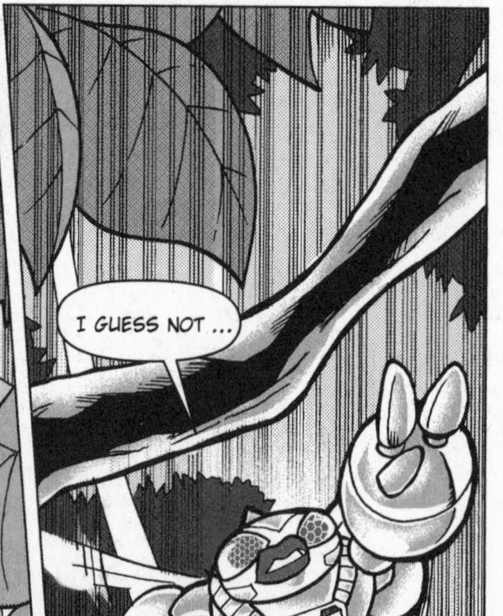
I GUESS NOT ...

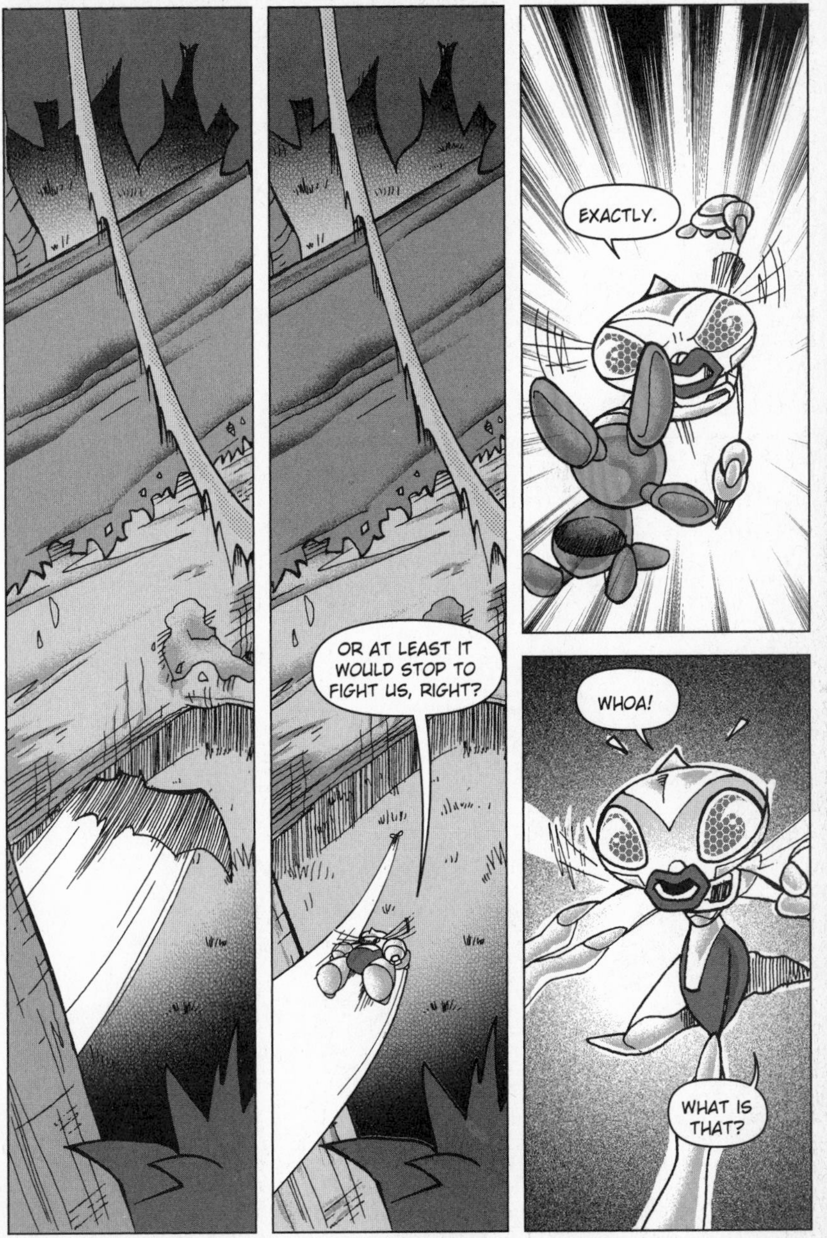
OR AT LEAST IT WOULD STOP TO FIGHT US, RIGHT?
EXACTLY.
WHOA!
WHAT IS THAT?

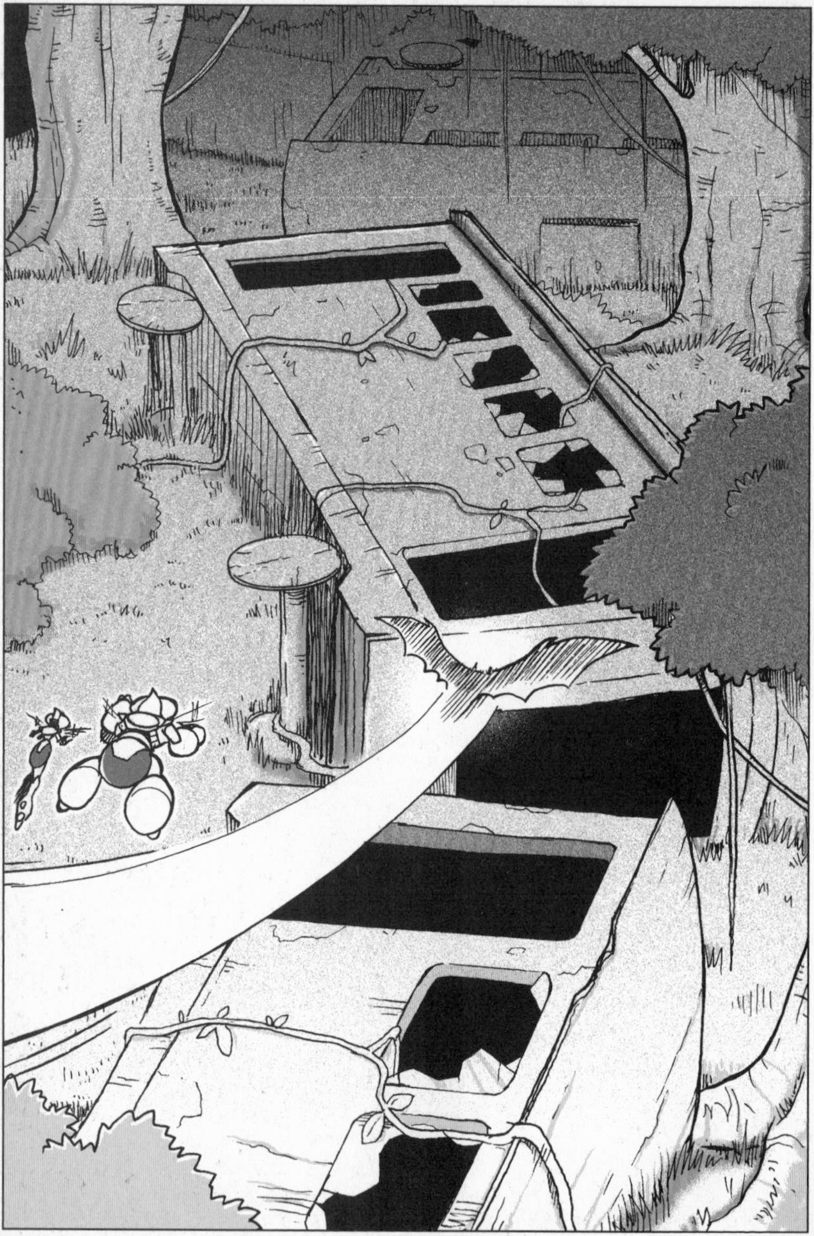

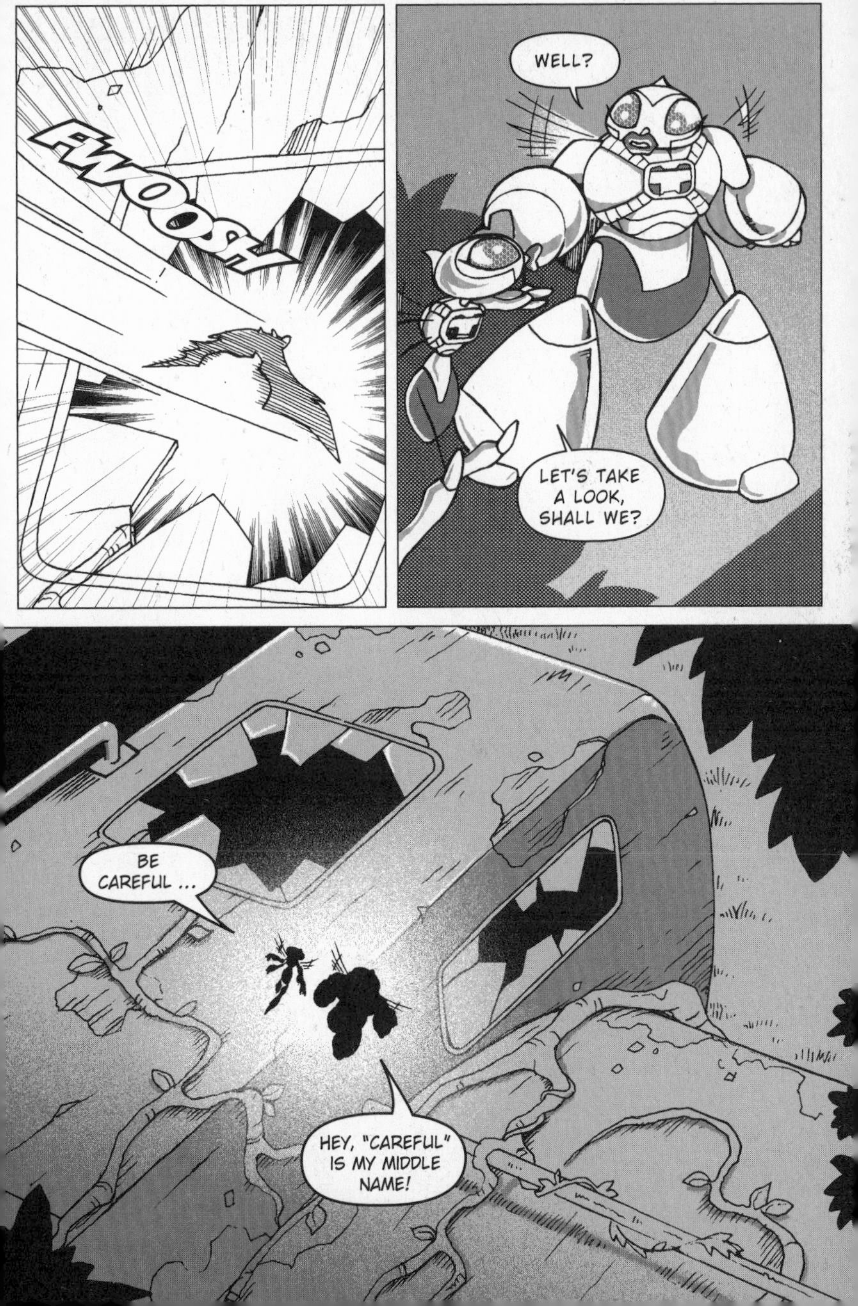
FWOOSH
WELL?
LET'S TAKE A LOOK, SHALL WE?
BE CAREFUL ...
HEY, "CAREFUL" IS MY MIDDLE NAME!

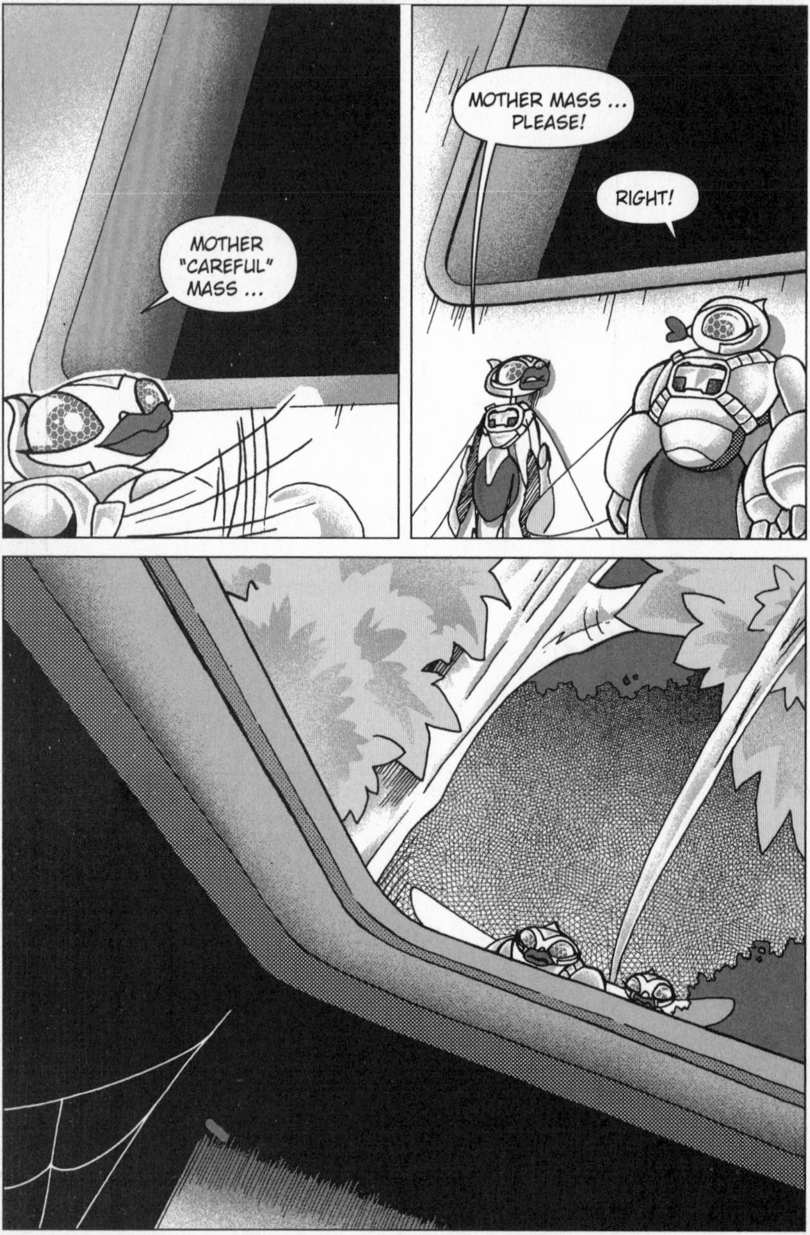
MOTHER "CAREFUL" MASS ...
MOTHER MASS ... PLEASE!
RIGHT!

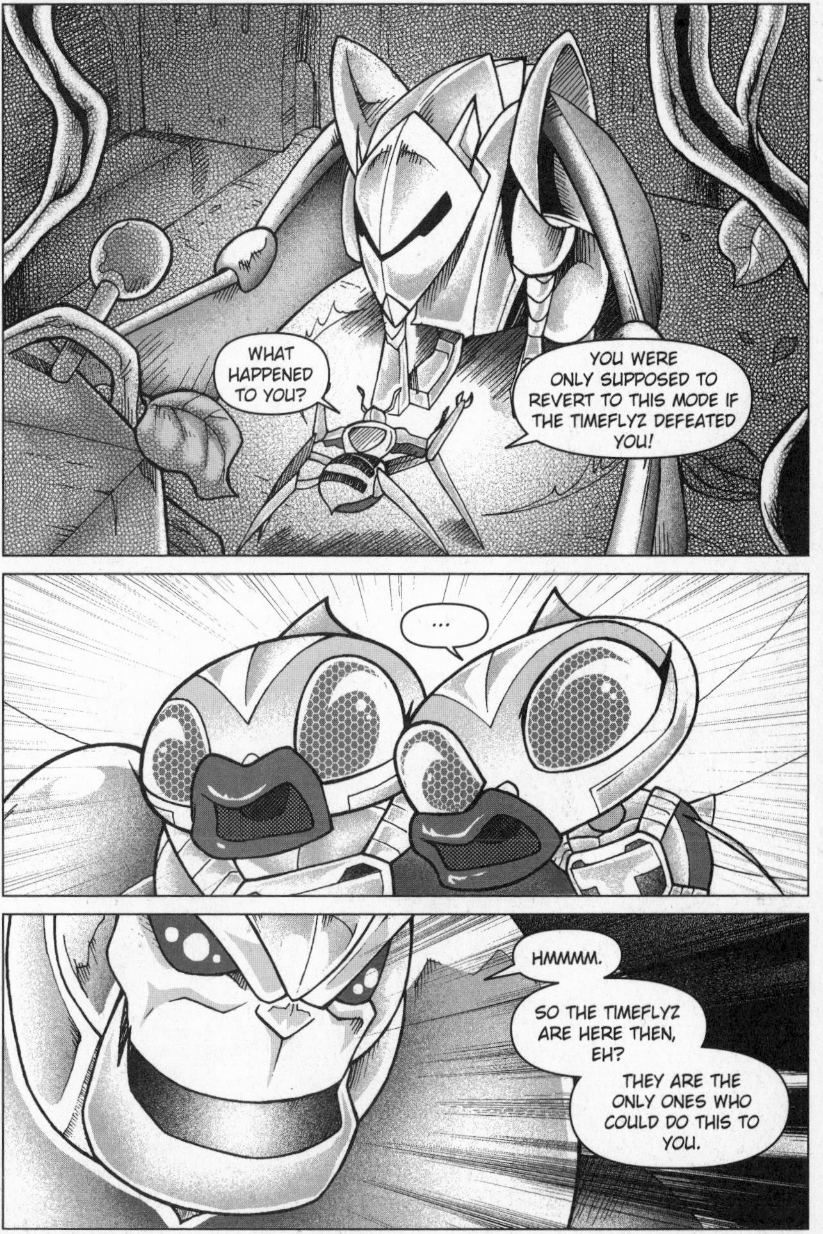
WHAT HAPPENED TO YOU?
YOU WERE ONLY SUPPOSED TO REVERT TO THIS MODE IF THE TIMEFLYZ DEFEATED YOU!
...
HMMMM.
SO THE TIMEFLYZ ARE HERE THEN, EH?
THEY ARE THE ONLY ONES WHO COULD DO THIS TO YOU.

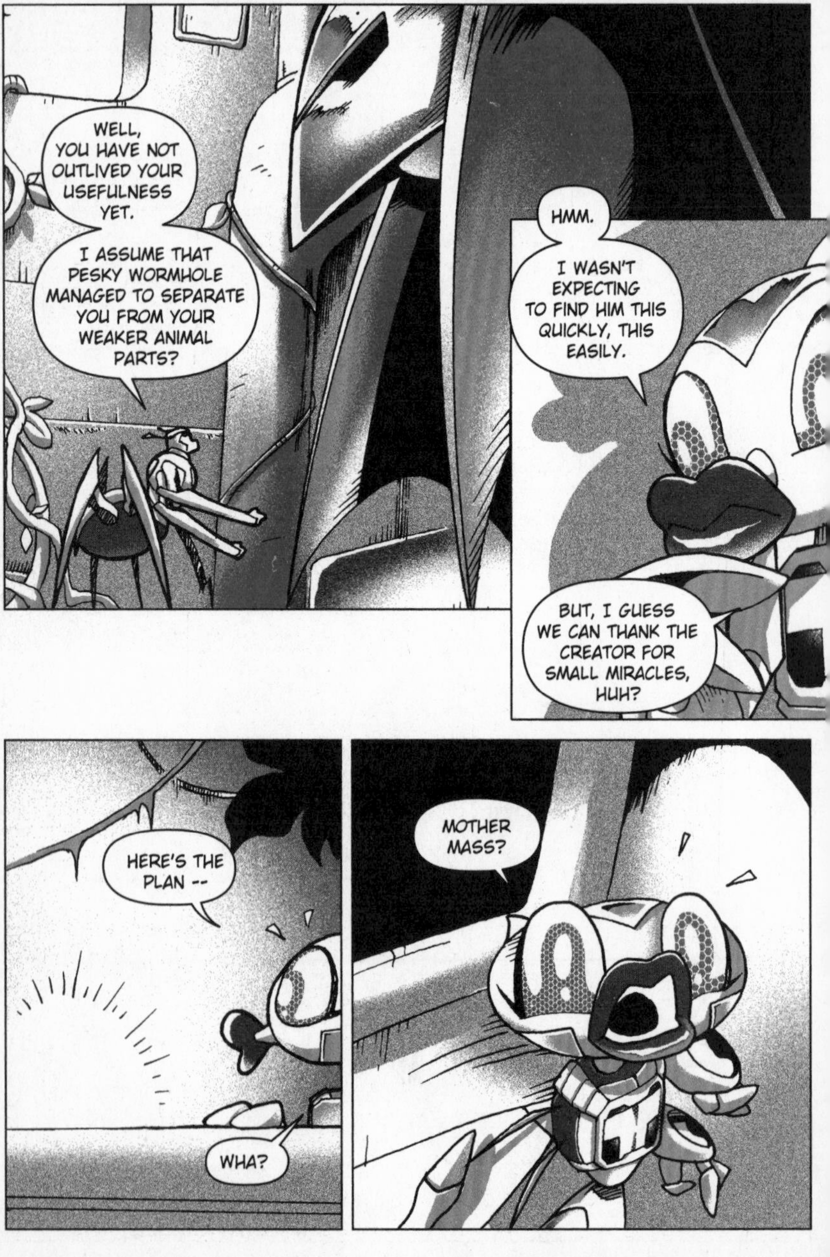
WELL, YOU HAVE NOT OUTLIVED YOUR USEFULNESS YET.
I ASSUME THAT PESKY WORMHOLE MANAGED TO SEPARATE YOU FROM YOUR WEAKER ANIMAL PARTS?
HMM.
I WASN'T EXPECTING TO FIND HIM THIS QUICKLY, THIS EASILY.
BUT, I GUESS WE CAN THANK THE CREATOR FOR SMALL MIRACLES, HUH?
HERE'S THE PLAN --
WHA?
MOTHER MASS?

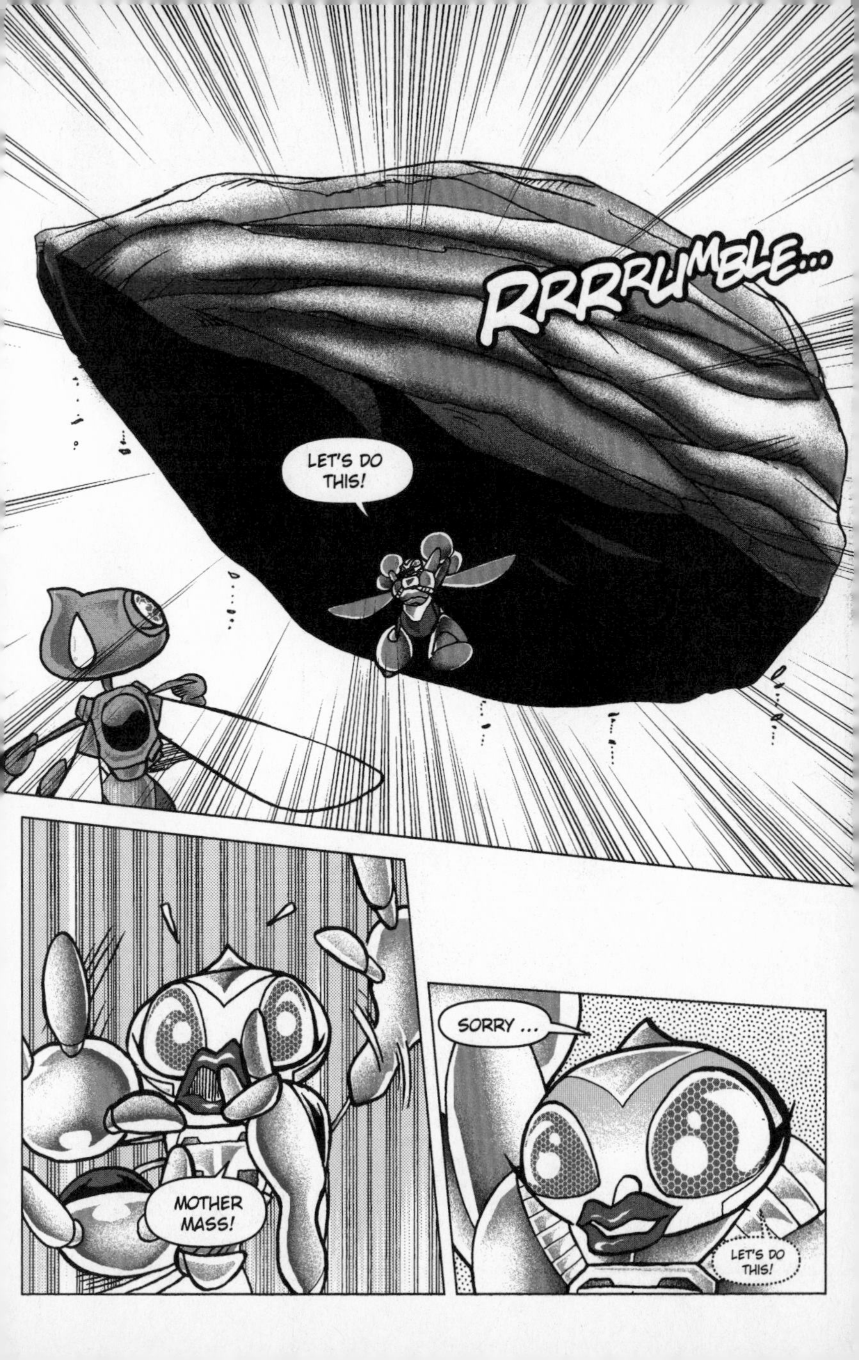
RRRRUMBLE...
LET'S DO THIS!
MOTHER MASS!
SORRY ...
LET'S DO THIS!

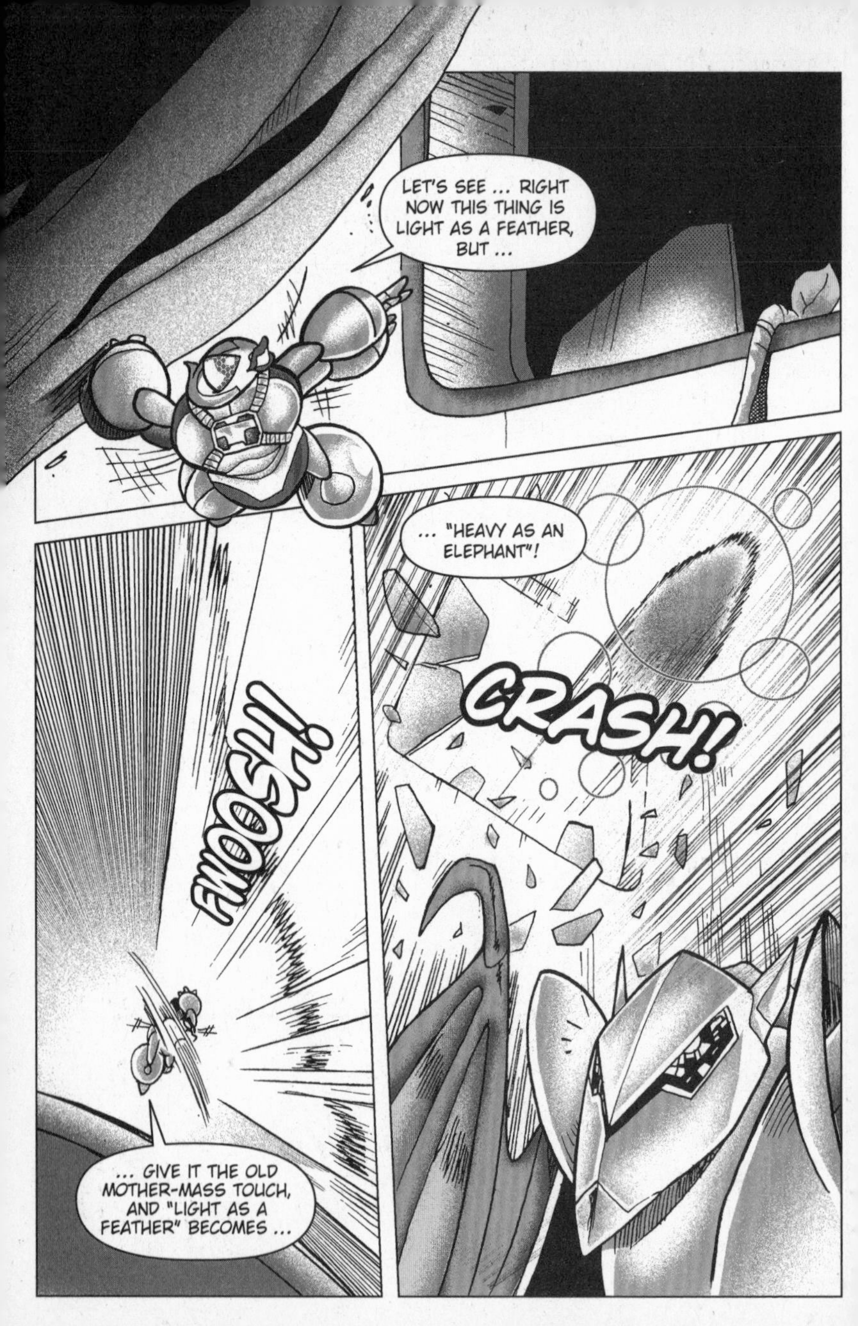
LET'S SEE ... RIGHT NOW THIS THING IS LIGHT AS A FEATHER, BUT ...
WHOOSH!!
... GIVE IT THE OLD MOTHER-MASS TOUCH, AND "LIGHT AS A FEATHER" BECOMES ...
... "HEAVY AS AN ELEPHANT"!
CRASH!

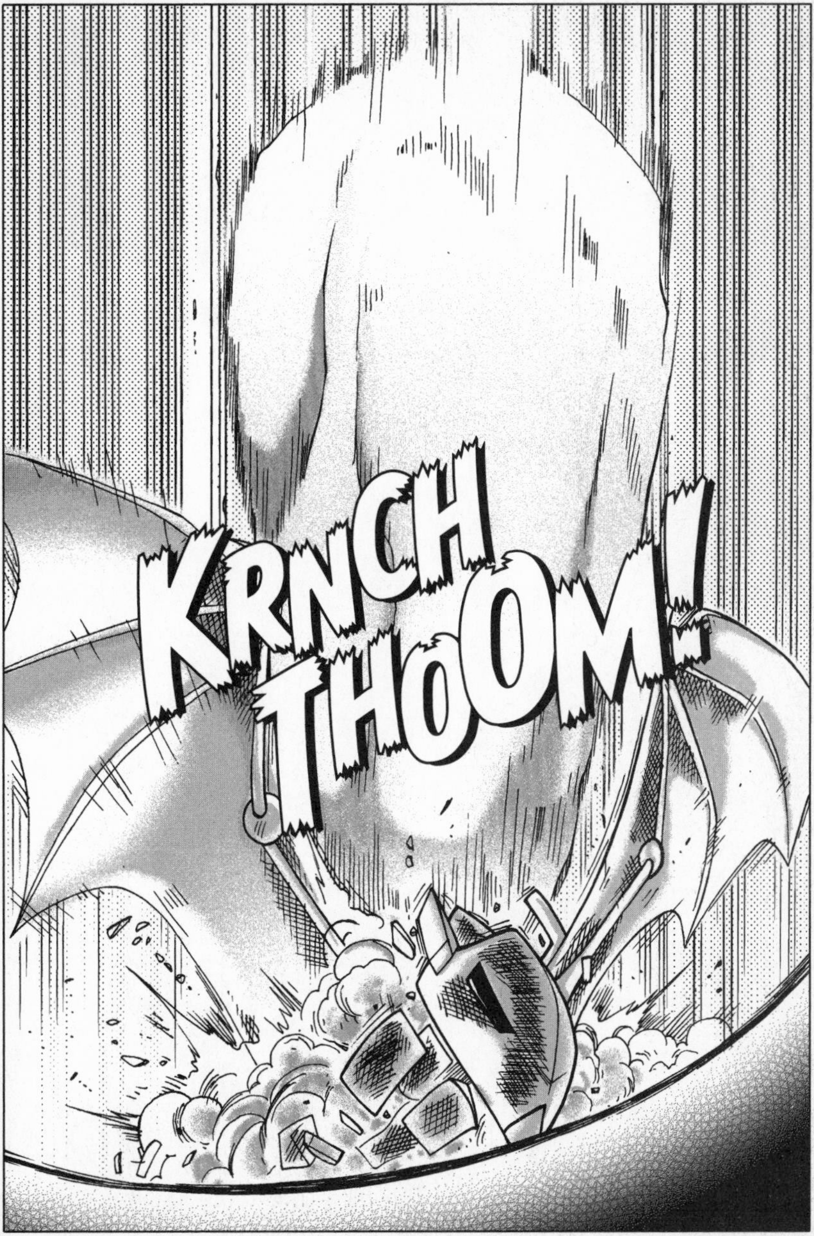
KRNCH THOOM!

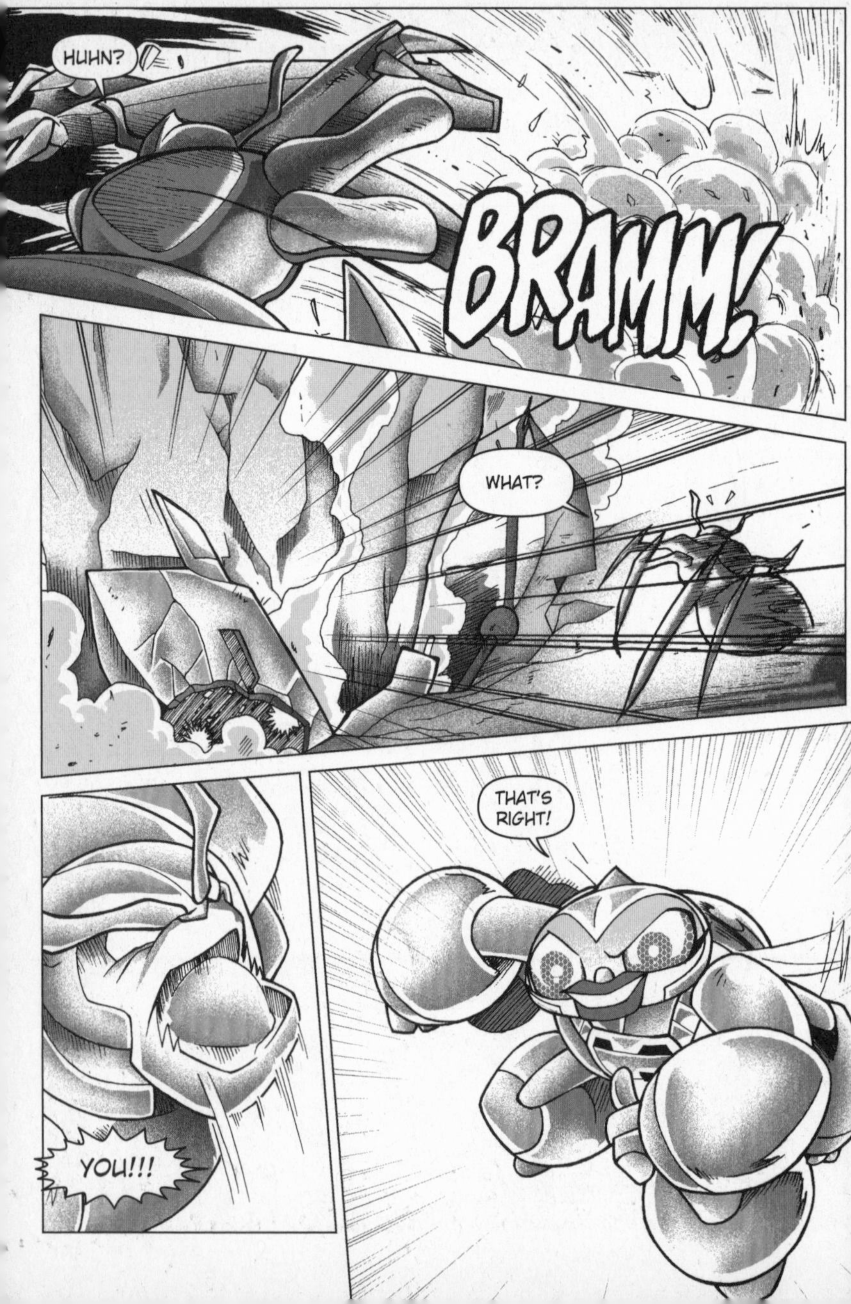
HUHN?
BRAMM!
WHAT?
YOU!!!
THAT'S RIGHT!

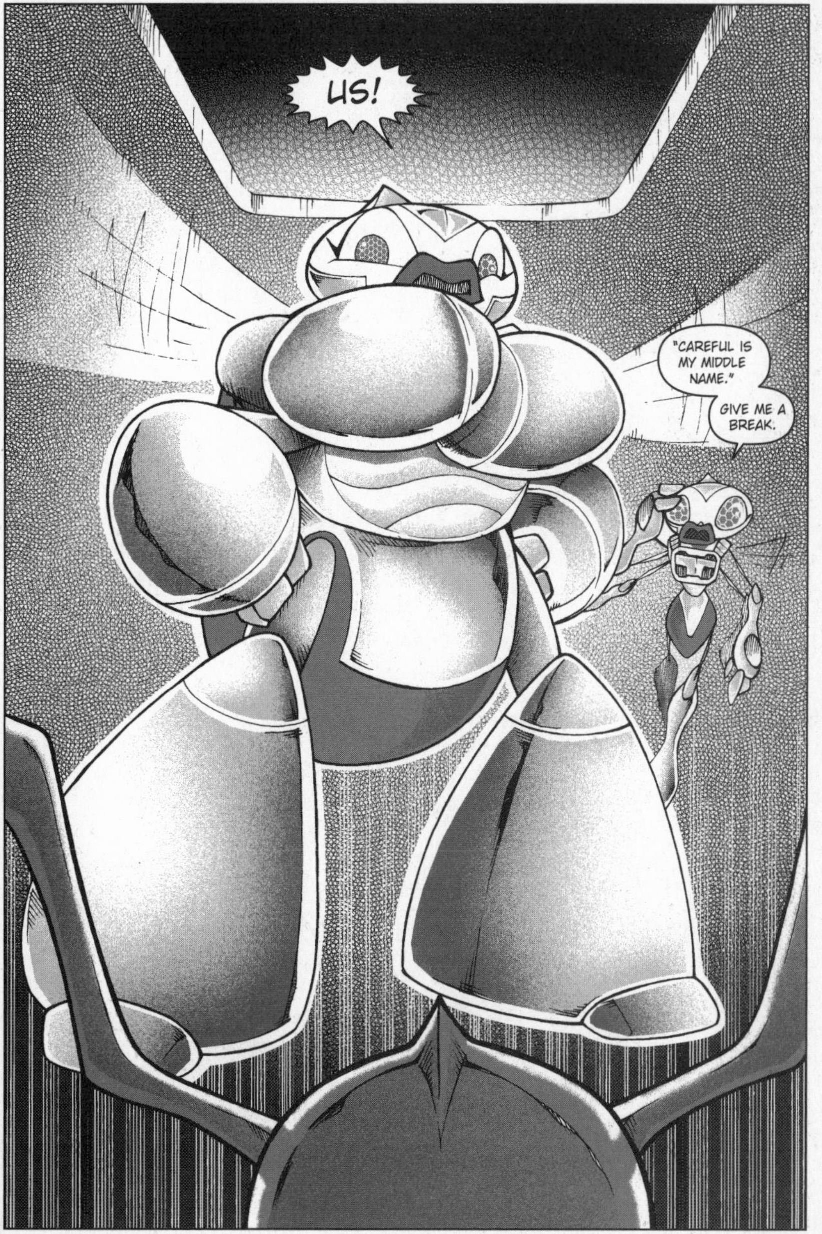

US!
"CAREFUL IS MY MIDDLE NAME."
GIVE ME A BREAK.

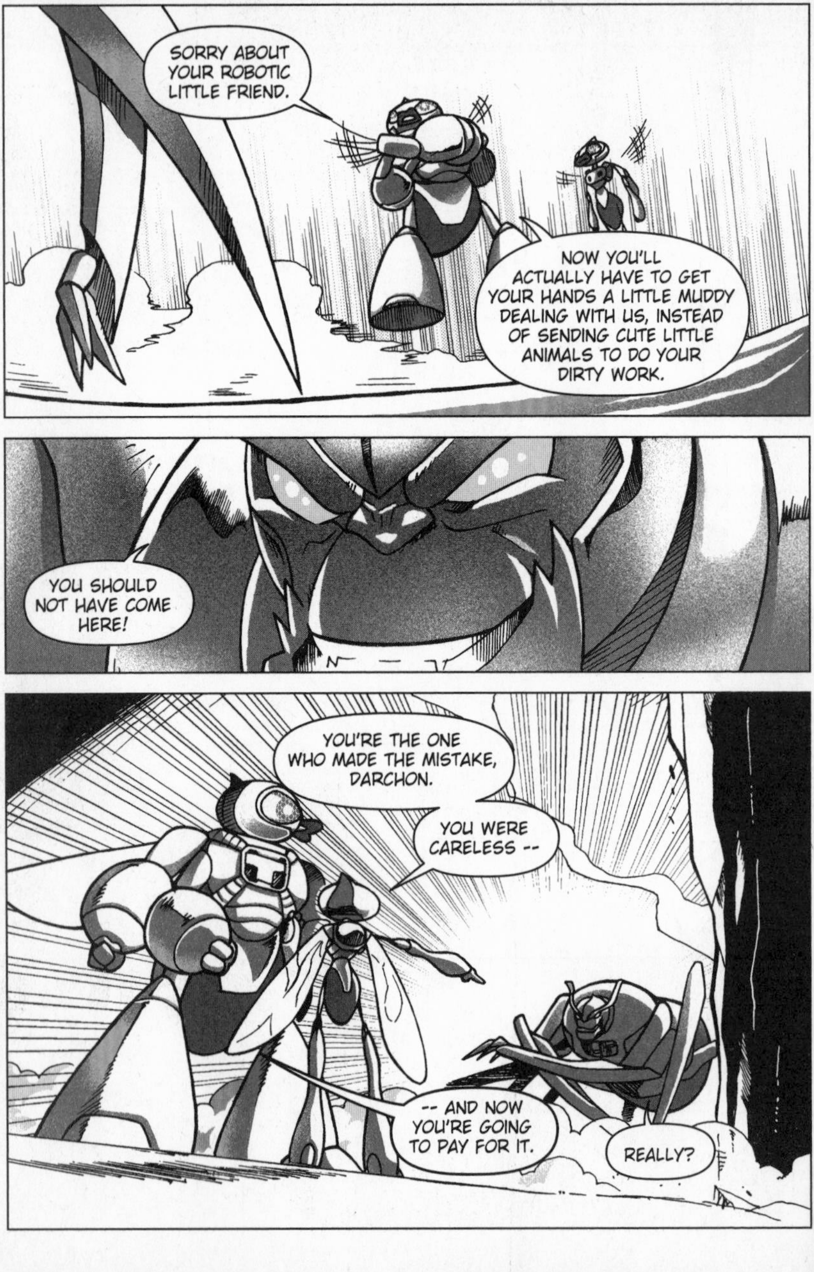
SORRY ABOUT YOUR ROBOTIC LITTLE FRIEND.
NOW YOU'LL ACTUALLY HAVE TO GET YOUR HANDS A LITTLE MUDDY DEALING WITH US, INSTEAD OF SENDING CUTE LITTLE ANIMALS TO DO YOUR DIRTY WORK.
YOU SHOULD NOT HAVE COME HERE!
YOU'RE THE ONE WHO MADE THE MISTAKE, DARCHON.
YOU WERE CARELESS --
-- AND NOW YOU'RE GOING TO PAY FOR IT.
REALLY?

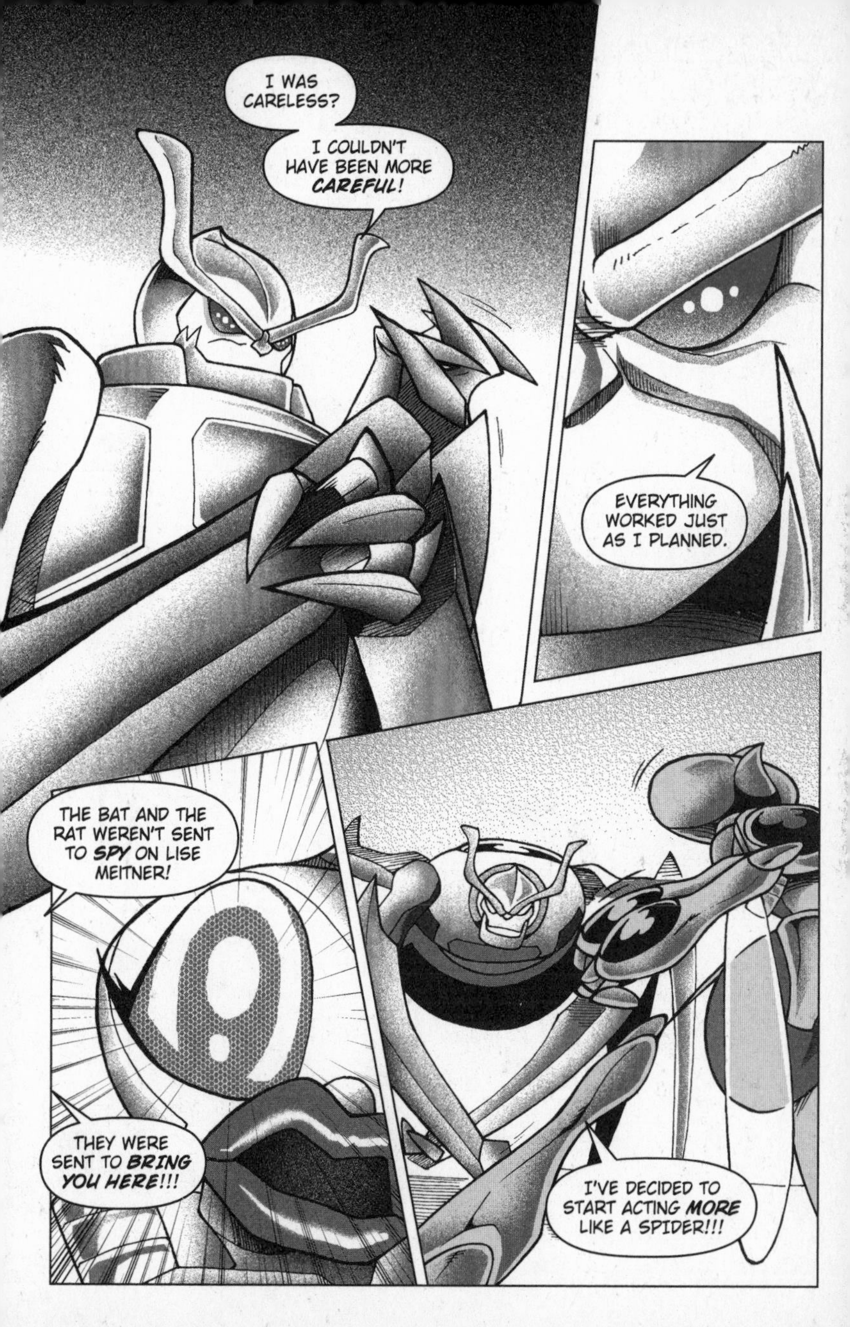
I WAS CARELESS?
I COULDN'T HAVE BEEN MORE **CAREFUL**!
EVERYTHING WORKED JUST AS I PLANNED.
THE BAT AND THE RAT WEREN'T SENT TO **SPY** ON LISE MEITNER!
THEY WERE SENT TO **BRING YOU HERE**!!!
I'VE DECIDED TO START ACTING **MORE** LIKE A SPIDER!!!

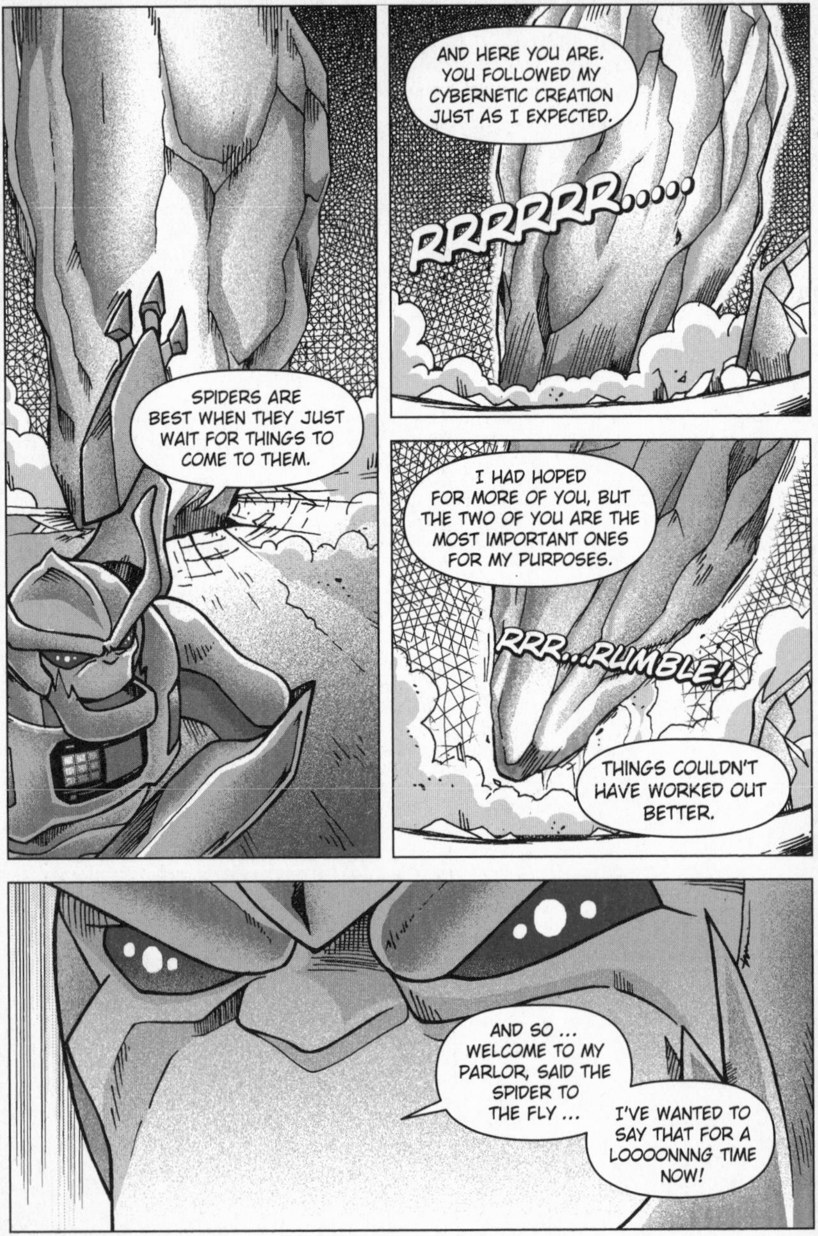
SPIDERS ARE BEST WHEN THEY JUST WAIT FOR THINGS TO COME TO THEM.
AND HERE YOU ARE. YOU FOLLOWED MY CYBERNETIC CREATION JUST AS I EXPECTED.
RRRRRR.....
I HAD HOPED FOR MORE OF YOU, BUT THE TWO OF YOU ARE THE MOST IMPORTANT ONES FOR MY PURPOSES.
RRR...RUMBLE!
THINGS COULDN'T HAVE WORKED OUT BETTER.
AND SO ... WELCOME TO MY PARLOR, SAID THE SPIDER TO THE FLY ...
I'VE WANTED TO SAY THAT FOR A LOOOONNNG TIME NOW!

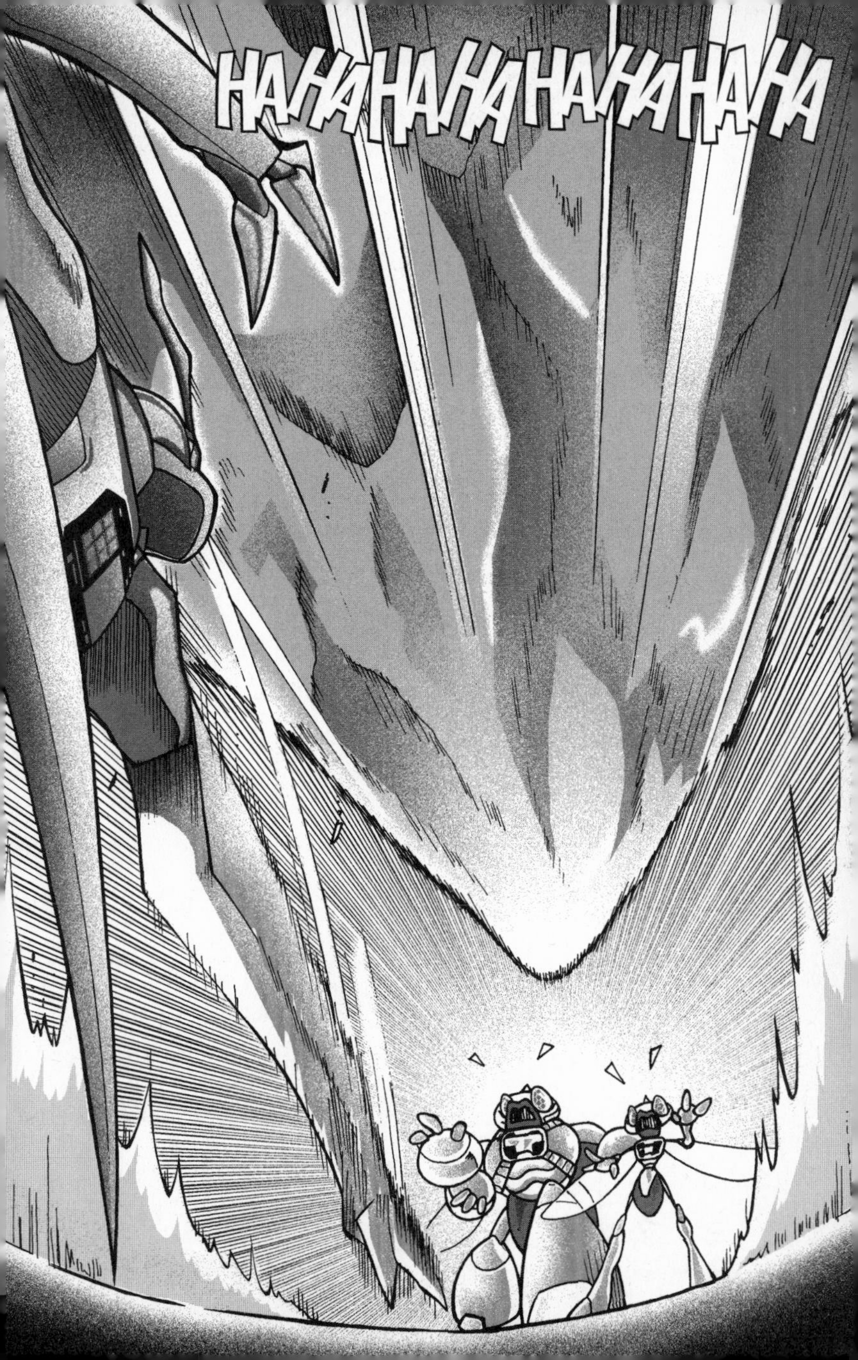
HAHAHAHAHAHAHAHAHAHA

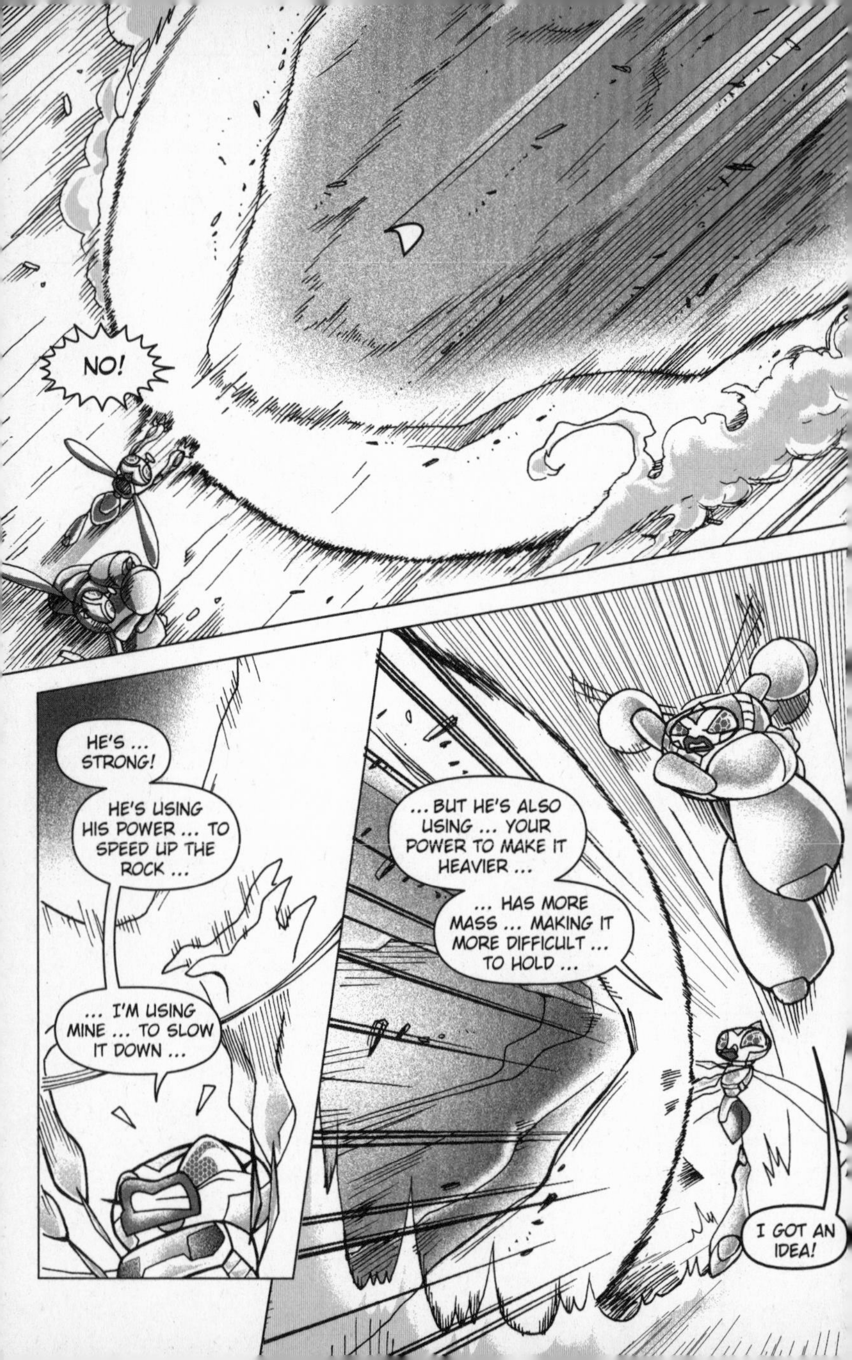
NO!
HE'S ... STRONG!
HE'S USING HIS POWER ... TO SPEED UP THE ROCK ...
... I'M USING MINE ... TO SLOW IT DOWN ...
... BUT HE'S ALSO USING ... YOUR POWER TO MAKE IT HEAVIER ...
... HAS MORE MASS ... MAKING IT MORE DIFFICULT ... TO HOLD ...
I GOT AN IDEA!

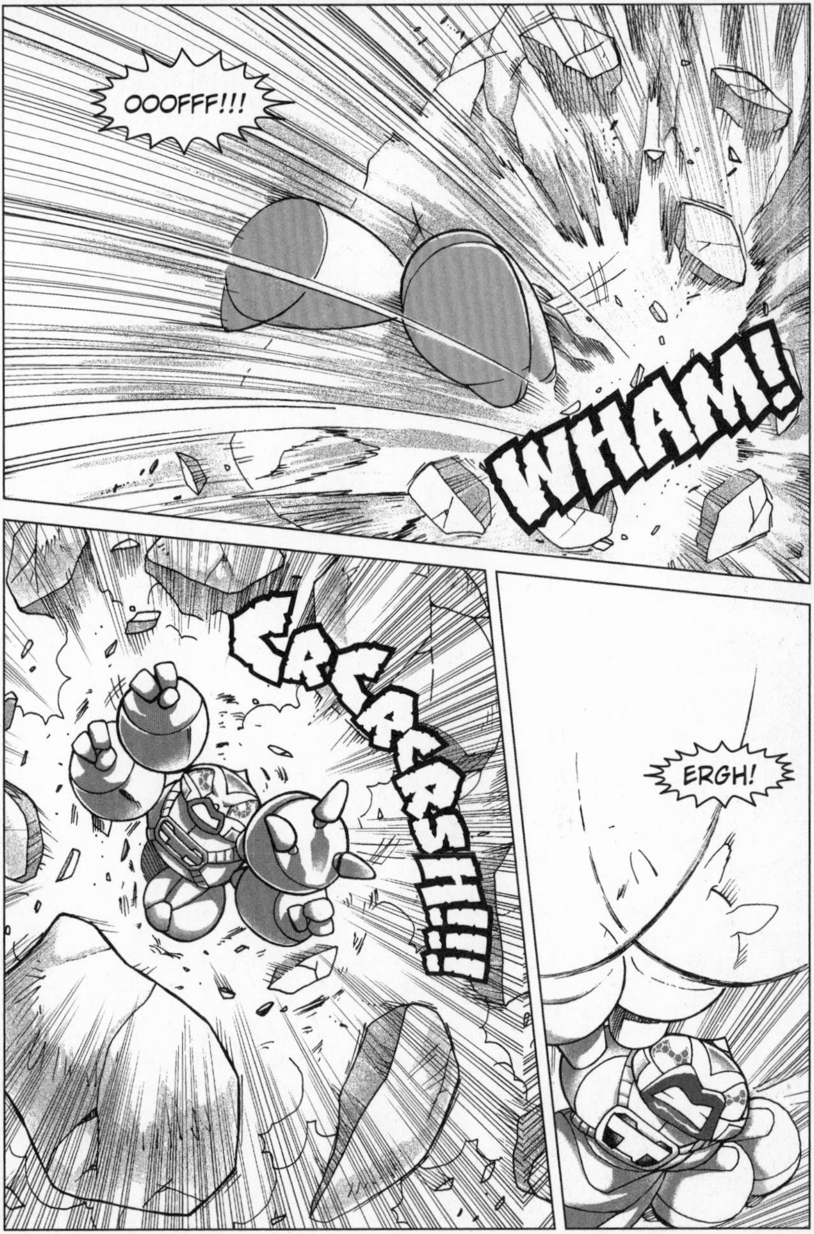
OOOFFF!!!
WHAM!
CRACRACRASH!!!
ERGH!

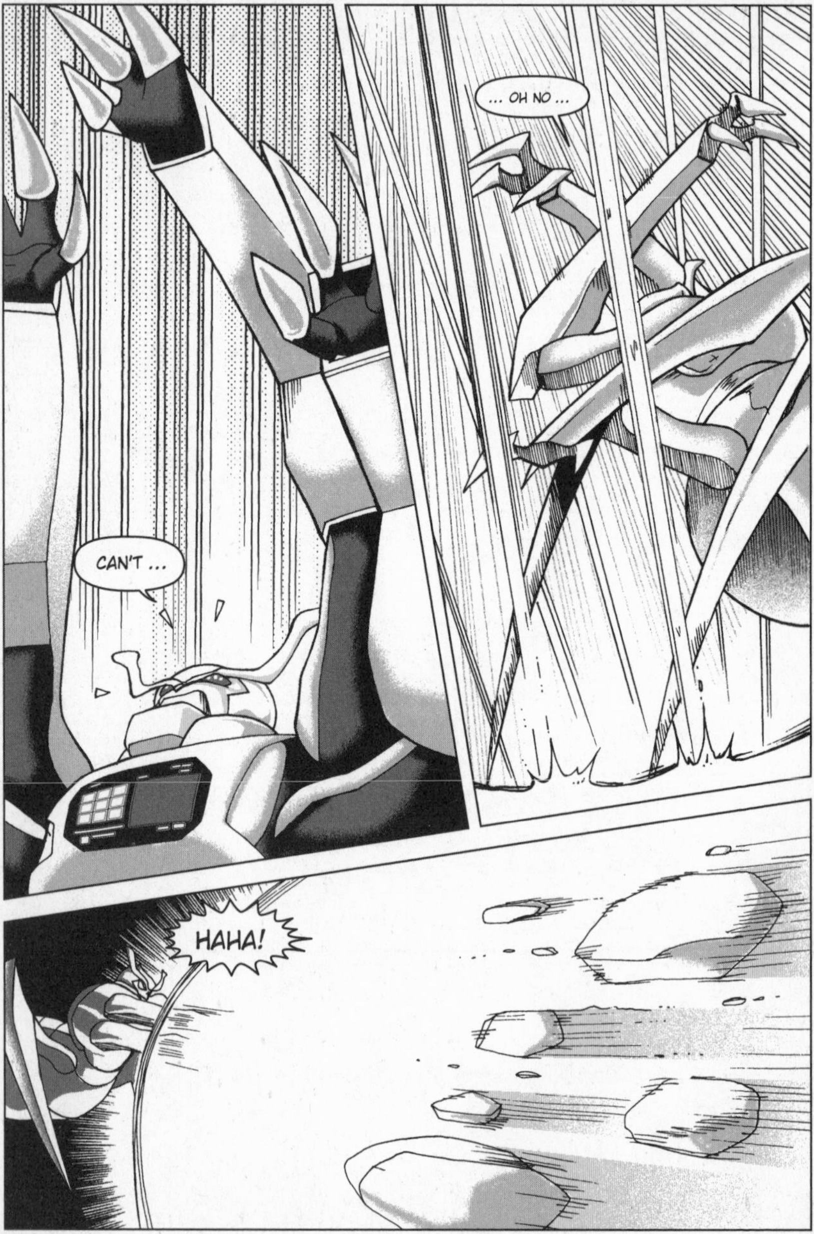
CAN'T ...
... OH NO ...
HAHA!

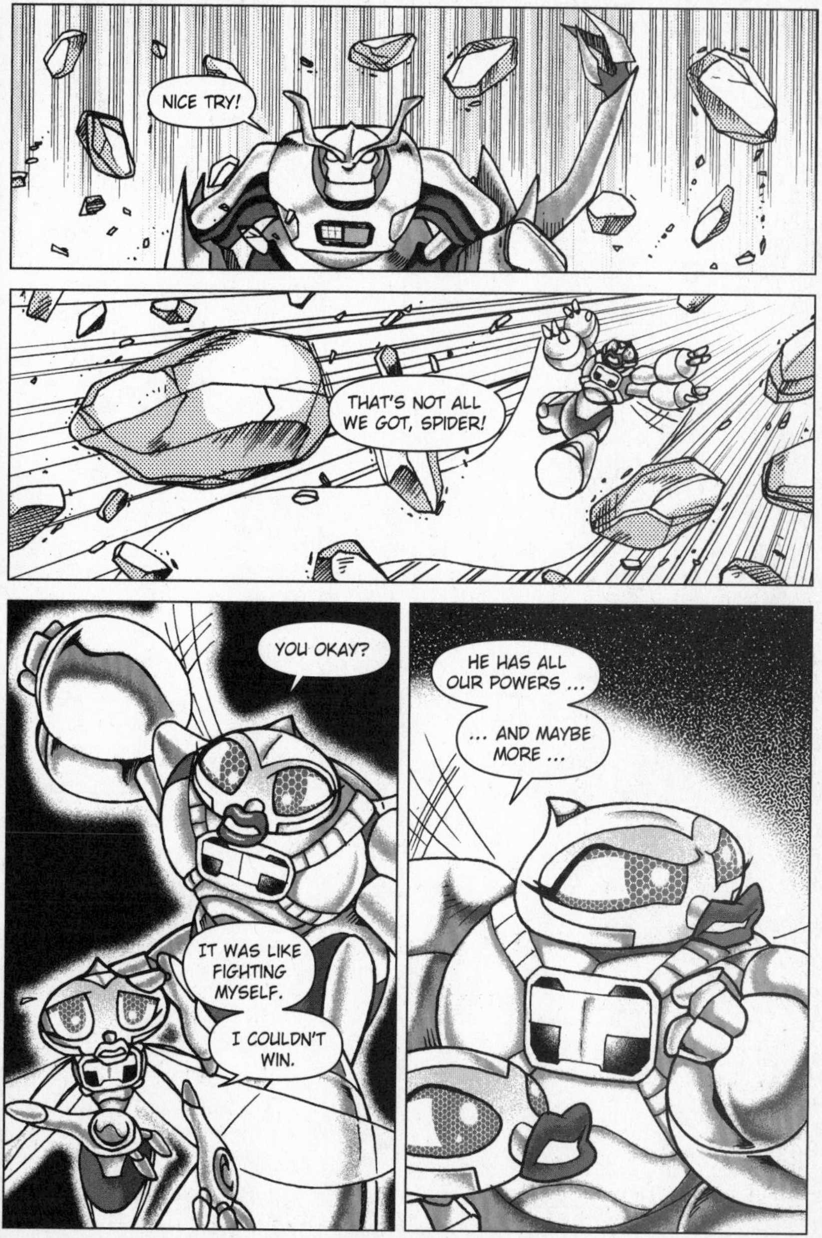
NICE TRY!
THAT'S NOT ALL WE GOT, SPIDER!
YOU OKAY?
IT WAS LIKE FIGHTING MYSELF.
I COULDN'T WIN.
HE HAS ALL OUR POWERS ...
... AND MAYBE MORE ...

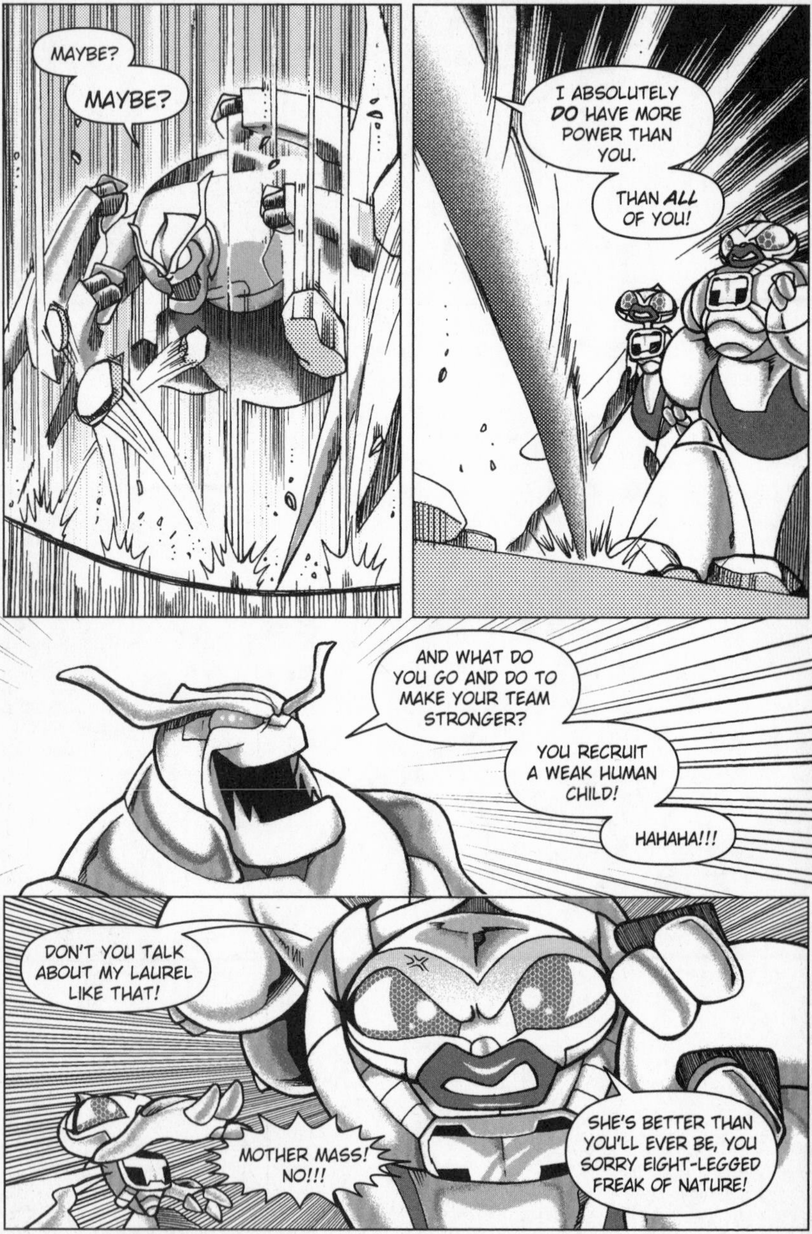
MAYBE?
MAYBE?
I ABSOLUTELY DO HAVE MORE POWER THAN YOU.
THAN ALL OF YOU!
AND WHAT DO YOU GO AND DO TO MAKE YOUR TEAM STRONGER?
YOU RECRUIT A WEAK HUMAN CHILD!
HAHAHA!!!
DON'T YOU TALK ABOUT MY LAUREL LIKE THAT!
MOTHER MASS! NO!!!
SHE'S BETTER THAN YOU'LL EVER BE, YOU SORRY EIGHT-LEGGED FREAK OF NATURE!

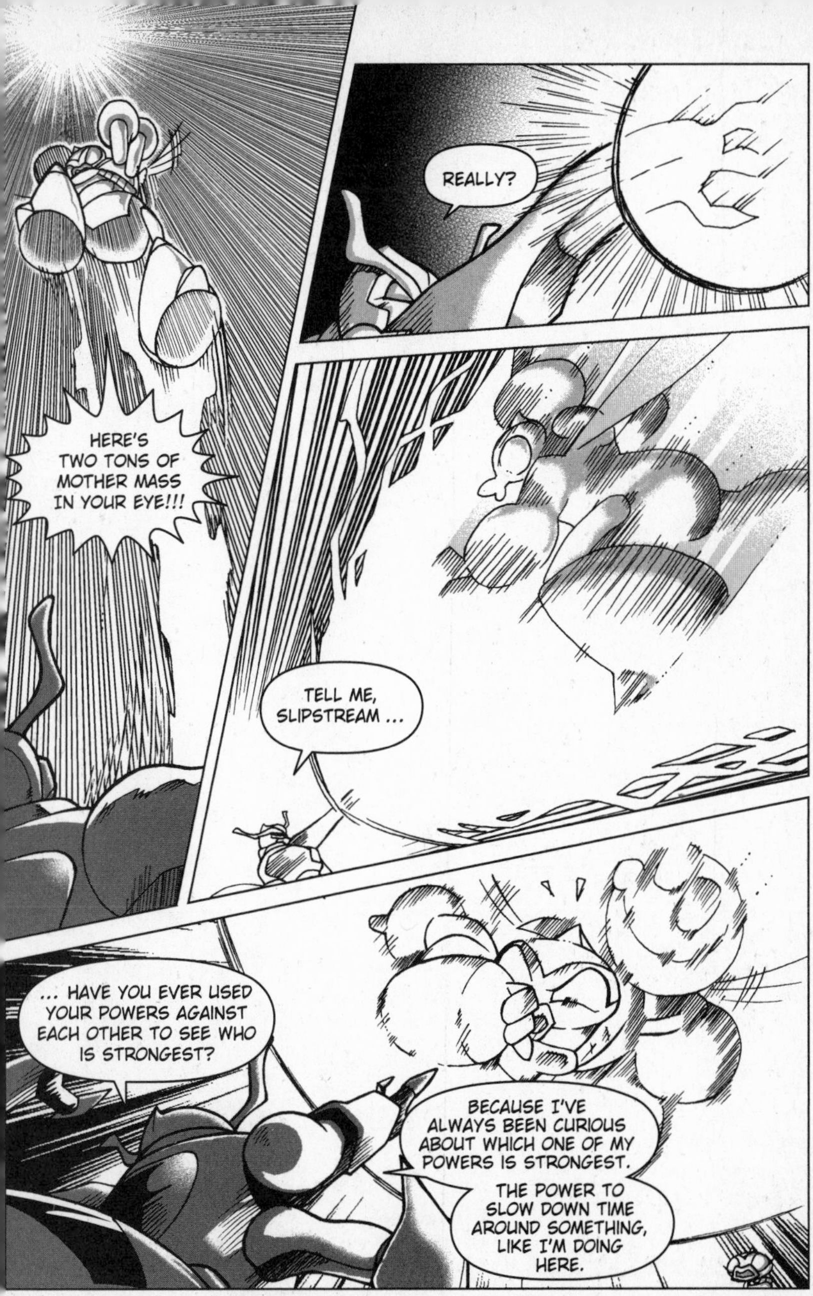
HERE'S TWO TONS OF MOTHER MASS IN YOUR EYE!!!
REALLY?
TELL ME, SLIPSTREAM ...
... HAVE YOU EVER USED YOUR POWERS AGAINST EACH OTHER TO SEE WHO IS STRONGEST?
BECAUSE I'VE ALWAYS BEEN CURIOUS ABOUT WHICH ONE OF MY POWERS IS STRONGEST.
THE POWER TO SLOW DOWN TIME AROUND SOMETHING, LIKE I'M DOING HERE.

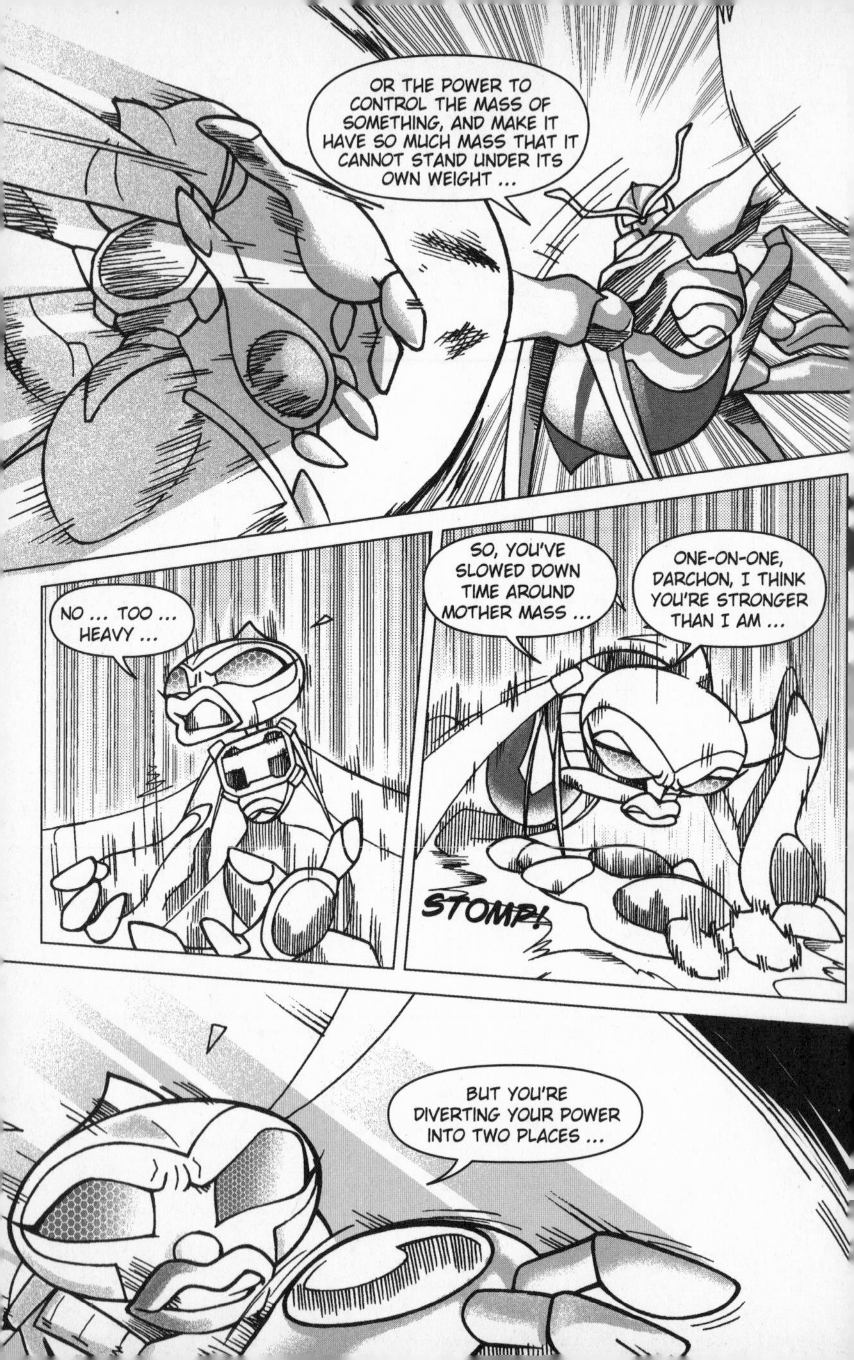
OR THE POWER TO CONTROL THE MASS OF SOMETHING, AND MAKE IT HAVE SO MUCH MASS THAT IT CANNOT STAND UNDER ITS OWN WEIGHT ...
NO ... TOO ... HEAVY ...
SO, YOU'VE SLOWED DOWN TIME AROUND MOTHER MASS ...
ONE-ON-ONE, DARCHON, I THINK YOU'RE STRONGER THAN I AM ...
STOMP!
BUT YOU'RE DIVERTING YOUR POWER INTO TWO PLACES ...

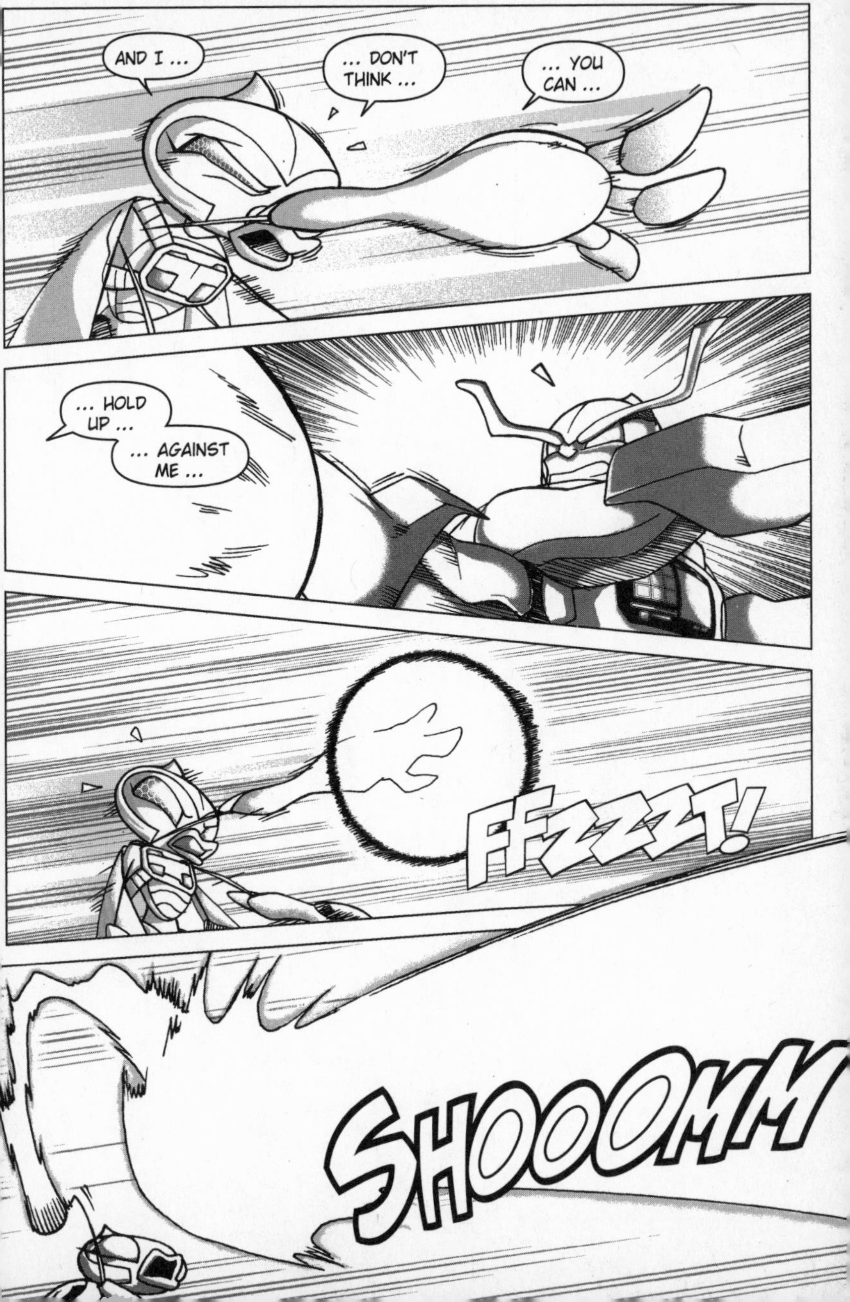
AND I ...
... DON'T THINK ...
... YOU CAN ...
... HOLD UP ...
... AGAINST ME ...
FFZZZT!
SHOOOMM

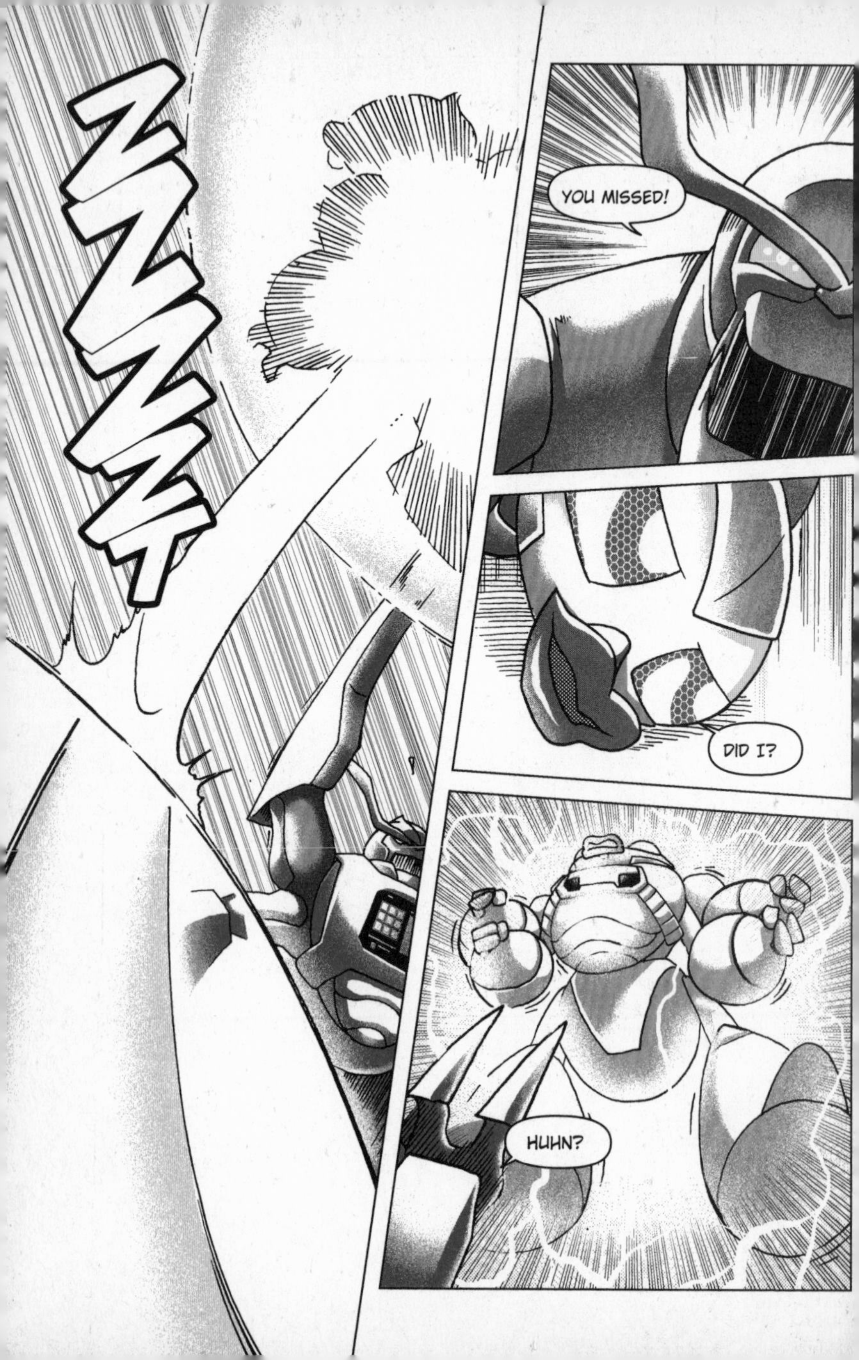
NNNNK
YOU MISSED!
DID I?
HUHN?

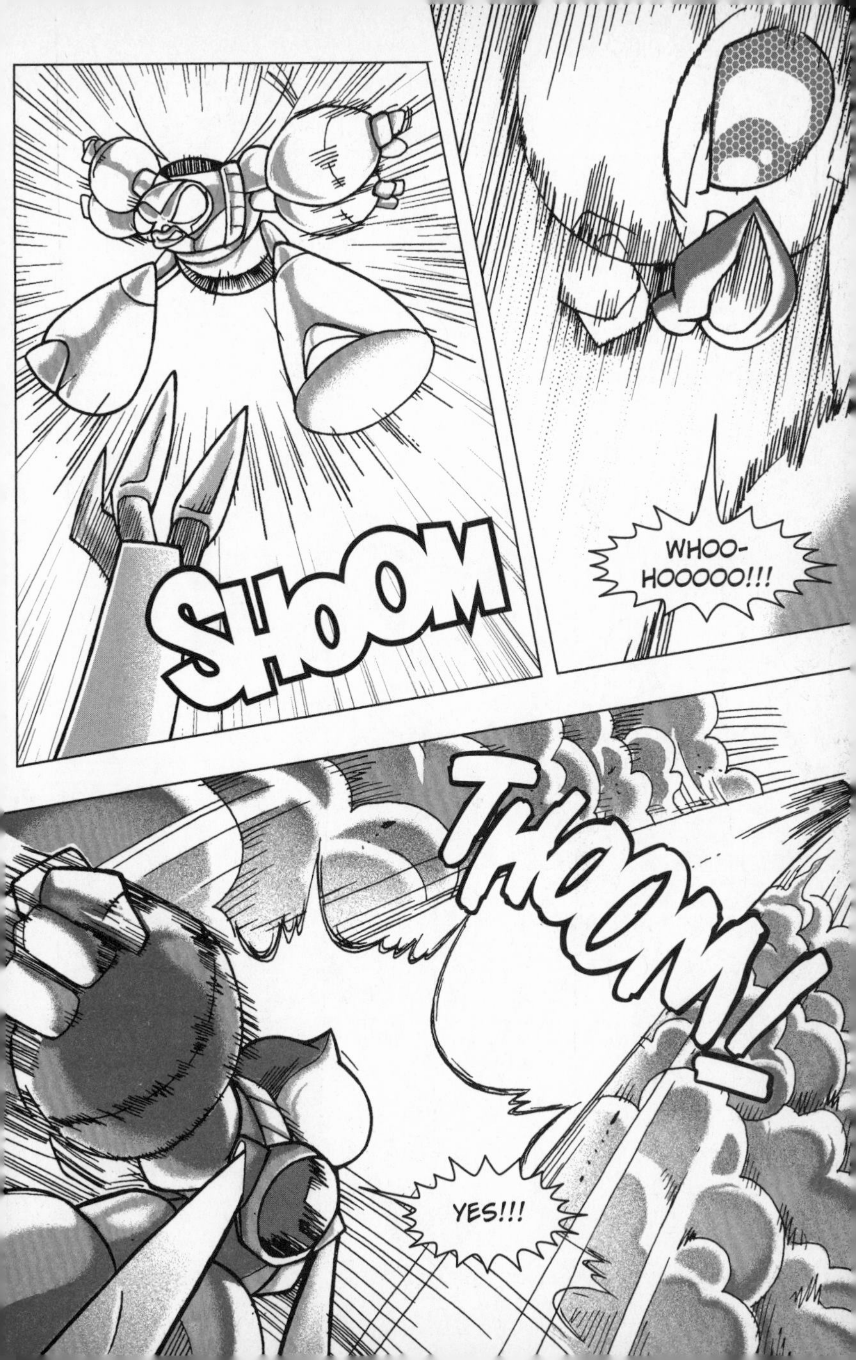
SHOOM
WHOO-
HOOOOO!!!
THOOM!!
YES!!!

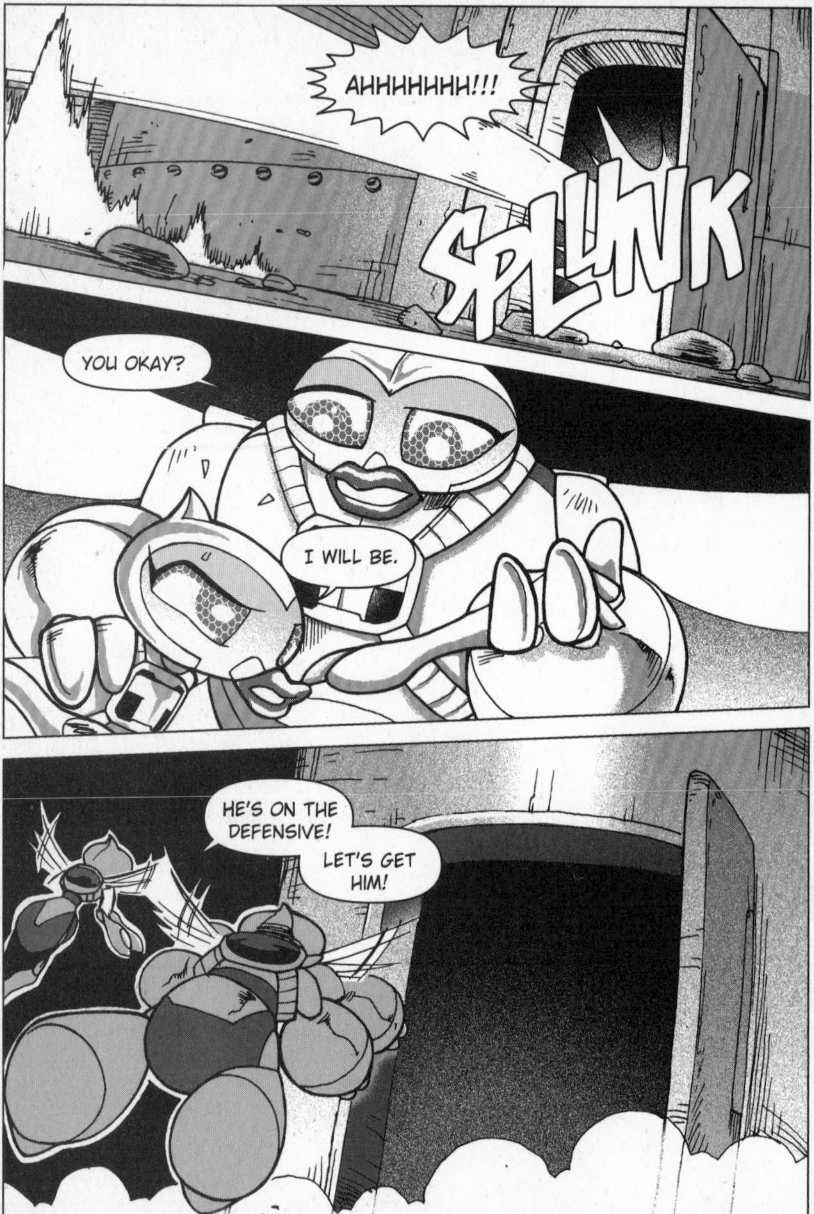
AHHHHHHH!!!
SPLUNK
YOU OKAY?
I WILL BE.
HE'S ON THE DEFENSIVE!
LET'S GET HIM!

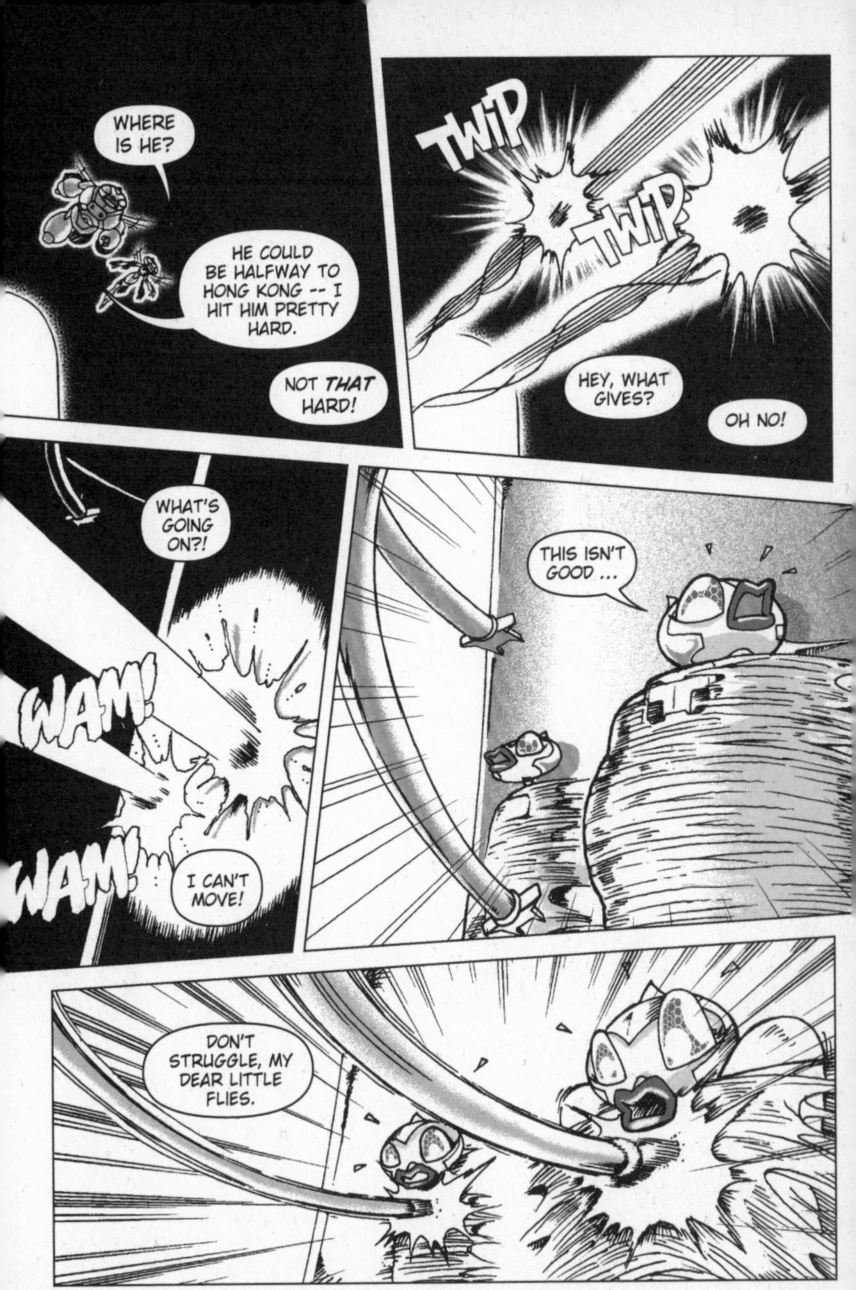
WHERE IS HE?
HE COULD BE HALFWAY TO HONG KONG -- I HIT HIM PRETTY HARD.
NOT *THAT* HARD!
TWIP
TWIP
HEY, WHAT GIVES?
OH NO!
WHAT'S GOING ON?!
WAM!
WAM!
I CAN'T MOVE!
THIS ISN'T GOOD ...
DON'T STRUGGLE, MY DEAR LITTLE FLIES.

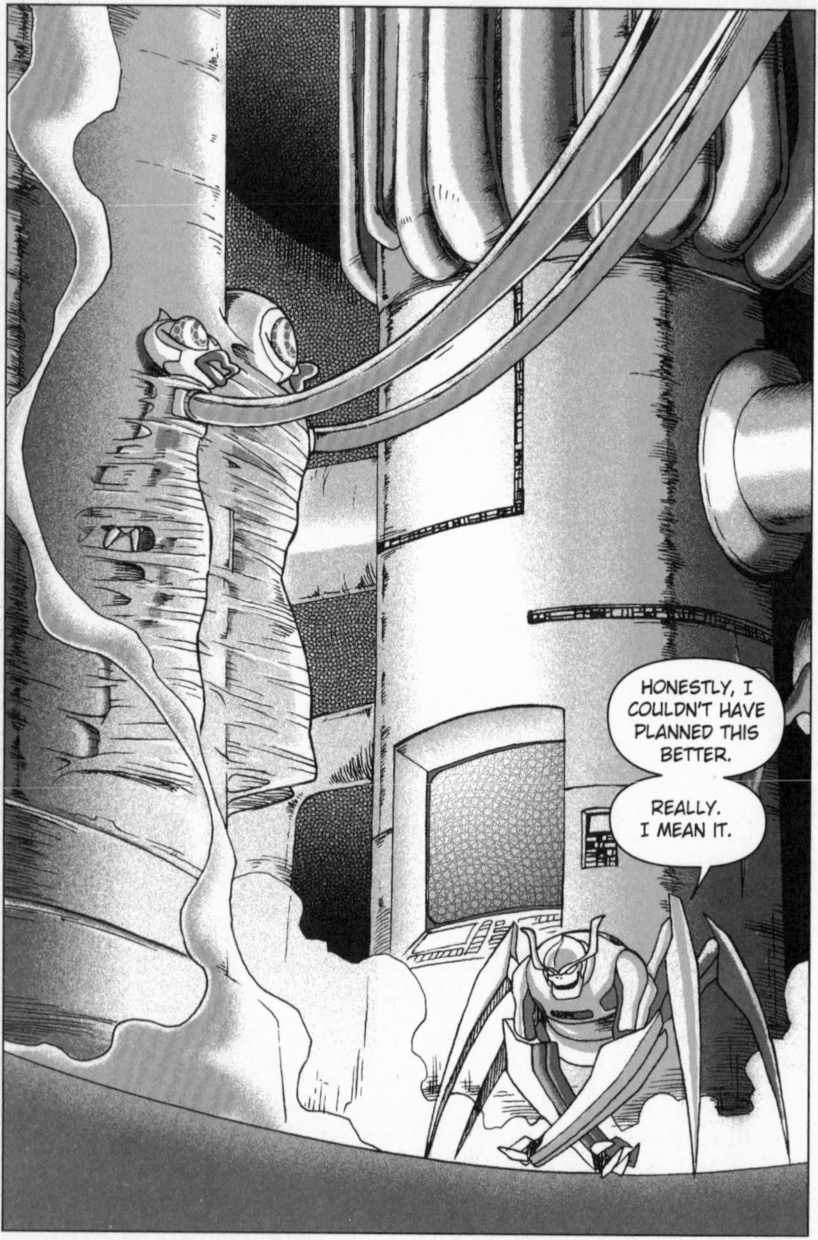
HONESTLY, I COULDN'T HAVE PLANNED THIS BETTER.
REALLY. I MEAN IT.

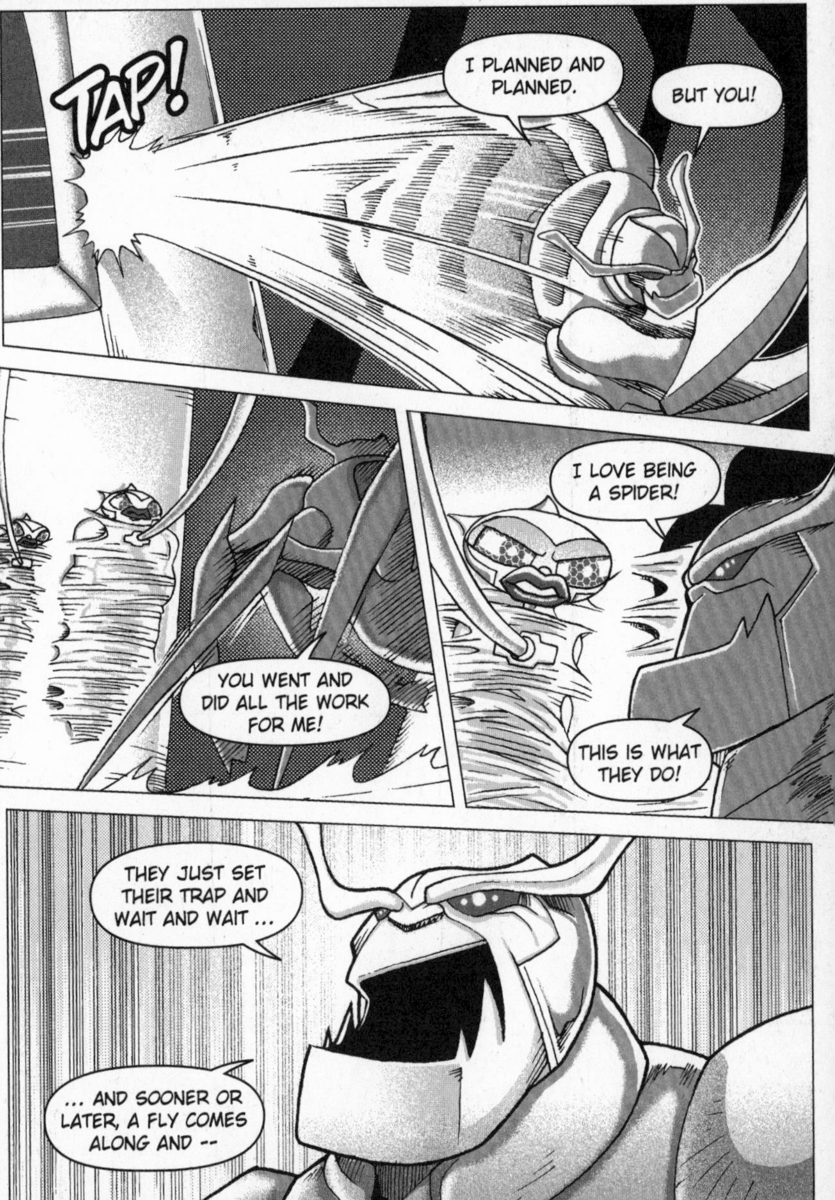
TAP!
I PLANNED AND PLANNED.
BUT YOU!
YOU WENT AND DID ALL THE WORK FOR ME!
I LOVE BEING A SPIDER!
THIS IS WHAT THEY DO!
THEY JUST SET THEIR TRAP AND WAIT AND WAIT ...
... AND SOONER OR LATER, A FLY COMES ALONG AND --

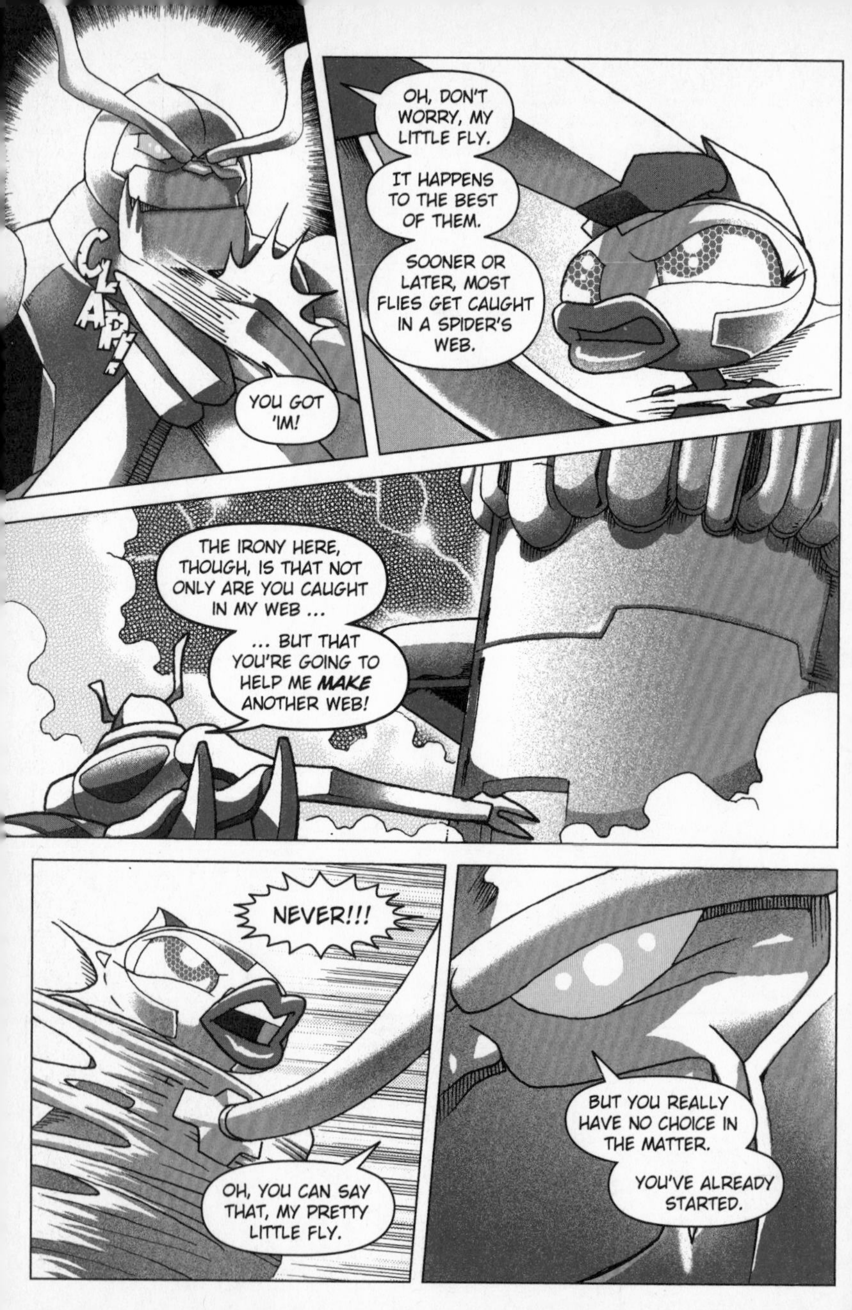
CLAP!
YOU GOT 'IM!
OH, DON'T WORRY, MY LITTLE FLY.
IT HAPPENS TO THE BEST OF THEM.
SOONER OR LATER, MOST FLIES GET CAUGHT IN A SPIDER'S WEB.
THE IRONY HERE, THOUGH, IS THAT NOT ONLY ARE YOU CAUGHT IN MY WEB ...
... BUT THAT YOU'RE GOING TO HELP ME *MAKE* ANOTHER WEB!
NEVER!!!
OH, YOU CAN SAY THAT, MY PRETTY LITTLE FLY.
BUT YOU REALLY HAVE NO CHOICE IN THE MATTER.
YOU'VE ALREADY STARTED.

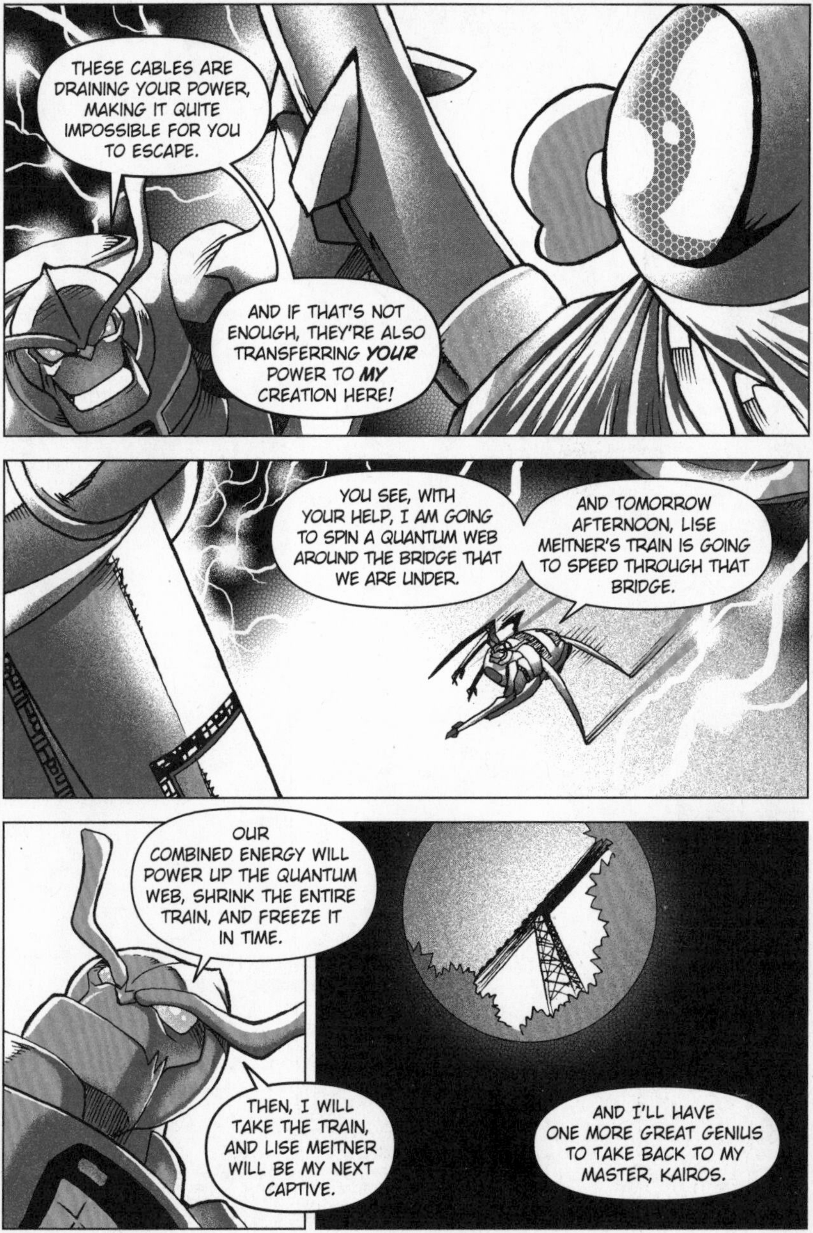
THESE CABLES ARE DRAINING YOUR POWER, MAKING IT QUITE IMPOSSIBLE FOR YOU TO ESCAPE.
AND IF THAT'S NOT ENOUGH, THEY'RE ALSO TRANSFERRING *YOUR* POWER TO *MY* CREATION HERE!
YOU SEE, WITH YOUR HELP, I AM GOING TO SPIN A QUANTUM WEB AROUND THE BRIDGE THAT WE ARE UNDER.
AND TOMORROW AFTERNOON, LISE MEITNER'S TRAIN IS GOING TO SPEED THROUGH THAT BRIDGE.
OUR COMBINED ENERGY WILL POWER UP THE QUANTUM WEB, SHRINK THE ENTIRE TRAIN, AND FREEZE IT IN TIME.
THEN, I WILL TAKE THE TRAIN, AND LISE MEITNER WILL BE MY NEXT CAPTIVE.
AND I'LL HAVE ONE MORE GREAT GENIUS TO TAKE BACK TO MY MASTER, KAIROS.

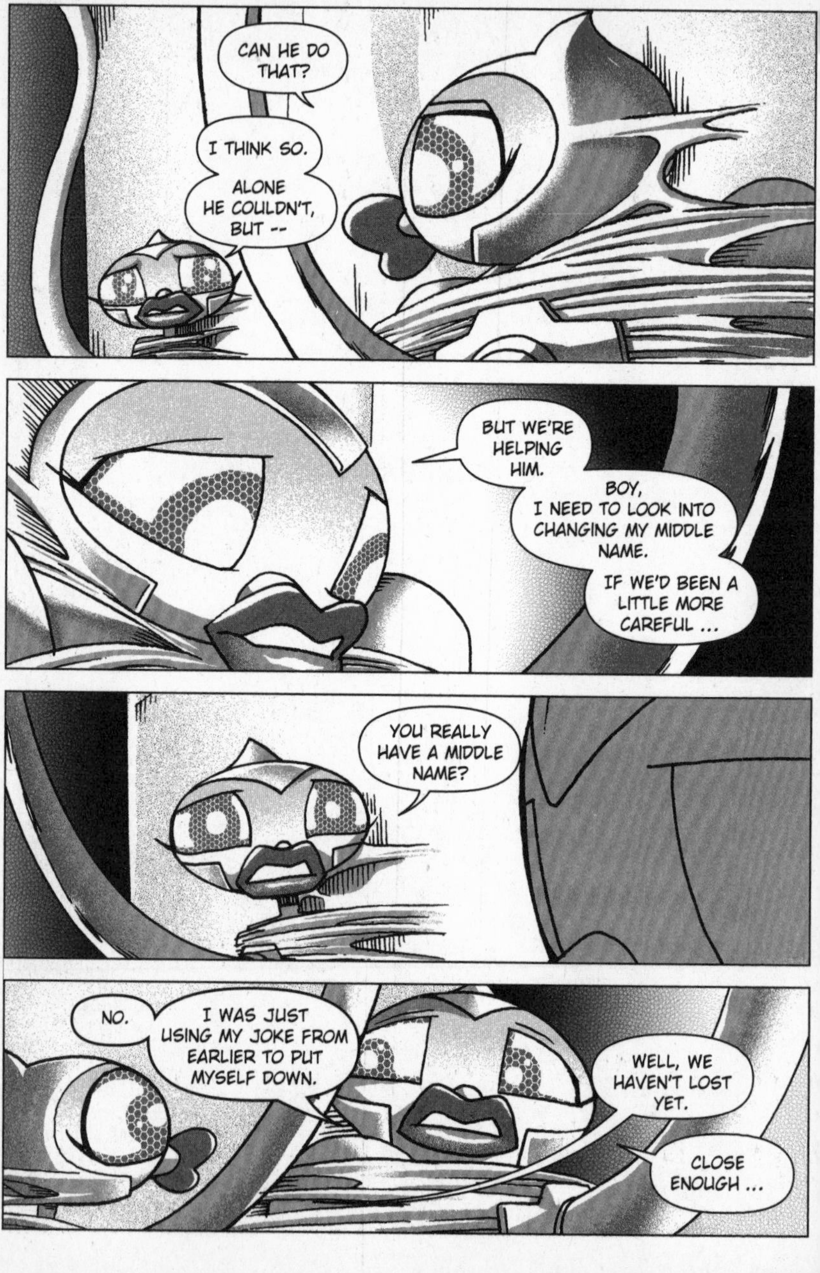
CAN HE DO THAT?
I THINK SO.
ALONE HE COULDN'T, BUT --
BUT WE'RE HELPING HIM.
BOY, I NEED TO LOOK INTO CHANGING MY MIDDLE NAME.
IF WE'D BEEN A LITTLE MORE CAREFUL ...
YOU REALLY HAVE A MIDDLE NAME?
NO.
I WAS JUST USING MY JOKE FROM EARLIER TO PUT MYSELF DOWN.
WELL, WE HAVEN'T LOST YET.
CLOSE ENOUGH ...

TAP!
TAP!
TAP!

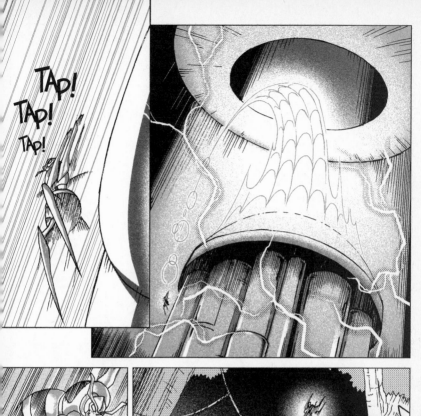

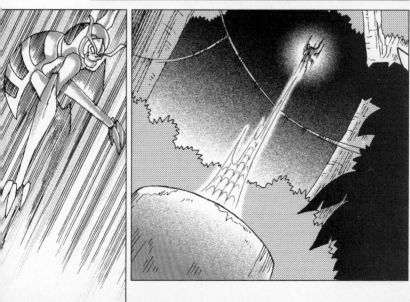

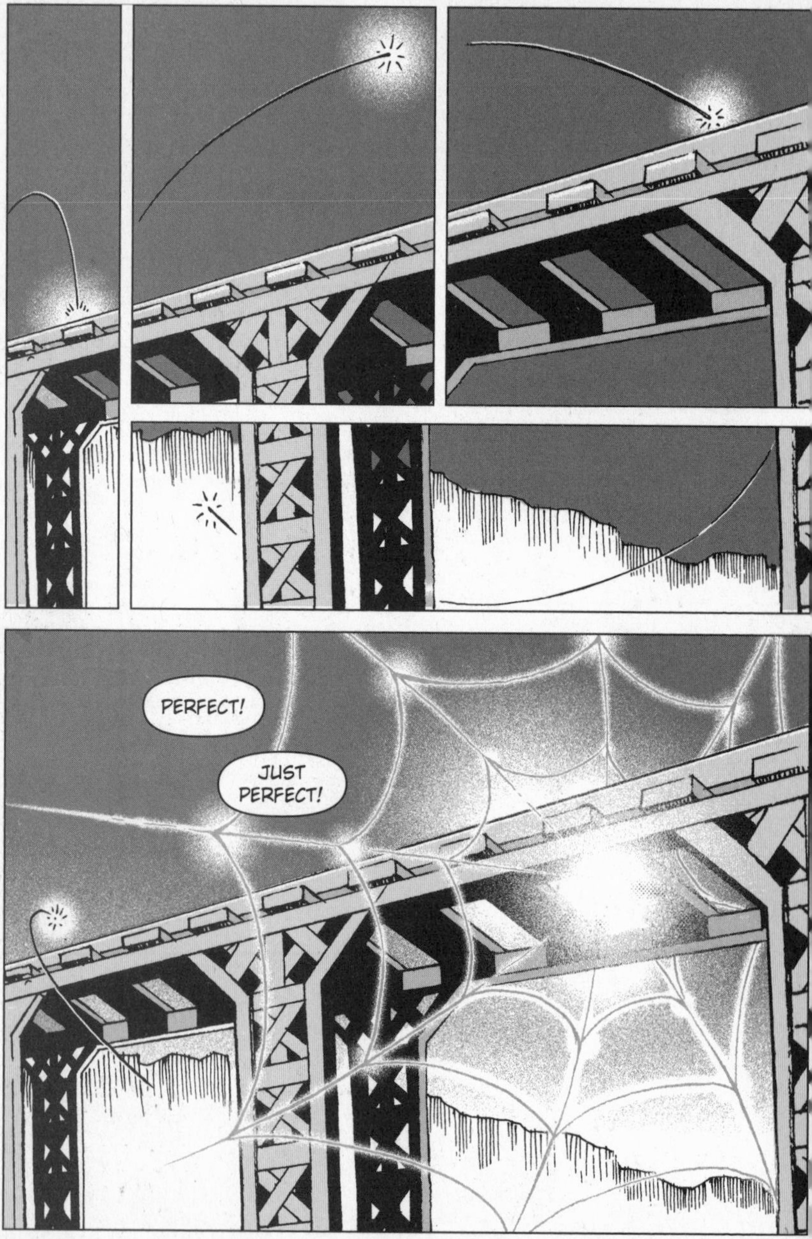
PERFECT!
JUST PERFECT!

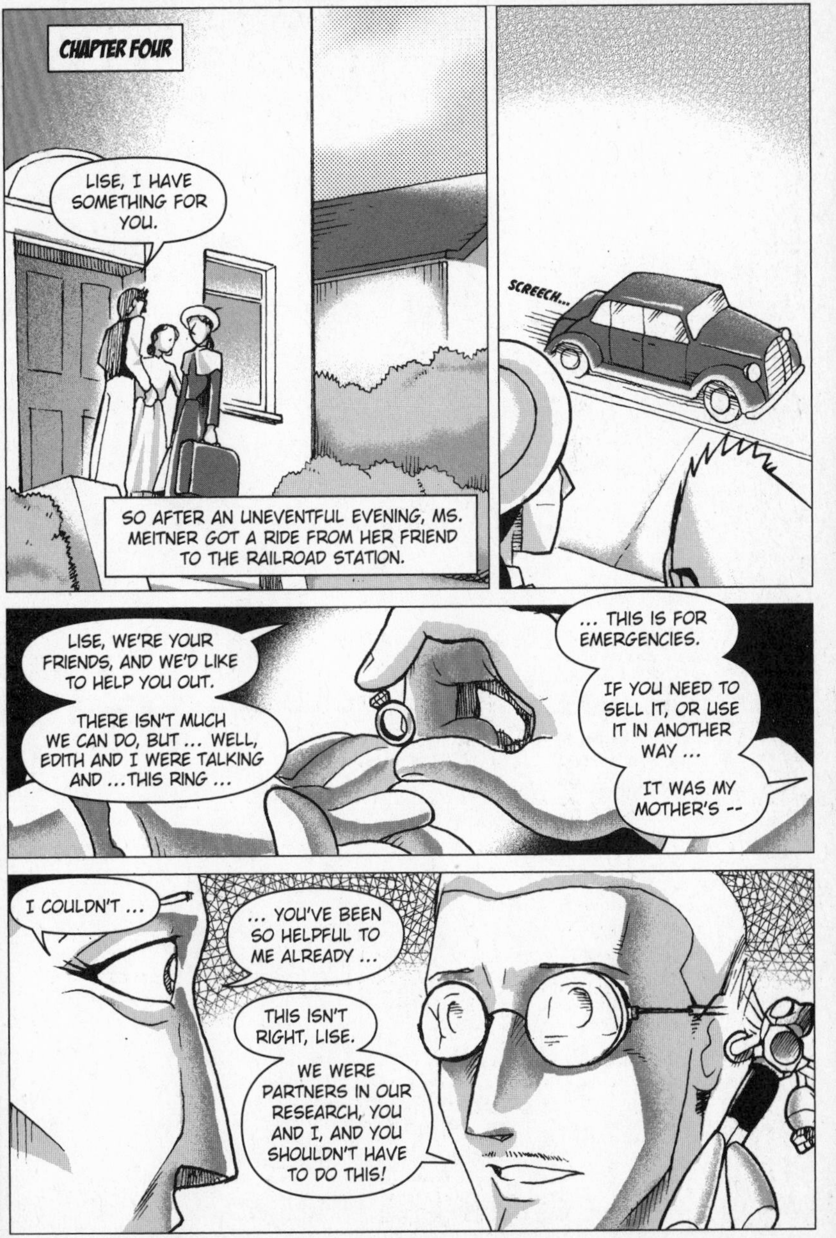
CHAPTER FOUR
LISE, I HAVE SOMETHING FOR YOU.
SO AFTER AN UNEVENTFUL EVENING, MS. MEITNER GOT A RIDE FROM HER FRIEND TO THE RAILROAD STATION.
SCREECH...
LISE, WE'RE YOUR FRIENDS, AND WE'D LIKE TO HELP YOU OUT.
THERE ISN'T MUCH WE CAN DO, BUT ... WELL, EDITH AND I WERE TALKING AND ...THIS RING ...
... THIS IS FOR EMERGENCIES.
IF YOU NEED TO SELL IT, OR USE IT IN ANOTHER WAY ...
IT WAS MY MOTHER'S --
I COULDN'T ...
... YOU'VE BEEN SO HELPFUL TO ME ALREADY ...
THIS ISN'T RIGHT, LISE.
WE WERE PARTNERS IN OUR RESEARCH, YOU AND I, AND YOU SHOULDN'T HAVE TO DO THIS!

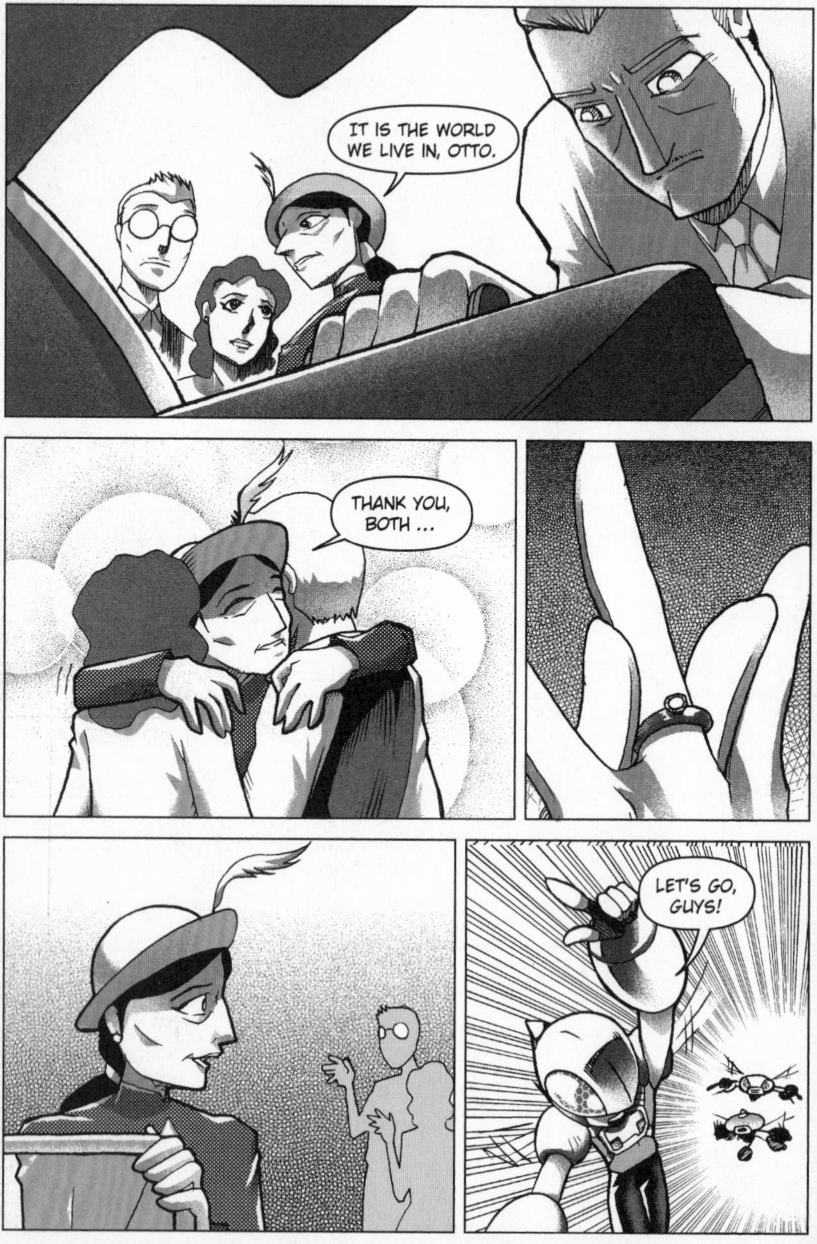
IT IS THE WORLD WE LIVE IN, OTTO.
THANK YOU, BOTH ...
LET'S GO, GUYS!

I KNEW HOW SHE FELT.

EVEN THOUGH SHE HAD ALL THESE FRIENDS HELPING HER, SHE FELT SO ALONE.

ALONE, AGAINST AN ALMOST IMPOSSIBLE TASK.

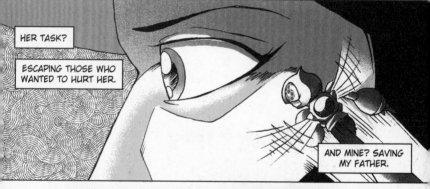

HER TASK?

ESCAPING THOSE WHO WANTED TO HURT HER.

AND MINE? SAVING MY FATHER.

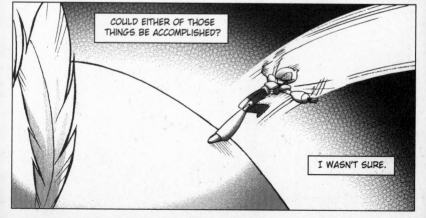

COULD EITHER OF THOSE THINGS BE ACCOMPLISHED?

I WASN'T SURE.

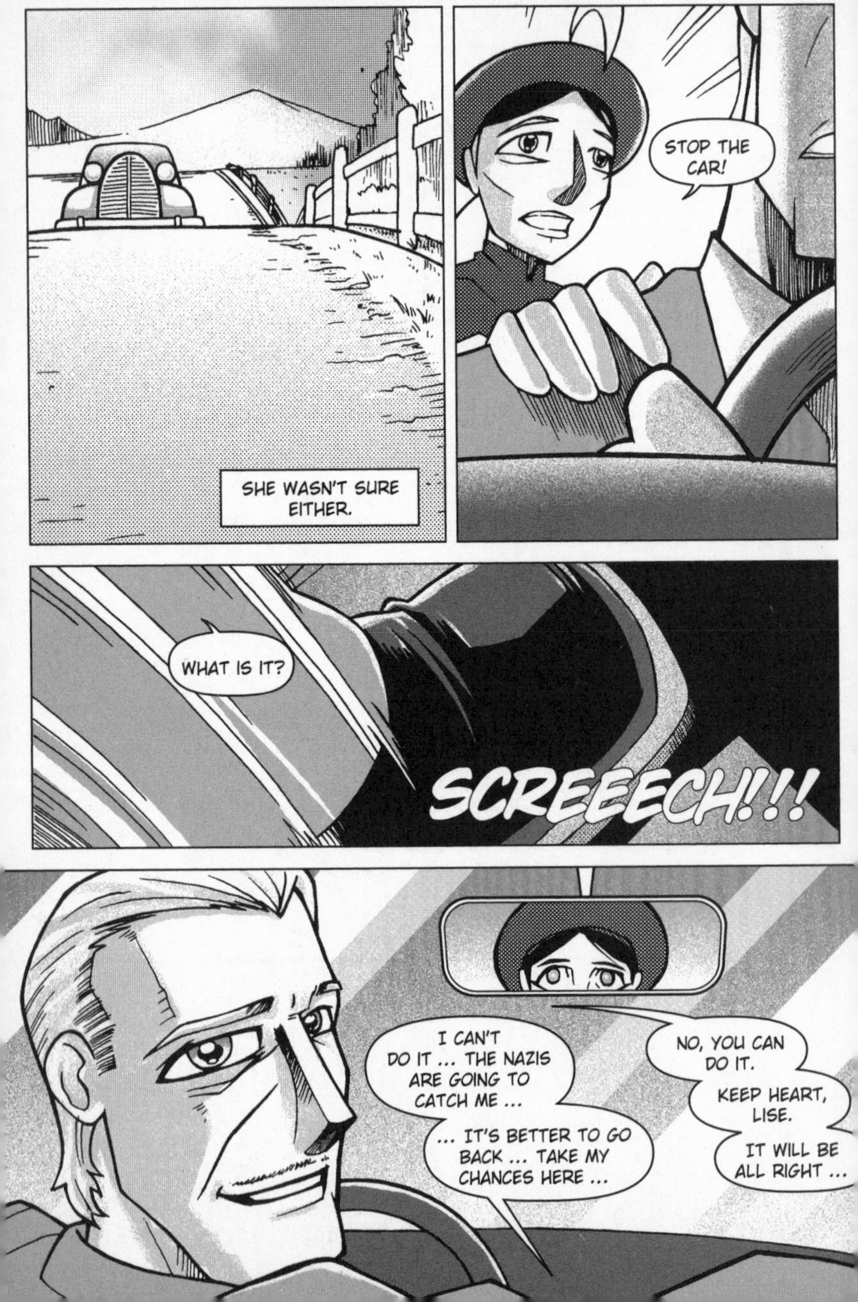
SHE WASN'T SURE EITHER.
STOP THE CAR!
WHAT IS IT?
SCREEEECH!!!
I CAN'T DO IT ... THE NAZIS ARE GOING TO CATCH ME ...
... IT'S BETTER TO GO BACK ... TAKE MY CHANCES HERE ...
NO, YOU CAN DO IT.
KEEP HEART, LISE.
IT WILL BE ALL RIGHT ...

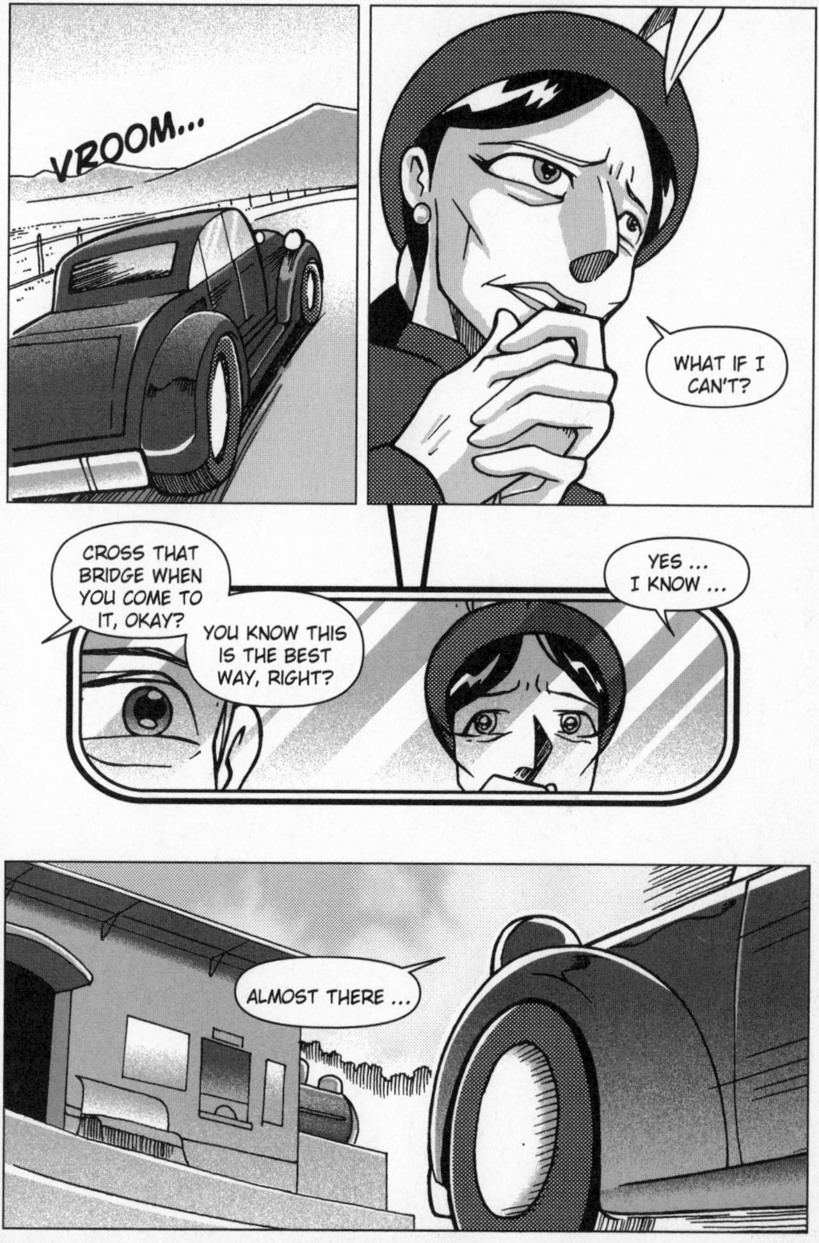
VROOM...
WHAT IF I CAN'T?
CROSS THAT BRIDGE WHEN YOU COME TO IT, OKAY?
YOU KNOW THIS IS THE BEST WAY, RIGHT?
YES ... I KNOW ...
ALMOST THERE ...

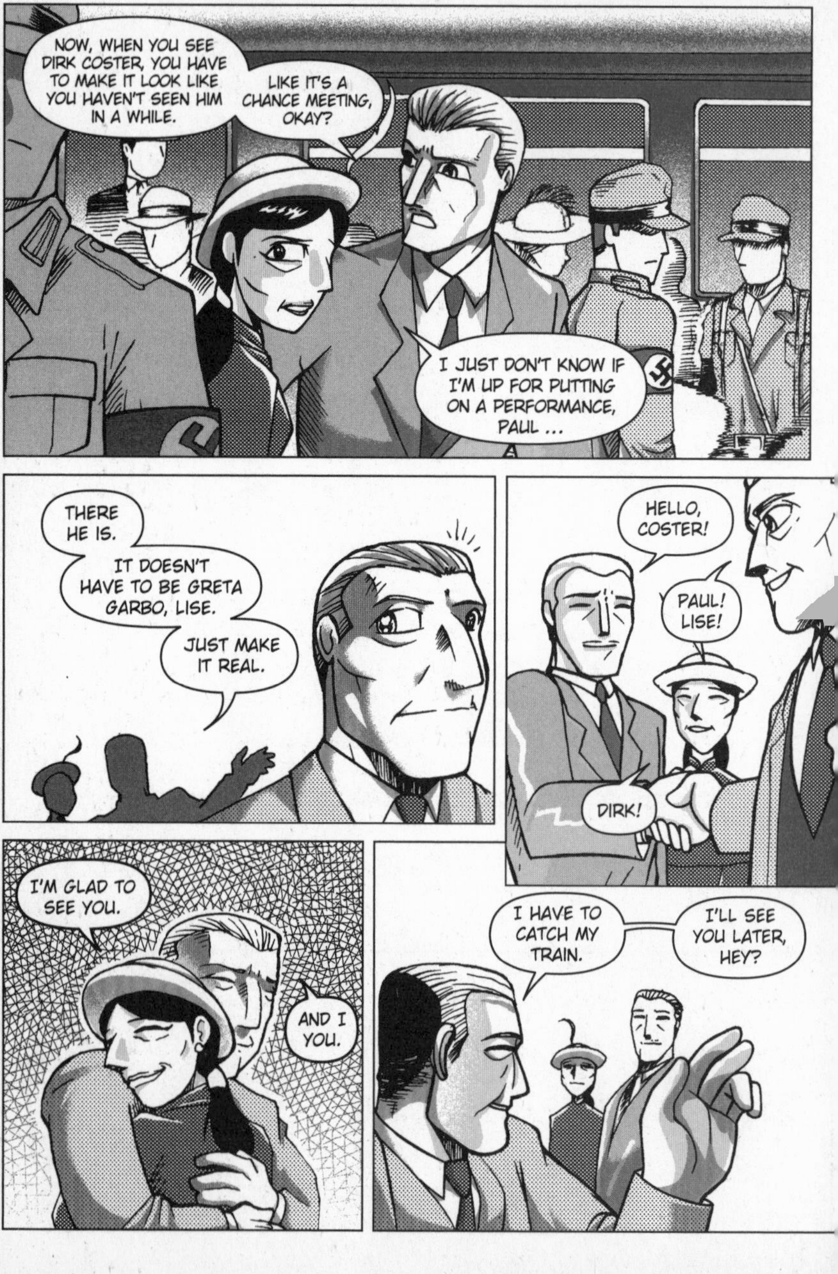
NOW, WHEN YOU SEE DIRK COSTER, YOU HAVE TO MAKE IT LOOK LIKE YOU HAVEN'T SEEN HIM IN A WHILE.
LIKE IT'S A CHANCE MEETING, OKAY?
I JUST DON'T KNOW IF I'M UP FOR PUTTING ON A PERFORMANCE, PAUL ...
THERE HE IS.
IT DOESN'T HAVE TO BE GRETA GARBO, LISE.
JUST MAKE IT REAL.
HELLO, COSTER!
PAUL! LISE!
DIRK!
I'M GLAD TO SEE YOU.
AND I YOU.
I HAVE TO CATCH MY TRAIN.
I'LL SEE YOU LATER, HEY?

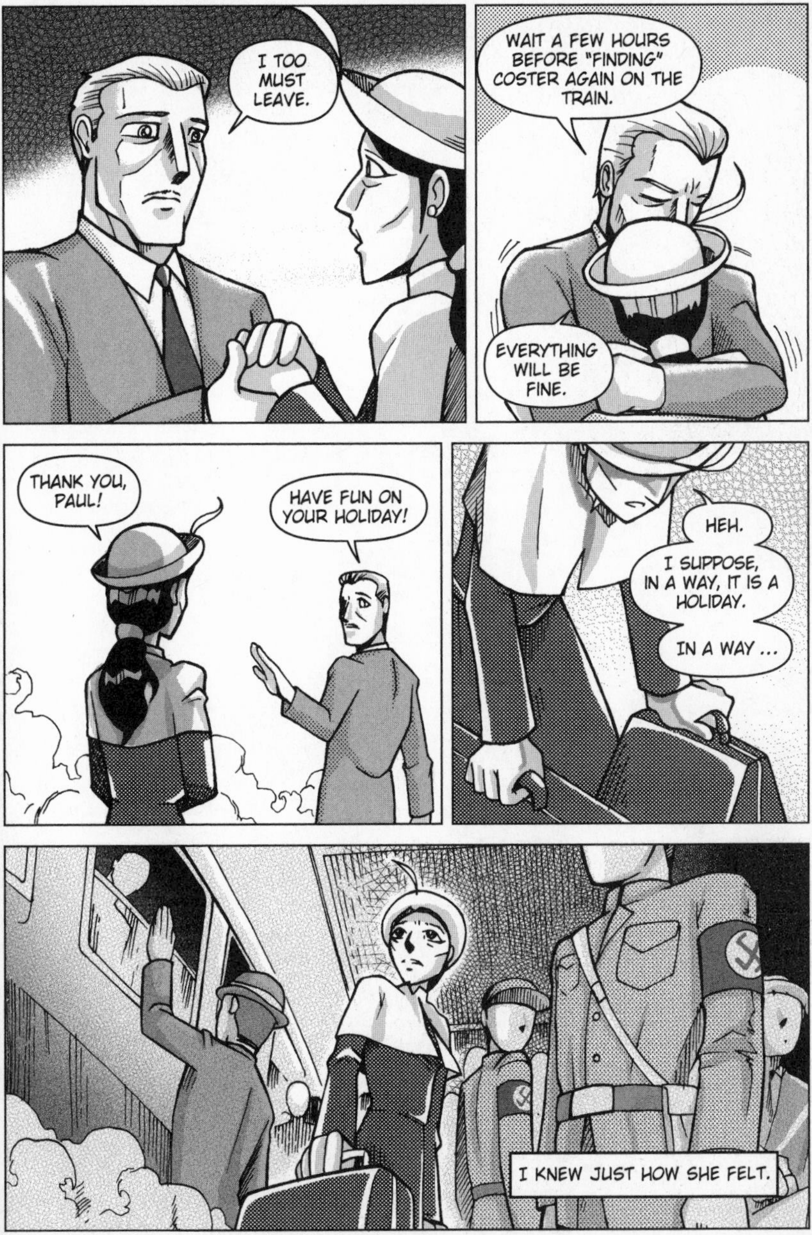
I TOO MUST LEAVE.
WAIT A FEW HOURS BEFORE "FINDING" COSTER AGAIN ON THE TRAIN.
EVERYTHING WILL BE FINE.
THANK YOU, PAUL!
HAVE FUN ON YOUR HOLIDAY!
HEH.
I SUPPOSE, IN A WAY, IT IS A HOLIDAY.
IN A WAY ...
I KNEW JUST HOW SHE FELT.

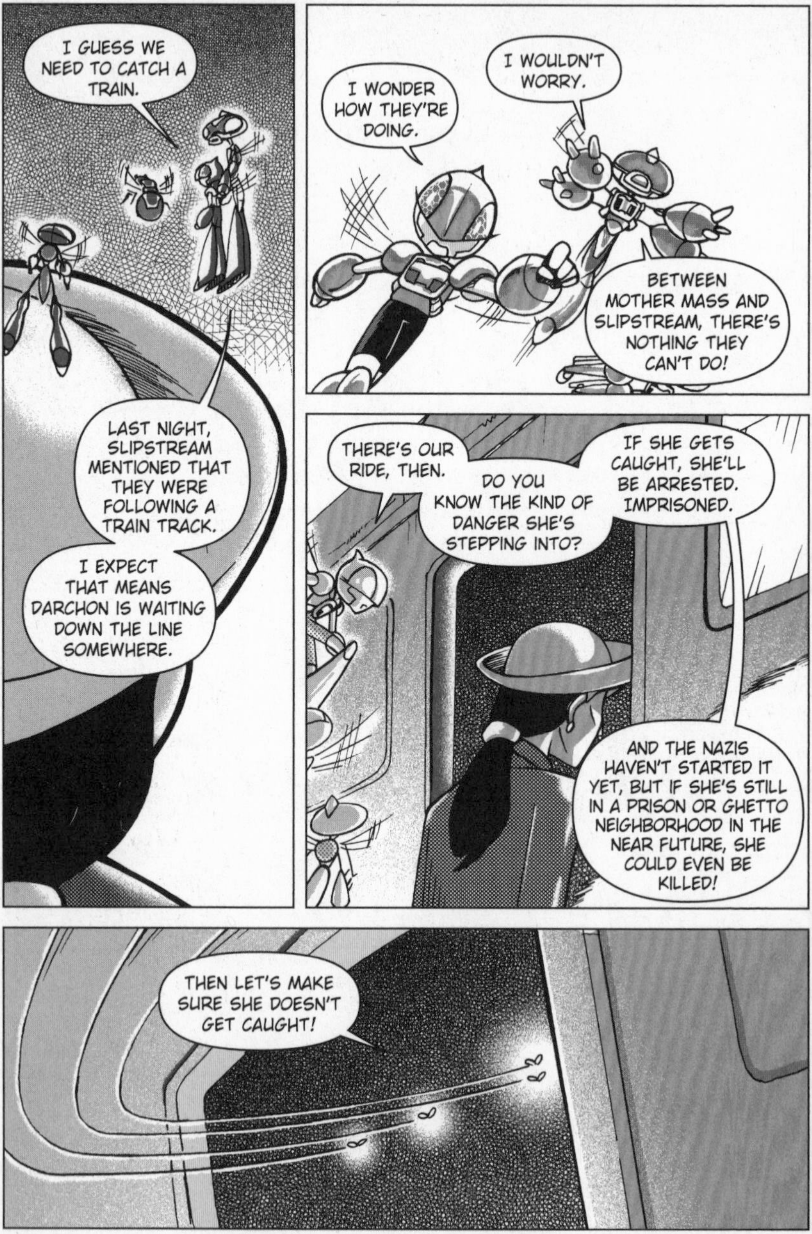
I GUESS WE NEED TO CATCH A TRAIN.
LAST NIGHT, SLIPSTREAM MENTIONED THAT THEY WERE FOLLOWING A TRAIN TRACK.
I EXPECT THAT MEANS DARCHON IS WAITING DOWN THE LINE SOMEWHERE.
I WONDER HOW THEY'RE DOING.
I WOULDN'T WORRY.
BETWEEN MOTHER MASS AND SLIPSTREAM, THERE'S NOTHING THEY CAN'T DO!
THERE'S OUR RIDE, THEN.
DO YOU KNOW THE KIND OF DANGER SHE'S STEPPING INTO?
IF SHE GETS CAUGHT, SHE'LL BE ARRESTED. IMPRISONED.
AND THE NAZIS HAVEN'T STARTED IT YET, BUT IF SHE'S STILL IN A PRISON OR GHETTO NEIGHBORHOOD IN THE NEAR FUTURE, SHE COULD EVEN BE KILLED!
THEN LET'S MAKE SURE SHE DOESN'T GET CAUGHT!

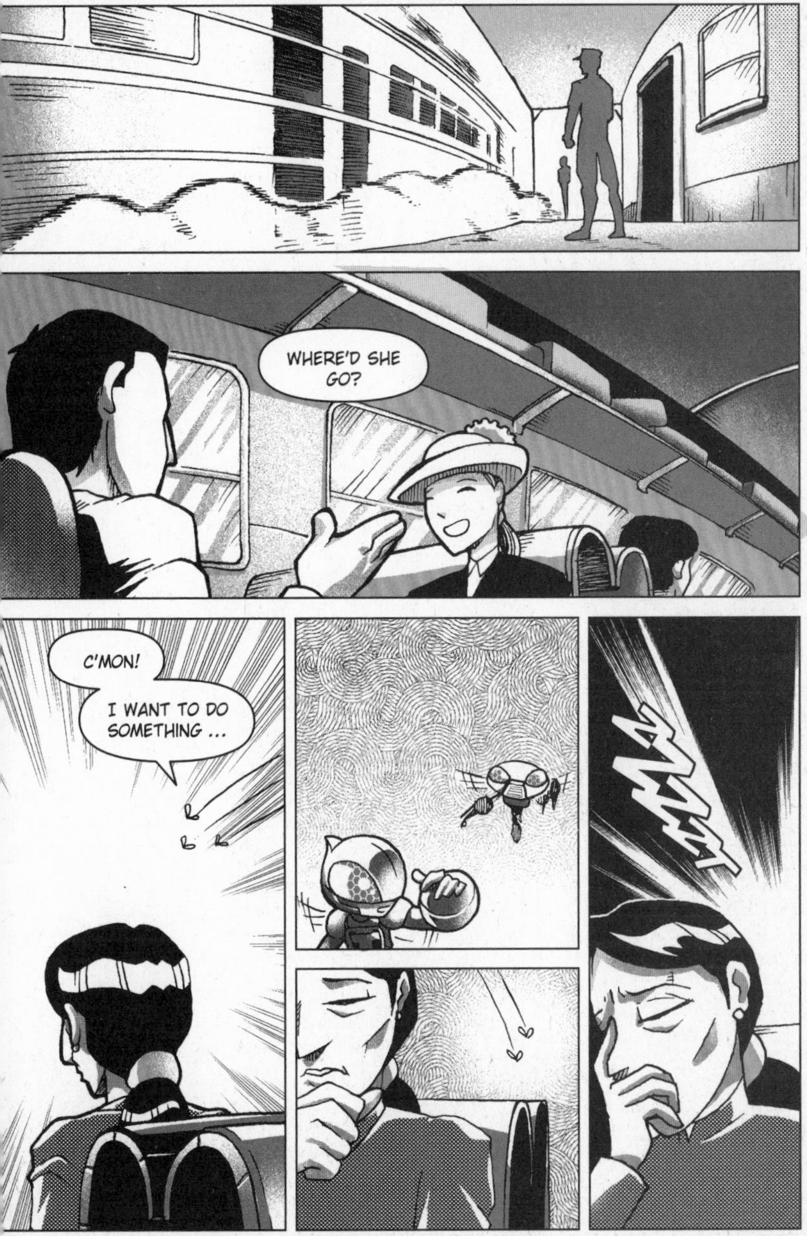
WHERE'D SHE GO?
C'MON!
I WANT TO DO SOMETHING ...

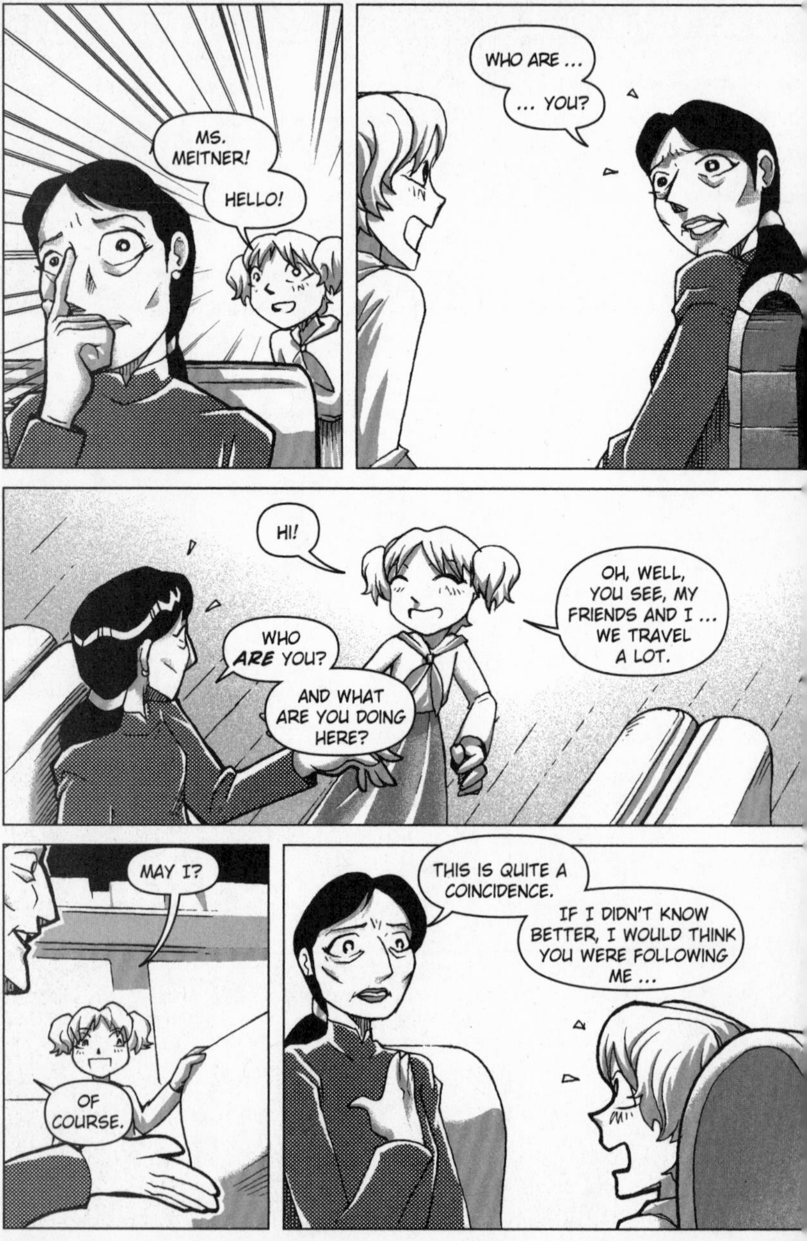
MS. MEITNER!
HELLO!
WHO ARE ...
... YOU?
HI!
WHO *ARE* YOU?
AND WHAT ARE YOU DOING HERE?
OH, WELL, YOU SEE, MY FRIENDS AND I ... WE TRAVEL A LOT.
MAY I?
OF COURSE.
THIS IS QUITE A COINCIDENCE.
IF I DIDN'T KNOW BETTER, I WOULD THINK YOU WERE FOLLOWING ME ...

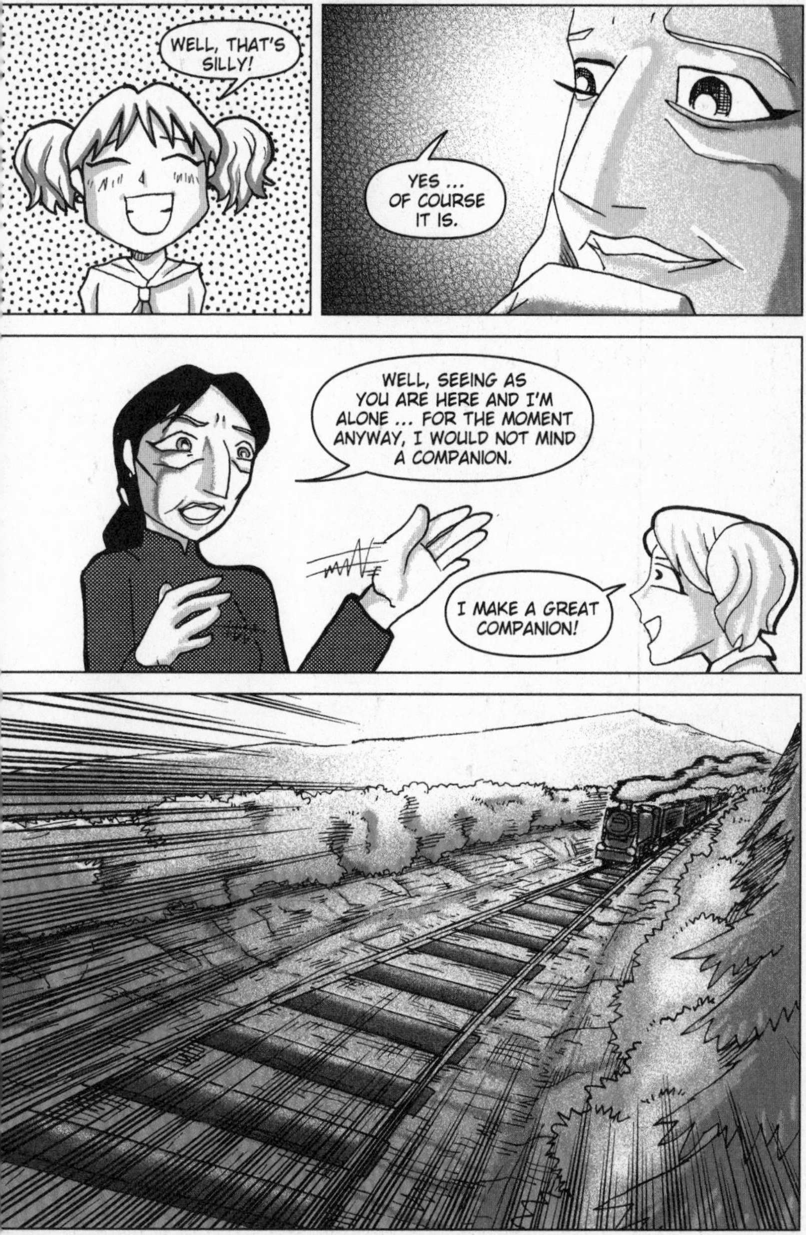
WELL, THAT'S SILLY!
YES ... OF COURSE IT IS.
WELL, SEEING AS YOU ARE HERE AND I'M ALONE ... FOR THE MOMENT ANYWAY, I WOULD NOT MIND A COMPANION.
I MAKE A GREAT COMPANION!

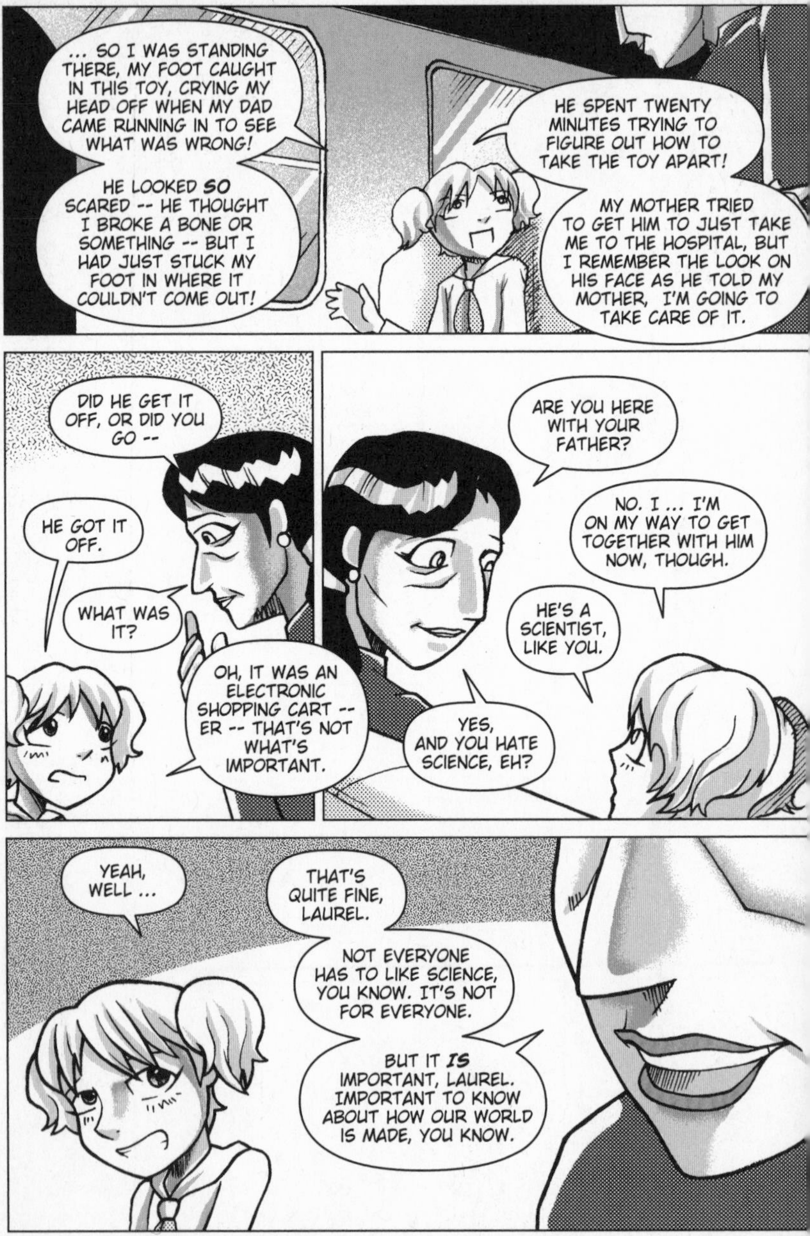
... SO I WAS STANDING THERE, MY FOOT CAUGHT IN THIS TOY, CRYING MY HEAD OFF WHEN MY DAD CAME RUNNING IN TO SEE WHAT WAS WRONG!
HE LOOKED **SO** SCARED -- HE THOUGHT I BROKE A BONE OR SOMETHING -- BUT I HAD JUST STUCK MY FOOT IN WHERE IT COULDN'T COME OUT!
HE SPENT TWENTY MINUTES TRYING TO FIGURE OUT HOW TO TAKE THE TOY APART!
MY MOTHER TRIED TO GET HIM TO JUST TAKE ME TO THE HOSPITAL, BUT I REMEMBER THE LOOK ON HIS FACE AS HE TOLD MY MOTHER, I'M GOING TO TAKE CARE OF IT.
DID HE GET IT OFF, OR DID YOU GO --
HE GOT IT OFF.
WHAT WAS IT?
OH, IT WAS AN ELECTRONIC SHOPPING CART -- ER -- THAT'S NOT WHAT'S IMPORTANT.
ARE YOU HERE WITH YOUR FATHER?
NO. I ... I'M ON MY WAY TO GET TOGETHER WITH HIM NOW, THOUGH.
HE'S A SCIENTIST, LIKE YOU.
YES, AND YOU HATE SCIENCE, EH?
YEAH, WELL ...
THAT'S QUITE FINE, LAUREL.
NOT EVERYONE HAS TO LIKE SCIENCE, YOU KNOW. IT'S NOT FOR EVERYONE.
BUT IT ***IS*** IMPORTANT, LAUREL. IMPORTANT TO KNOW ABOUT HOW OUR WORLD IS MADE, YOU KNOW.

HERR ALBERT EINSTEIN SAID, I WANT TO KNOW HOW GOD CREATED THIS WORLD. I AM NOT INTERESTED IN THIS OR THAT PHENOMENON, IN THE SPECTRUM OF THIS OR THAT ELEMENT. I WANT TO KNOW HIS THOUGHTS; THE REST ARE DETAILS.

INTERESTING, ALTHOUGH I DO NOT THINK HERR EINSTEIN BELIEVES IN A GOD WHO CARES ABOUT PEOPLE.

DO YOU?

I DON'T KNOW.

I DON'T KNOW.

I'VE HEARD THAT BEFORE.

MY FATHER LOVED THAT SAYING OF EINSTEIN'S. MOM MADE A FRAMED POSTER OF IT FOR HIM.

AND WHEN MY FATHER STUDIED OR RESEARCHED ANYTHING, THAT'S WHAT HE TRULY BELIEVED HE WAS DOING. "LEARNING ABOUT SCIENCE WAS LEARNING ABOUT GOD," HE SAID.

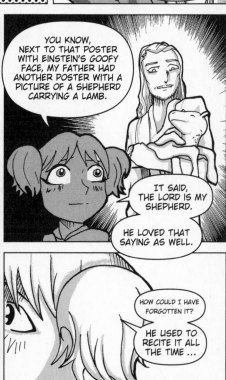

YOU KNOW, NEXT TO THAT POSTER WITH EINSTEIN'S GOOFY FACE, MY FATHER HAD ANOTHER POSTER WITH A PICTURE OF A SHEPHERD CARRYING A LAMB.

IT SAID, THE LORD IS MY SHEPHERD.

HE LOVED THAT SAYING AS WELL.

HOW COULD I HAVE FORGOTTEN IT?

HE USED TO RECITE IT ALL THE TIME ...

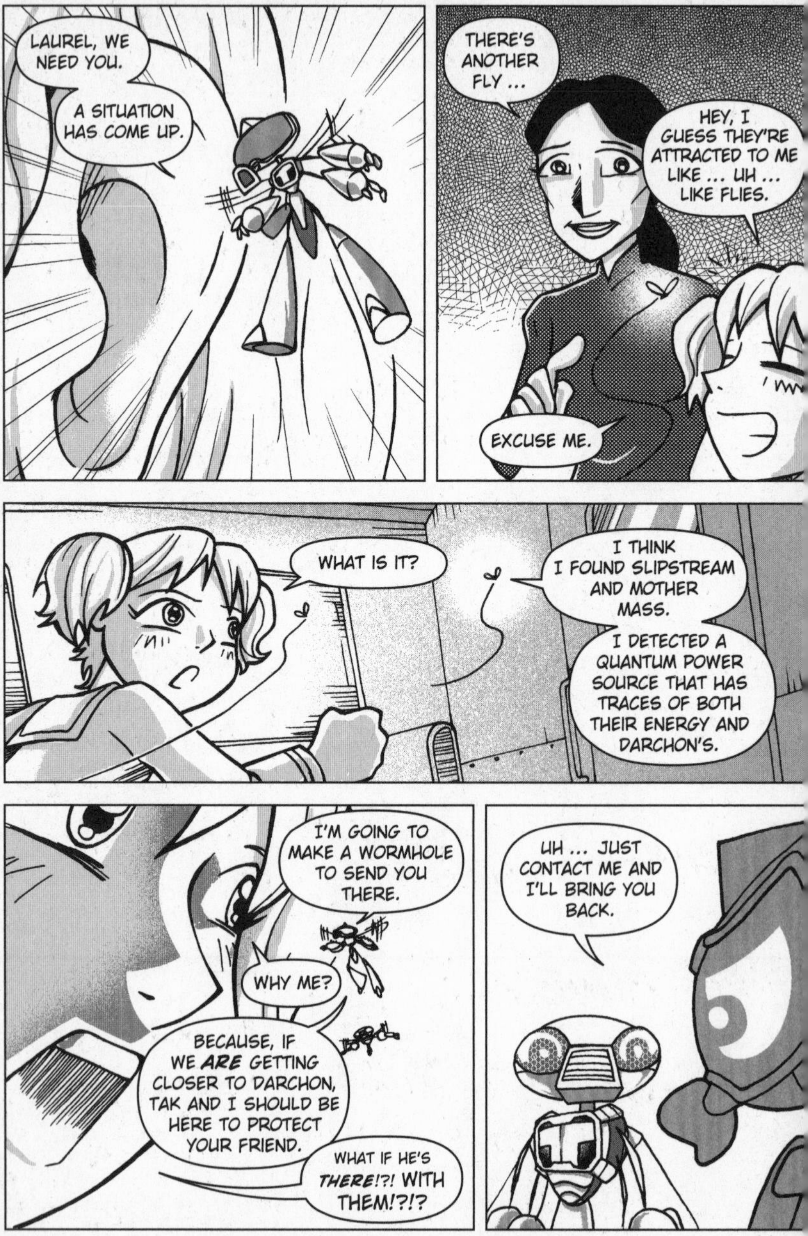
LAUREL, WE NEED YOU.
A SITUATION HAS COME UP.
THERE'S ANOTHER FLY ...
HEY, I GUESS THEY'RE ATTRACTED TO ME LIKE ... UH ... LIKE FLIES.
EXCUSE ME.
WHAT IS IT?
I THINK I FOUND SLIPSTREAM AND MOTHER MASS.
I DETECTED A QUANTUM POWER SOURCE THAT HAS TRACES OF BOTH THEIR ENERGY AND DARCHON'S.
I'M GOING TO MAKE A WORMHOLE TO SEND YOU THERE.
WHY ME?
BECAUSE, IF WE ***ARE*** GETTING CLOSER TO DARCHON, TAK AND I SHOULD BE HERE TO PROTECT YOUR FRIEND.
WHAT IF HE'S ***THERE***!?! WITH THEM!?!?
UH ... JUST CONTACT ME AND I'LL BRING YOU BACK.

ALL RIGHT, WORMHOLE.

I'LL TRUST YOU.

I'M READY ...

DON'T TRY ANYTHING HEROIC, LAUREL.

JUST ... BE CAREFUL.

JUST FIND OUT IF MOTHER MASS AND SLIPSTREAM NEED HELP AND CONTACT ME.

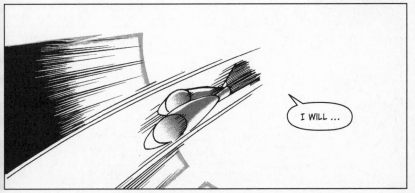

I WILL ...

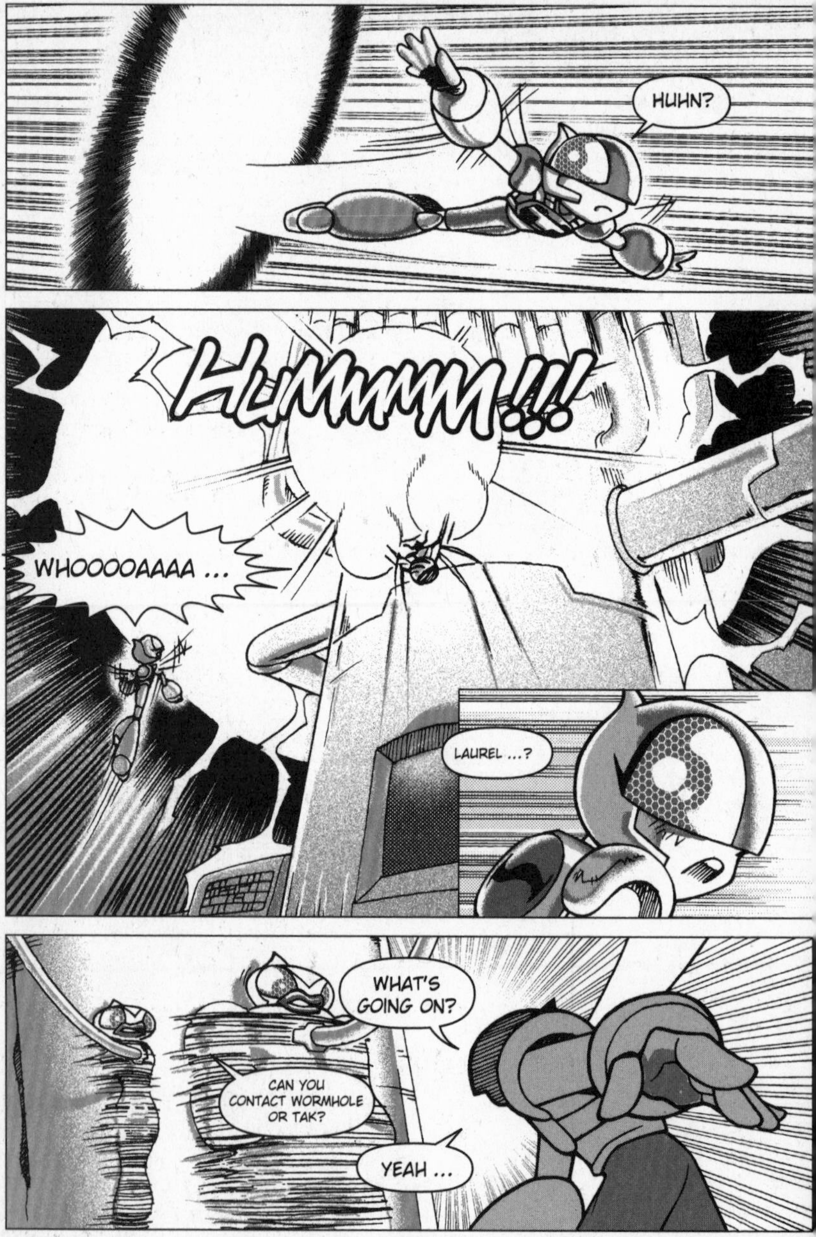
HUHN?
HUMMM!!!
WHOOOOAAAA ...
LAUREL ...?
WHAT'S GOING ON?
CAN YOU CONTACT WORMHOLE OR TAK?
YEAH ...

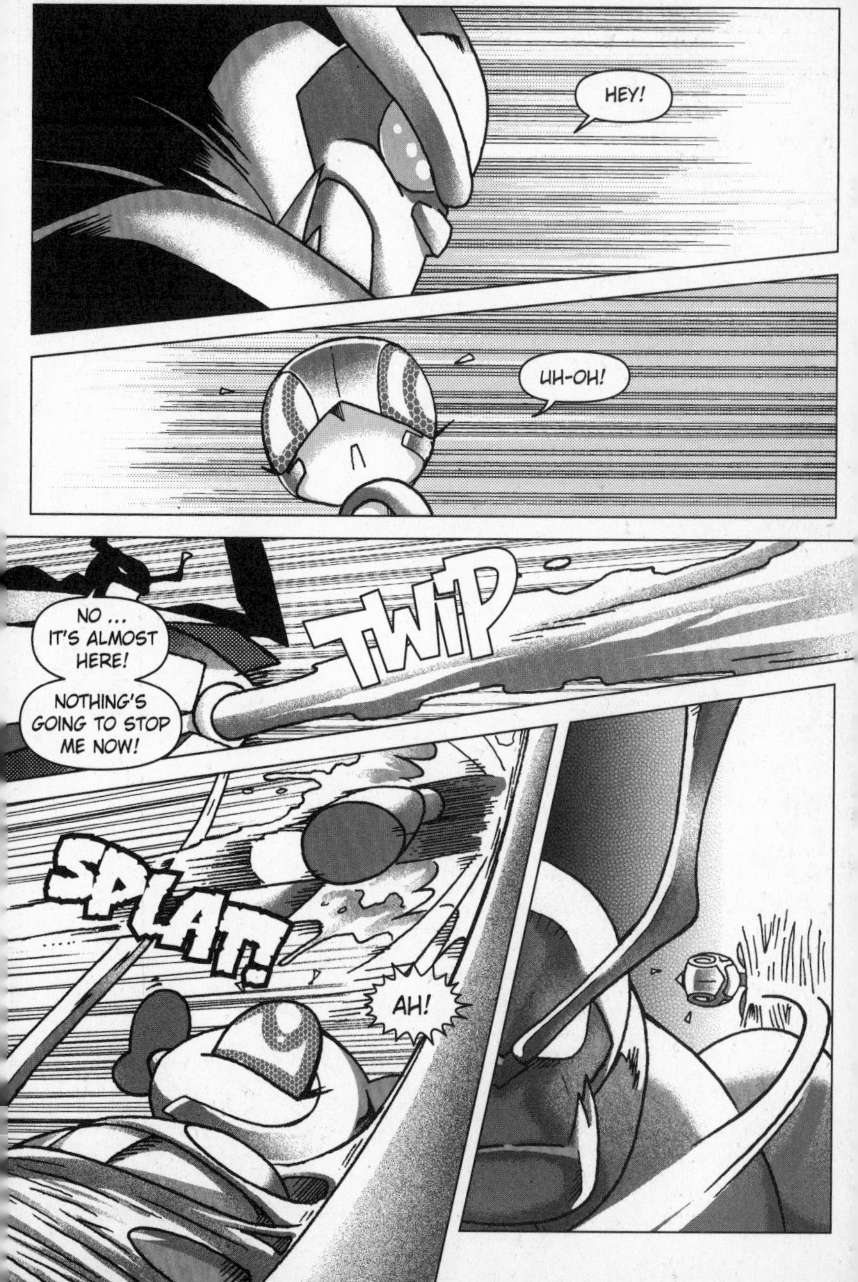
HEY!
UH-OH!
NO ... IT'S ALMOST HERE!
NOTHING'S GOING TO STOP ME NOW!
TWIP
SPLAT!
AH!

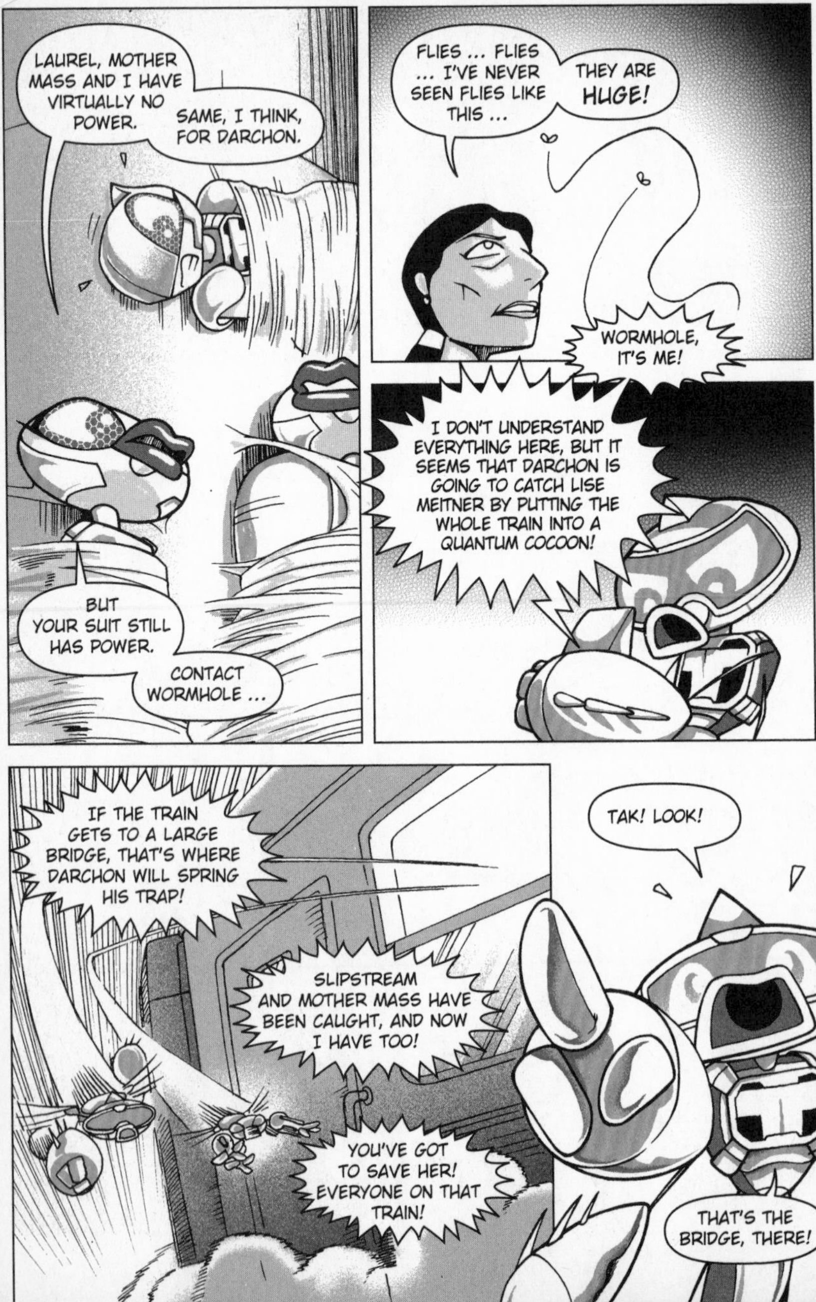
LAUREL, MOTHER MASS AND I HAVE VIRTUALLY NO POWER.
SAME, I THINK, FOR DARCHON.
BUT YOUR SUIT STILL HAS POWER.
CONTACT WORMHOLE ...
FLIES ... FLIES ... I'VE NEVER SEEN FLIES LIKE THIS ...
THEY ARE HUGE!
WORMHOLE, IT'S ME!
I DON'T UNDERSTAND EVERYTHING HERE, BUT IT SEEMS THAT DARCHON IS GOING TO CATCH LISE MEITNER BY PUTTING THE WHOLE TRAIN INTO A QUANTUM COCOON!
IF THE TRAIN GETS TO A LARGE BRIDGE, THAT'S WHERE DARCHON WILL SPRING HIS TRAP!
SLIPSTREAM AND MOTHER MASS HAVE BEEN CAUGHT, AND NOW I HAVE TOO!
YOU'VE GOT TO SAVE HER! EVERYONE ON THAT TRAIN!
TAK! LOOK!
THAT'S THE BRIDGE, THERE!

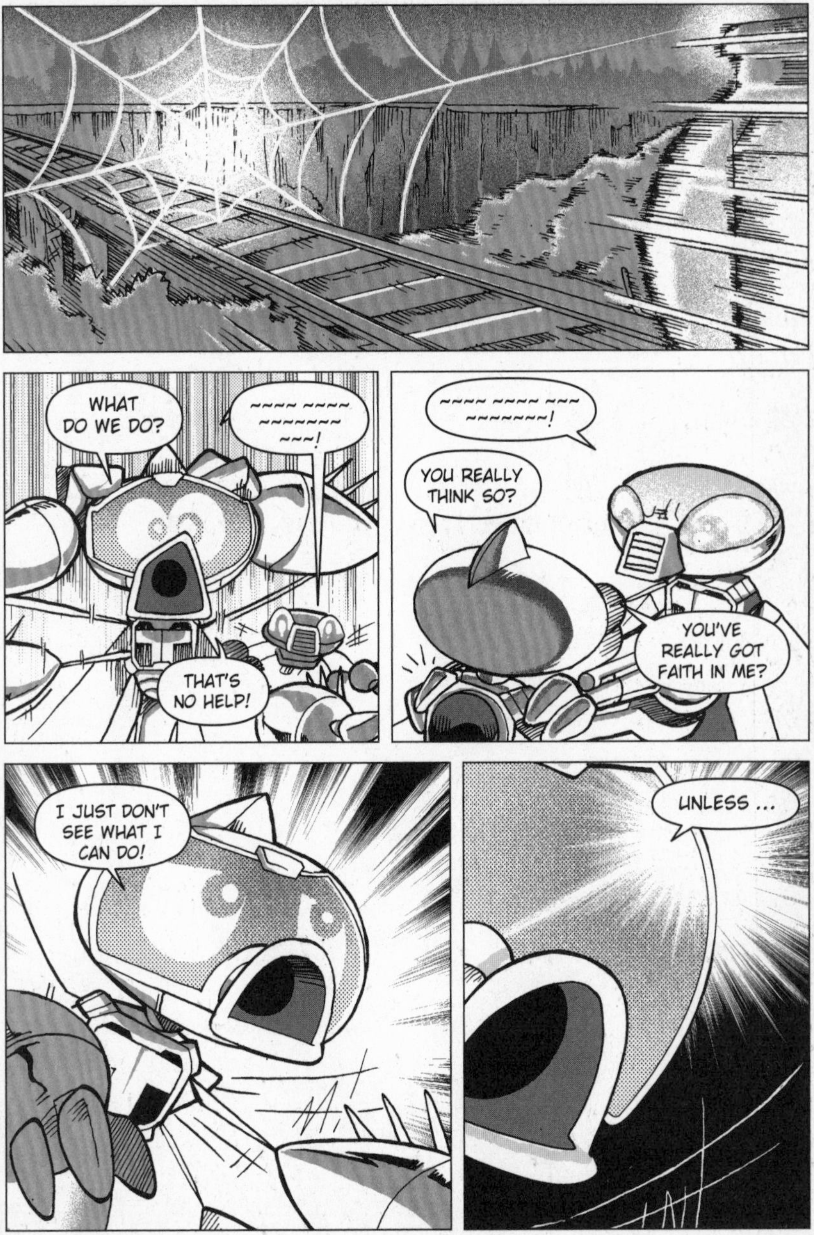
WHAT DO WE DO?
~~~~ ~~~~ ~~~~~~~ ~~~!
THAT'S NO HELP!
~~~~ ~~~~ ~~~ ~~~~~~~!
YOU REALLY THINK SO?
YOU'VE REALLY GOT FAITH IN ME?
I JUST DON'T SEE WHAT I CAN DO!
UNLESS ...

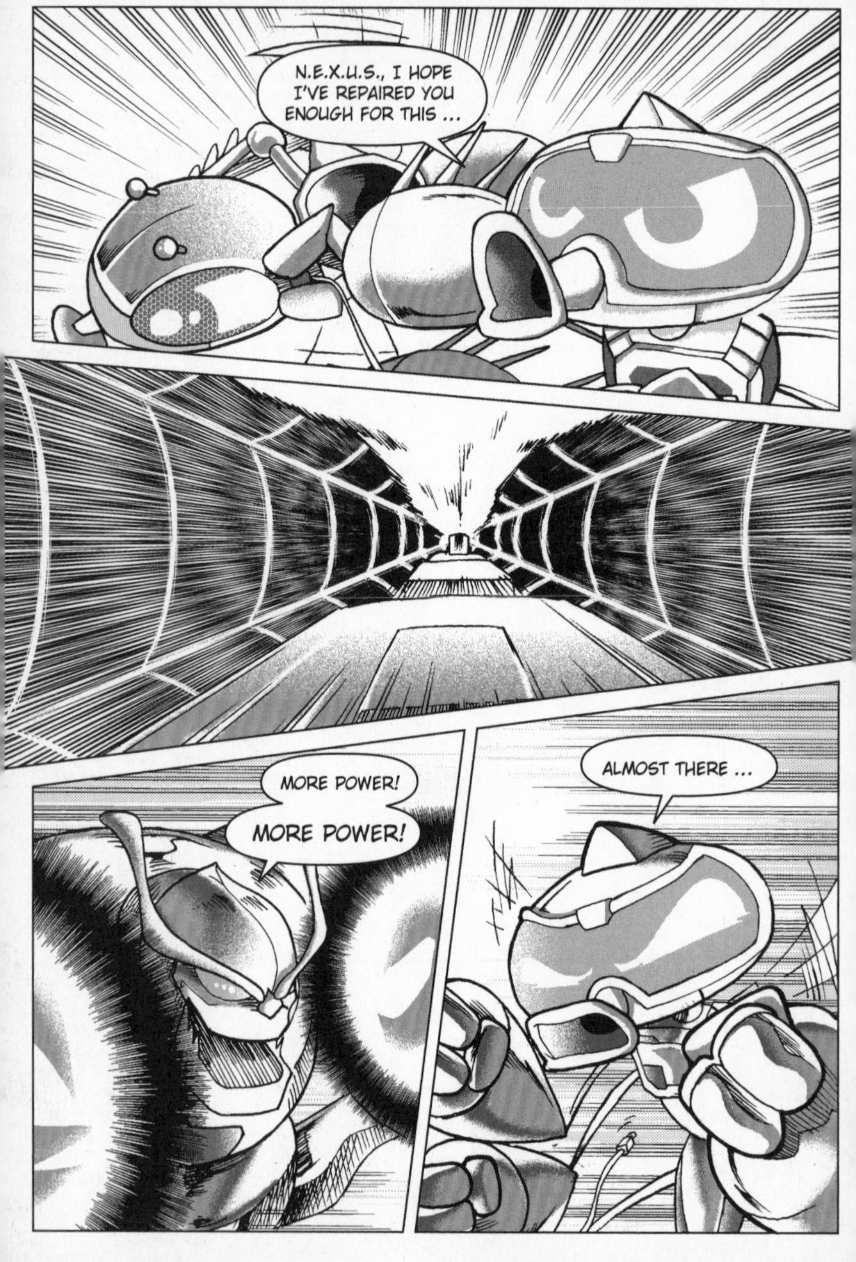
N.E.X.U.S., I HOPE I'VE REPAIRED YOU ENOUGH FOR THIS ...
MORE POWER!
MORE POWER!
ALMOST THERE ...

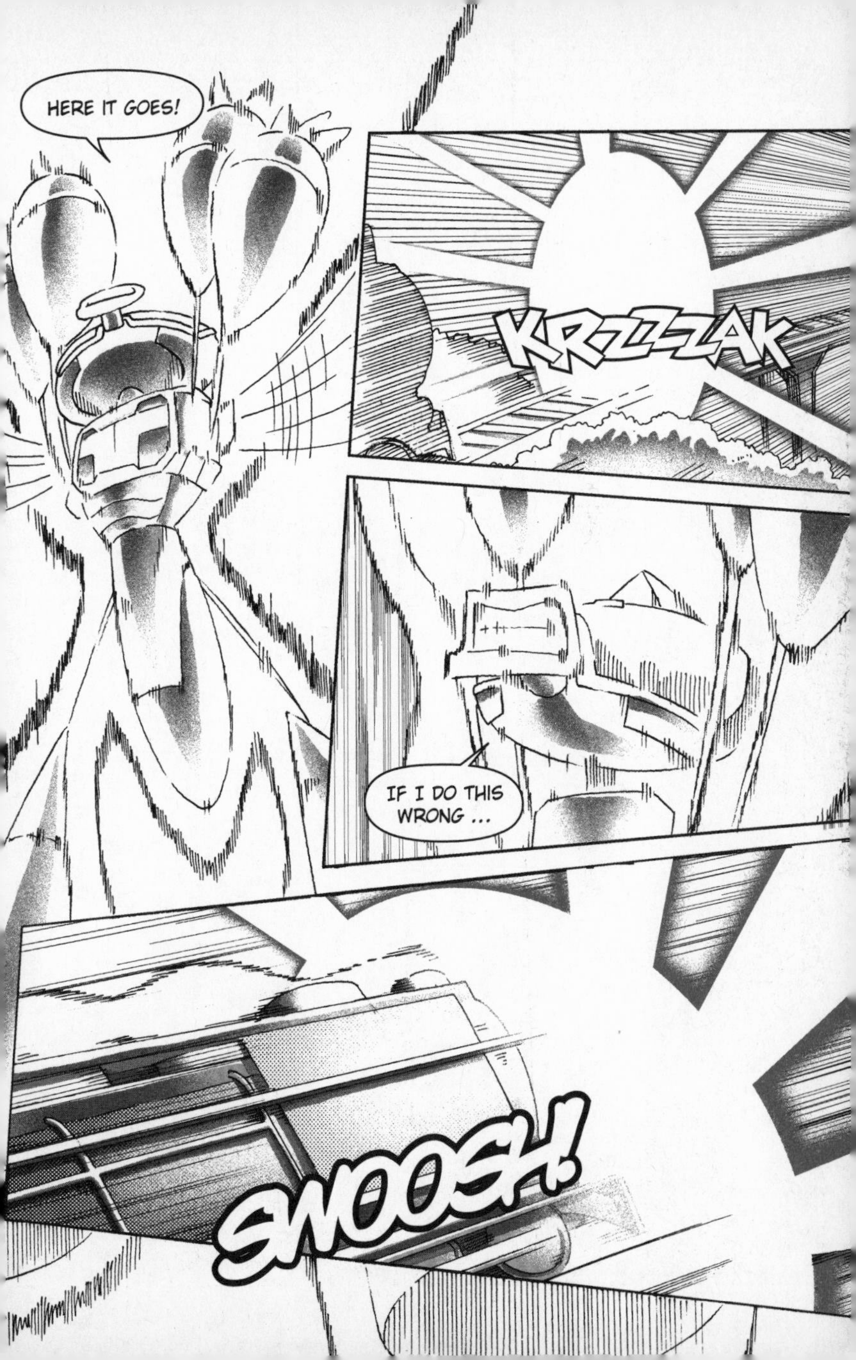
HERE IT GOES!
KRZZZAK
IF I DO THIS WRONG ...
SWOOSH!

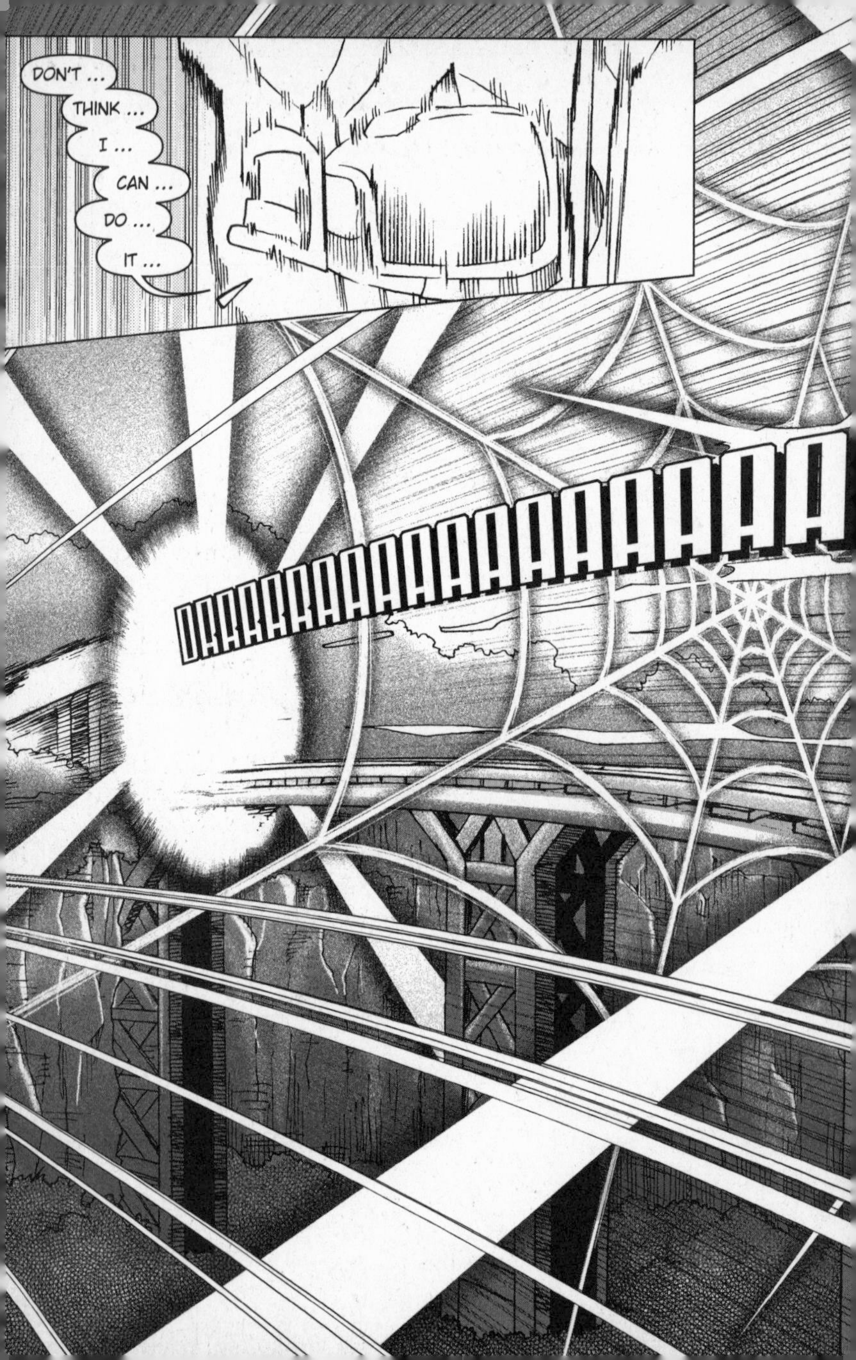
DON'T ...
THINK ...
I ...
CAN ...
DO ...
IT ...
DAAAAAAAAAAAAAAAAAA

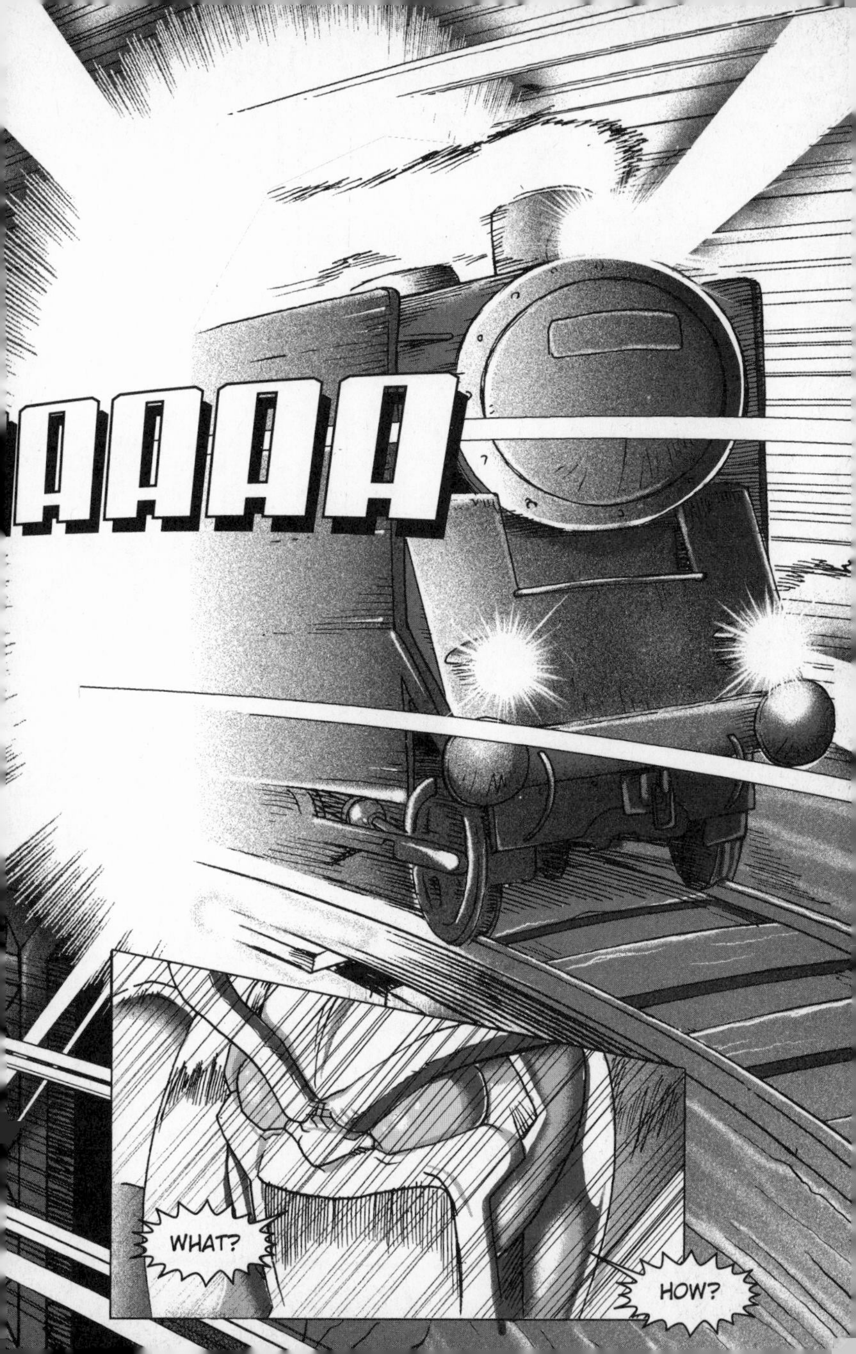
AAAAA
WHAT?
HOW?

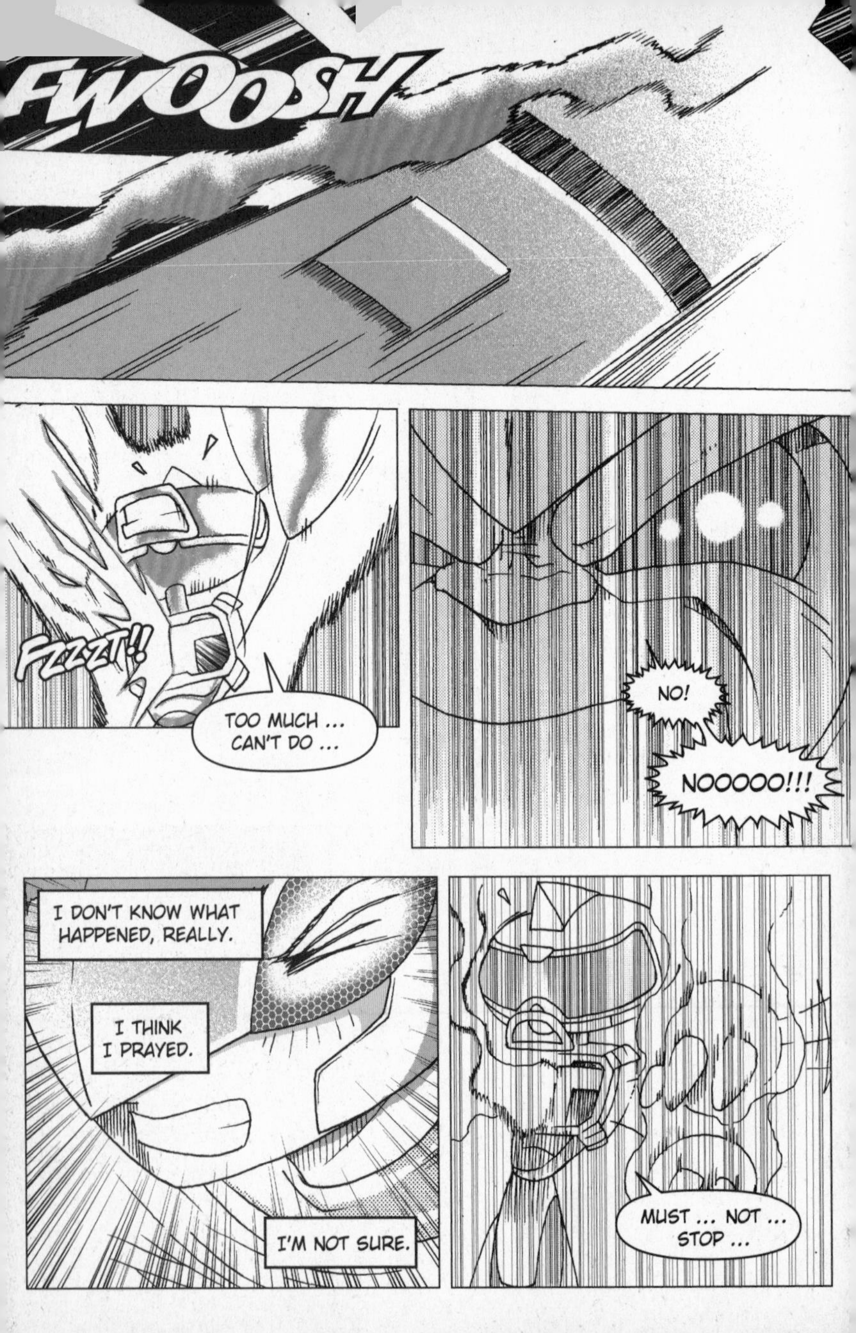
FWOOSH
FZZZT!!
TOO MUCH ... CAN'T DO ...
NO!
NOOOOO!!!
I DON'T KNOW WHAT HAPPENED, REALLY.
I THINK I PRAYED.
I'M NOT SURE.
MUST ... NOT ... STOP ...

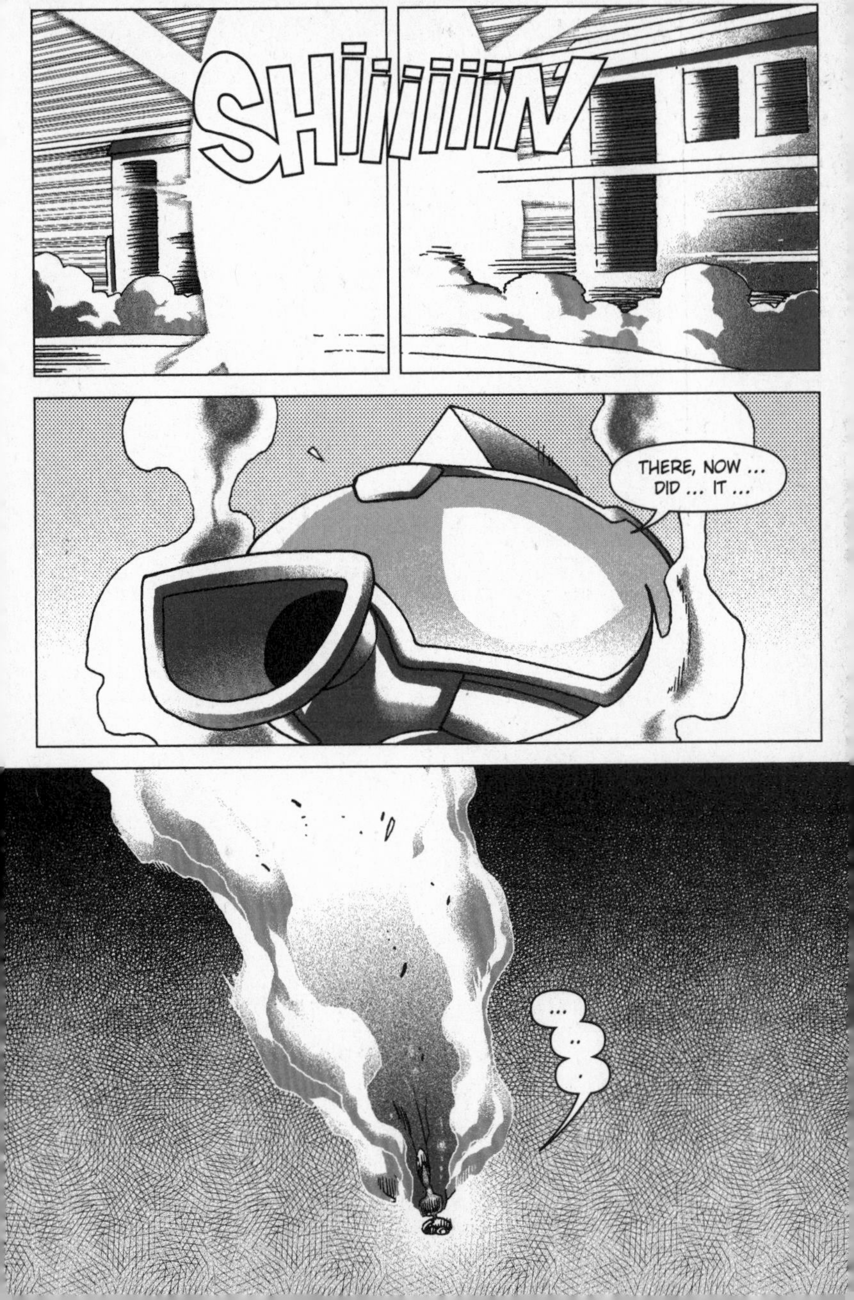
SHIIIIIIN
THERE, NOW ... DID ... IT ...
...
...
...

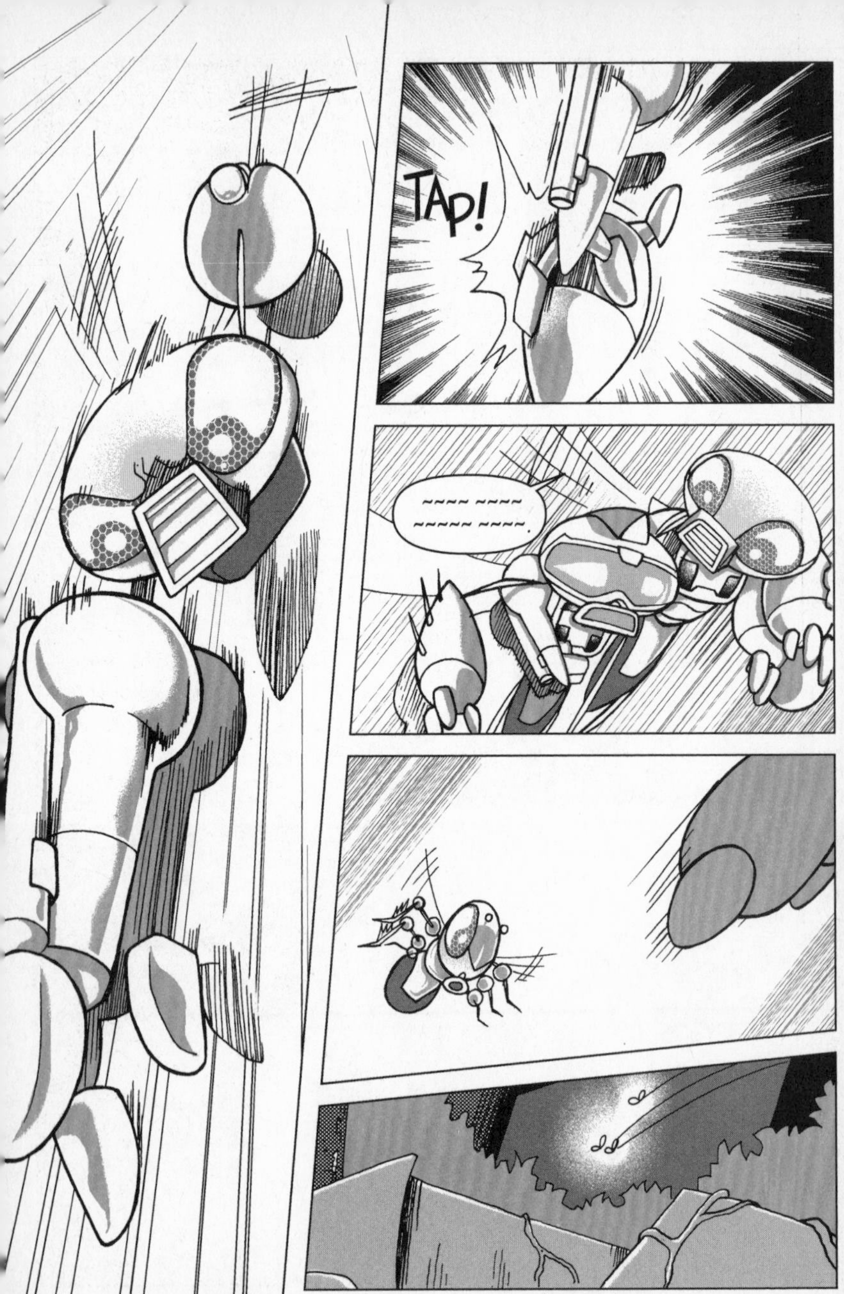
TAP!

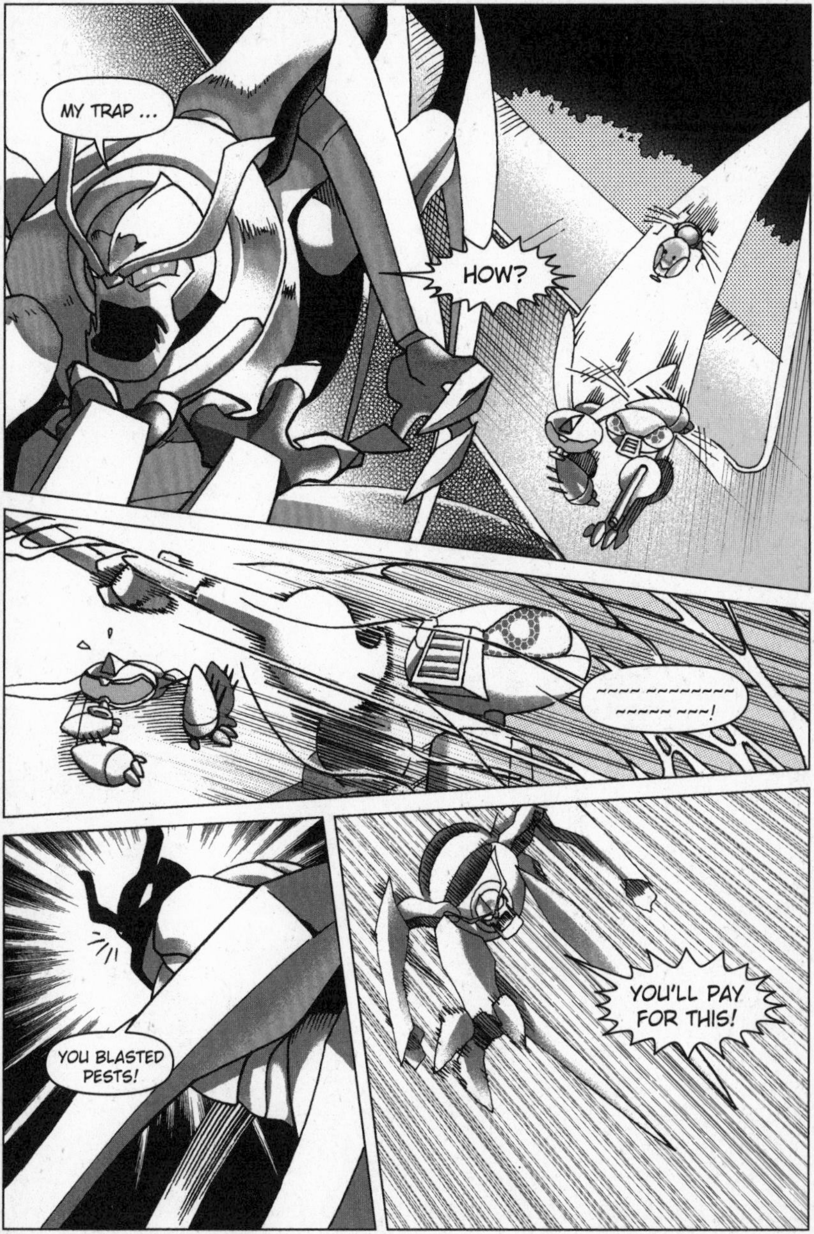
MY TRAP ...
HOW?
~~~~ ~~~~~~~~ ~~~~~ ~~~!
YOU BLASTED PESTS!
YOU'LL PAY FOR THIS!
~~~~

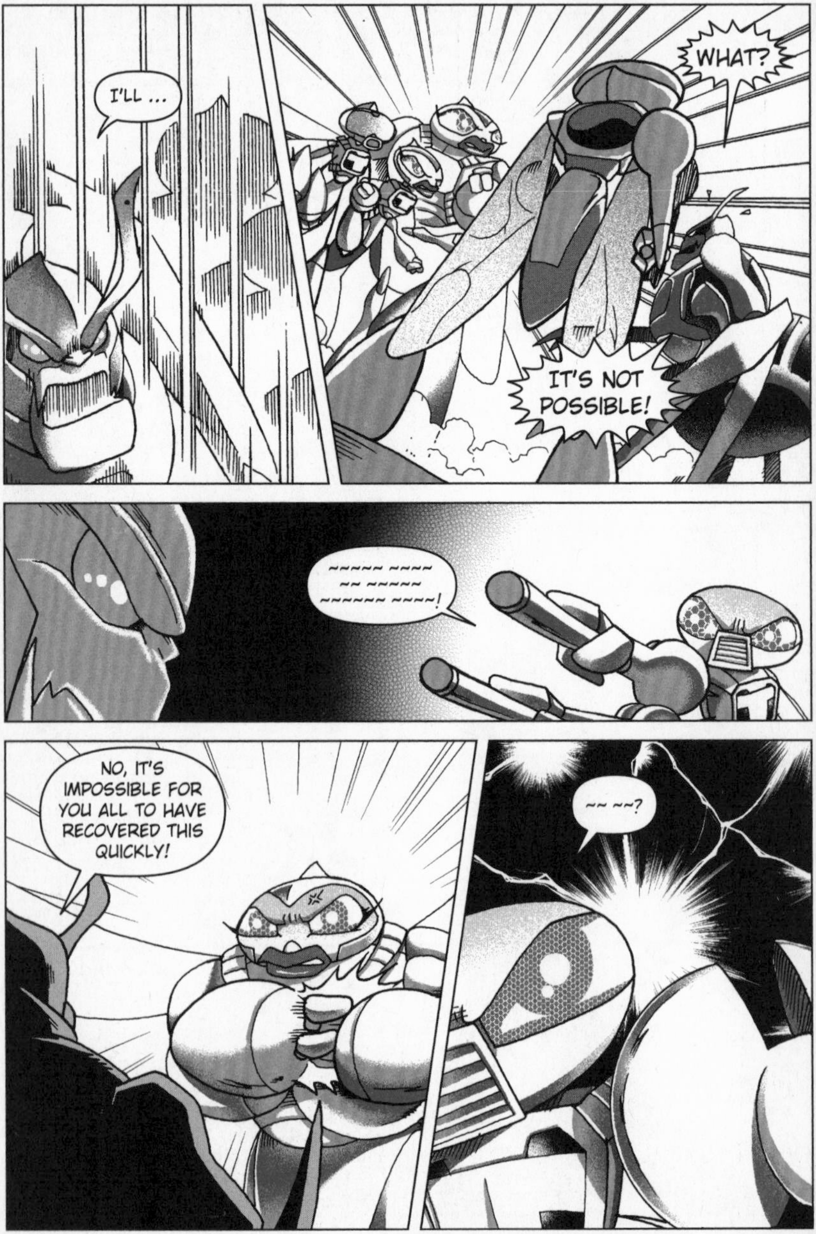
I'LL ...
WHAT?
IT'S NOT POSSIBLE!
~~~~~ ~~~~ ~~ ~~~~~ ~~~~~~ ~~~~!
NO, IT'S IMPOSSIBLE FOR YOU ALL TO HAVE RECOVERED THIS QUICKLY!
~~ ~~?
~~~~~

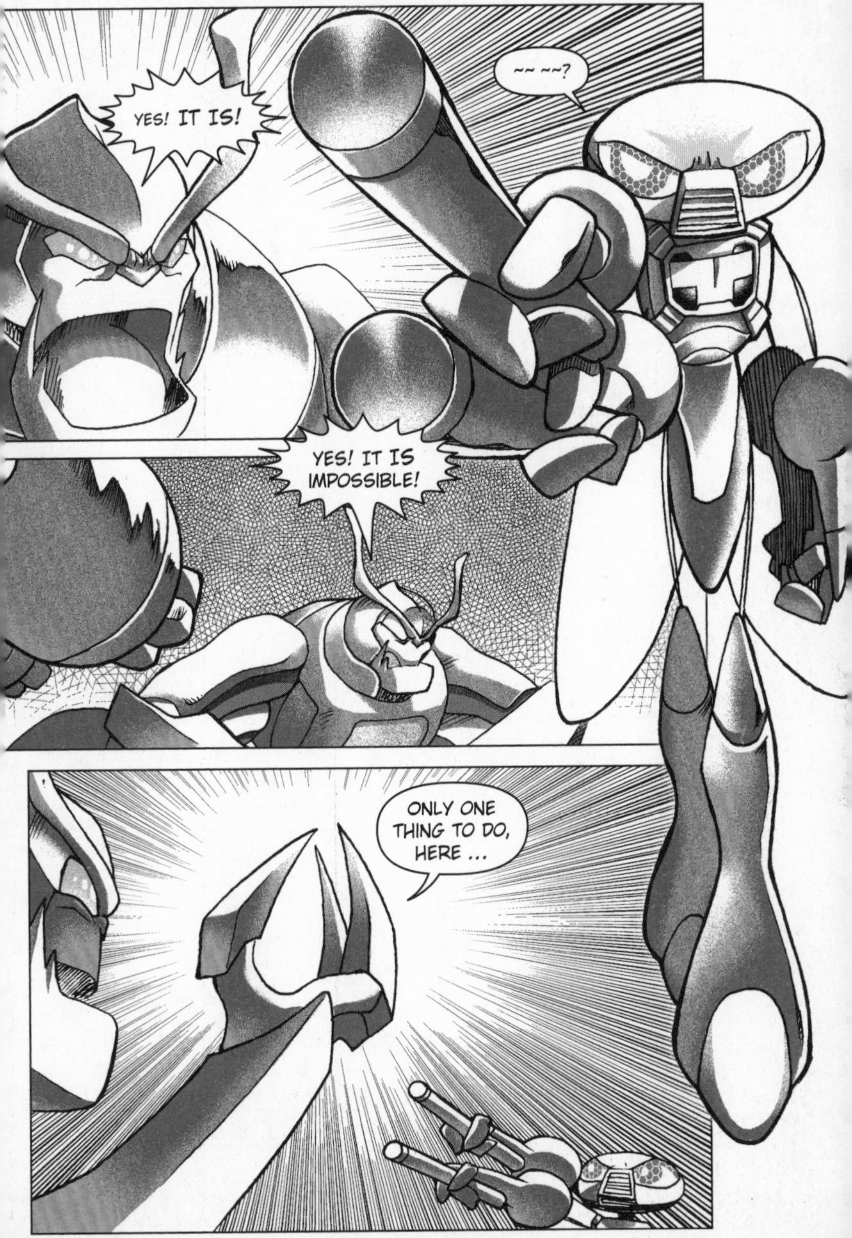
YES! IT IS!
~~ ~~?
YES! IT IS IMPOSSIBLE!
ONLY ONE THING TO DO, HERE ...

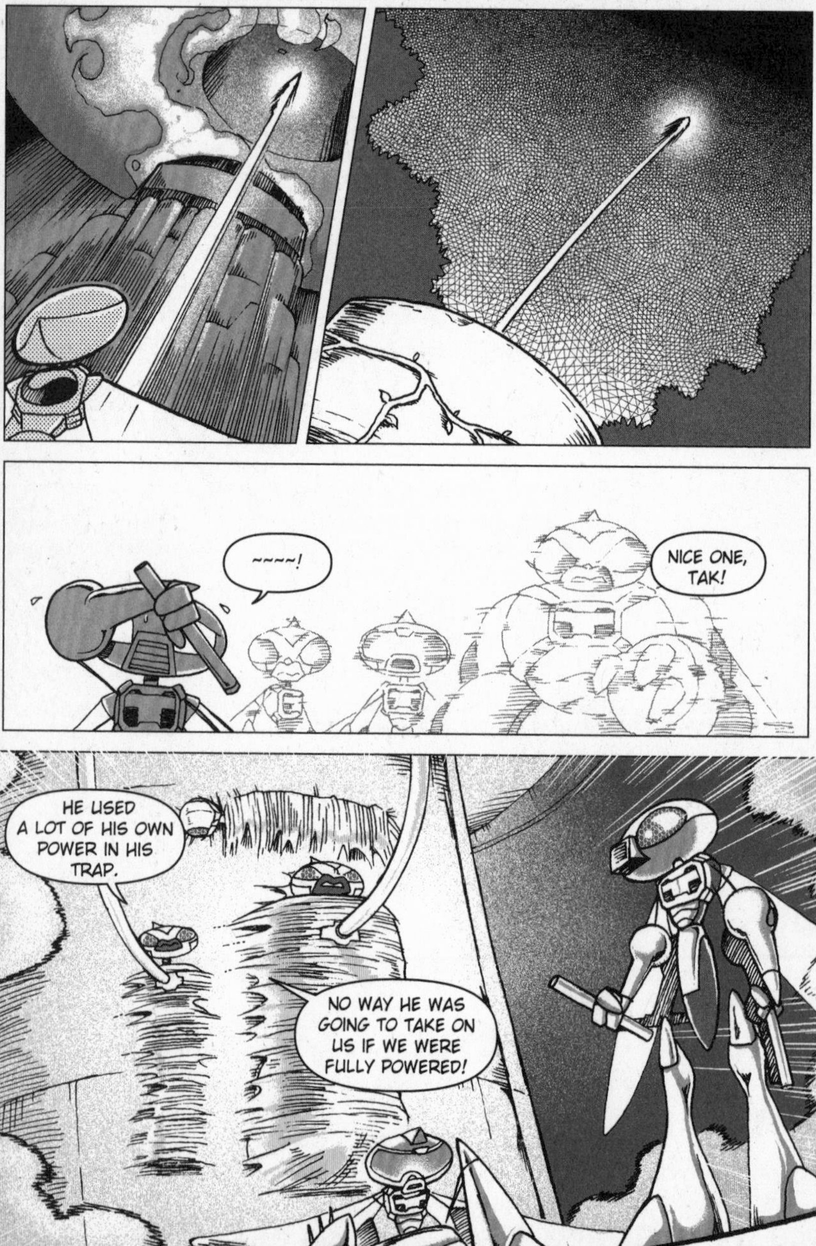

NICE ONE, TAK!
HE USED A LOT OF HIS OWN POWER IN HIS TRAP.
NO WAY HE WAS GOING TO TAKE ON US IF WE WERE FULLY POWERED!

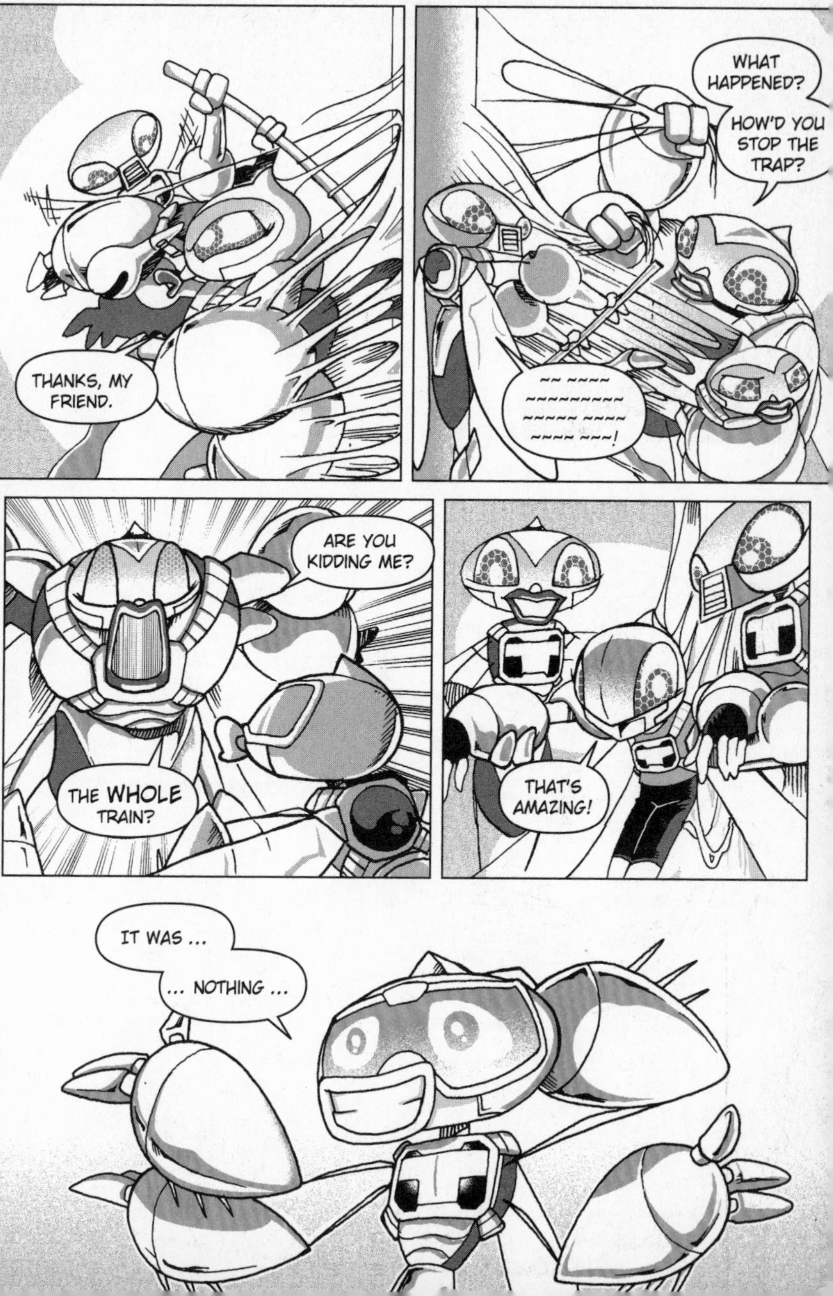
THANKS, MY FRIEND.
WHAT HAPPENED?
HOW'D YOU STOP THE TRAP?
ARE YOU KIDDING ME?
THE WHOLE TRAIN?
THAT'S AMAZING!
IT WAS ...
... NOTHING ...

AFTER DARCHON LEFT, WE USED WHAT ENERGY WE HAD LEFT TO GET BACK ON THE TRAIN.

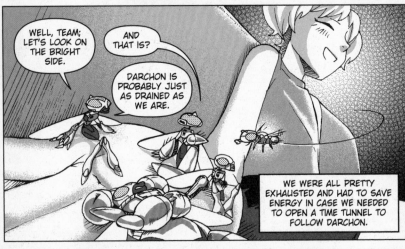

WELL, TEAM; LET'S LOOK ON THE BRIGHT SIDE.

AND THAT IS?

DARCHON IS PROBABLY JUST AS DRAINED AS WE ARE.

WE WERE ALL PRETTY EXHAUSTED AND HAD TO SAVE ENERGY IN CASE WE NEEDED TO OPEN A TIME TUNNEL TO FOLLOW DARCHON.

WELL, IF HE OPENS A WORMHOLE THROUGH TIME, AS LONG AS HE'S ON THIS PLANET, WE'LL KNOW.

I'VE GOT N.E.X.U.S. UP AND RUNNING ... MOSTLY.

WE SAVED LISE MEITNER ...

THAT'S GOOD. RIGHT?

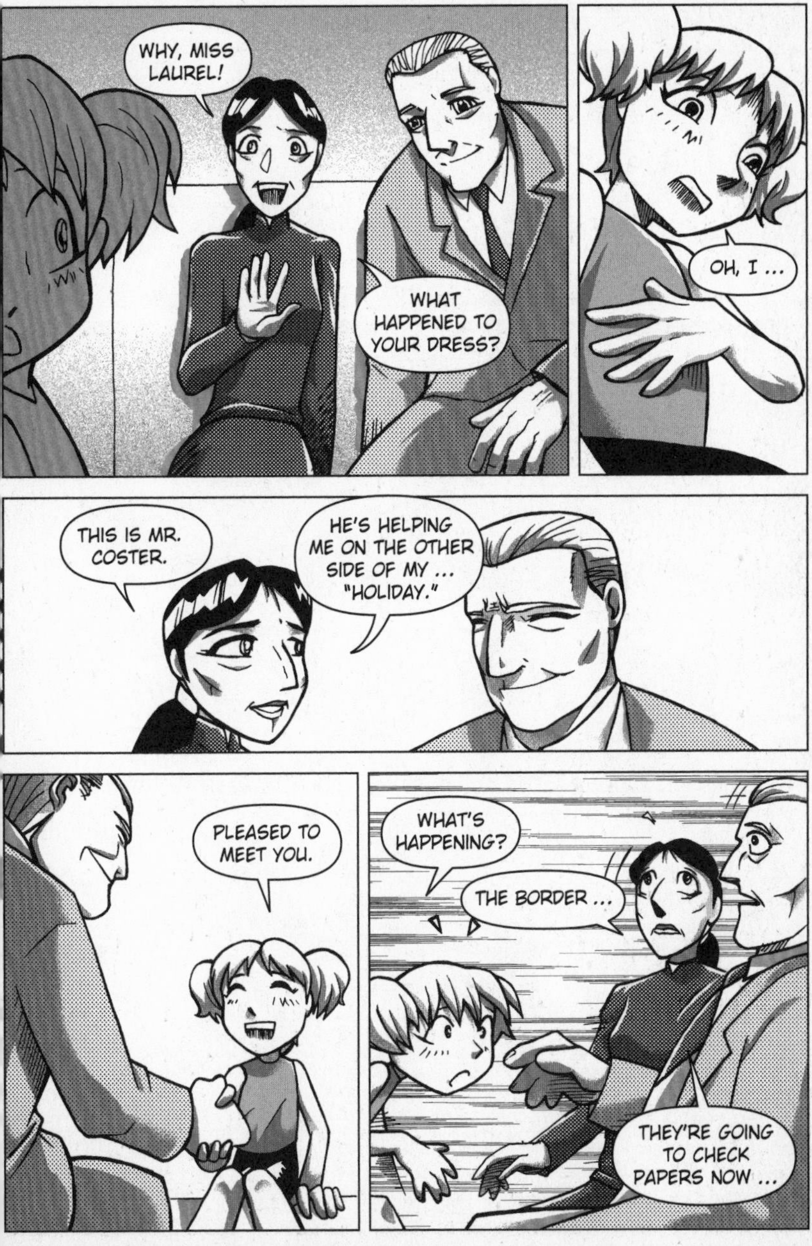
WHY, MISS LAUREL!
WHAT HAPPENED TO YOUR DRESS?
OH, I ...
THIS IS MR. COSTER.
HE'S HELPING ME ON THE OTHER SIDE OF MY ... "HOLIDAY."
PLEASED TO MEET YOU.
WHAT'S HAPPENING?
THE BORDER ...
THEY'RE GOING TO CHECK PAPERS NOW ...

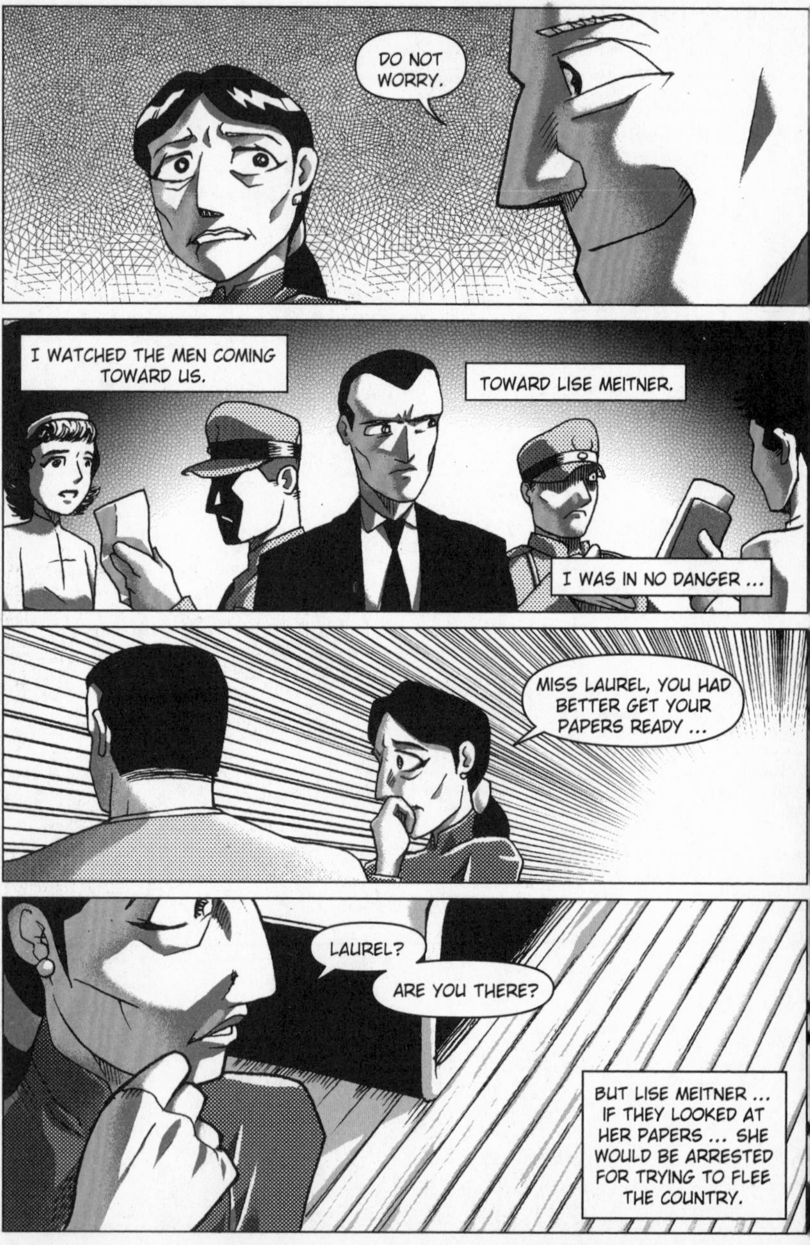
DO NOT WORRY.
I WATCHED THE MEN COMING TOWARD US.
TOWARD LISE MEITNER.
I WAS IN NO DANGER ...
MISS LAUREL, YOU HAD BETTER GET YOUR PAPERS READY ...
LAUREL?
ARE YOU THERE?
BUT LISE MEITNER ... IF THEY LOOKED AT HER PAPERS ... SHE WOULD BE ARRESTED FOR TRYING TO FLEE THE COUNTRY.

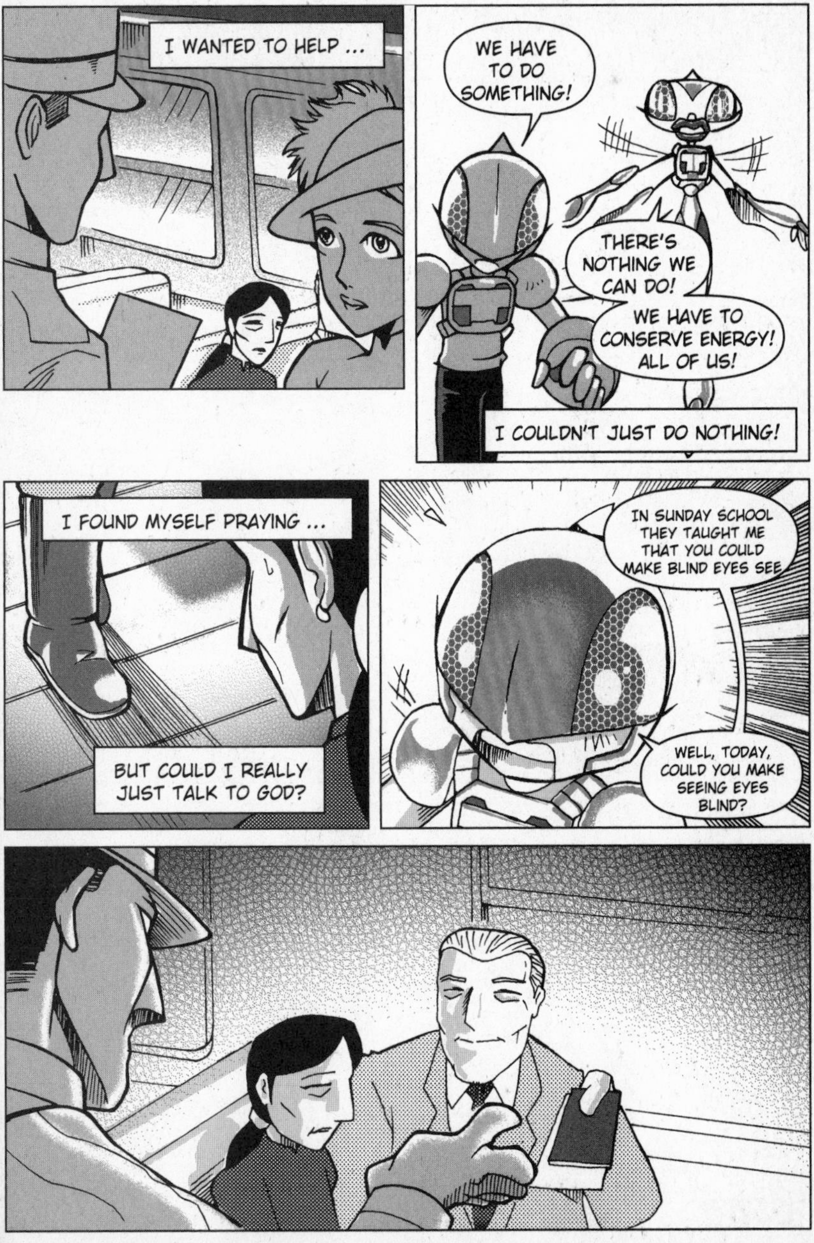
I WANTED TO HELP ...
WE HAVE TO DO SOMETHING!
THERE'S NOTHING WE CAN DO!
WE HAVE TO CONSERVE ENERGY! ALL OF US!
I COULDN'T JUST DO NOTHING!
I FOUND MYSELF PRAYING ...
BUT COULD I REALLY JUST TALK TO GOD?
IN SUNDAY SCHOOL THEY TAUGHT ME THAT YOU COULD MAKE BLIND EYES SEE
WELL, TODAY, COULD YOU MAKE SEEING EYES BLIND?

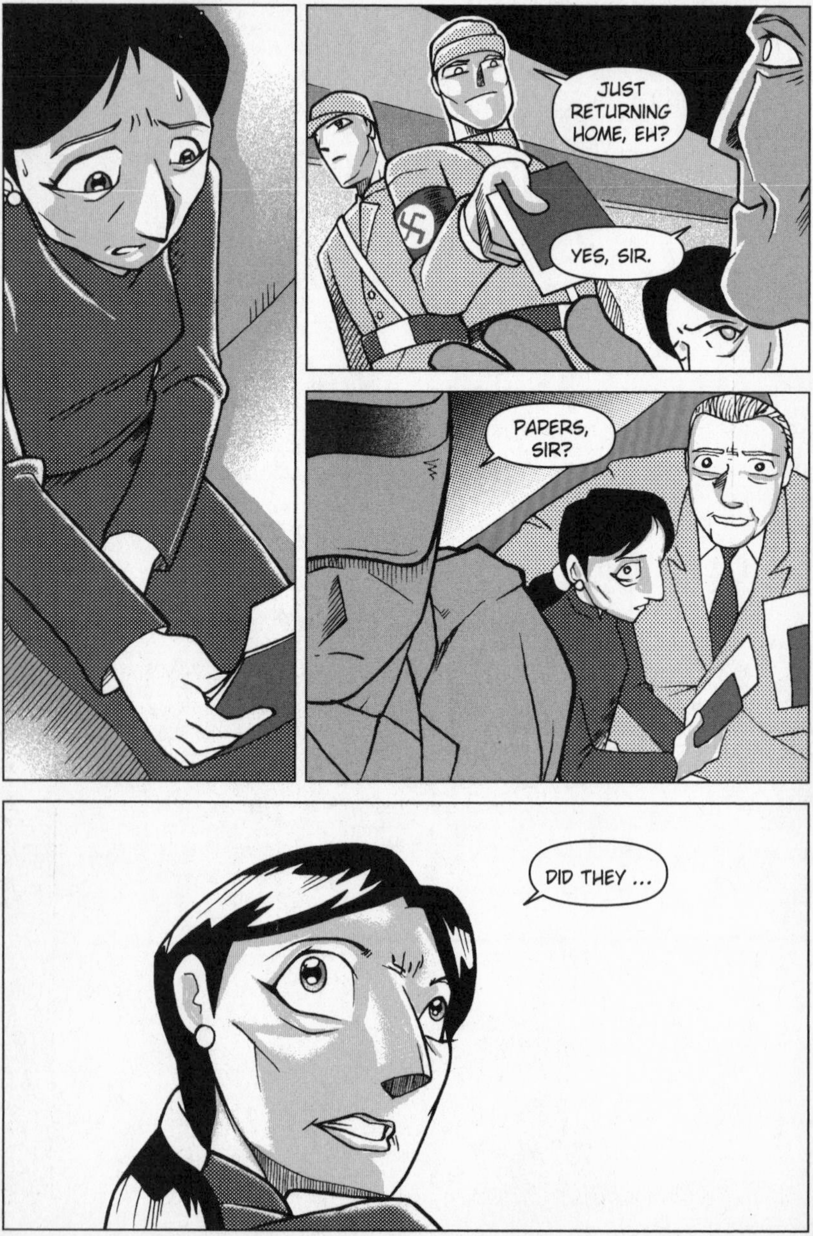
JUST RETURNING HOME, EH?
YES, SIR.
PAPERS, SIR?
DID THEY ...

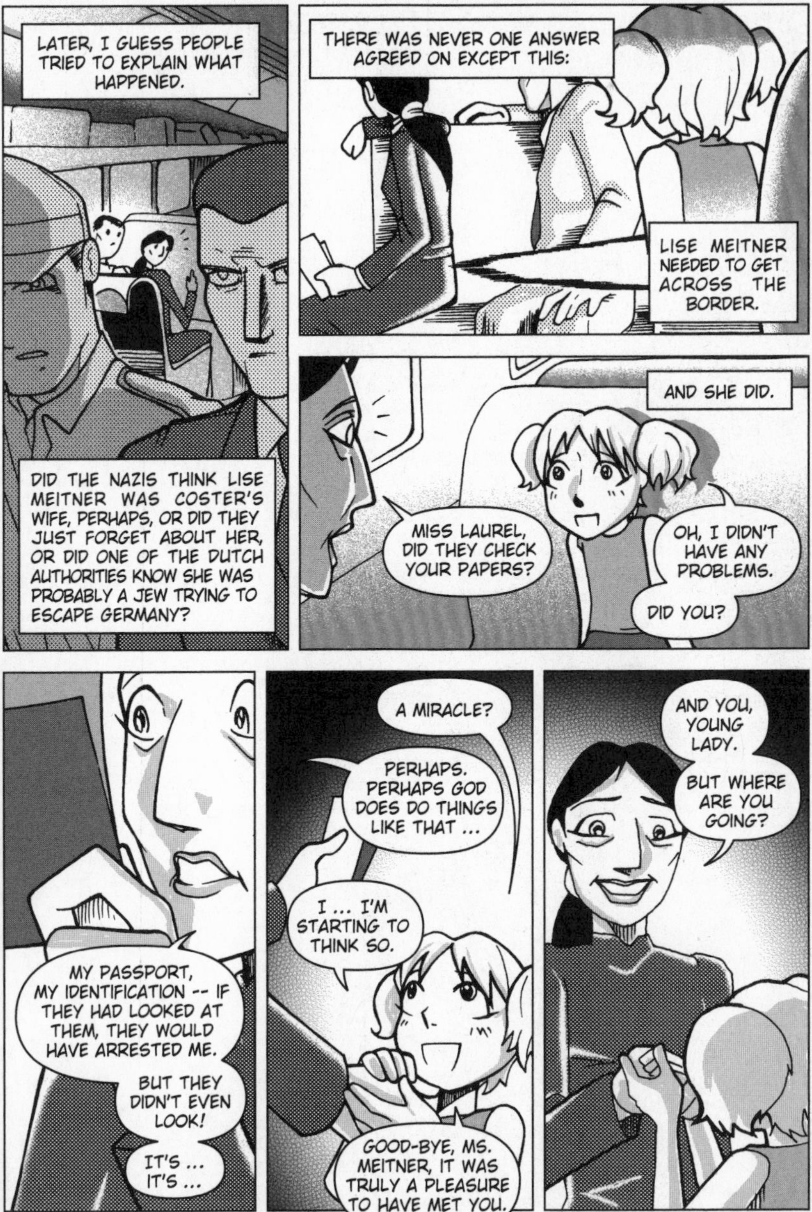
LATER, I GUESS PEOPLE TRIED TO EXPLAIN WHAT HAPPENED.
DID THE NAZIS THINK LISE MEITNER WAS COSTER'S WIFE, PERHAPS, OR DID THEY JUST FORGET ABOUT HER, OR DID ONE OF THE DUTCH AUTHORITIES KNOW SHE WAS PROBABLY A JEW TRYING TO ESCAPE GERMANY?
THERE WAS NEVER ONE ANSWER AGREED ON EXCEPT THIS:
LISE MEITNER NEEDED TO GET ACROSS THE BORDER.
AND SHE DID.
MISS LAUREL, DID THEY CHECK YOUR PAPERS?
OH, I DIDN'T HAVE ANY PROBLEMS.
DID YOU?
MY PASSPORT, MY IDENTIFICATION -- IF THEY HAD LOOKED AT THEM, THEY WOULD HAVE ARRESTED ME.
BUT THEY DIDN'T EVEN LOOK!
IT'S ... IT'S ...
A MIRACLE?
PERHAPS. PERHAPS GOD DOES DO THINGS LIKE THAT ...
I ... I'M STARTING TO THINK SO.
GOOD-BYE, MS. MEITNER, IT WAS TRULY A PLEASURE TO HAVE MET YOU.
AND YOU, YOUNG LADY.
BUT WHERE ARE YOU GOING?

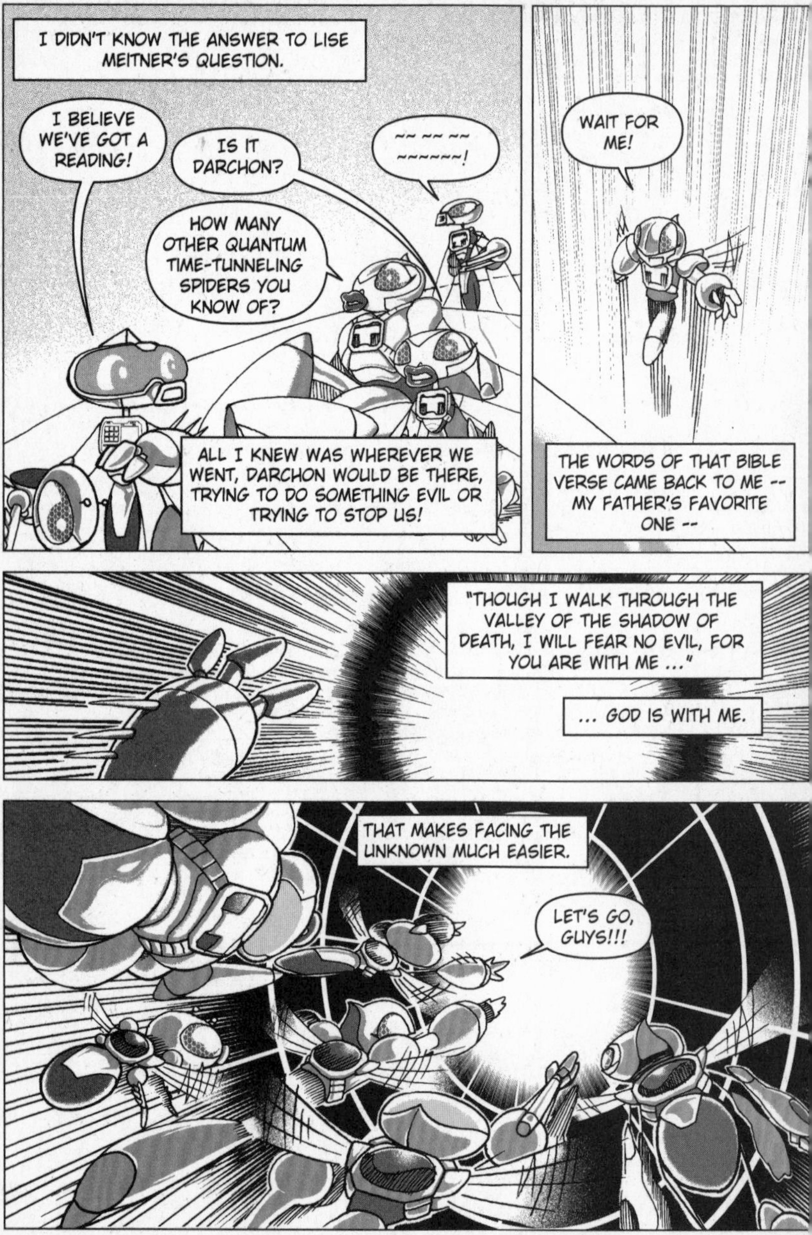
I DIDN'T KNOW THE ANSWER TO LISE MEITNER'S QUESTION.
I BELIEVE WE'VE GOT A READING!
IS IT DARCHON?
~~ ~~ ~~ ~~~~~~!
HOW MANY OTHER QUANTUM TIME-TUNNELING SPIDERS YOU KNOW OF?
ALL I KNEW WAS WHEREVER WE WENT, DARCHON WOULD BE THERE, TRYING TO DO SOMETHING EVIL OR TRYING TO STOP US!
WAIT FOR ME!
THE WORDS OF THAT BIBLE VERSE CAME BACK TO ME -- MY FATHER'S FAVORITE ONE --
"THOUGH I WALK THROUGH THE VALLEY OF THE SHADOW OF DEATH, I WILL FEAR NO EVIL, FOR YOU ARE WITH ME ..."
... GOD IS WITH ME.
THAT MAKES FACING THE UNKNOWN MUCH EASIER.
LET'S GO, GUYS!!!

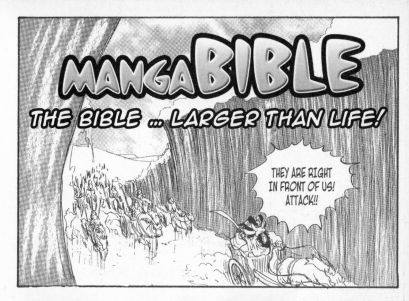

HAND OF THE
MORNINGSTAR
WHA-AAM!
IN THE BATTLE BETWEEN GOOD AND EVIL,
IT'S HARD TO TELL WHO'S ON WHICH SIDE.

HAND OF THE
MORNINGSTAR

Advent

Available Now!

HAND OF THE
MORNINGSTAR

Resurrection

Available Now!

HAND OF THE
MORNINGSTAR

Confession

Available Now!

HAND OF THE
MORNINGSTAR

Emergence

Available May 2008!

AVAILABLE AT YOUR LOCAL BOOKSTORE!

VOLUMES 5–8 COMING SOON!

ZONDERVAN®

We want to hear from you. Please send your comments about this book to us in care of zreview@zondervan.com. Thank you.

[redacted]

Grand Rapids, MI 49530
www.zonderkidz.com

ZONDERVAN.com/
AUTHORTRACKER
follow your favorite authors

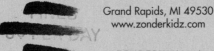